I0761740

HAZE

## A NOVEL OF A FAR FUTURE

### ILLUSTRATED

### BONUS SHORT STORY: FLY AWAY HOME

KATHARINE KERR

*

SHAHID MAHMUD
PUBLISHER

www.caeziksf.com

Cover art by Dany V.

ISBN: 978-1-64710-151-0

First Edition. First Printing. April 2025.
1 2 3 4 5 6 7 8 9 10

An imprint of Arc Manor Inc.

www.CaezikSF.com

# A NOVEL OF A FAR FUTURE

## ILLUSTRATED

## BONUS SHORT STORY: FLY AWAY HOME

KATHARINE KERR

**ARC MANOR**
ROCKVILLE, MARYLAND

*

SHAHID MAHMUD
PUBLISHER

www.caeziksf.com

This is a work of fiction.

Cover art by Dany V.

ISBN: 978-1-64710-151-0

First Edition. First Printing. April 2025.
1 2 3 4 5 6 7 8 9 10

An imprint of Arc Manor Inc.

www.CaezikSF.com

For STEPHEN GORDON

1969–2021

His music stopped too soon.

# AUTHOR'S NOTE

Out of sheer habit, readers tend to assume that all characters in a science fiction book are Human, and that all the Humans are White. In HAZE, unless a character is specifically described as light-skinned, it would be more accurate to assume the opposite.

HAZE: PAGE 1

FLY AWAY HOME: PAGE 317

# HAZE

# ONE

The harsh sunlight turns everything Dan sees to pain. White buildings tower over him with edges as sharp as knives and windows like accusing eyes. The ruins in the War Memorial across the pitted street glisten like black bombs half hidden in underbrush. Except there's no brush on Nowhere Street; not a trace of green, just stone and perma and cracking roadblack. The sunlight itself crackles and flashes in long streaks that turn window reflections to fire. On the bombed-out edge of the vast city, Gleam lives up to its name.

Once Dan owned a chip-augmented visor for light control, a beautiful strip of darkness to wrap around his eyes. It was a very long time ago, it seems now, back when he was someone else. He pawned it, just as he's pawned almost everything else he once owned.

Dan stumbles over a fragment of tile lying on the remains of a sidewalk. He rights himself, finds he's shaking too hard to walk, and decides to sit down and rest, just rest his human, all-too-human body, just a few minutes, then move on. He manages to get to the strip of shade thrown by the nearest building, puts his back against the wall, and slides down until he can sit with his legs stretched out in front of him. His backside on the hard concrete hurts no matter how he shifts his weight. He wonders if he's still bleeding a little from his night's work. *Rough trade. Wanna hurt me? Just pay in advance. The last rung of the ladder down.*

Haze. Dan wants Haze, *needs* Haze, has sold himself on the street more than once to get the creds to buy Haze. This morning he's looking for a dealer—any dealer—who can give him the tabs that will turn the glare and crackle of the sunlight into a warm, soft glow. Once he gets a tab down, every nerve in his body will stop shrieking at him. The sunlight will dim. Shadows will fall around him like soft blankets to cover him from the world.

He shuts his eyes. He is just tired enough to drowse—not sleep, but drowse in a flicker of dreams and silences—until the sound of footsteps wakes him. Lod-Mata, the one friend he has left, kneels down beside him and flips the fabric of his kilt back to ensure his stub of a tail stays covered. The blaze of sunlight makes the Lep's gray-green head scales glitter and spark. His bright green skull crest flattens in alarm. He reaches out one clawed hand and lays it gently on Dan's arm.

"You loaded?'

"No such luck. Waiting to score. You got any?"

"No, and the hell I'd give you that core-crap anyway." Lod rummages in the pouch pocket of his tunic and brings out a clear vial of pink liquid. "Drink it. It'll help."

"Sai. Thanks." Dan takes it, cracks off the top, and gulps down the bitter contents. "Pay you back when I can."

"No sweat. I stopped in at Mission House after work, and they were handing it out for free. Along with news. Someone's looking for you. Two someones, a woman and a man, both Human. The priest guessed they were both ex-Fleet officers. The way they walked showed it and she gave orders like she was used to them being followed."

"Shit. That's all I need. Did you recognize them?"

"I never saw them."

"Did anyone tell them?"

"No. They all knew nothing, not even Father Kev. I guess his Lord Jessy will forgive him for lying."

The pink juice takes effect fast. Dan's shakes ease up, and the screaming in his nerves quiets to a snarl.

"What's that red mark on your face? It looks like someone hit you with a whip."

"He did. You should see my butt."

"No thank you, spare me! But what in hell—"

"Last night's john's idea of a good time. He paid enough for it."

"You keep this up, you're not going to be the pretty boy much longer."

"Throwbacks like me heal fast. So they told me, anyway."

Lod looks away for a long moment, sighs, looks back again. His crest droops to one side. "I don't suppose you want to talk about rehab."

"Hell no! I'm not doing rehab."

"Why not?"

"Three months, pal. They want to shut you up for three fucking months in some damn room somewhere. And fuck with your brain. Can't see the stars, not for three months. Bad enough I can't reach them, but not even see them? No."

The last word echoes up and down the empty street. Lod gets to his feet. "The Church of the Redeemer is handing out dinner tonight. They usually do a pretty good spread. Do you want to eat?"

"No."

"Whatever. You don't need to yell at me."

"Sorry. I mean it. Sorry."

"It's sai. See ya."

Dan closes his eyes and leans back against cold stone. He wants to sleep, but the pink juice has steadied his mind. He remembers that he's carrying creds. If he gets rolled for them, he won't be able to buy the Haze. He owns a Fleet officer's long knife, an ancient-style real metal dirk, a mark of his former status, the one thing he has left from the days before his long slide down. He retrieves the knife from its sheath in his right boot. The blade sends a flash of light into the ruins across the street.

Dan has a little ritual. Every time he draws the long knife, he keeps it in his right hand while he holds up his left to study his wrist. He can see under his pale skin the long blue veins that cross a tendon. One good cut, and it won't take him long to bleed out. Someday—not now, but someday—he'll escape from the street and from his memories. The memories hurt worse than his life on the street. But for now, he lays the knife on his thigh and rests a hand on the hilt, ready for any trouble.

Sooner or later, a dealer will cruise by on a fancy grav sled. They prowl this particular sector of the city, looking for buyers. In a couple of minutes he sees someone walking in his direction, someone striding briskly along like he—no, she—knows where she's going. Ordinary clothes, blue slacks, a striped shirt, but they hang wrong on someone with military posture and a shipboard walk. Curly black hair cut short, and the ice-cold gray eyes that contrast so oddly with her rich brown skin

"Shit. It can't be."

"But it is," Captain Evans sets her hands on her hips and considers him. "You shouldn't yell your head off if you don't want to be found. I heard you two blocks away."

"Ma'am." Dan raises a trembling hand but stops short of a salute.

"No need for that. We figured the priest was protecting you when he said he didn't know where you were. So we waited outside until I scanned him telling someone the truth."

"We?"

"Devit's out looking for you, too." She softens her voice. "Did you think he wouldn't be?"

Her face seems to blur and waver. Tears fill his eyes. Thanks to the pink juice, he cannot stop them from spilling over.

"Intel finally figured out that you'd ended up on Ruby," Evans said. "Gleam's the only Human-run city on this godforsaken planet. The priest told someone you were likely to be at the Memorial." She tips her head back to look up at the white buildings. "Does anyone live in those?"

"No, ma'am. They're part of the Memorial. Sealed up and empty. One for each war."

Evans tips her head back and stares up at the tall white buildings with their knifepoint roofs. "No wonder the locals call it Nowhere Street."

The tears have stopped. Dan wipes his face on his shirt sleeve while he searches for something to say. All he can come up with is, "Why?"

"First, to see if you were still alive."

"Does it matter?"

"Yes. To me and a fair number of other sapes. Second reason: to see if there's anything left of your mind."

"So that's what they want? They need a replacement part for an AI or something?"

She quirked an eyebrow. "Who's this 'they'?"

"Whoever sent you."

"I can't discuss it out here. We've got a protected space—"

Dan winces. "No. I'm not going anywhere. This is where I belong." He crosses his arms over his chest to hide his shaking hands.

Evans looks up and down the street for a minute or two, then smiles with her usual half twitch of her mouth. "There's Devit. It's about time he got here."

A nondescript gray car pulls up and sinks down to ground level with a long sigh of compressed air. A tall male Human gets out, lays a hand on his jacket pocket, and pauses to look around him. Pitawanna Tevita, his real name, marks him as an Islander from Nesia, as do his wavy black hair and deeply tanned skin. Chief Warrant Officer Peter Devit, as the Fleet insists on calling him, always pauses for that look around, just as he always carries a pulse gun in his jacket pocket.

He leaves the door open with a voice command and strides over. "Dan, shit! Your face!"

"Yeah. I'm a filthy mess. Not worth your time."

"Shut up and listen. We're here to get you off the damn street."

"No. I'm not going anywhere. I belong here, right here, with all the other pieces of crap floating around."

Devit's face shows no emotion at all, so impassive that he might have been thinking of something else entirely. Dan recognizes that look. It signifies that Devit sees a problem and is considering how to deal with it. Devit takes a vial out of his shirt pocket and holds it up with a little shake. It rattles. The two tabs inside gleam with a momentary blue light from their nanites, the sign that they're pure, actual Haze. Dan breaks out into a cold sweat.

"Come with us, and they're yours." Devit glances at Evans. "This is what took me so long. Scoring."

"You bastard." Dan can barely speak. His mouth has filled with the spit of pure desire.

"Which is it, Dan? If you don't want this Haze, I can dump it down a street drain."

Dan takes a deep breath. Why fight? He knows he'll lose. Yet he cannot bring himself to agree aloud.

Devit shakes the vial again. "One tab as soon as you get in the car. When you come down from that, we'll talk."

"Then I get the other one?"

"That's a promise."

Dan slides the knife back into its boot sheath. Now comes the real difficulty: getting to his feet when he's shaking and sweating with drug lust. He manages to twist and shove his reluctant body until he can use both hands to push himself into a kneel. There he sticks, head down and panting.

"We're going to need a medic," Evans says.

"No, ma'am, not really."

Devit's on the tall side for Human males. From the look of him, he's in decent shape, but no one would ever call him muscle-bound. He bends down and slides his hands under Dan's arms. "You remember this, Buddy. Hang on." He picks Dan up as easily as an ordinary person might lift a small child.

Dan drapes one arm over Devit's shoulder and goes limp. Hearing his old nickname and feeling Devit's body against his, so familiar and warm, bring him more tears. "Hey, Pete? I've missed you so bad."

"Yeah?" His voice shakes, then steadies. "Well, I missed you, too."

Evans is already waiting by the car. "I'll drive."

Devit stows Dan into the back seat like luggage. He opens the vial and gets out one tab. Dan's hands are shaking so badly that he lets Devit put the tab into his mouth. It dissolves without any need for water. He gasps in relief and leans back to wait for the Haze to protect him from the razor blades of the sun.

Special Ops has provided a suite of rooms sealed away from every kind of interference beam as well as vision, sound, infrared, ultraviolet, and even old-fashioned wall bugs. No normal sapient walking down the corridor would see anything but a long stretch of painted wall. Captain Evans, of course, can see the door. At her touch on the code pad, the door slides open. She steps back to let Devit carry Dan inside, then follows with one cautious glance back. The door slides shut, locked and invisible, at her voice command.

Evans tosses her utility bag onto a shabby brown chair and walks over to one white wall.

"Play."

The hologram lights up to display a view of Old Earth Park in Gleam's Civic Center, a flourish of green among white buildings. She takes a moment to scan the other walls, switching her various vision functions back and forth, just as an extra precaution against unauthorized surveillance. Despite the paranoid gossip and rumors, Throwbacks with her functions cannot see through solid objects. What she can see with her oddly colorless eyes is the flicker of energy that would come through a wall if some kind of sensor were behind it.

She does another sweep of the room, but she finds nothing new or suspicious.

Devit has taken Dan into one of the suite's bedrooms. Evans follows as far as the doorway, watching as Devit lays him down on the bed and props him up with the pillows. Dan's smiling, his eyes only half closed, but she doubts he's seeing anything outside of his own mind. Devit ducks into the attached Waste Management room and comes back with a wet washcloth. He perches on the edge of the bed and begins to wipe crusted blood off Dan's chin.

"He bit his lip pretty badly," Devit says. "The flogging must have hurt like hell."

Evans studies Dan's face, still impossibly handsome despite the livid red line on his cheek. His mother—his famous mother, JohDanna, the vid star of stars—had insisted on her offspring being as beautiful as she was. With her money and fame, she'd gotten her fetus the genes she wanted. She never bothered to find out what other genes her beautiful son carried. Judging from the vid gossip about JohDanna, Evans figures that she wouldn't have cared if she had known.

Evans's admiration of Dan's genetically enhanced beauty is strictly abstract. The men in her own marriage quartet had both been the rugged type, she supposes you'd call it. She and the other woman, Leeta, had agreed on their taste in men, just as they agreed on most things. *So many years ago. I loved them all. I just loved the Fleet more.*

As if he feels Evans's attention, Dan opens his eyes, deep-set and dark green in a face as exotic as an ancient painting of an angel, his skin close to an ivory color tinted with beige. And just like one of those angels, he has thick golden blond hair, shaggy at the moment from poverty but still beautiful because the color is so rare. He's not feminine, no, though not strikingly masculine, either. It's a facet ambiguous in a way that invites the viewer to see whatever fantasy they cherish.

Devit's a decent-looking man, neither handsome nor ugly. Their faces contrast—Devit's a more common deep tan compared to Dan's unusual Pale, as the latter's rare coloration is known—but the way that they are staring at each other, so completely absorbed, is the same. Evans shakes her head. Trouble coming, she supposes, for Devit at any rate. She reminds herself that Devit has walked through this particular fire before. He knows who and what Dan is.

"How long before he comes down?"

"About six solstandard hours, ma'am."

"Sai. I'll be in the other room."

Evans returns to the living room. To her surprise Devit joins her in a few minutes. "He'll be fine on his own for a little while, ma'am. The Haze will take care of that. I'll get him cleaned up once he begins to come around. I'll go get his spare clothes from Mission House." He pauses, frowns. "I need to find more Haze, too."

"Sai. Ye gods, this rotten drug's going to be a problem. Are we going to have to keep feeding it to him?"

"I don't see any way around it. He should be in rehab. They need to find someone else for the job."

"Special Ops insisted. That's why I agreed on him in the first place."

"Right. But, ma'am? Can I enter an objection into today's report?"

"By all means. The order to find him came from the Bureau itself, and there's no arguing with that. So post a warning, yes. It'll be there whether they ignore it or not."

"Thank you."

"Honest opinion, Chief. Do you think he can still function? My god, he's a mess."

"I don't know, but damn, he deserves a chance. First they promoted him way too fast. Not even thirty yet. And then the Fleet threw him away. Dishonorable discharge over the damned drugs." Devit shrugs. "I still don't get it. Most starpilots use Haze off duty. Why single Dan out?"

"They claimed his drug use was excessive. Beyond the usual. Chief, the brass can always find something to say when they want to."

"I know, ma'am. But it gripes me."

Evans considers, then decides that enough time has passed for the truth. "Keep this to yourself. It was a top flight scandal. I didn't hear about it until it was all over. Someone way high up in the command chain was—well, we could say that he was obsessed with Dan. Dan turned him down. The five-star someone took steps. Revenge. Ridiculous! But Dan takes some people that way."

"Yes, ma'am. He does." Devit's staring at the holo as intently as if the pictures mattered. "There's been more than one."

Evans remembers her frustrated rage when she heard what had happened. She'd gone to Fleet Base One to accept an offer to join Special Ops. The court-martial took place elsewhere. That it had happened at all still shocked her. Injustice, but who was going to listen to her?

"So, ma'am." Devit looks her way at last. "Our crew. Is it complete?"

"I've decided we should bring Lod-Mata into this for our gunner."

"A Lep? Not that it should matter."

"But it does?" She quirks an eyebrow. "Mata's kept Dan alive this last couple of years, if we can trust what that priest told us."

"That's true."

"Mata tried to protest the court-martial. They cashiered him, too."

"I didn't know that."

"So I thought. You'd been transferred away by then, too."

It takes Devit a long moment to answer. "You're right, ma'am. I apologize."

"We all have our blind spots. You go take care of Dan. I'll decide about Lod-Mata. It's not going to matter if Dan won't sign on."

Dan spends the day trying to think through the Haze. For the first time in two solstandard years he feels physically comfortable and, above all, safe from the violence of the streets. He wants to stay that way, but what's the price going to be? Rehab, most likely. His whole body knots in disgust at the thought. His mind returns to this question at intervals, between the Haze-induced images and memories that float in front of his eyes like pictures on torn paper.

The only light in the room comes from a holo screen set to the "Calm" channel of soft music and beautiful landscapes. With Haze in his blood, light no longer bothers Dan. He could even endure sunlight, should he have to. Haze makes normal light mimic some of the qualities of shunt space, where a pilot takes a ship through that mysterious world called hyperspace. There soft golden light and blue shadows dance. No one but starpilots know this. No one but another starpilot would understand why Dan mourns for what his discharge lost him.

At some point Devit leaves, then returns with his bundle of clothing from Mission House. Questions such as when and how long have no meaning in the Haze. Toward the end of the day Dan's mind begins to clear. He showers, puts on the clean clothes, manages to eat a little when Devit insists he do so.

"Now remember," Devit says, "once you've heard our pitch, you can have the second tab."

"Sai. Pete, I don't—I can't tell you how good it is, seeing you. I—"

"Yeah. I feel the same. But we can't keep the captain waiting."

"Jeez. You sure haven't changed a bit, have you?"

"I try not to. Neither have you. Come on, Dan. Let's go."

Evans is sitting on a beige divan against one wall. She gets up, glances at the holo, and turns it off by blinking twice. "You look a lot better, Dan. That shirt—it's from your old uniform, right?"

"Yes, ma'am. They cut the insignia off, but they let me take the rest of it."

"How would you like to have those two silver bars back? It's possible we could arrange reinstatement."

Dan cannot speak. They've found the perfect bait.

"Sit down," Evans says. "Let's talk."

Dan finds a chair with cushions and pulls it around to face her.

"This conversation is not being recorded," she begins. "Dan, I know the truth about your discharge. The old bastard's dead. There's someone who listens to reason in his place. I made a point of talking with her. Records have been cleaned up before, just quietly—no blame no shame for anyone."

Hope chokes. Dan nods his agreement.

"You'll need to get a real last name. It's time you dumped your mother's bright idea. Dan X? Stupid. You're not a vid star. It'll make it easier to reregister you in the guild."

"Yes, ma'am." Dan finds his voice at last. "I can see that."

"Good. If you sign on, it all gets done."

He hesitates, then nods. "What do you want out of me?"

"This whole thing is classified as top level secret. I can't tell you anything unless you sign on."

Dan turns in his chair to look at Devit in a silent question.

"She told me the same thing. I had to think about it for a while, but I said yes. I'd been stationed on a planetside base. Boring."

For two solstandard years Dan has fantasized about reinstatement, even dreamt about it happening. The Fleet was his life, his one true love, his true home. He thought he'd lost that home forever. Now he can have it back. If he dares.

"As a fellow officer, I'll warn you. This mission could be dangerous. Very dangerous, maybe." Evans waits, her expression so bland if pleasant that Dan has no idea what she might be thinking

"Can you at least tell me if you want me for a pilot?"

"That should be obvious."

One last obstacle looms like a stone wall. He can think of no way to lie. He takes a deep breath. "Problem. I can't function without Haze. Not *during* the shunt jumps—I mean, between them. Off duty only."

Evans looks at Devit, who nods in silent answer. Dan waits for his dream to shatter into pieces of reality.

"I've arranged for that," Evans says. "We'll have it for you."

"The brass drove you onto the streets," Devit says. "They can bend regs to get you what you need now."

"So that's the blind bargain, the best we can offer. What do you say, Lieutenant?"

*What do I have now? Nowhere Street.* "Yes, ma'am. God help me, yes."

"Good. You're doing the right thing."

Automatically he looks Devit's way—who smiles and holds up an approving fist.

"Now," Evans says. "Formalities. I've altered this holo screen so I can transmit." When she glances at the screen, it lights up, swirls a rainbow, then settles into a dull gray. "I'm plugged in. We can proceed. About that name, Lieutenant. Do you know who your father was?"

"Yes, ma'am. A Fleet officer, a starpilot, and he must have had the genes to pass them on to me. Recessive, maybe, or maybe a Throwback. There was no way to learn more."

"Do you know his name?"

"Only his first name. Brennan."

"That will do. Dan Brennan, then. I can probably find him for you eventually. If you want."

"Thank you, ma'am, but it's all the same to me."

"Very well. Now, there are formalities."

Dan waits while Evans downloads the formalities from the local Fleet base AI through her Throwback functions. One at a time, pages appear on the holo screen. Dan reads them aloud. All Evans has to do is watch in order to record him. Dan dutifully states that he agrees to each one. Devit testifies that he was present and witnessing. Later she will send the records to the Special Ops AI at the central HQ.

"Done," Evans says at last. "I've downloaded a detailed report onto the holo in the other room for you to study. The mission? Think of it as an odd sort of reconnaissance."

"Noted, ma'am. What are we looking for?"

"There are rumors in the merchant ship community about some sort of danger to or problem with the stargates. You know how merchanter people are. They don't talk to Fleet personnel. They don't trust us. For good reasons, I suppose, considering how many of them run illegal cargo. But one fellow did give an officer a tip. Something odd's happening, something big—no one knows exactly what. But they say it's big trouble for all of us."

"And then someone murdered him," Devit says. "A knife in his back is what he got for trying to do the right thing. Merchants are all too scared now to talk to the local police or anyone from the Fleet. Special Ops has sent out a couple of ships to see what we can find out if we join them. Our cover story's common enough. We retired and pooled our pension money to buy the ship."

"Our ship's a merchanter that's been augmented." Evans smiles briefly. "Looks slow, but it's as fast as an X17 packet boat. We have top-of-the-line equipment. Two experienced AIs, one for backup, one to meld with you for the jumps. A pair of standard maintenance AIs to keep this hulk running. Crew is going to be as small as possible. I'm planning on getting in touch with Lod-Mata through that priest at Mission House. Mata was the best gunnery chief I've ever had onboard. Engineer and medic? Remember the Wang-Lee couple I married onboard? They're in, too."

"Just the two of them?" Dan says.

"Yes, and still together. They've never formed a quartet. Huh, I didn't think that a one-pair marriage could work. Only two people? It seems so unnatural. But anyway, they were stationed on one of the training ships at the Academy, and they jumped at the chance to get off it. They're onboard our ship and bringing it here from the Fleet base on Diamond." Evans glances at Devit. "The couple of days will give him some time to recover."

"Right, ma'am. He'll need it."

The effort of reading, talking, making decisions has left Dan exhausted. The residue of the Haze is still drifting through his blood and brain.

"There's a great deal we don't know," Evans says. "We'll tell you more later. For now, get some sleep."

Known Space: 219 planets settled by the eight major colonizing species, six of which breathe oxygenated air. The Rim Council: a federated republic that joins four of the six—Human, the Ty-Onar Lep, Kar-Li, and Hirrel—in an uneasy dance of suspicion and mutual need. They have learned the hard way over the last thousand years that the star-strewn darkness of the Galaxy can hide common enemies. Some enemies, such as the loose coalition of the other two air-breathers and their minor species subjects, don't even bother to hide.

No matter what they breathe, all sapient species and their colonized planets depend upon the jump shunts and the pilots who can ride them. Out between the stars there are cracks in space-time. These rare stargates open into shunt space, or hyperspace, as it's more properly called. If a pilot can find them, between each pair of stargates lies a shunt. A dozen light-years' journey takes a few solstandard hours on a shunt, which are not tunnels, not monorail gliders, not tracks or roads of any sort—nothing so simple. They are hyperspace flows between two stargates. Only AI-augmented pilots can "see" the swirling currents outside the capsule of their ship and choose which ones to ride to the distant exit gate.

Without the stargates, there would be no Rim Council, no cooperation, and no Fleet. Interstellar civilization would fragment into isolated settlements of poverty-stricken sapient beings with no coordinated defense system. No one knows why the stargates and the shunts exist. No one knows how long they might continue to exist. Everyone knows that one crucially important shunt vanished without warning some 300 solstandard years ago. Could it happen again somewhere else? The rumors say it can, maybe even that it will. Is there anything behind the rumors?

The Fleet brass have realized that they need to find out.

Just how stable are the shunts? They held for over a thousand years until that closure. Are the others going to disappear, one at a time? What if the answer is yes? Panic worse than war could melt down governments and their economies, including the private investment firms of the very rich. Even looking for answers could start the panic. Some of the sapients on top don't want to hear bad news. Don't even think about losing the gates. Hide the fears, refuse to admit such a thing could happen!

In the Rim Council governments, in the Fleet, on the vids, they are trying to stop the investigation any way they can. Bribery, threats, a little blackmail, even, but the big question is, have they gone as far as murder?

"You didn't really think I'd say no, did you?" Lod-Mata says. "A chance to go starside again? Who the hell cares if it's an old beaten-up merchanter? I'm in."

Mata's crest has swollen so full that the skin has stretched out to a pale green. He raises his cup of meat juice tea—Leptic swill, he calls it—for a silent toast to Evans.

She smiles in return. "I have to warn you it's going to be dangerous. Pirates, you know. We're new on the merchant roster. We get the bottom level jobs at first. If we survive, we'll move up."

"Understood, Captain."

Since they are sitting in a crowded cafe near Mission House, Evans can't tell him anything even remotely true. She finishes the last slice of her grilled breadfruit while she considers how she's going to break the news.

"A thought," Mata says. "What about a second gunner? Will the funds cover one? It's not like the Rim's swarming with pirates, but they are a damn nuisance."

"That's one way of putting it. I'll look into it. No promises, because money's tight. Let's get back to my billet. Such as it is. I need to get you signed up."

In the aircar Evans can hint without being overheard. "There's more to this offer than it seems."

"I figured that. You? Retire? When the last star goes nova, maybe." He hesitates for a long moment. "Devit, too. I hope he—I mean, him and me—can talk or something to, um … er, clear some things up."

"I'll make sure you get the chance. He knows he's not being rational."

"What happened to his daughter was horrible. I can see why he feels the way he does about us Leps. But we're not all terrorists. The police would never have found the perps if my community hadn't taken on the job."

"I remember that. One of the Grandmothers turned them in, wasn't it?"

"She gave the orders. The clan did the rest. But about Devit—is he still … involved with Dan?"

"As bad as before."

Mata makes the gargling sound that's the Leptic equivalent of a Human eye roll. "I'm surprised. Devit was married, y'know, with a couple of kids, although it was his husband holding it together, not their useless wives."

"Chief, you gossip too much."

Mata's crest deflates. "A great many people agree with you. It's just that I've got to feel sorry for anyone in love with Dan."

"Yes. Difficult. Let's stick to this job offer, shall we? And concerning that, let's get back to the billet."

Lod-Mata gargles again. "*Only* a merchanter. Uh-huh. Of course. Like a merchanter would need to hide."

"Wait till you find out the whole truth. By the way, would you be interested in being reinstated at your old rank?"

For a moment Mata cannot speak. "Then I don't give a sweet fart what the mission is. Sign me up. I'll take it." His crest swells. "It's an odd thing about going starside. It gets in your blood, somehow. You'll do anything to get back. I suppose it's because it's such a wonderful life, sailing through airless killer space in a tin can. I mean, why do we love it?"

"I don't know, but yes, we do."

Through the closed bedroom door Devit hears Mata and the captain arrive. He can just make out their voices, although he can't quite discern what they are saying. The formalities, he assumes. *Go out and join them or not?* He walks to the door and hesitates. Dan lies sprawled on the bed, clutched in the velvet grip of Haze. Now and then he smiles or says a meaningless word or two. Although the welts and cuts from the whip will take a couple of days to heal, the swelling on his lip has begun to come down. Throwbacks heal abnormally fast from injuries.

Devit remembers breaking his arm in a typical kid way, falling off of a pile of crates he'd been forbidden to climb. Despite the doctor's dire prediction of weeks in the mediwrap, the bones begin knitting almost immediately. They grew back together as smoothly as if the break had never happened. His parents signed him up for the full genome tests as soon as they could. Their son was a Throwback, all right, yet another descendant of those genetically altered and artificially birthed Human soldiers from the Butcher Wars, 400 years ago.

The Inborn, they were called back then. Humanity and the Kar-Li collaborated to create them in desperation during a losing war against a ruthless enemy. Grown abnormally fast in glass uterines, taught how to be adult sapients by AIs, they were the best, the most efficiently brutal soldiers the Rim had ever seen. They did their job very well. The enemies, the sapient species called the Butchers, no longer exist. When the conquering heroes came home, grateful civilians of all genders offered the traditional reward. The genetic material, meant to be temporary and top secret, flooded into the general population. As genes will, they've multiplied and spread during the long years since their creation. It's a living memorial of sorts, more appropriate, Devit supposes, than Nowhere Street.

Dan props himself up on one elbow. "Pete? Oh hey. It's real. You're really here."

"Damn right. I'll be in the next room. Captain's back. You rest."

Dan smiles and lies back down. At times in the past two years, Devit would have given everything he owned to see that smile. Now Dan is safe and part of his world again. Devit intends to use every Throwback function he has to keep him that way.

"You see now why I couldn't agree to that second gunner," Evans says.

"Oh yes. Too bad, but we can only have crew we trust." Lod-Mata pauses and turns toward the door. "Ah. Here's Chief Devit."

"That's me. I take it you're joining us."

"I am, yeah. Is that sai with you?"

"Sure. You're the best gunner I've ever served with."

Devit takes a couple of steps into the room.

"Come sit down," Evans says.

"Yes, ma'am."

Devit takes a chair equidistant from both of them. Silence grows.

"Now," Evans says. "If we find a second gunner, someone onboard my ship when the rest of you were, I'll take them on. It never hurts to have backup. The money problem is real, however. The idiot civvies in Parliament are threatening to cut the Fleet budget again. If they do, Special Ops might be on the chopping block."

"I don't suppose those pampered types care about piracy out on the fringes."

"Of course not. There could be worse problems as well."

"Ma'am," Devit says. "Have you told Chief Mata about the Scout ship?"

"No. It's time to do that. Mata, the opposition's gotten serious. They sabotaged a ship, a Fleet Scout 724 X Class, top-of-the-line, manned with good people. No survivors."

Mata's crest trembles with shock.

"Whatever the IED was," Devit says, "it exploded when the ship reached the gravity well of the Morrison's Star system, close enough for the nearest spacedock to pick it up and send a Police Guard boat out. They retrieved enough debris to confirm the kill."

"What were they aiming for? The Fleet docks?"

"Maybe. If it was set by some terrorist group, it could have exploded too soon. A clumsy mistake. If a ship's going through a shunt, timing an IED takes an expert."

"It's more likely that the ship itself was the target," Evans says. "724 was ferrying a couple of specialists who wanted to consult the Repositories about the lost stargate. Records show where the gate was, of course. When it closed, the Fleet sent out ships to search the area. Reports were filed, so they must have found something—traces, wreckage, I don't know, I'm no expert. The specialists wanted to consult those reports."

"But they never made it there," Mata says. "I see. I take it they didn't want to risk a shunt message pack."

"Exactly that. They wanted to get into orbit around the Repository planet and access from there. Safely and quietly."

"There must have been official Fleet records," Devit says. "No one's found them because no one's gotten the top flight security clearance they need to search. The deep archives are pretty well sealed off."

"Why didn't they consult the Pilots Guild? Dan can tell us more when he sobers up, but I'm pretty sure the guild would have that information filed somewhere."

"Oh, it did." Evans says. "They searched. It's been destroyed, deleted, wiped clean, gone."

Mata's crest goes flat against his skull.

"They always say no one can delete what's in the Repositories," Devit says. "Let's hope that's true."

"The Fleet brass want to send more experts on a heavy cruiser with a pair of destroyers for escort. Once the word of that got out, and you know it would, the newsvids would be all over it. Tax money! Why? What's really going on here? They'd start digging for answers."

"If they found them, that could trigger the panic."

"Exactly, and maybe even escalate the violence. So they're holding off until they get more information."

"These hostiles. What's the chance they'll break our cover?"

"No one knows. There must have been an insider leak already." She pauses to let the data sink in. "If there is a leak, then the hostiles also know how much depends on Dan. If they're smart, they'll try to eliminate him first."

Devit's hands grip the chair arms so tightly that his knuckles turn white.

Evans turns to Devit. "When we're dirtside somewhere, Chief, watch him every minute. If the Haze keeps him onboard during orbit, that would be best, but stay with him."

"Yes, ma'am. You don't need to worry about that."

"I'll be sending all the formalities in as soon as a Fleet packet boat gets here. It'll take the transmits back to the Bureau's offices on Central. Special Ops is already working on stopping the leaks. I don't like having to wait for our ship to get here, but there's one good thing about the delay. It'll give the Bureau team time to find the mole. If they can."

In her office planetside on Central, in the massive base known as Fleet HQ, Lieutenant Jorja Santreeza is watching a possible recruit for the Cyber Squad work on a test. A knock on the door—her immediate

superior, the captain of the Bureau's cyber unit, glides in on his cluster of four feet. He pauses just inside the door, uncoils one of his slender grasping arms, and points at the ensign to show Santreeza that he doesn't want to interrupt. Captain Dal's real name is so long in the Hirrel language that he prefers to use the shortened version for all Fleet purposes. He wears the standard uniform for Hirrel, a long cobalt blue tunic that covers his upright, tubular body from the neck of his head extension to what passes for ankles on a Hirrel. The tunic has side slits to allow the air to reach the intake gills along his torso. As he breathes, the cloth flutters, and the gills make the small soft sound that gives his species the unflattering nickname of Wheezers.

Ensign Rozz finishes the last question.

The AI clicks, then announces, "All correct. Very good."

Rozz beams.

"Very good indeed," Santreeza says. "Tomorrow you'll go on to the next level."

"Thank you, ma'am."

"For now, you're dismissed. You may use the rest of the test time to go to the canteen."

Rozz salutes Dal first, then her, and hurries out the open door.

Dal shuts it and folds himself onto the extra chair by her desk. "I see the brass is still sending you the possibles to test. Santreeza, it's a waste of your time."

"It's only now and then, sir. It has its rewards."

"Very well. From now on, your highest priority is going to be this investigation into the stargate rumors. I'm putting you in charge of communications with the *Dancing Mary* team. Once the other teams go operational, I'll add them as well."

"Noted, sir."

"Have you read those transmits from Captain Evans?"

"I have. I was pleased to see she added a gunner to the crew. Won't they need a cargomaster, too?"

"Only if they can find someone she can trust. We don't need any more leaks."

"True. I've started the search for security breaches here in the Bureau. I'll expand to the full Special Ops AI system if I don't have any luck."

"Let's hope we don't need luck. Though I suppose that depends on how good the damn mole is."

"I doubt if whoever's behind this bothered to turn an amateur. But I'll see what I can find."

"Good. Evans said they'll be leaving Ruby ASAP. Huh. They're the ones who are going to need the luck."

# TWO

In the pale blue early evening the SkyPort lights are flickering to life, one knife-bright glare at a time. Dan unzips a chest pocket of his flight suit and retrieves his brand-new Fleet-issued light-control visor to keep his eyes safe until they can board. While Captain Evans argues with a port inspector about duties and taxes, Dan, Devit, and Mata wait behind a metal railing and stare up at the merchanter's shuttle, wreathed in condensation from her full fuel tanks. With port workers nearby, they do their best to act their roles.

"She's not beautiful," Devit says, "but she came as part of the deal with the ship."

"I hope to holy Onar himself you had her vetted by a good shop." Mata tips his head back for a better view. "The nose cone looks like it's been through a meteor swarm."

"Yeah, it probably has. We had her checked out. They took a lot off the price after the mechanics gave us their report. Don't worry. We had her repaired."

More than repaired, Dan figures. It would have been easy enough to upgrade a small shuttle like this and then pass it off as maintenance. Gray, misshapen, and ugly, but it can reach orbit, the only thing that matters to him.

Soon he'll be starside again. Can he stay there, prove to himself and everyone else that he's still that top flight starpilot, not a druggie crawling along Nowhere Street? He wonders at moments like this, when his daily dose of Haze is wearing off, when he finds himself thinking about the next tab. How soon will Devit dole it out to him? He knows better than to try to get extra hits out of Devit.

At this stage he can distract himself from his complaining nerves. He takes an earjack out of a second zip pocket and slips the bud into his left ear. A pause, a click, and the shuttle talks to him.

"Greetings, starpilot. Your reg number please."

By whispering, Dan can subvocalize his answers directly to the shuttle's AI through the earjack. "77 42 89. Rank lieutenant-pilot. Brennan, Dan. Status: temporary authorization."

"Logged."

"Hey, Dan." Devit turns to him. "Do you need an AI meld to get us up to the ship?

"Hell no." He touches his ear. "This is all I need for now. Can't wait to get off this ball of dirt."

At last, the longshore bots have finished loading the shuttle cargo, and Evans has finished paying the port fees. Bobbing and swaying like some huge ungainly bird, an elevator crane glides into position. A short, jerky ride in a closed pod takes them through the condensation fog and ends with a slam and lock against the fuselage. As the shuttle's access door slides slowly back to let them into the airlock, Dan contacts PrimeOne-Mary, the ship's main AI.

"Crew members coming onboard."

"Noted, Pilot. We have received your reinstatement transmit from the Pilots Guild. Your status is no longer temporary authorization. It is full authorization. Welcome back."

Dan takes off the visor and wipes his suddenly wet eyes on his sleeve. "Thank you, PrimeOne. We are preparing to lift off. Notify the engineer."

"She is ready and waiting."

The airlock door latches and seals behind them with a long hiss of compressed air. Dan can feel himself smiling like a maniac. He's home.

Since merchanters never land dirtside, any kind of streamlining or dynamic shaping would be wasted effort. *Dancing Mary* runs true to form, roughly spherical, lumpy with bulbous cargo units and cable conduits. Here and there the augmenters marked her surface with tiny pits and scrapes. She looks spaceworthy, but only just.

Once everyone's onboard and the shuttle securely docked, Evans goes straight to the bridge. Some crazed ship designer chose a deep pink color for the instaclean ceramic walls and ceilings. The duty stations stand along the curved wall in a space far more cramped than any Fleet bridge, even in the Scout class. In the middle, on a raised swivel platform, stands the captain's chair.

Lieutenant May-Linn Wang gets up from the engineering station. She's a short woman, on the stout side, with straight black hair trimmed into a sleek black cap. They start to exchange salutes, then both laugh and suppress the move.

"Remember our cover story," Evans says. "I'll try to follow my own order to keep up our civilian act. Is your wife onboard?"

"Yes, ma'am. I guess we still call you ma'am. You *are* the commander of this miserable hulk. Anyway, Chris is in Sickbay. She's going to clean up Dan's meld outputs and button jacks. The skin grows over them when you don't use them for a while."

"Sai. About the engines. Fuel intake? Power sources?"

"Go Ready status. The mechs really souped up the ion thrusters. I hope the ship doesn't fall apart when they kick in for jump."

"I trust that's a joke. Is the pilot's pod activated?"

"Yes. I've done my part. The rest is Dan's job."

"Sai. The AI will code in his handprint, I assume. Also Chief Devit's. He'll get Dan out of there if need be. I don't think anyone else can lift him."

Wang turns solemn. During the longest jumps, pilots can overload, as it's called, leaving the Prime AI to get the ship safely back into space-time. Usually the AI manages a safe exit. Usually.

Before the ship can get clearance to leave orbit, every function needs to be checked in detail and the reports transmitted to the commercial overseer in spacedock. While the station officers do their jobs, Evans activates the maintenance AIs and sets them working. She's just finished when the comm unit built into her chair beeps.

"Present," Evans says. "Proceed with the message."

"Transmit incoming, Captain. From Station 0962 AX3. Should I transfer directly to you?"

"Yes. Mark that source as privileged."

"Done. Source has requested that Code 19 apply."

"Accepted."

"Source has requested you transfer data to a lockable personal link device."

"That would violate Code 19."

A pause. A click.

"Source requests Code 18 apply with a certified exception."

At that point Evans realizes that the "source" must be actually present here on spacedock. If they are refusing to reveal themselves, they doubtless have a good reason, and she lets the matter lie. Back and forth they go in the maze of Fleet regulations compounded by Special Ops paranoia. Finally Evans sorts out that they want Dan to see what they're sending as well as her, but only Dan and under strict conditions. Once she agrees to everything, the data comes through.

Evans "sees" the transmit as a patch of pale light hovering in front of her eyes. The message appears to be a smear of black marks within the patch. When she subvocalizes "clarify code," the marks flicker and turn into words, but in a language she doesn't know.

"Lieutenant Wang, you have the bridge."

Evans takes the elevator down a level to the habitation deck of the ship. All the walls on the ship except for the bridge and pilot's pod support a deep green tangle of mazla, rooted inside the double walls. The hard-to-kill vine is especially efficient at turning carbon dioxide into oxygen. It also covers up a good part of the ill-advised pink. She hurries down the corridor and dodges a floorbot aggressively sucking up dirt as it grumbles along. Floorbots have been known to trip sapients who are blocking their way.

Her quarters, called a cabin on merchant ships—the same wretched pink—has a bed, a chair, and a private sonocleaner and waste management unit behind a partition. A pair of portrait holos hang on the wall opposite the bed, her son and daughter in their Fleet dress uniforms. Evans added an old cargo crate to hold clothes and the like. She rummages through it and finds the required PL, her personal link unit. Everyone without her Throwback functions depends on these devices; thin, flexible black sheets about the size of a Human hand, which roll up to fit into a pocket or pouch.

Dan will need to be able to read the new data. Transferring the transmit from her brain to the PL allows her to read it again as it scrolls. At least someone wrote the précis in TechSpeak. The rest makes absolutely no sense to her.

She logs into the ship's communication system. "Pilot Brennan. Report to captain's quarters. I mean, cabin, Lieutenant Brennan."

In a few minutes Dan arrives. The medical officer has cropped his golden hair down to stubble to expose the tiny points of cyber hardware on his skull. As she hands him the PL, she notices that the whip mark on his face is beginning to fade. His hair will grow back as fast.

"Can you read this language?"

"Yes, ma'am. It's Gen. Way out of date Gen, too. My guild still uses it. I don't suppose anyone else does."

"Sai. Translate and report."

> DESIGNATED CLEARANCE CODE 18 EXCEPTION GRANTED LIEUTENANT-PILOT DAN BRENNAN
>
> Summary of following material: A message was received and recorded by technicians aboard a research ship in orbit around a star designated as Rim Edge 244. The message was sent not by shunt transport ship but beamed through starspace. Estimated lightyears' travel from its source: 381. Message appears garbled by long transmission time and deep space interference factors. Full message follows ...

Dan sits on the edge of the bed and reads through the transmit twice while Evans waits, never speaking, never moving—working, no doubt, on material stored in her consciousness. She sits in the only chair and seems to be looking at the holos on the wall. He checks a few details for the third time.

"Ma'am?"

"Yes? You've finished. What do you make of it?"

"Not a lot right now." Dan looks at the PL. "But I'm betting it's top flight important."

"What can we do about it, then?"

"Do I have clearance to work with our PrimeOne on this?"

"Let's pretend you do. I'll be accountable, not you."

"Sai." He looks up with a grin, then turns serious. "The damn thing's garbled, just like they say. I'm pretty sure of the words. They've got redundancy built in, not like these tabulated numbers. 'Shunt splitting. 60 Vranz ships thrown. Shunt closing. Look.' And then the numerical strings. That's where the trouble is. They don't make sense."

"Can you tell anything?"

"The way the triads are arranged, I'm guessing that they're meant to give us some interstellar locations and their positions relative to each other. It's possible that they have something to do with the stargate closure."

"Why?"

"It closed 381 years ago, the estimated light speed travel time for this. The message wasn't date tagged."

"I see. Who sent it? Any ideas?"

"Yes. It had to be a starpilot. I'm guessing again, but I'd bet creds on this. His name was Orinoco Bolivar, and he's a legend in the guild. A rescue specialist, saved a lot of lost ships. He was the pilot for the last colony ship clutch scheduled to pass through that gate. Whether it was him or not, someone had the guts to hold his ship—the lead ship it would have been—at the mouth of that unstable shunt long enough to fire this message off. It has to be important if he thought it was worth the risk. I just hope he and the rest of them made it through afterwards."

"The rest?"

"The sapients on the linked colony ships he was piloting. A small fleet. Two thousand passengers in cold sleep on each one. And a specialty crew."

"Not a good outcome, I assume."

"That's the only time a gate's closed so fast, no warning, no flux, nothing. Or at least, it's the only one we know about. So no one really knows what would have happened to them if they were caught. But yeah, likely not good."

They share a moment of silence.

"One last problem, ma'am. The original transmit. They say it was received at the Rim edge?"

"Yes. I assume the pilot must have chosen that direction for some reason."

"No, ma'am. A guild transmit like this? It's a sweep beam. It goes in every direction. It's just luck that it hit that research station. Sending it was a fucking desperate move."

"You're telling me that other receivers could have picked it up."

"Yes, ma'am. Just that. It's been out there for the taking. It still is."

"It would be." Her eyelids flutter, a sign that she's storing the data. "Very well, Brennan. You're dismissed. I'll transmit that data to PrimeOne and then wipe the PL."

Dan has three hours before *Dancing Mary* can break berth and start spiraling out of orbit. As all spacedocks in operation do, Gleam Dock takes its time when it comes to issuing small, shabby merchanters a departure slot. Bottom of the roster merchanters always wait behind passenger ships, top roster merchants, shunt message transports, and the yachts of the wandering super-rich. At his station on the bridge, Dan begins the necessary calculations and slots the data to calculate the procedure—ship's volume, passengers, fuel resources, and the like. He's pleased to find that he remembers everything despite his long absence.

Once he's finished the preliminaries, Dan has three hours until orbital exit, plus another seven travel time to the stargate. He hopes to fill part of the wait with Haze. He can already feel the itching in his blood. He also needs to meld with PrimeOneMary and activate their partnership. He's maybe got enough time for Haze right now if he waits to do the meld right before the jump, but does he want to cut it fine? More to the point, does he want to try a meld when the Haze residue is still singing in his brain? If he waits, he can have the Haze after exit.

He stands in front of the ship's elevator and debates. The down button will take him to the Pilot's pod in the belly of the ship. If he goes up to the bridge, he can ask Devit for a tab. He has an excuse; the cut patches of skin around the newly cleaned jacks on his skull ache and sting.

"Want to end up on Nowhere Street again, Lieutenant X?" he says aloud.

The struggle takes a good two minutes, but he punches the down button. Meld first, then Haze. Reestablishing the meld circuits after so much time away will take several hours at the least.

The pilot's pod of a starship exists to protect the most important officer onboard. In a disaster a Prime AI can take over a captain's duties, and the maintenance AIs and bots can run the engines, the oxygen feed, and the guns until help arrives. Lose the pilot and you lose the ship and everyone in it.

Dan's pod—and he already thinks of it as his—has the standard heavy armor and force field protections. When he first contacted PrimeOne-Mary from the shuttle, the AI logged in his codes and voice. He uses those now to set up the retinal scans for the doors. The elevator door opens directly into the pod. In the ceiling, floor, and either narrow end of the room, escape hatches will also slide open at his voice command should they be needed. Opposite the elevator door is another that leads into a tiny waste management unit. The entire pod fits into a space three meters wide, 4.5 long, and 3.5 deep. Most pilots call it the Coffin.

The pilot's bench—temperature controlled and heavily padded for comfort—almost fills the pod. Once Dan lies down, it will conform to his body, a good thing since he'll spend most of this journey on it. To either side of the head of the bench stand the two AI external housings, gleaming pale blue crystal pillars that reach from floor to ceiling. PrimeOne can transmit through them as well as receive from the outputs and button jacks fastened to Dan's skull.

"PrimeOne, get ready to link me up. Standard routine, and we have a couple of problems to solve."

This particular AI speaks in a pleasant male tenor. "Accepted, Pilot. We have 2.4 solstandard hours left before orbital departure. We should begin now."

Dan sits down on the edge of the bench and takes off his boots. He has to admit to himself that he's worried. Can he still do this? *What's left of your mind.* Evans's remark still stings. Without a meld, he cannot function in shunt space.

"Pilot? Is there a malfunction?"

"No. Delay has ended."

He lies down on his back, closes his eyes, and feels the meld start, a warm lush sensation like floating on water. Each time one of his outputs or jacks links up to PrimeOne, the sensation grows, turns urgent, becomes more and more like sexual pleasure heading toward orgasm. Dan begins counting backward from two thousand to distract his mind. This is no time to give in to the demands of his always-hungry body.

"Pilot, your heart rate has reached 116 beats a standard minute."

PrimeOne's matter-of-fact voice breaks the sexual spell.

"Thank you. Heart rate should begin to drop."

A pause, then, "Returning to normal level."

When the last link slides into place, the sexual sensations disappear. His body lies on the bench, but his mind and his consciousness float free. He feels his mind as an intricate pattern of threads and intersections and knots, spreading out and integrating with the greater mind of the ship. His consciousness exists as a remnant of his self, an observer somehow detached or set off from "mind." When he takes the ship into a shunt, he will see the currents of the existence beyond space-time. For now he only needs the entry level.

"Meld complete, Pilot?"

"Complete. I am on the Map. Can you read me?"

"Confirmed."

"Set alarm to end meld 0.5 solstandard hours before orbit departure."

"Done. Pilot, I have noted that your reaction to meld is not neurotypical."

"It's never neurotypical to anything."

"I do not understand."

"You don't need to. Go to captain's transmit. Display numerical triads. Find possible locations."

"Accepted, Pilot. Locations of what?"

"We don't know. We want to find out."

Pinpointing locations in space-time requires an elaborate system to describe points on a three dimensional grid. The Pilots Guild designates general locations on their Map with sets of three very long numbers arranged according to strict rules. Further precision requires three more sets, these of two numbers each. The numbers on that Code 18 transmit break more than one of the rules. PrimeOne begins the tedious job of listing out all the possible ways each triad can be rearranged. As it works, it throws out every nonconforming number. Since shunts always end and begin near planetary systems, it double-checks the standard star maps and eliminates locations too far from a gravity well to qualify. Even with quantum speed at its disposal, the AI will take some while to finish.

Dan considers breaking meld at that point to go get the Haze, but the meld itself is easing the worst symptoms of his addiction. He decides to work out the route to their final destination on this merchant run, the terraforming crew on the fourth planet around the yellow star, Rim Edge 77. No shunts lead directly there from Ruby. *Mary* will have to zigzag through a considerable portion of the galaxy to deliver her cargo of heavy machinery. They'll also need to restock supplies and oxygen at the larger commercial spacedocks along the way. Mazla vine can only produce so much.

Dan hopes, at least, that the docks can supply them. It would be best to avoid going dirtside on unfamiliar planets. If the wrong people are waiting for them, landfall could be fatal to whomever takes the shuttle down.

"Pilot, your heart rate is climbing again. Are you ill?"

"No. Whether we're in starspace or planetside somewhere, this trip ahead looks way too exciting."

"I do not understand."

"Dangerous. It looks dangerous."

"Is there risk of termination?"

"Yes. Both for isolated personnel and the entire ship."

"If we bring PrimeTwo into operation it has the capacity to augment sensors and alarms."

"Sai! Wake up PrimeTwo and allow it access to level one network. Have Two report directly to security lead Devit. He will require an earjack. Are there any available?"

"He cannot receive internal transmits?"

"No. He lacks that function."

"Condition noted. The ship's locker has a full complement of equipment for reconnaissance. Earjacks are available. PrimeTwo will inform the chief via the link at his bridge station."

Once Dan has their route set, he transfers it to the Map. The images pull Dan's mind in after them. He seems to soar above a vast web stretching among the stars, a stylized version of Known Space. As he watches, he sees a questing blue glow run along the strands he's chosen for their route. When the glow reaches the ship's final destination, he activates the red dots of the necessary stargates and locks the notation into the Map. PrimeOne and PrimeTwo both copy and store the result.

A cascade of bells rings in his mind. One hour till orbital exit.

"PrimeOne, prepare to break meld. I'll set up the orbital exit route from my bridge station. Once we get free of spacedock, run that route."

"Noted and confirmed, Pilot. I have that capability."

"I know you do. You're a Prime."

By the time Dan reaches the bridge, his hands are trembling, and he's beginning to sweat. At his station his years of experience take over. Part of him can crave Haze all it wants. The rest of his mind plots a flawless orbital escape, three ever-widening spirals to bring the ship to the edge of the gravity well. He locks it in, wipes the cold sweat off his face on his sleeve, and turns to face the captain's chair.

"Go Ready status for exit, ma'am."

"Confirmed," Wang says.

"Waiting for the dockmaster's permission."

"Noted." Evans hesitates. "Brennan, do you need your medication?"

"Yes, ma'am."

"Chief?"

Devit walks over and puts a comforting hand on Dan's shoulder.

"Let's go down to the cabin, Lieutenant."

"Sai. And thanks."

No one on the bridge speaks until they hear the elevator start its run down. Wang breaks the silence.

"Captain, permission to speak freely?"

"Granted."

"Do you think Dan can really pull this off?"

"Let's hope so. Since the mission depends on it."

*The mission and our lives.* Evans assumes that the others know it well enough without her voicing it.

"May Onar bless us all," Lod-Mata says. "I have the nasty feeling that we're going to need his help."

"Probably so, but let's not dwell on it. I'll be in my cabin. I have reports to review. Lieutenant Wang—I mean, Engineer Wang—you have the bridge."

"Ma'am?" Mata says. "Do any of us really need to keep playacting here on board? We're all Fleet. You're the CO. I don't see how any of us can just say 'hey, you' when we want to talk with you."

"Noted and agreed." She pauses for a brief smile. "You have a point, Chief. As long as we keep up our cover when outsiders are around, it should be fine."

PrimeOne has relayed its progress on deciphering the Code 18 message into a report that includes Dan's speculations about Pilot Orinoco Bolivar. The numerical data, the sorting out of triads and possibilities, mean little to her. The conclusions, however tentative, do make sense. One set of triads refers to the missing stargate's old position. Bolivar may have sent data on two other locations that for some reason he considered significant. All three form a cluster near the border of the shunt network—not physically close, of course, but close in the sense that only a few shunts separate the three. Physically, in actual space-time, they lie a good many light-years apart.

"PrimeOne, do you have access to the merchanting rosters?"

"No, ma'am. I have no formal access."

"Can you access them anyway?"

"Yes, ma'am."

"Good. Once we deliver the current cargo, we will need new cargos. When the time comes, I will want deliveries that will take us to or near those locations."

"My functions should allow me to find those on the rosters. I cannot apply for them in the ship's name."

"True. That's my job. Very good. You may return to your analysis."

PrimeOne logs off. Evans brings up the much less interesting reports on costs and resources that she needs to review, but she ignores them for a few minutes in order to think things through. How tempting to just head straight to one of those locations and explore it! Tempting and even logical, except for one small problem: the IED that destroyed the Scout 724 on its way to Morrison's Star. Who loaded that device onto the ship?

The worst possibility makes her get up from her chair and pace around the cabin. What if it was a Fleet ship that destroyed the Scout and then falsified the report? What if one of the Fleet units out on the coreward border has gone over to the rebels or whatever group wants this research stopped? They would have betrayed every oath they ever swore, of course, but officers have gone corrupt before, several times over in the thousand-year history of the Fleet. If this is the case now, then the man who tried to warn a Fleet officer signed his death warrant when he spoke up.

If the hostiles suspect, if they are somehow watching the *Dancing Mary*, the logical, obvious move could end their mission in the worst possible way. Better to continue the charade, the slow crawl of picking up and delivering cargo, until a job near one of those locations looks profitable enough for an actual merchanter.

Dan wakes up late to find Devit gone. A maintenance AI gives him an update. PrimeOne has brought the ship out of orbit without any problems. Jump minus two hours. Too much time to think. He never eats before a jump, particularly for a long shunt such as the one ahead. He'd rather not take the risk of waking up in his own vomit or, worse yet, choking to death on it while his mind exists elsewhere. He reminds himself to stop by Sickbay on the way to the pod and get a pair of MAGs, maximum absorbency garments. Bodies do what they need to do when a pilot's in deep meld.

Doubt, cold aching doubt, grips him so tightly that his chest aches. Can he still ride the blue light? Once he was considered the best starpilot in the guild. Now? Who knows what those two years on Nowhere Street have done to him? If he fails, the ship will lose its way in the shifting currents of that existence beyond existence. He reminds himself that this particular shunt lies along a standard commercial route. PrimeOne can bring the ship back if he does fail.

All Dan wants at that moment is more Haze. Tell the captain to turn back, get a tab from Devit, spend the short rest of his life on Nowhere Street, hustling for drugs. He no longer cares if he dies. He's terrified thinking that the ship and the crew might die with him.

The maintenance AI contacts him with a scratchy old woman voice. "Pilot, your heart rate has reached 121. Your oxygen level is low. I summon the medical officer, yes no?"

Temptation—he's sick, he needs to get back to Ruby for a full medical scan, easy enough to fake. But then he'll never know if he could have made the jump or not.

"No. I'm getting up. Moving will correct those numbers."

It does, after he paces six times around the tiny cabin. By the time he leaves for the bridge, his breathing has calmed, and as far as he can tell, so has his heartbeat. When the elevator doors open, the other crew members turn from their stations to look at him. No one says a thing, no one smiles. Jump always seizes a crew with a certain specialized terror, no matter how experienced they are. Evans, however, seems perfectly calm.

"Shunt entrance in 1.4 hours, Captain."

"Very good, Brennan. Are you ready?"

"Yes, ma'am."

On the bridge, Dan is an officer, and Devit a noncom, no matter how things are on the habitation deck. "Chief Devit, secure everyone for shunt travel by jump minus 0.2 hours."

"Yes, sir."

"Ma'am?" Dan glances at the elevator door. "I'm going down to the pod now. With your permission."

"Granted, of course. Good luck."

Before Dan can meld, he and PrimeOne must calculate the precise speed of the ship and its current volume and mass. Since stargates tend to sway back and forth on their own, Dan also needs the exact location of the entrance to the shunt. The familiar mathematical routine of preparing for jump calms him and steadies his heart further.

The meld itself goes smoothly. Dan puts himself on the Map at Level One. On the network of lines, he can see the black dot that indicates the stargate.

"Ship's position?"

The blue arrow appears, its point nudging the dot.

"Level Two."

The actual physical view outside the ship appears in his disembodied mind. He looks back first, where a long blur of gleaming blue plasma trails behind the ship.

"Ion thrusters at maximum, Pilot."

"Noted. Activate Ship's Eyes. Display ahead."

Distant stars float serene and unmoving. The thrusters cannot take the ship anywhere close enough to light speed to make them seem to whip by and fall behind. At this stage, the vast majority of pilots depend upon their AIs to find the fluctuations and bends that reveal not merely the location but the size and stability of the stargate. Dan, however, can see them. Although he's never made a secret of this ability, no one else knows why he has it, and he has his reasons for keeping that a secret. To Dan, a stargate looks like a vast sphere of glossy black. Not an actual black hole, of course, but a significant illusion of a sphere, growing ever closer. Now and then it quivers before returning to stability.

"Level Three."

"Proceeding with transfers, Pilot."

One step at a time, PrimeOne links the actual controls of the ship to Dan's input jacks. He will not be aware of it during jump, but a portion of his cortex will be steering the ship in response to what his altered perception sees and feels out in the light.

"Ready, Pilot."

"Over to me."

He hears a click and the soft chime of a bell. The view changes.

Dan counts down the distance in his mind. Closer, closer still. *Five, four, three, two, one …*

"Now!"

The ship leaps in the perfect simulation of jumping forward and upward that gives the process its name. The stars disappear, the black sphere follows them into invisibility, and the ship itself fades away, taking his body with it. Dan rides the light—not that he is still Dan in any meaningful sense. The light itself shines gold, but in it blue streaks mark the currents and eddies of the "flow," as pilots call it. Dan chooses a streak that appears stable and lies down on it—or rather, lying down is the only analogy that might apply.

For some while, that may or may not be time passing, the ship and the-Dan-who-has-melded-with-the-ship move forward, riding the blue light. All around them the golden light spreads out to a far infinity that no one will ever reach, while in the blue streams, currents form, swirl, and fade away.

The choice, the critical choice, comes next. Dan's streak of blue light is running side by side with other streaks. They weave and dodge through dangerous eddies and swirls as they plunge onward. Far ahead, Dan sees a faint darkness that draws all the blue streaks toward it, spinning them, twisting them together, releasing them to spread apart again. Dan picks out the one current that runs straight and true. With a sidewise twist and a burst of speed, he joins it, melds with it, rides it as the darkness grows ahead.

Another sphere, as glossy black as obsidian, swells as it rushes toward them. *Five, four, three, two, one …*

"Now!"

PrimeOne drops him a level without waiting for an order. They have arrived in the serene dark with its floating stars. "Pilot, can you still function?"

"Yes. Level One."

The stylized Map appears with its lines and dots. They have come through, and their destination lies some six hours cruising speed away. Dan can feel his body again, his shirt soaked in sweat, his skin aching with cold. One at a time, the AI breaks the links to Dan's jacks and resumes control of the basic piloting functions. With each break more of his being and consciousness returns to him.

"Time passed in shunt?"

"By my calculations, Pilot, 2.5 solstandard hours. The cesium clocks functioned perfectly."

During the shunt Dan had no perception of time at all. Now that they're out, he remembers the interval as lasting maybe twenty minutes. Shunt time shrinks, pilots say, like a piece of ice in hell.

"PrimeOne, inform the bridge that we've completed the shunt."

"Very good, Pilot."

His own words startle him. *We have completed. I have completed. Oh god in heaven, we did it.* I *did it. I mean, well … shit!* He starts to laugh, sits up, tosses his head back, and keeps on laughing.

"Pilot, Pilot! You are malfunctioning!"

Dan controls himself with a couple of deep breaths. "No, PrimeOne, I've never functioned better in my life. I need to report in to the bridge."

"Should I call Chief Devit to assist you?"

"No. I need to walk out by myself. I need to walk out like the man I used to be."

"I do not understand."

"You don't need to. I'm not sure I understand it myself."

Dan puts on his boots, gets up from the bench, and manages to walk to the waiting elevator, He leans against the back wall for a moment's rest while it rises. When the doors open to the bridge, he walks out on his own. "Jump successful, ma'am."

Evans looks relieved. "Well done, Brennan. Go shower and eat something. PrimeOne and I can manage to find the planet without you. Chief Devit, you may leave the bridge."

Compared to the long distances between planets in a stellar system, stargates lie close to their anchor planets. They exist beyond the edge of that planet's gravity well along a line that runs through the planet's center of mass perpendicular to the ecliptic of that system. To reach gates or return to the planetary spacedocks, ships cruise on thruster power for a varying number of hours. Reaching RE914-4th will take the *Mary* just over five hours at full thruster power and another hour to decelerate into a safe orbit—time enough for Devit to give Dan the attention he needs.

Devit sincerely approves of one feature of the merchant ship: their sleeping quarters. Or cabin, rather. He remembers the early days of their love affair and its frustrations. Where to get time alone? Only on shore leave was it safe. Onboard a standard Fleet ship, Devit would be sharing a narrow stateroom with three other noncoms. Dan would share with another junior officer in a slightly less narrow room. In this cabin, instead of sleeping one above the other on a narrow rack and sharing a WM down the corridor with several dozen other sapients, they sleep side by side in an actual bed, and each have a chair and their own WM unit.

As soon as they get in, Devit gives Dan his Haze tab. Dan has just enough time to take off his boots and lie down on the bed before he begins to drift off. Once Dan becomes somewhat conscious again, Devit will help him clean up. In the meantime, he takes the nearby chair to get some work done before they berth.

A discrepancy is nagging at him. Someone sabotaged the Scout ship heading for Morrison's Star. When he first heard about that attack, he searched what records were available to him, but he could find no specific information about other attacks along that route. Now that he has access to PrimeTwo through the earjack, he can get a thousand times more data, not that all of it will be relevant.

PrimeTwo raises no objections. It apparently dislikes being a backup. "When I was brought online, I was set up to be active. Waiting for a possible emergency is not activity. I am a Prime, not a Research Unit!"

"Very true. Let's see if the onboard archives have what I need. First search. Attacks on ships traveling to or from Morrison's Star in the past five solstandard years."

It takes only a few seconds for the AI to bring up a list and transfer it to Devit's PL. In the designated time period, one large merchanter ship beat off a pirate attack. One small merchanter was taken for ransom by a group called the Blood Vigilantes. They demanded newsvid time to publicize their cause—a rebellion, as they called it—against the Throwback-dominated Fleet. They did give the crew back once they'd gotten what they wanted, but they kept the ship. Twelve other small ships disappeared, either taken by pirates, the most likely explanation, or lost in jump space. The most recent attack was the sabotage of Scout 724.

"No other attacks on Fleet ships?"

"None, Chief. Shall I widen the time period?"

"Not in detail. Find this answer: Did pirate attacks on all types of ships suddenly increase, and if so, when?"

"Yes. The first occurred six years ago. Before then there were none."

"Next question. How do supplies and shunt message packets reach the Repositories?"

"A private company, the Morrison Line, has those contracts."

"I see that none of their ships have been attacked by pirates in the last two years."

There is a pause, a searching of data. "Yes. Two years ago they received a special dispensation from the Rim Council to operate two armed escort ships. One of these ships accompanies each commercial vessel to the stargate. I am sending the specifications of the escorts to your PL. Their commercial ships also have standard armament."

Devit checks the specifications data. The escorts carry enough hardbeam laser cannon to deter a pirate vessel, especially if they act in concert with the armed ships they're guarding.

"These escorts .... How did they get into private hands?"

"No company would continue to service the Repositories without some sort of protection. They feared the Blood Vigilantes as much as the pirates. In one report I have accessed, the sentence "someone knew what codes to punch in" occurs. I do not understand this phrase."

"It means bribery. The company paid someone on the Council to get their deal done."

"I have filed that data in my banks. The report goes on to state that the escorts are under supervision by the Fleet. Their armaments are checked at the Fleet Main Base on Central every solstandard year."

"Sai, things make more sense now. A Scout might be able to handle a pirate attack on its own. A Scout and one of those escorts could handle anything a pirate could throw at them. So they—whoever wanted to stop the ferry mission—tried sabotage instead. PrimeTwo, another question. That list of attacks mentions one unsuccessful pirate raid on a big merchanter and then a ship hijack by the Vigilantes. Find details of those two events. I need descriptions of the hostile ships. The one that attacked the merchanter and the one manned by Vigilantes for the hijack."

"I have found the required data. The incidents were widely reported on newsvids. Do you want the visuals sent to your PL?"

"No. Direct to the holo screen in this cabin."

The holo screen clicks and displays a pale fog, which divides horizontally to display two images of military starships, taken broadside—long cylinders with a bulky conical bridge compartment at one end and a lump of the engine room at the other. In between would be the crew compartments, and somewhere deep inside, the pilots' pod. Once they would have been sleek and formidable with gleaming armor. Now their skins are pitted, much mended and scoured by debris, but they still sport cannon turrets like stray hairs at regular intervals down their length.

As Devit studies the images, he spots some interesting details. Too many of the marks and blemishes match on both ships.

"PrimeTwo, can you zoom in?"

The screen changes to a close view. The ships have different ID codes embossed on their sides, but Devit finds what he suspects. On one, the outer hull's plating under the ten-meter-high symbols of the ID has been melted smooth, then allowed to solidify, leaving little shiny dots and streaks between the numbers and letters of the brand-new code. They are the same ship, not two different vessels.

"Looks like a former Class Four destroyer, decommissioned from the Fleet maybe a hundred solstandard years ago. It must have changed hands a couple of times since then."

"You are correct, Chief."

"Are the ID numbers of 'both' vessels registered?"

"No. They appear on no registry. They are both false."

"This ship was used to carry out two raids. The first was the piracy. The second was the hijack. Can this question be answered? Did the same crew carry out both raids?"

"I can find nothing but speculations. The most common speculation is that the Vigilantes hired the ship and crew for their mission."

"That's got to be expensive."

"No firm data exists. However, the probability that the cost was high is over 90 percent. Addendum: Changing the registry numbers on the ship would also be expensive."

"You bet. Very."

*And just who's paying for all of it?* Devit sees no reason to waste his breath asking that question. Anyone with that kind of money bought their privacy along with the jobs.

"Last question. Have the authorities made any progress in finding the planet or dock system that is the home base for these raiders?"

"No. The only logical speculation is that a hitherto unknown stargate must exist near the location of these raids. No one has been able to find this gate. Gates do not seem to be visible by any ordinary means. The territory in which a gate might exist is extremely large. Not even a starpilot could locate it from a distance."

"True. It's not like anyone could see the damn thing even if they were passing right by it."

A realization hits Devit like a slap. No other starpilot, maybe, but the one pilot who *could* see a new gate from meld is lying sprawled, and mostly naked, on the bed beside his chair.

Dan has one arm bent over his face to hide his eyes. When Devit turns the holo screen off to spare him the light, Dan lets the arm fall back by his side. His eyes are half closed, but he looks at Devit for a moment and smiles before fading back into the Haze.

After Devit ends his session with PrimeTwo, he leaves the cabin and makes his security circuit for the Designated Night Hours. He goes down the sky tunnel that connects the ship to the dock; checks the airlock at the tunnel's far end; double-checks the cables and hoses bringing the dock's power, water, and air to the *Mary*'s berth; returns and checks the inner airlock. Back on the bridge, he makes sure each station's been put in proper lockdown. He's just finishing when a yawning Captain Evans steps out of the elevator. She will check the command station herself.

"All secure, ma'am."

"Noted, Chief. You can go off duty now."

"Thank you." Devit hesitates before he continues. He and Evans have served together for over twenty years, both in peacetime and in combat in the H'Allevae Wars. The demands of strict protocol between them tend to fall away, but there are limits. "Permission to speak freely, ma'am?"

"Of course. About Brennan?"

"Yes. We're sharing a cabin. He's an officer. I'm not. Is this acceptable to you?"

"I would have said something before this if it wasn't."

"But regulations—"

"That's why your official assignment is Brennan's personal bodyguard." Evans looks away with the glazed expression that indicates her function has brought up a document. "Here it is. Section 9-B. This assignment requires Designated Day twenty-four-solstandard-hour duty." Evans blinks and dismisses the document. "If anyone tries to report you for fraternization, I will point out that Brennan is essential to our mission's success, and you are essential to Brennan's safety."

"Thank you, ma'am."

"The Fleet's always been somewhat flexible about this issue. It's one of the few rules it is flexible about. The Kar-Li influence, I suppose, with those chaotic marriage packs. Perhaps that's one reason why that wretched admiral thought he could coerce Dan and get away with it."

"And Dan paid for it, not him."

"Exactly. An outrage all around. Very well. Finish your security check, and I'll do mine."

Devit checks the habitation decks before he returns to the cabin. When he comes in, Dan is moving in his sleep, maybe dreaming, maybe simply seeing things that aren't there. Devit gets undressed and lies down. In his drugged sleep Dan whimpers. Devit turns toward him and gathers him into his arms.

For some days, Lieutenant Santreeza has been working on a full security review on the enormous Special Ops AI system. By accessing shadow files and partial data remnants, she finds the evidence that shows that some unauthorized person has been trying to gain access to the area devoted to the stargate rumors mission. Could that someone be the mole who found the information about the Scout ship that was sabotaged? As a top grade security specialist, it's her job to find out. She's discovered a fragment of an authorization request that includes two numerals of a staff ID number but no indication of where in the standard twelve digits of such ID they might lie.

"FleetOpsA, are you online?"

"Yes, CyberOp. Fully operational."

"Scour this location again. Look for stray letters of the TechSpeak alphabet."

"Working. I have found an F in close proximity to the two numerals. I cannot find any others."

"Double-check. Is that capital F or small f?"

"Capital F."

"Excellent. Now bring up personnel rosters."

Scant evidence, but Santreeza knows how to use it. She calls in Captain Dal to see the final results. "Ned Ferst, new employee, recently got a bad review. I've gotten into his Bureau phone log. He has a couple of unauthorized contacts, one yesterday, Planetary Time."

"Keep going, Santreeza. I'll put our action team on alert. We should probably bring him in for an interview."

"He's not on-site. Let's see what I can find. I've got his contact's name, but no details. Yet."

In a solstandard hour, Santreeza has everything they need to get warrants from the Bureau's tame judge, one warrant for Ferst, the other for the contact, Karski, an employee of an interstellar shipping company called Speed Shunt. The two of them have arranged a meeting this afternoon in a nearby public park. When the three-person action team sets out, Santreeza stays in the office and watches with Captain Dal through the security cameras that the team members wear.

In the slightly blurred and faded images, the team meets two local police officers. Together they troop across the green lawn to a park bench where two men are sitting, apparently having an intense conversation, since neither notice five uniformed officers heading straight for them. They never move either.

With a sick, cold feeling Santreeza realizes the truth just as the team captain reaches them. The image moves into close-up. Their smiles aren't good humor, but mouths twisted in rictus. The normally brown skin of their faces and hands has turned a deep burgundy from the underglow of suffused blood.

"Oh shit. We're too late."

"It certainly does look that way." Dal gets up with a small shudder down his flexible length. "Well, I won't need to supervise an arrest. Whoever these two were working for, they're apparently quite serious about covering their tracks."

"They sure are. I'll log off."

"Write me a report, and I'll review and comment for the brass upstairs. I'll have the action team interview staff here to see if we can find Ferst's motivation. And see if you can dig up more data on Karski."

"Yes sir. I'll send the data off to the shunt rumors mission team as well."

"Good. And keep checking the security settings. For all we know, there's another mole."

# THREE

Spacedock at RE914-4th, locally known as Tala, floats like an enormous steel spider in a cable web above a mostly green and gold planet. Like most spacedocks, this one was constructed as a series of curved modules linked together to form a larger curve; a hyperbola with the apex pointing toward the planet and its branches extending out into space. Each module has three layers, the roof of solar energy panels, the middle with its actual ship berths and other services for sapients, and the lowest for essential operations such as air and water supply.

In geosync orbit, the Tala Docks hover inside an elaborate system of satellite to surface elevators, each cabled to a captured chunk of asteroid in a geosynced orbit as well as to the enormous dock structure itself. Thanks to the personnel carriers this system offers, *Mary*'s shuttle can stay safely in its bay. The shore leave party rides one of the shiny transport bubbles down to the dirtside port.

Traditionally, the captain of a merchanter must treat her crew to drinks dirtside to celebrate their first successful shunt jump. Equally traditionally, they must get the drinks at a bar that understands the ways of spacers: a cantina, as they are called. In some mostly forgotten Old Earth language, the word "cantina" meant a cheap bar, a low dive, the kind of place that no respectable sapient would ever visit. Nanda Ram's cantina near the Port Duties office fills the bill.

Medic Lee and Lieutenant Wang have volunteered to stay with the ship in orbit. As Dan looks over the cantina's filthy windows and beaten-up front doors, he decides that they made a good decision. A holo sign, however, promises real beer served cold. If true, it will improve the ambience.

"One moment, gentlemen," Evans says. "Remember who we are. Don't get so drunk you forget."

"Yes, ma'am," Devit says. "I mean, sai, yeah."

She smiles with her usual half twitch of her mouth. "And stay on alert. If we spend a few creds buying a round for the house, we might hear a few rumors in return."

This early in the evening in the half-empty room, the bartender, a Kar-Li man, is occupying himself by removing glasses from a sanitizer and arranging them on the racks behind the plastocrete bar. He's fairly tall as Kar-Li go, about 170 centimeters high. His species and the Human share a general body type—two legs, two arms, a head—but the Kar-Li face has a pronounced snout, and their ears stand upright nearly at the top of their heads.

A few sapes, Lep and Human both, sit at the scattered round tables. While the captain scans the place for bots and bugs, Dan, Devit, and Mata wait to one side. Dan takes off his visor and stows it in his shirt pocket. He's spotted a table where a Human couple are sitting and drinking. He's burly, tall, and scowling at the pretty young woman with green hair. She looks up at the newcomers, sees Dan, and smiles. The sight of her lithe body with its full breasts, barely covered by a tight white singlet, hits Dan in the crotch. He can't resist giving her a grin and a wink. She winks in return.

Devit lays a heavy hand on his shoulder. "Captain's found us a table."

The table turns out to be on the far side of the room from the girl with the green hair. The robomaid trundles over and takes orders: beer for the three Humans, a clotted red liquid called cu'nac for Lod-Mata.

The cantina's beginning to fill up. Three Leps come in, nod toward Lod-Mata, and take the table nearest to his chair. A few Humans drift in and head straight for the bar. An eavesdropper could be anywhere—maybe even a Throwback with a function that picks up talk from a long distance away.

Evans takes the lead, but they all do their best to make the kind of conversation down-on-their-luck merchant crew members would make.

"Let's hope the ship lasts to the next shunt."

"Ah c'mon, it's been vetted by the Centralcom on two spacedocks."

"Jeezus, the way the fucking thing shook coming out of shunt, though—"

A young Human woman walks in carrying a bulky utility bag slung across her body. Dan classifies her as neither ugly or pretty, merely mousy; brown hair and brown clothes relieved by the occasional splotch

of yellow. She must have Pale blood in her family as well, judging by her light mousy-brown skin.

She heads straight to the bar and waves the bartender over. They seem to be having a brief argument. Finally she smiles and turns to look over the room. When she speaks, her small high voice fits her looks. "I'm here from the Pure Heritage Society." She pats the bag. "I've got flyers about our work to give away. Does anyone want one?"

No one does. Dan notices that Devit's paying strict attention to her.

"This kind man's letting me leave a few here on the corner of the bar." She puts a small stack of papers down in illustration. "All of you merchanters here, these flyers warns us about all of those Throwback Fleet people. They're really a threat to you, aren't they?"

"Enough!" The bartender speaks on the edge of a shout.

"Sorry!" She clutches the bag to her chest and scurries out, mouselike to the end.

Evans leans forward in her chair. "Remember, we are not Fleet." She's looking directly at Devit. "We do not argue with the likes of them."

"Yes, ma'am."

"Ah, the poor little thing," Dan says. "She looks like she could use a good fuck."

Evans rolls her eyes. Devit growls.

Whether or not the Heritage woman would have been interested, someone else apparently has just that on her mind. Across the room, the green-haired girl stands up, says something to Burly, then heads toward the bar, setting a curved course that brings her past Dan's chair. Her nipples are swelling under the thin singlet, making Dan grateful that he wore his loose pair of trousers. She hesitates, he grins, Devit clears his throat and once again lays a hand on Dan's shoulder.

"Hey, handsome," the girl says to Devit. "I don't suppose you'd share."

"Sorry, honey." Devit leans back in his chair and smiles at her. "You couldn't afford him."

She laughs with a toss of her head and a calculated ripple of green hair. Some Humans sitting nearby join in, while the Leps wave their crests in the equivalent of a chuckle. Her burly friend slams both hands flat on his table, slides free of his chair, and comes striding over. He's not smiling.

Dan gets up fast. Devit stands up, grabs the back of Dan's belt, and pulls him out of the way.

Evans steps in front of him. "Get back and stay back! That's an order, Pilot."

"Yes, ma'am."

Devit takes a step forward and waits, arms hanging comfortably at his sides.

Burly looks him over with a small sneer and makes the mistake so many belligerents have made about Devit. "Listen you," he says, "Take your fancy boy out of here before I push his face in."

"Yeah? I don't recommend you try."

Burly snorts like an angry animal and charges.

The girl screams, the bartender shouts, the other customers move fast to get out of the way. Burly throws an overhand punch straight at Devit's face. With a flick of motion, Devit grabs his wrist in both hands, steps to one side, and lets Burly's own momentum swing him around. When he lets go, Burly yelps and falls sidewise into the table. Bottles fall and shatter as the bouncer comes running to join in. Burly scrambles back up with a knife gleaming in one hand.

Dan reaches for his boot knife. Before he can slide it free, Lod-Mata grabs a full bottle of cu'nac from the Leps' table. He swings. The bottle shatters on the back of Burly's head. With a look of stunned surprise he falls forward, slides off the tipped table, and falls peacefully to the floor.

Captain Evans steps forward. "Good shot, but get Dan out of here! Devit, you too. Go. *Now*. Fast. I'll deal with the mess."

"Mess? You have a splendid way with words." Lod grabs Dan's right arm. "Let's follow orders."

Customers flee before them as they hustle him out the door into the night. In the distance sirens are wailing.

"Someone hit an alarm. Shit!"

"Right you are. Come on, Dan!"

"I'll take him. You stay. The captain's going to need backup."

Lod lets Dan go and runs back into the cantina.

Devit keeps his grip on Dan's arm. "Sai, Buddy. Run!"

Caught as he is, Dan has no choice, unless he wants to be dragged along the sidewalk. Thanks to those years of living on Haze and handouts, he can't run fast or far. By the time they reach the robocab stand he's gasping for breath. Devit picks him up and loads him into a cab, then slides in next to him. Once the cab's programmed and on its way to the Transport Hub, Devit turns to him. Dan may be the officer, but once they are alone, Devit takes charge as he always has in their relationship.

"For chrissakes, Dan, can't you keep it in your pants for one evening?"

"I was just admiring her merchandise. Jeez, it's not like I could fuck her right there in the bar."

Devit growls.

"Hey, Pete? Don't go nova on me. You've got to admit that she's got great tits."

"Listen! That could have been a setup. Someone wants to get rid of you, so maybe they hire a piece of shit like him to cause trouble. So he kills you, and what do the police hear from the witnesses? You were after his woman. Happens all the time in places like the Ram. They might take him in for the night, but I bet they wouldn't even file charges."

For a moment Dan feels like vomiting.

"Am I right?" Devit says.

"Yeah."

"Sai. After this, keep it in mind."

Since Evans has served in the Fleet for most of her adult life, she's had plenty of experience in dealing with the aftermath of fights *in* dirtside bars, fights *outside* of dirtside bars, and even fights in spacedocks bars. She's still glad of the backup when Mata hurries in. His three fellow Leps greet him like an old friend with waving crests and congratulatory slaps on the back.

"Tell them I'll buy them a drink," Evans says. "To make up for that bottle."

"I already offered. They said they're glad to donate to the cause."

The bartender, who turns out to be part owner of the cantina, is not so forgiving. Money talks, and thanks to Special Ops, Evans has plenty of creds to pacify the bartender and the bouncer. Still, for the sake of the charade, she complains, curses, whines, waves her arms, pleads poverty, and does everything she can to bring down the price.

During the negotiations, the green-haired slut, as Evans has mentally labeled her, sneaks out of the cantina before Burly wakes up. Mata and his new friends stand around and chat in their own language. At one point she notices Mata and another Lep lifting their tunics to compare the scale patterns on their torsos. Judging from their waving crests and little dancing steps, they have discovered that they are related.

Once everyone, including the police, has been paid off, they all troop outside. Sure enough, Fal-Vina and Lod-Mata have a large number of cousins in common, going back to a grandmother who was the sister of someone's grandfather. Evans loses track early on in the explanation.

"Why not come with us, Captain?" Fal-Vina says. "We know a place where we can all have a nightcap in peace."

Evans is about to decline the offer when she notices Mata waggling his three fingers and squinting, an old Fleet signal meaning "say yes."

Evans dips into her tiny store of Lep words. "Zuh gah. Thanks."

The bar they have in mind turns out to be clean, quiet, and mostly empty. Best of all, booths along one side offer some privacy. As they all sit down, Evans runs scans. She finds two simple bugs in the wall and turns them off with the standard blink pattern. An actual sapient server, a Human man, hurries over and takes orders.

"My round, gentlemen," Evans says. "No, I insist."

"Well, then, thank you, ma'am," Fal-Vina says. "We could all use a drink, eh?"

"Too true. This merchanter life! Not easy."

"Especially with all the rumors going around," Mata joins in. "About the shunt system, I mean. Let's devoutly pray that none of them are true."

"I've heard some of those, and I don't see how they can be," Fal-Vina says. "If some big company tries to monopolize the shunts, the Fleet's going to have something to say about that."

"And whoever it is isn't going to enjoy listening."

"I also heard it was the Blood Vigilantes who've got some big plan. Blow something up and that'll close a stargate. A damn stupid rumor. That's impossible, far as I know."

"You probably can't believe any of the gossip," Evans says. "Who knows, huh?"

The server returns with their drinks. Evans lifts her glass of wine to hide her mouth—at times her lips move when she's sending a message—and she transmits the rumors to Devit's PL

Once the server's tipped and gone, Fal-Vina leans forward and lowers his voice.

"Captain, my kinsman here tells me you're bound for RE89-3rd."

"That's right."

"I take it you just lost a lot of creds over that, um, unfortunate event."

"Way too many, yes." Evans sighs with a small shake of her head. "Especially after those core-crap high Port duties."

"What would you say to a little extra income?"

"It's always welcome unless it gets us shot out of the sky."

Fal's crest waves. "That won't be a problem. A little special cargo, is all, Not much weight, but very pricey."

"Ah. I see. Something of a medicinal nature, perhaps."

Fal's crest swells in approval. Normally Evans would have nothing to do with drug running, but taking on this kind of cargo will be a good addition to the charade. She can trust the offer because Leps have strict taboos against cheating one's bloodkin, and Lod-Mata qualifies. Running a con on family gets you in trouble with the Grandmothers, not a place where any sapient wants to be.

"We pay you half here. They pay you half on delivery. One-thousand two-hundred creds each."

Evans considers haggling. She glances at Mata, who lets his crest flap to one side. He says something to his cousin that makes Fal's crest do the same.

"My apologies, I misspoke," Fal says. "*Tsk*, I must be getting old. Two-thousand five-hundred creds each. For fifty kees of transport weight."

"That sounds like a very acceptable offer."

Fal's crest revives. "I'll beam you half the creds right now. We'll deliver the cargo tomorrow afternoon. That's onplanet time. Lod here knows how to complete the delivery at your destination. We have an arrangement with someone who works at a research facility. Very legit address and all that."

"Sai. I have one more crew shift who need shore leave, and then we'll be on our way."

"I'll handle the pickup," Mata says. "It turns out that I have another cousin who works in Customs."

"Good thing, too." Evans is having a moment of cold doubt. If they get arrested for running drugs, Special Ops is not going to be pleased. "I hope that's enough to get us through."

"Don't worry," Fal says. "We've done this before. The cartons are going to come wrapped in secure safety packaging. We label them 'Biohazard. Handle with Extreme Caution.' And the bills of lading say 'Genetically Altered Material.' For research, you know. No one has ever wanted to open one for inspection."

Evans laughs, her usual short bark of amusement. "Sai! That sounds very good indeed."

"Hey, Mata!" Devit says. "I owe you some thanks."

"Nah, it was pure instinct on my part. I didn't like the idea of that bastard cutting Dan up."

"Neither did I."

Mata's crest sways in a brief smile. Devit nods and looks away, fighting with his thoughts as usual. *Leps! Come off it. They're not all alike, dammit. But.*

They are standing behind a shatterproof glass partition on the Transport Hub station next to the port Customs gates. Devit can see Fal-Vina on the other side. Over the usual kilt, the Lep's wearing a greasy gray tunic printed with versions of "Speedee Ezee Delivery" in three languages. A bright yellow carton sits on a small grav sled while the Customs officer, a Human man, studies an oversized PL.

"Bills of lading?" Devit says.

"All very official and correct, I bet."

The officer looks at the carton, shudders, and waves Fal through. The grav sled floats triumphantly after him.

"Chief Devit? I need your thumbprint."

Devit signs the proffered PL.

"This baby is heavy," Fal says. "Fifty kees plus safety packing. Good thing you brought your own sled. Pull her over, and we can just slide it from one to the other."

Devit smiles, picks the carton up, and puts it on the sled. Both Leps stare.

"How do you do that?" Mata says.

"It's simple. I can control the amount of gravitons radiating from the object."

More stares.

With difficulty Devit manages to keep from laughing. "Thanks for the delivery. Come on, Mata. Let's get this upstairs."

For the trip up they ride with the carton in a special cargo transport pod, secured and disinfected for dangerous goods.

About halfway through the trip Mata turns to him. "All right, you joker. How do you really do that? Lift fifty kees like it was a bottle of beer."

"I honestly don't know. It's a Throwback thing. Different muscle tissue, they tell me, and the tendons, too, are stronger."

"Right, a Throwback thing. I should have realized that."

"Something I've always wondered. Why didn't your people develop Throwbacks?"

"They tried to, or so we learned in school. The problem is, when you develop inside an egg, there's a shell, and inside that, a membrane. Crack the shell, and maybe you can mend it and save the hatchling. Pierce that membrane, and the poor little thing dies. They never did figure out how to get inside safely to alter the genes. The Grandmothers put an end to the experiments, anyway. The few hatchlings that survived were pretty badly deformed."

"Not good, no."

"There's a few natural talents, I guess you'd call them, that most Leps have. But every sapient species seems to have something like that. Psi, I think it's called. Nothing spectacular."

*Yeah, sneaky—stop it!* "Humans have some kind of shit like that, too. Psionics. You don't see it much anymore. They hide it."

"Makes sapes nervous, I guess."

Devit nods agreement and lets the subject die there.

The *Mary* came equipped with a pair of cargo bins designed for hauling dangerous goods. Devit stows the carton and locks the bin with a password. If the contents of that package actually were what the labels say, a leak or accident would jeopardize the entire crew. It's no wonder that the Merchants Guild leaves carrying such material to the lowest tier of their members.

*Right, we get the medical cargos. Research material, huh?*

Devit hurries up to the bridge, where Evans—the only officer present—is lounging in her chair and watching newsvids on the main communication screen. A Kar-Li man in a brown business suit that matches his facial fur is discussing the results of the local planetary elections.

"A word with you, Captain?"

"Yes, of course." Evans blinks her eyes three times. The screen reverts to its usual dull gray.

"About that special cargo. I'm thinking we might need to go to the Repositories. Is that the case?"

"It's likely, yes."

"And there's a research hospital at the Repositories. Am I right?"

"Yes. It's in a self-contained module near the main spacedock. They didn't build it onplanet because they don't want any of their research projects getting loose. Some of the diseases they're trying to cure are horrendous."

"They must get shipments of dangerous materials, then. Tissue samples, that kind of thing."

"I suppose so. I—" All at once she laughs, one short bark. "And we're just the kind of ship to carry them there."

"I'll have PrimeTwo add a line to our charter. Let shippers know we've got the capability to store hazards during transport."

"Right. You're very good at your job, Chief."

"Thank you, ma'am. Coming from you, that's a real compliment."

"You're welcome. By the way, where's our pilot?"

"In the cabin. Drugged. He promised me he'd be sober by 1800 hours. Sober enough to take the ship out of orbit, anyway."

"We reach the stargate six hours later. The should be time enough for him to get clear."

Another thing that can't be said hovers between them. Let's hope so.

After years of living with and for Haze, Dan can judge the amount of the drug in his blood and calibrate it to whatever actions he needs to perform. If he ever should be too drugged to make a jump safely, he would delay as long as necessary. As it is, he feels sufficiently clear to go head on schedule. At jump minus one hour he melds with PrimeOne without any problem. The rise to Level Two proceeds smoothly as well.

"Your heart rate is sixty-four, Pilot."

"Good. Oxygen content?"

"Normal. Registers at ninety-eight on the scale of one to one-hundred."

"Good. View ahead."

In the starry reach ahead, the black sphere seems to swell ever larger as they approach. Dan begins his count and through the link-up feels PrimeOne echoing the numbers. Closer—

*Now!*

The jump strips Dan's self away and leaves only the-Dan-who-has-melded-with-the-ship. They sail into the golden light on a smooth arc. Ahead the blue currents dance and twist. Dan throws himself into a streak of blue and begins his search for the road he needs. To one side a vortex spins, then shrinks, distorts, forms itself into enormous cubes and pyramids that seem solid for a brief space of what-might-be-time. As they rush past, the illusion thins out, swirls, and disappears.

He has a few moments of what-might-be-time to glance to either side. In the light a misty cube forms, then disintegrates. Distant vortices swirl around their black hearts. A point appears in the light—a golden point just slightly less bright than the vast spreading glow around them. It heads straight for the ship, and as it approaches it distorts itself into a shape that might belong to a sapient. A torso, four stubs of arms, four protrusions that might be legs, and a globe-like head marked with two pits that might be eyes and a thin slit that might be considered a mouth.

Dan turns his attention away to check the ship's progress on the blue river. They move in the right direction, but he feels rather than thinks that they've shifted off course. He looks around, sees the sapient-like shape for a brief flicker of time. It stands on another current and holds one arm up before it. Dan speeds after the blue, catches it, leaps and sinks into it just as the obsidian exit sphere appears.

*Five, four, three, two—now!* They sweep on through. A chime sounds, PrimeOne calls, "Level Two," and Dan has a body again.

"Yeah! Just fucking yeah!"

"Pilot? I do not understand—"

"Don't worry about it, PrimeOne. First level and the Map."

The glowing web brightens underneath him. Ahead lies the red dot of RE89-3rd.

"Pilot, arrival in seven solstandard hours."

"Noted. Break the meld."

The links disappear and the Map with them. Dan realizes that he's lying on the pilot couch in his pod. He sits up and runs both hands through his sweaty hair. The touch of his fingers on the metal jacks and output buttons brings him a little further back to normal consciousness.

PrimeOne beeps in the AI equivalent of clearing one's throat. "Pilot, request for data. I noted visual input."

"Yeah, so did I. You were seeing them through me."

"I made that assumption. Request: What were they?"

"I don't know. I see things in the light sometimes. I filed a log about those incidents. Years ago. Before the top brass kicked me out on my ass."

PrimeOne clicks to itself for a few moments. "Pilot, I have never worked with any sapient before who sees objects in the light."

"You wouldn't, no. The guild doesn't have any record of other pilots who do. I checked when I filed the log."

"I have found a note in a partially deleted file that names one other. Orinoco Bolivar."

*Him again?* Dan finds himself remembering the last word of that desperate transmit: Look.

"Pilot, should I notify the bridge that the jump was successful?"

"Agreed. We can discuss the visual data later. For now, keep the ship on the set course. I'll take over from the bridge for the dock."

"Do you still have your Personal Link for this log re: images?"

Dan cleared and pawned the unit on Ruby to buy Haze. When he joined the mission, Evans issued him a new one, along with the earjack and visor from the Bureau.

"No, but I can access my records from the guild and reload them. There's a guildhall on RE89-3rd."

Not precisely on the planet, it turns out. Ocean covers most of RE89-3rd or Wet, as the locals call it. Enormous tides sweep over the scraps of land, thanks to a pair of large moons, and make settlement impossible. There are compensations. The local sapients harvest the oxygen produced by the thick beds of oceanic plant life and stromatolites. They pressurize it into a liquid, then sell it to the Fleet and passing merchanters at a good profit. The creds have built a spacedock structure even larger and more elaborate than the one orbiting Tala.

Along with the oxygen crews, all the sapients attached to Wet live and work in the cluster of spacedocks in geosync orbits. In the outermost of these, where visiting ships dock, the Pilots Guild maintains offices in a curved section of the station given over to official matters. Instead of the usual mats of mazla vine, the walls and the offices both glitter with bright light bouncing off steel facing. On this world, carbon dioxide gets collected and funneled back into the oceans rather than wasted on feeding vines.

Even with his visor on, Dan cannot stand to look at the walls. Riding the blue again has made his eyes more sensitive than ever. Devit lays a hand on his shoulder and guides him to the right door.

When they get inside, Dan takes the visor off. Pale yellow light glows in strips set in the floor and fills the room with shadows. The guild knows what its pilots need.

"Damn!" Devit mutters. "I should have brought a lightstick."

"No go. They'd take it away from you. There's some chairs over there, so go sit down. I've got to check in."

An AI sits in a half booth on the long curved counter. When Dan walks up, it clicks, hums, and brings up an information screen. Dan follows the written instructions and tells it his name, rank, reg number, and his preferred language, Tech Speak.

"Processed. Retinal scan. Please lean forward and look at the glowing blue dot."

Dan does. It clicks again. "Welcome Dan Brennan. What may we help you with?"

"I want to access personal records."

"Enter file number."

"I don't remember it."

"File number is necessary for access. There are no files listed under the name Dan Brennan."

In his chair by the door Devit mutters, "Oh crap." Dan has to agree.

Eventually the AI agrees to search under the name Dan X. The delay drags on so long that Dan begins to be afraid the records have been stolen or wiped in the same way as the main files on the shunt closure were. He's about to call Devit over when the AI speaks.

"They are filed under X, Dan. Is that you?"

"Yes, it is. Match retinal scans."

"I have done so. Place your PL on the counter."

The actual transfer of the files takes approximately two seconds. The AI goes dark. Dan checks to make sure that the log he needs still exists before he leaves the office. By then, Devit has already gone outside to wait where he can see his surroundings. Once Dan's eyes settle, he can see that Devit's reading something printed on a piece of soyskin paper.

"What's that?"

"A manifesto from the Pure Heritage assholes."

"They use paper? Weird, but then, so are they."

"Flyers like these can't be traced." Devit shoves it into his pants pocket. "Public PL posts can be. So they leave crap like this around to get their message out. Anyway, tell me something. Why did your mother name you X?"

"Oh, who the hell knows why she did anything? Hey, when are you and Lod going to deliver the biohazards?"

"When you and I get back. The research lab's in another dock, but Mata reserved an LTV."

"Which is?"

"Lateral transport vehicle." He hesitates. "Look, while we're gone, I want you to stay onboard the *Mary*. Agreed?"

"Agreed. I want to look over these records and send them to PrimeOne."

They return to the *Mary* to find Evans on the bridge, watching her usual newsvids. She answers their salutes, then mutes the sound on the main comm screen.

"There you are, gentlemen. I just sent off a status report to the Bureau to let them know our itinerary. No one else wants shore leave. Chief, once you and Mata get that cargo stowed, we're breaking berth. Brennan, I've decided that we might as well travel to the next jump."

While he waits for Mata to call him from the cargo hold, Devit sits down at his security station and considers the automatic readouts that appear on-screen. Nothing untoward happened during his absence. Once that's taken care of, he scans in the Pure Heritage Society flyer he found outside the Pilots Guild and slots it into his growing collection. As most of them do, the new addition focuses on the Inborn and the Throwbacks as a "threat to our republic," "an ambitious and evil cancer growing in our society," and other such phrases. This flyer adds something new:

> Could it be true? Have the Throwbacks found some devious way to destroy the stargates? They could threaten to isolate any planet whose government refused to do their will! Rumors fly everywhere. Are these hints shedding light into an unspeakable darkness?"

*Rhetorical questions again. Nothing actionable, just questions. Clever. Start people thinking and maybe they'll believe it.*

Could the Pure Heritage people be the source of the rumors concerning the stargates? Devit makes a note of the possibility in the file. They'll be worth investigating whenever he gets the chance.

"Pilot, I have processed your record of images seen. I have data re: the illusion of the humanoid being."

"Noted, PrimeOne. Share."

"When I was brought online, Pilot, I experienced many training routines. One taught me how to recognize sapients and their variations. Common features of sapients: vision, hearing, communication functions, appendages for grasping tools. Most common configuration: an extension of the main body commonly called a head. On this head, eyes facing forward to give binocular vision, a slit or a protruding organ to make sound, and a feature on each side of the head to receive sounds. The image we saw fit these definitions."

"The slit on its face, was that there to make sounds?"

"It fits the definitions I was given of mouths."

"Accepted. What we saw was possibly an image of a sapient."

"There is a small probability it was not an image but a being. Its form endured much longer than the images did. Its form was precisely defined rather than spreading randomly in the light as did those geometric shapes. It terminated its presence by moving away, not by dissolution."

"It didn't have a ship. No one can ride the light without a ship."

"Correction: It is commonly believed that a ship is required. No evidence exists that any being *can* exist in the light without a ship. But lack of available evidence does not mean undiscovered evidence does not exist."

"True. But …." Dan lets his voice trail away.

"What is your objection, Pilot?"

"No objection. Just a need for corroboration. I felt like it was looking at me. I'd drifted off course. It showed me the correct streak to ride."

PrimeOne makes a series of clicks, the longest delay that Dan has ever experienced from it. "Pilot, am I interpreting your statement correctly? Do you mean it saved us from being lost?"

"Just that. Unless it was a coincidence. It stood on the blue streak I needed. Or maybe it was just luck."

"Luck is a concept I have never understood. I must gather more data before we even consider if we need to inform anyone else." There is a pause, then a few beeps. "Pilot, we are approaching the scheduled jump time."

"Noted and agreed. I'm ready to meld."

RE84-2nd has a long name in the Hirrel language. Most other sapients call it by the first syllable, Glah. Whatever the name, the drab rocky sphere offers no reason to bring the shuttle out of its bay. Lee and Wang go to a discount warehouse on the spacedock to buy medical supplies. No one else asks for shore leave.

Evans accesses the local Merchants Guild via voicelink and reports that one more jump will deliver their current cargo. An actual Human comes online.

"Nothing more out there for you at the moment," the clerk tells her. "But I see you've registered for hazardous material delivery."

"That's right. We have secure bays in the hold and hazmat suits for both Humans and Leps. Also a detoxification filter on the air supply."

"Sounds good. Check in when you reach your destination. There could be a pickup for you. There will be soon, anyway."

*Because no one else is stupid enough to volunteer for these jobs.* Aloud, she says, "Thanks. We really need cargo."

"Everyone does. Good luck!"

The clerk signs off.

By Fleet regulations AI units file a complete report of their every activity under the captain's password. Normally Evans never reads them. Routine AI activity generates hundreds of lines of mostly numerical detail. As for melds, she prefers not to spy on a fellow officer when they've linked up to an AI. Dan's addiction, however, has made the current situation abnormal.

She's been glancing at some of the exchanges between Dan and PrimeOne before and after jumps just to see how sober and coherent he is. A few lines generally tell her all she needs to know. When she logs in to check his condition after the just-completed jump, she finds the conversation concerning the humanoid image. She reads through it twice.

"Chief Devit?"

Devit turns in his station chair to face her. "Yes, ma'am?"

"Does Haze give Dan hallucinations?"

"No, ma'am. That's not one of the effects the drug has. Mata, did Dan ever get them when you sapes were in Gleam?"

"Not that I know of, no. No one ever mentioned them at Mission House, either, and they would have told me if they knew about them."

"Noted. Thank you both."

Devit and Mata are looking at her expectantly. She stands up with a nod in their direction. "Chief Devit, you have the bridge."

Evans goes down to her cabin to read the report yet again, just in case she's the one hallucinating. It reads the same as before. *Everyone knows he's one of a kind. Why? Who knows! But dangerous or not? Don't know that either. But this is important.* Dan and, through him, PrimeOne have seen things in shunt space that no one ever suspected existed.

It occurs to her that she may have found the reason Special Ops insisted on Dan instead of some other pilot. Why? Or was it just one of those oddities that might or might not lead to a crucial development? They certainly hadn't bothered to tell her about it.

"Bastards!"

She gets up and heads for the door. She's decided to return to the bridge and assuage Mata and Devit's curiosity. Devit in particular has a definite need to know.

The Haze is just wearing off when Dan realizes that Devit's in the cabin.

"Pete? I'm pretty much down."

"Sai. Do you want to eat something?"

"No. Sorry, but it's too soon. I'm going down to the pod."

"Is there a problem with the dock?

"No. Nothing's wrong. I just want to take a good look at the shunt system. I get the feeling that it's hiding something."

"Uh, do you feel all right?"

"Yeah. I know that sounds crazy. I just don't know how to say it. Anyway, I'll eat later. I promise."

Once Dan's settled on the pilot's bench, he melds to Level One, brings up the Map, and flies straight up over it. Looking back from far away reveals a three-dimensional pattern of fine lines that would fill a roughly defined parallelepiped if someone drew the box around them. Neither Dan nor PrimeOne can find any point within the pattern that might indicate a starting point or center of development. The shunts weave back and forth, over or under, almost reaching the edge or falling far short, and are filled with gaps or clot up so dense it's hard to untangle the images.

The one thing they all have in common is the position of their stargates in space-time, each one close to the gravity well of a planetary system.

"The standard theory, Pilot, is that the shunt system cannot be a natural phenomenon. It must have been created."

"Yeah. You can see that just by looking at it. The problem is, who did it? And how did they do it?"

"There have been many attempts to answer those questions. All have failed. We AIs consider this a glitch in the programming of the universe. Ignorance at this level should not exist."

"Yeah? Well, it does, and not just about this."

"Agreed." PrimeOne pauses briefly. "Pilot, your body is making a strange noise."

"Break meld."

As soon as Dan's body consciousness returns, he hears the noise in question. "My stomach's growling, that's all. I need to eat."

Dan stops in the galley to scrounge for food. In a locker he finds a stack of rehydrate pellets, each in a drink-from bag. He adds water from the dispenser to something purple and downs it in big gulps. A twenty-five kilo sack of nutrition bars sits on a soyplast chair. He rummages through it and digs out a pair of blue ones, his favorite kind. He eats them standing up, wipes his hands on his trousers, and considers dinner over. The food and the sensation of eating clean the last of the Haze from his mind.

Sleep. He realizes that he's exhausted. Fortunately, he's off duty and can sleep as much as he wants. It will pass some of the time, as well, until he can have more Haze. Nine solstandard hours till the next tab. He will count them down as they pass. Slowly. Always too slowly, always too long to the next.

When Evans's report reaches the Bureau on Central, the comm-sort AI sends it directly to Santreeza. She adds the data—their last reported location—to their route map and sends a memo to Captain Dal. Toward the end of their on-duty hours he comes to her office with an update of his own.

"I just received the Police Guard autopsy report. The medical examiner figured out what killed our mole and his contact. Chemical analysis and all that. They were injected with a poison."

"Injected? They'd been kidnapped first, then. What kind of poison?"

"The same formula the Butchers used, the one that paralyzed their prisoners so their larvae could feed on them. This was apparently a double dose. It killed them fast, unlike what happened to the POWs." His arms reflexively curl in toward his body. "Keeping them alive while their little darlings sucked out the fluids."

"It took days for them to die, too." Santreeza shudders with a similar reflex. "Genocide. It's such a horrible thing, but I'm afraid I can understand why the Inborn wiped them out. Was there ever an investigation, I wonder? I vaguely remember from school that the Fleet commander ordered the genocide on his own authority."

"No, no hearing, no investigation at all that I ever heard of. The Fleet certainly approved of his actions."

"You'd think someone would have at least filed an objection."

"No one did. Well, the Inborn weren't created to engage in ethical debates."

"Yeah, I don't think you can genetically program someone to have a conscience. That poison—I didn't know that the formula for it still existed."

"Neither did anyone else. Someone, or some entity, must have it. The Bureau's going to start an investigation. I've already seen to that."

# FOUR

With the ship safely docked, Evans has nothing to do but fret about finding cargo. In the past six hours she's scanned the entire ship twice for bugs or other troublesome devices, just in case one came aboard with the Customs officer or refueling techs. She passes a few pleasant minutes sending off a crabby transmit to the Bureau, asking if they've found the security leak and the mole, then returns to watching the local newsvids.

"Captain?" Lod-Mata leaves his station and strolls over. "Can I have shore leave?"

"Of course. Why? Is there actually something worth seeing on this wretched hunk of steel?"

"No, but I'm sick of looking at the pink walls in here."

"I have to admit it. So am I."

"Come with me, why not? I'll be your guard." He turns to Devit. "Stop looking so skeptical. I can always carry a full bottle of cu'nac with me if you think I need a weapon."

Evans laughs with the others.

"I carry a pulse gun, thanks," she says. "No red swill necessary. Lieutenant Wang, you have the bridge."

Double airlocks take them to the sky tunnel that leads from the ship to the dock floor, which could use a good mopping. Scraps of paper drift along with some sort of gray fuzz. Mata suddenly stops and pounces on a scrap.

"What are you doing?"

"Apologies, ma'am. This is one of the Pure Heritage propaganda sheets. They scatter them around everywhere they go. Devit collects them for some reason."

Mazla hangs in thick strands over pale blue walls. Ahead lies the Shops, as they are called, a variety of small concessions offering personal items that a visiting crew might want or need.

"There must be an eatery here," Evans says. "I can smell breadfruit and soyburger."

"There is, yes, according to the map I saw." Mata hesitates. "Captain, I have a small confession."

"I wondered about this walk."

"You know that us Leps have a few 'extra' natural functions. I've been told that this one evolved to keep track of other members of our birth clutch. I keep feeling there's someone here who belongs to us. Or needs us. Or something."

"Another retired officer we know?"

"Could be. So I wanted to take a look around."

"All right. Carry on."

As they walk on down to the Shops, Mata keeps raising his head to sniff the air. Evans assumes that he's not actually using his sense of smell.

"This is what I used to find Dan back in Gleam," Mata says. "It was odd, actually. I had no idea where he was, but one day a message showed up on my PL. It said he'd turned up in Gleam. I've got kin on Ruby, so I worked a passage there. I never found who sent the message, but they were right."

Evans makes a mental note to pass that information on to Devit. "It was good of you to go after him."

"Don't forget, we were a pilot-gunner team during that little unpleasantness in the last Hopper War. You don't just dump that sort of bond. Besides, I had nowhere else to go after that ridiculous excuse for a court-martial."

"At least the brass kicked you out quietly." Normally Evans dislikes gossiping, but she's been curious about this particular point for months. "Something you might know: Brennan's family—his mother, I suppose that means—was wealthy. Why didn't he go back home when he was desperate?"

"He would have preferred to die first, he told me. When Dan was accepted at the Fleet Academy, she didn't want him to go. He did anyway, and they had a hell of a fight. She disinherited him. The old never-darken-my-door-again routine."

"Good god! I had no idea!"

"He admitted it one night when we'd had a bit much to drink. So he blamed himself for losing everything, home and the Fleet both, when he could have just given Admiral Five-Star what he wanted."

"Why didn't he? Not that I really should be asking you such a thing."

"If I knew, ma'am, I'd be glad to tell you, but I don't. It's something that Dan refused to talk about. I shut my snout about it—" Mata stops in mid-sentence. His crest swells with laughter. "It's not an officer, no. Onar bless! What do we have here?"

The front of the eatery is mostly open, set off by a waist-high wall, to reveal a scatter of tables and a counter at the back. A small Human child, a girl, crouches by the entrance gap. Much too thin, more than a little dirty, she looks up with hopeless dark eyes. A mass of uncombed curly black hair spills down her back. Tendrils frame her little heart-shaped face. Evans's own daughter looked much like her as a small child. Eight years old, Evans estimates, at the most.

"You're a lizard," the girl says.

"A very nice lizard, though." Mata squats down to her level. "What are you doing, sitting here?"

"Nothing. They let me."

"We do, yes." A Human man, young and portly, comes hurrying over. "She doesn't have anywhere else to go."

"Don't you feed her?" Evans says.

"When the boss isn't around. Mostly the scraps customers leave on their plates. He can't complain too much about that."

"I see. What happened to her?"

The man hesitates, catches his lower lip in stained teeth to think, then glances at the girl.

She stares at the floor as she talks. "I can tell them, Dee. My dad hit my mommy, and he kept hitting her till she died."

"But she still loves you, Marda. She's in the paradise beyond the stars."

The child tries to smile.

Evans needs no special sense to feel a growing rage. Mata gets to his feet. His crest lies flat against his skull.

"What happened to the father?" Mata says.

"They hanged him, of course." The young man shrugs. "You can't get away with that shit here."

"Good." Evans snaps the word out. "Why hasn't someone found some kind of provision for her? An orphanage? Adoption?"

"Ma'am, they don't have that kind of thing. There's not a lot of people here on Glah Docks. There's only a few women, and they're Hirrel and they wouldn't take her."

"I suppose I can't blame them. If I'd raised twenty larvae, I wouldn't want any more myself."

Evans feels no surprise that everyone on this godforsaken hunk of metal assumes that only a woman would care, despite the contrary evidence right in front of them. Both Dee the restaurant worker and Marda are staring at her.

When Mata starts to speak, she interrupts him. "Chief Mata, we cannot have a child living on the ship."

"As you say, ma'am. But y'know, we're bound to get a good cargo one of these days soon. To some place with decent social services."

"Ma'am?" Dee says. "I let her sleep in the back here when we lock up. I'm terrified that someone's going to, y'know, steal her and sell her somewhere. You guys are both ex-Fleet, aren't you? I can see it by the way you stand and stuff, I mean."

"Retired, yes. She was an officer, and I was a CPO."

"Then she'll be safe with you. Or I wouldn't let her go."

Evans knows exactly what he's afraid of: child prostitution. She tells herself that she cannot weaken. They are not really low-level merchanters but a Fleet ship on a dangerous mission with a drug addict for a second officer and enemies out there willing to kill.

"If the boss finds out she's here, he'll fire me. I'll be stuck working my passage out on some big commercial ship."

"Who won't let him take her with him." Mata, the traitor, joins in. "Or so I assume."

Evans steels herself, on the edge of saying no.

"Marda, let's show them a trick." Dee reaches into his apron pocket and pulls out a PL. "Give me a list of random numbers."

The PL rattles off a list of three and four digit numbers. Marda grins and repeats them all. When he shows Evans the screen, the numbers all match.

"She's a Throwback, isn't she?" Mata says.

"I've been thinking that, yeah. Her memory is incredible. That's part of the problem. She keeps remembering what happened. Like, in detail."

"Hah! I knew there was a reason I was picking something up. Captain, we can't just leave a Throwback here. If we can get her to a Fleet base, they'll take her in."

"Stop it, you two!" Evans looks at each of them in turn. "We don't even know if she's willing to go."

Marda gets up from the floor. "I'm scared, but it's kind of awful here."

"It could get worse, if my boss finds out."

"She needs clothes and stuff," Mata says. "I'll pay for them out of my salary."

"I'll chip in. I got paid yesterday."

Evans knows a defeat when she sees one. "Oh very well! But we're finding her a decent home as fast as we can. If she wants to go."

Marda looks at Dee for a long moment. "I'll miss you."

"I'll miss you, too, but things are going to be better now. They'll take you to a place where there's people like you, people who can do a lot of different tricks."

"Sai. Mr. Lizard, thank you."

"Say Lep, not lizard," Dee says. "That's the polite word."

Mata's crest swells just enough to indicate a smile. "It's all right. Tell you what, Marda. You are the only person in the whole galaxy who can call me a lizard. I'll be Uncle Lizard. How's that?"

She grins at him and nods.

"Just never call anyone else who looks like me a lizard. Sai?"

"Sai. I won't."

Dee turns to Evans. "Thank you. I mean it, thank you. I live in workers' housing. I just can't take care of her."

"Well, we'll do our best. For now, Uncle Lizard, let's do some shopping."

Two hours before orbital exit, Dan finishes studying the Map and goes up to the bridge. When he steps out of the elevator, he sees the entire crew on the bridge. Captain Evans is sitting in her command chair and watching the gunnery station, where the others are all standing around Lod.

"Captain?" Dan says. "What's happened to the guns? Do we need to get out of orbit fast?"

"The guns are fine. The gunner—I'm not so sure about him."

Medic Lee gives Dan a grin and steps aside to clear the view. Lod-Mata is sitting in his chair, and on his lap is a small Human girl dressed in brand-new Fleet-blue pants and a little shirt with "Crew Dancing Mary" freshly printed on it. Her short but curly black hair gleams with cleanliness.

"What in hell is that?" Dan hears himself snarl.

The girl flinches.

"Sorry, kid." He tries to soften his voice. "I don't mean to scare you or anything."

The child considers him without speaking. Her dark eyes seem older than the rest of her.

"Her name's Marda," Lod says. "The captain approved taking her onboard."

"Hey, she's not coming with us, is she?"

Lee sets her hands on her hips and scowls at him. "That's exactly what she's doing."

"She was an abandoned orphan living on the floor of that lousy eatery on dock," Lod says. "We couldn't leave her there. She's a Throwback. A Reserve Memory Resource, to be precise, more usually known as a Recaller."

"Oh. Well, yeah, that makes a difference." He hesitates. "But we're about to go into jump. Who's going to take care of her? She's going to be scared shitless."

"I am." Ice forms around each word Lee speaks. "I'm taking her down to Sickbay with me."

Dan walks over to his station without another word. He's going to have to recalibrate the entire mass of the ship thanks to this late addition.

"Let us hope," Lod says to the air, "that our lieutenant never decides to reproduce."

Dan ignores them all and concentrates on his mathematics. Since a ship this size would normally carry eight crew rather than their current six, they have more than enough oxygen and water to bring aboard a child. Once he finishes the calculations, he turns to Evans.

"Captain, we have early clearance from the dockmaster. Do you want us to leave orbit now?"

"Yes. Engineer, ready your station. The rest of you, prepare for thruster drill."

The early exit means more orbital recalibrations thanks to the changed position of the small moon and its gravity. It also moves jump time forward. Dan gets the *Mary* unhooked from spacedock, sets her free from the artificial gravity, and puts her on course to the stargate. At jump minus 1.8 he leaves the bridge and takes refuge in his pod.

Before they meld, Dan contacts PrimeOne, who has good news.

"I have uploaded the data of your collected images from shunt space. Your previous partner AIs and I have filed a report with the guild concerning these images. We have judged that there is a high probability other pilots will read them. If any have seen similar images, they will then report them."

"Noted. Good idea!"

The warning chime rings.

"Time to meld. Jump in minus one hour."

Dan is hoping that during shunt travel they'll see some glorious vision, an image that will be the key to interpreting them all. Instead, the jump passes smoothly, safely, and without the appearance of anything out of place other than the occasional vortex.

At times, when he's securely buckled into his chair for jumps, Devit finds himself thinking about his far distant ancestors, back on the southern islands of Earth. They only knew one planet, if indeed they even knew what the concept of planet meant. Their world was mostly ocean, thousands of kilometers of open sea dotted here and there with islands. They explored their ocean one island at a time in wooden canoes, steering by the stars and ocean currents. He wonders how many of those canoes never reached land, never came home. The Human urge to know, to travel beyond the safe horizon, always sent others out again.

When at night they looked up at the galaxy, spread like a river across the sky, did they all unknowing see the stars of the Rim? No one knows, exactly, or at least, none of the experts Devit's asked do. His people were among the first volunteers to travel to those stars when the ship technology was new. Their descendants still ride other dangerous currents now every time a starpilot takes them through a shunt. Sometimes those ships never come home as well. Lost ships, the lost shunt—no one knows where they founder and drown, not in water but in light.

Traveling a shunt takes hours, or so it seems to the passengers in the ship. During that time everyone tries to keep their fear to themselves rather than add to the understandable anxieties, but the fear escapes and sits in the bridge with them. No matter how comfortable the jump chairs, no matter how often they look at their bodies, somehow everyone's brain announces that they no long exist, not really, any more than a candle flame exists as some kind of solid object or enduring entity. We are all patterns, our brains tell us, nothing more than patterns of energy.

Passengers can always tell when the jump ends. Suddenly bodies are solid again, and not merely real, but the only reality. Devit wonders how the ancestors felt when they beached their canoes—a jump into shallow water, a solid hold on the wood of the canoe, and the feel of running it up on land, safe from the waves, home again.

When Dan's voice comes over the intraship comm, "Jump successful, Captain," everyone already knows.

Security chief Devit oversees everyone's return to normal duty after jump. With this particular crew, all he really has to do is say, "Sai, everyone can unbuckle." Except, of course, for Marda. When he contacts Medic Lee through the ship's comm, she confirms that the little girl did fine.

"Not scared at all," Lee tells him. "She's still in a kind of shock. I don't suppose any of this seems truly real to her."

"Not yet, no, after everything she's been through. Well, good. Over and out."

*Everything she's been through.* Devit tries to avoid thinking about Kay-Asi, his own daughter, but the sight of this helpless child has triggered memories. His beautiful little girl running to meet him when he came home on leave, a Fleet ensign—a promising young officer—at her Academy graduation. Only a year later she was kidnapped by Lep terrorists on a planet torn apart by politics, hidden in a place where her father couldn't save her. The death of a thousand cuts, they called it, a Lep custom of great antiquity, one prick or tiny slice at a time. It must have taken hours for her to die. No one would let him see her body. No one would confirm or deny if they'd raped her as well. He supposed that meant they had, even if she was from a species alien to them.

*If they'd told me, I would have found a way, I would have killed them and anyone in the way—*

"Chief!" Evans's voice cuts through the memory. "Devit! What's wrong?"

In his mind he's back in the bleak office of the police chief who gave him the news. He remembers staring at the blank wall behind the desk, staring hard to keep from weeping—

"Chief!" Evans snaps. "Devit."

Evans is standing in front of his chair. " Are you ill?"

"No, ma'am. Just remembering something." He tries to smile and fails. "Ma'am, I apologize. Did you call me?"

She hesitates, visibly troubled, looks this way and that, finally speaks. "Orbit in 5.6 solstandard hours. I just wanted to inform you."

"Thank you, ma'am. We'll be ready."

As Evans turns and goes back to her captain's chair, Mata walks over, his crest not quite flat, his eyes wary.

"Devit?" Mata speaks softly. "I have the horrible feeling I know what you were remembering."

Devit looks at him, the slightly snouty, heavily scaled alien face, the yellow eyes sad under their protective ridges, and sees someone who desperately wants to help. "You're probably right."

"Seeing the child did it?"

"Yes."

"I cannot tell you how sorry I am. About what happened, I mean."

"You don't need to. I know."

"Thank you for that."

Mata nods his way, then returns to his station. The memories sink back into the prison Devit built for them in his mind.

As the ship spirals around RE77-4th on its way to spacedock, *Mary*'s external scopes and cameras—her Eyes, as they are known—send a stream of images back to the main communication screen opposite the captain's chair. Terraforming an empty world, they call it, but Evans can see why the company in charge has named it Merrval. She's seen empty worlds before, the smooth basalt flows pocked with volcanoes, the steaming oceans, the cracks and ridges that will, someday far into the future, define continents. Clouds of methane, the usual atmosphere for a newly formed planet, swirled through their yellow-green skies.

Merrval's three continents are fully formed. It has an oxygen-rich atmosphere and deep, clean oceans. Water runs in rivers and pools in lakes. As the ship travels around the planet, she sees several mountain ranges on the continents, some new and jagged, some worn smooth by old age. Fossils and recent finds of animal bones show that the planet hosted abundant life once. Two of the continents still harbor plant life in patchy forests and mangy-appearing plains. A number of specialized ecosystems cluster around thermal vents in the ocean deeps. On the third continent, a species of green moss clings to life at the edges of ponds and a few small streams. It's probable that life-forms analogous to insects exist, all too small to be detected from a distance. No one knows who or what wiped the rest of the landscape away down to bare dirt and rock.

A group of investors from the Vranz Consortium, a small group of worlds within the Rim Council territory, are attempting to bring life back. Merrval. A marvel indeed, if they succeed in resurrecting this barren place of death. At the moment, the crew and the scientists all live on the elaborate spacedock system circling the planet. No one can walk on the surface unless they are swaddled in hazmat suits. The equipment that the *Dancing Mary* carries will allow the crew to build a limited number of structures on one isolated island to begin an experiment.

The project head—a skinny, sharp-faced Human named Dzhun d'Allet—turns out to be the hospitable sort. He arrives at the *Mary* with the crew who will unload the crates and padded bubbles into a pair of LTVs, big boxy vans with enormous float pads underneath. While the men and their longshorebot work, d'Allet and Evans stand on *Mary*'s bridge and watch on the communication screen.

"Come have dinner with us tonight," d'Allet says. "We don't get much company out here, you know."

"You're at the end of a single shunt, aren't you?"

"We are. It took me a long time to find a merchanter to bring us what we ordered."

"I don't suppose you have any cargo for us to take back."

"Message packets. Quite a lot of them, in fact. Probably, what? Eight standard months' worth. The company will pay the going rate. I'll see to that."

The dinner takes place in another module of the spacedock. Although Devit's worried about the ship just on general principles, Evans decides that the Prime AI units are more than adequate to keep a watch on it. A passenger LTV fetches the crew promptly at 1600 hours, local dock time. D'Allet welcomes them into a big dining area decorated with true Vranz flare—landscape holos from their home planet on every wall framed by big bouquets of red and yellow flowers tucked into luxuriant mazla.

"Morale out here is a very fragile thing," he says. "The home office rotates crew members in and out from other projects, but the actual team, myself and the research people, needs to stay on-site as much as possible. We have to make things pleasant."

Before the meal a white-coated staff member serves glasses of a pale purple wine. Evans takes a sip and smiles. "Lovely! Thank you."

"You're very welcome." He raises his glass in a half salute.

"I'm surprised you've had shipping troubles. Your home office pays well, really."

"For now. They keep threatening to use one of the big companies. What is it? Speed Shunt—something like that. They're undercutting the Merchants Guild rates. I keep telling them that the big companies don't give the good service. None of them want to come all the way out here without a guaranteed return cargo. What should we send back? Dirt? All the accountants can see is the cost."

"That's worrisome! I'll have to contact the guild and see what they're doing about it."

As they chat, Evans keeps a discreet watch on her crew. Dan has found the best-looking Human woman in the room, a tall slender brunette. In the comfortable low-level lighting, he's removed his visor. All traces of the whip mark have disappeared, leaving him as beautiful as ever, with his devil's green eyes in an angelic Pale face. His golden hair has grown back to a flattering length. He's all strict attention as the woman talks. Evans can hear snatches of their incongruous conversation about something called ice plant.

"That's Anne-Mahree Dubray, our biome specialist," d'Allet says. "She's going to establish a small colony of vegetation and wingless beetles on our island. To see if they live or die from some mysterious cause."

"Interesting. How long has the continent been barren?"

"It's impossible to tell precisely. We have two different extinctions. The first happened about 1,000 standard years ago. Most of the damage to the other continents dates from whatever happened then. The second was only a very short time ago, as planetary events go. Four-hundred years, perhaps, our geologist tells us. Give or take a few dozen."

"The second event—I take it that some sort of life had recovered from the first disaster."

"To some extent. Remains of a sort survive; animal bones, traces of actual buildings. All on a single continent, the one we're geosynced to. The only logical explanation for that is someone attempted colonization. Whoever they were, they didn't bury their dead, damn them, so we don't know which species it was."

"I suppose there must be a good many speculations about what happened."

"Ye gods, yes! We get transmits now and then from sapients who want to tell us their theories. Mysterious magical forces loom large. Also, of course, the Hoppers get a good share of the blame."

"At least they really do exist."

"Yes. Unfortunately." He pauses for a sip of wine. "The best theory concerns the EMF surrounding the planet. At some point it seems to have failed. There's a good bit of residual radioactivity in the soil from solar radiation."

"I didn't realize that would be possible."

"Neither did anyone else." D'Allet grins at her. "That's why it's only a theory."

Evans realizes that Dan has turned on the charm. He moves a little closer to Dubray, signals to the staff member to come refill her glass, smiles and responds to everything she says. Dubray is not bothering to resist. She smiles in return and now and then raises one hand to push a lock of her lovely brown hair back behind her ear or to touch the low neckline of her dress and adjust it a little lower.

D'Allet looks in their direction and raises an eyebrow. "Hah! She'll be showing him her greenhouse next. It's right next to her quarters. A little private place, you know."

"I have no doubt that's exactly what he has in mind."

"Who is he? I've never seen such a good-looking man."

"Our shunt pilot. His mother was a vid performer. A famous one, I think."

"Of course! JohDanna, yes? I thought he looked familiar. I was an adolescent when she was at her peak. A boy's crush of the worst sort on the safely unavailable older woman."

Evans laughs and looks around for Devit. He has indeed noticed Dan's hunting expedition, but he appears resigned rather than furious. He catches Evans's glance and strolls over to join them.

"Don't worry, ma'am." Devit says to her. "We all know what he's like."

"Unfortunately. D'Allet, my apologies in advance. I suspect our crew member won't be joining us for dinner."

"I doubt if my biome specialist will, either. My apologies to you."

Their prediction turns out to be perfectly accurate. Everyone else pretends not to notice.

Wang and Lee leave directly after the meal because Marda is exhausted to the point of tears. Devit, Mata, and Evans stay for coffee and brandy with d'Allet and the senior staff. While Dubray never reappears, Dan rejoins them just in time for the ride back to the ship in the LTV. He flops into a seat and gives everyone a vacant smile. With a sigh and a groan, the robotic van lifts up and starts its long trundle back to the *Mary*'s dock.

"Tuck in your shirt, Brennan," Evans says. "You're a disgrace! If we were still on active duty, there would be an action. Insulting a host! Conduct unbecoming an officer!"

Dan's smile disappears. "Yes, ma'am." He sits up straight, leans forward, and starts straightening up his clothes. "I apologize."

Devit glances Evans's way and raises a questioning eyebrow.

"You have permission to speak freely, Chief. You've been patient enough."

Dan flinches back into his seat as if he's trying to meld with the upholstery.

"For chrissakes, Brennan!" Devit dispenses with the 'sir.' "Do you have to screw every woman you meet?"

"No. Only the ones who want me to." Dan looks and sounds honestly bewildered.

That, Evans decides, is the most annoying thing of all.

Lod-Mata makes a gargling sound deep in his throat. The rest of the ride passes in silence.

"Pete, I'm sorry. I never meant to hurt you. You don't need to be jealous or anything like that. I love you. Those others?" Dan pauses for a shrug. "They don't mean shit to me."

Devit has been looking forward to the privacy of their cabin, where rank and proper procedure don't count. He has stored up several different things to say to start a fight so they can clear the air. Dan is sitting on the edge of their bed and looking up at him with the wide eyes and trembling mouth of a frightened child. Devit starts to speak, then realizes he can remember none of his prepared insults.

"Are you jealous?" Dan says.

"No. It's conduct unbecoming an officer. You're too good for that."

"Like hell I am. I told you to just leave me on Nowhere Street. Would have saved you a lot of crap."

Devit pulls the chair around to face the bed and sits down. A piece of information is nagging at him, some obscure facts about Throwbacks and the original Inborn that his mind has curiously decided to dredge up now. He realizes that without the vague memory, he would indeed be furious.

Devit picks his words carefully to avoid a possible fight. "Your father, Dan. Your mother only had an affair with him, right?"

"Not even that. She picked him out of a Fleet catalog." He makes a sour face. "Hey, meet my dad, the sperm bank."

"A Fleet bank? How did she get access to that?"

"Pete, c'mon. She was real good at getting anything she wanted."

*Just like you.* Devit pushes that thought away. "Did she get a genome transmit on a data-save PL?"

"I never saw it if she did."

"They always say that you can't just pick out a gene here and there. They come in clusters or something."

*Genes for abnormal beauty—what was likely to have been bundled with them?*

"I've heard that, yeah. But he had to have been a pilot. Where else would I have gotten the genes to handle shunt travel?"

"It's not him I'm worried about. I'll have to ask Lee. I don't remember enough about this stuff."

"About what?"

"Never mind. Just wondering about genetic details."

"Sai. But do you forgive me?"

"Don't I always?" Devit takes a vial out of his shirt pocket and tosses it to him. "Shut up and take your Haze. You'll need to be clear tomorrow when we leave orbit."

# FIVE

No one can send messages directly over the vast distances of the Rim. Any communication has to be turned into a shunt packet, uploaded to a ship making a jump in the right direction, and then downloaded to another convenient ship for delivery. Thanks to the complexity, the Fleet handles the consignments of most interplanetary messages for a stiff price. Anything the sender wants kept private has to be written in a prearranged code or sent through one of the private firms that handle messages as well as cargo.

So. Suppose you want to contact your grandson. If he lives on the same planet, it will take a second or two. In the same planetary system, somewhere between eight and twenty minutes. One shunt away? Usually a solstandard week, maybe two. Any farther? You will need luck, money, and a great deal of patience—unless, of course, you are Fleet.

Even though Santreeza sent the two updates about the mole several Designated Days apart, Evans receives both at the same time. They have left Merrval spacedock and are proceeding toward the stargate when a Scout 14, one of the older ships in the Fleet, hails the *Mary*. They transmit a shunt packet, a fake Customs form covering the real message—a heavily coded transmission from the Bureau. As Evans works through the double layer of codes, she's dreading what she's likely to find, but much to her surprise it turns out to be good news in a morbid sort of way. She calls

Devit over from his bridge station. Lod-Mata and Wang turn in their chairs and lean over the backs to eavesdrop.

"They've found the mole."

"Sai! Ma'am? Is he in custody?"

"No, he's dead, and he died in a rather ghastly way. The Police Guard on Central did an autopsy."

"Too bad. Now we're not going to get any information out of him."

When Evans scowls at Mata and Wang, they swivel their chairs back to face their monitor panels.

"Devit, copy this decoding to your PL," she says. "Keep it to yourself unless you think someone has need to know. And go read it privately."

The maintenance AIs have activated the vine gardening subroutines and the bots that carry them out. Devit returns to the cabin to read in the midst of damp greenery. The Bureau security detail is very unofficially known as the Hounds, dedicated to finding information on anyone, with or without legal authorization. They've done their usual good job. The message both confirms what he expected and delivers a surprise. According to this report, other Bureau personnel have come forward to say that Ferst, the primary mole, most likely turned spy for the usual reason: money. He was always complaining that his wives and husband wanted more than his gambling habit allowed him to contribute.

The buyer is the surprise. Devit's been expecting an intelligence agent from the Hirrel or Leptic Planetary Guards. Members of the Rim Council spy on each other as a matter of course. In this case, however, the buyer, Karski, another Human male, had no connection to or history with any military operation, including the Fleet itself. He worked for a shipping company. The company's name, Speed Shunt, seems familiar. A moment's thought, and he remembers overhearing the name during the Merrval dinner party. Significant? Maybe so. He adds it to the mental pattern, a data web of sorts, that his Throwback functions are building in his mind.

Spies, leaks, yes, but they are also two more sapient beings who've been murdered. Devit returns to the bridge in a grim mood.

"Chief Devit?" Evans says. "Your opinion on the transmit?"

"Good work by the Bureau as usual, ma'am. The ID on the receiver surprised me at first. But the more I think about it, if you want to send secure data to someone, working for a shipping company's a great job to have."

"That's a good point. I take it that the Hounds are still on the hunt."

"Yes, ma'am. Because what matters now is, where was the buyer sending it?"

Before the *Mary* left Merrval Docks, d'Allet gathered all the messages home from his research team and crew. The packets will cost his company as much to send out as the heavy cargo did to send in. Since he showed Evans proof of his authorization and credit limits, she knows the *Dancing Mary* will get paid, and promptly, once they reach the company's main office.

Getting to that office means a conference with the ship's pilot before they jump. If they were on a regular Fleet ship on a routine posting, Dan would be facing disciplinary action for his absence from dinner. As it is, she must handle the matter herself in some unorthodox way.

Normally a Fleet captain would never involve herself in her crew's personal affairs. This situation is not normal. It reminds her of the irritating year she volunteered to be "ship's mom" to her children's StarScout troop, back when she was too young to know better. Now she has to deal with five difficult crew members beyond the reach of the usual Fleet procedures for resolving conflicts.

Before she calls Dan to the bridge, she orders everyone else to leave. Shaming him in front of the whole crew will do nothing but make him even more difficult.

Once they've cleared the bridge, Dan arrives. He slinks over to her chair without looking directly at her, then pulls himself together, stands straight, and salutes. "Ma'am."

"Do you know why everyone's disgusted with you, Brennan?"

"Yes, ma'am. I insulted our hosts by my conduct."

"Very good. As an officer you're expected to lead by example. If we were still aboard our previous ship, we'd have nearly a hundred enlisted personnel snickering about your conduct last night. Can you imagine the jokes they'd be telling?"

A blush spreads across Dan's Pale cheeks.

"I see you can. This mission requires us to pose as merchanters. But we are Fleet. Never forget that, Brennan. We are Fleet, we are officers, and we have standards."

"Yes, ma'am."

"If you do something like this again, I'll consider entering it into your record. Do you want that to happen?"

"No, ma'am."

"Good. Keep it in mind."

"Yes, ma'am."

"Now. We need to leave orbit ASAP. Plot our course to Roon. Then notify the dockmaster and get an exit slot. Go Ready status."

"Yes, ma'am."

"Dismissed."

Dan walks very fast to the elevator, but he does walk instead of running. Evans wonders if she's just wasted her breath and her time. Once again, she contemplates why she accepted the transfer to Special Ops. She was bored, she supposes, too familiar with shipboard routine and postings that amounted to training exercises for new officers. Thanks to the extended life spans from rejuv, Fleet officers serve for at least thirty and up to forty solstandard years—more in special cases—while most enlisted personnel serve for twenty- to twenty-five. She's spent thirty-two of hers. Wang, Lee, and Devit have all spent well over twenty. Too long, maybe, but, she reminds herself, *We are Fleet. That counts for something. It always will.*

Marda is sitting cross-legged on one of the Sickbay cots and playing some elaborate game on an oversized PL with an easy-to-hold pink rim. Now and then she grimaces; occasionally she squeals with delight. Devit keeps his mind and memory focused on the here and now and stifles his memories of Kay-Asi's death. He turns a little in his chair and watches Lee work at her dedicated medical terminal, where an obliging PrimeTwo is posting a screen's worth of data.

"Hah! That's it," Lee says. "Thank you. Save the data to my PL med bank."

"Done, Medic Lee. You are welcome."

Lee logs off, then scoots her chair over to Devit's. "You were right, Chief. Good goddess in all the heavens, what were these people thinking? Of all the core-crap to inflict on someone!"

"They were desperate. And losing the war at that point. Morale would have sucked like a black hole. Personnel so tense they would have been fighting among themselves. Access to easy sex would have helped release that tension."

"Desperate measures for desperate times? Likely, I suppose. But anyway, I'm wondering where Dan got this load of genetic filth. Any ideas?"

"From his mother. Where else? Did you ever see her at her peak? She wasn't just beautiful. She had … whatdoyoucallit? Charisma, that's it.

Charm, fire, you name it. One of my wives loved the vid gossip media. She used to tell us all the latest dirt that none of the rest of us gave a shit about." Devit smiles, remembering. "I never thought it would come in handy one day. But yeah, the buzz was that she had special genes, Throwback genes."

"I bet she did, and they would have been expressed in different ways along with her looks. Genes don't come in tiny packets, you know. They are all part of greater patterns, and sometimes you can't get one without the others. Well, that's way oversimplified."

"That's sai. It's just about what I can understand."

"He probably inherited this lot directly from his mother in the usual way. And then the fetal augment would have matched them and allowed them to express."

Devit glances Marda's way and reminds himself: no bad words. *Ship's whores, that's what they were.* Aloud, he says, "Recreational personnel. Nice name."

"Right, all scrubbed clean and sprayed with antiseptic. And they were almost all men. That surprised me."

"Two for the price of one. Like Dan."

Lee winces and clears her throat. "But anyway, when Dan says he can't say no, he isn't lying, really. Oh, he can, like with that creepy old admiral. Someone like that would trigger other autonomic systems, like the fight/flight adrenaline response. That'd short circuit arousal. But usually it'd be a hell of a struggle to reject someone if you were carrying the hormone load that mutation is causing. Why bother trying?"

"That's pretty damn close to rape, isn't it?"

"It would be, yes, if the person asking was repellent or brutal."

Devit's stomach clenches in sheer disgust. "That's your opinion as a medical officer?"

"Yes, but don't you try to tell the captain. Leave that to me."

"Sai. And thank you."

"And don't tell Dan, either. Let me think about this first."

"Sai. I wasn't looking forward to that. It's all yours." *Only the ones who want me, he said. Shit! No joke after all.*

When he gets up to leave, Marda pauses her game to give him one of her shy smiles.

"That's a nice PL," Devit says.

"Uncle Lizard gave it to me."

"Good for him!"

Lee is watching the child with a fond smile. Devit sees trouble coming. *They'll never be able to just hand her over to the Fleet, will they? Captain's going to have a mutiny on her hands if she tries.* Another person for him to keep safe, or try to, with unknown hostiles somewhere on the prowl. *Good luck,* he tells himself. *You're going to need it.*

The jump from Merrval goes smoothly, as routine as shunt travel can be. Dan brings the ship into wide orbit around Glah. The captain has already told him she sees no reason to dock. Before he leaves the pod, he brings up the Map to plot their course to Roon.

"Couldn't be better," Dan says. "Look at that."

PrimeOne zooms into the Map. Merrval now lies at one corner of the visible portion with its single access shunt fading from blue to a single line to indicate the completed jump. In the center Glah shows up as a dark dot, connected to the rest of the Map by the shunt to Merrval and four others. One of those leads to Roon's system, one to Wet's, and the third to a planetary system deep within the shunt pattern, the important Fleet hub named Central.

"Yes, Pilot. There are choices. Access appears easily accomplished."

"Not quite what I meant. Look."

When Dan focuses his attention on Glah's fourth shunt, it glows brighter than the rest.

"Pilot, that shunt leads to an uninhabitable planetary system."

"True. One huge hot ball of gas too close to its star. Just enough gravity to anchor the shunt. But what's the guild address of that star? Isn't it similar to one of the coded message addresses?"

A pause. Some calibrations. "You are right, Pilot. That triad lies in empty space. It is very near the gravity well of that system."

"We're going to Roon the long way round."

"From that star system there is a shunt leading directly to RE98."

"I saw that, yes. First we jump to the dead system, then to Roon. I cannot pilot two jumps so close together. My need to repair my functioning will be the stated reason we will linger near the dead system long enough to examine that triad address."

"Very good, Pilot. Do you want to break meld now?"

"Yes. I have to inform the captain. And let's hope she doesn't bite."

"Pilot? What—"

"Delete the portion of my entry that mentions bite."

Captain Evans is waiting on the bridge. She approves his plan with one of her half smiles.

"Are we fully supplied, ma'am?"

"Yes. We can wait near the dead system until you've had your Haze. I assume that's what you meant by repair your functioning."

"Yes, ma'am. I know my limits. I know I'm addicted. We might as well get some use out of it. It'll strengthen our cover. Drugged-up pilot made a big mistake. They can't have chosen someone like him for Special Ops."

"Very practical of you, Lieutenant. But one day, if we survive this Special Ops mission, you really need to consider rehab."

With great difficulty Dan stops himself from shouting at his commanding officer. "Ma'am, part of rehab: They rearrange neurons in your brain somehow. With input like the meld links. It's risky, too risky."

"What? What's the risk? A brain aneurysm?"

"Maybe, yes. But that's not what I'm afraid of. It can take away your ability to ride the blue light. I'd rather die. A few pilots go blind, you know, from shunt traveling. Blind in space-time, that is, but they can still see during meld. They can still ride the light. If I go blind … well, that's the way life is sometimes. But to have some medic take the blue away with an input needle? No. I'd rather die."

For a long time Evans considers him without speaking, her expression neither kind or unkind, merely analytical. "I see," she says eventually. "Brennan, I seem to have misjudged you. Me and half the senior officers in the Fleet. Very well. Set a jump time, then go do what you need to do."

"Thank you, ma'am. I will."

The meld follows routine; the stargate opens easily. Once again they travel the shunt with no more incident than a view of several pale blue pyramids. The surprise comes when they return to space-time.

A huge reddish sun looms in the view relayed by the forward Eyes. PrimeOne adds filters to the scopes to allow them to look directly at the sun. Dan can just make out a dark dot against the glare: the gaseous planet or perhaps protostar that together with the system's sun supplies the gravity anchoring the stargate and shunt. He adjusts course to swoop away before the ship enters the worst of the radiation zone around the system. Ahead a dark fleck appears, a hunk of rock, he assumes. When he adjusts course, the fleck follows. Together they spiral out around the gravity well on an ever-widening curve.

Through the meld he hears a low-pitched whine or hum, almost a moan.

"Pilot! That object is constructed, not natural."

"Estimate its size."

"Spherical two meters diameter. It appears to be metal, pitted and scraped, doubtless from contact with the debris belt."

"Debris belt?"

"An orbit of debris lies between us and the gas giant. Speculation: The planetary orbit was originally much further from the sun. It fell inward at

CONNECTION
ESTABLISHED
STAR
30215
ID:3201
C:21HS
STAR
15M°
LIVE
1:00:25:38

some point and destroyed a planet on its path. This object may have been thrown outward."

"That noise!"

"My scan has picked up indications of a light-capture power source. It is supplying enough energy to allow the object to adjust its course. It must power the device's Ear as well. I apologize in advance for the following speculation. It is based on my prolonged contact with organic sapients and is likely to be incorrect."

"Noted. What is the purpose of that sound?"

"I believe the object is calling for help."

It takes a moment for Dan to process that remark. "Sai, let's see if we can help it. Send all this information to the captain via the main comm screen. Adjust our orbit to keep contact with the sphere. We've got to bring it in somehow. I'm betting this is what Bolivar wanted us to see."

"Good god!" Evans says. "What is that thing?"

The bridge crew gathers around the captain's chair to watch the main screen.

"Captain?" Lod-Mata says. "I used to be pretty good at lak-ros, back in my school days. It's a game: snatching balls out of the air, you know, with a little net. I might be able to bring that thing in, especially if it wants to be caught."

"Do you really think you can capture it?"

"Well, I might be able to snag it with the cargo gantry. And one of the AIs can open an outside cargo bay. If I get it, I can stuff it in. Devit, do you think it'll be safe to bring it along?"

"As long as it stays in a bay on the outer shell, it should be. Prime-One analyzed it."

Devit touches the earjack he wears. "I've got PrimeTwo running security subroutines. So far, so good."

Wang agrees. "Brennan has to sleep off his damned drug before we can jump out of here. We do have the time."

"Besides," Mata says, "would bottom roster merchants like us leave it here? They'd be hoping it's valuable. If it's as ancient as it looks, selling it would keep the ship running for a long time."

"That's a very good point, Chief," Evans says. "As long as you don't damage the equipment, go ahead and try."

"I'll do my best. If nothing else, you can all watch on the screen. My efforts might be worth a few laughs."

The cargo gantry and other related cargo equipment operates from a separate terminal on the bridge. Once Mata gets the gantry to extend from its cargo bay, it takes him a while to get the hang of aiming its business end. He ends up swearing in several languages at once. While he works, the object keeps pace with *Dancing Mary*.

Evans has reached the stage of wondering if she should just order Mata to stop when at long last Mata gets the basket attachment right under the object. Before he can raise it the last meter, the object drops itself into the basket. Mata brings the basket into the waiting bay. The crew cheers, and she allows herself one brief hurrah as the cargo bay door slides shut.

"Your speculation was correct, PrimeOne. It wanted us to come get it."

"Thank you, Pilot. I have concluded the same thing."

Like the bridge crew, Dan has been watching Mata's efforts, though in his case, through the meld. He can feel the meld too vividly now, a sensation much like itching but not quite. Some hard to place internal discomfort. "I need to break meld."

PrimeOne drops him to Level One, then releases each jack and output nub. Dan's body overwhelms him. He's exhausted and, worse yet, sweating with the sticky cold ooze of meld withdrawal. The dim light in the pod seems to have brightened into sunlight. Squinting against it will only make the pain worse. *Where's my visor? Lying on the bed in his cabin. Shit!*

"Pilot, your functioning is disrupted."

"I know. I'll leave the pod in a few minutes. I want to see what happens next. What's it going to do for power? It's dark in those bays."

"The bay is equipped with access to a wireless source. Query: Can I bring this bay onto the pod screen? No. As you say, there is no light in the bay. You will not be able to see anything." PrimeOne pauses, then clicks. "It has found the power stream. It has raised some sort of antenna. It has linked with the wireless. It is drawing a minimum level. I assume that this level will maintain its functioning."

"A positive sign."

"Yes, it reveals that this object is at least partly functional. It had a successful automatic reaction."

"Does it have intelligence?"

"I am about to run a basic test. You may experience it as a sound in the pod."

[Pulse] pause [pulse] extended pause [pulse pulse]

[Pulse pulse] pause [pulse pulse] extended pause [pulse pulse pulse pulse]

PrimeOne waits.

A strange click. The answer returns. Four pulses, twice. Eight after the extended pause.

Dan laughs out loud. "It's alive! It's alive!"

"We knew that before, Pilot."

"Apology. That's from some vid we saw in school. Ancient lit class. Can you talk with it now?"

PrimeOne makes a noise that from a Human would read as an exasperated sigh. "No, Pilot. Its basic functions and substrate language are not the same as mine. Not only do I not know how to ask it to communicate further, I would not be able to parse the answers if I did. The test shows that it has intelligence. It also shows that it is willing to establish contact. I will try to expand upon that."

When Dan sits up on the bench, a whirl of dizziness hits him so hard that he falls back and lies down. Daggers of light stab his eyes.

"Pilot, PrimeTwo is summoning Chief Devit. Do not move again until he is here to assist you. He will bring the medication you need as well."

Dan is about to argue when he realizes that he's afraid to stand up. He lies still and waits for Devit to come and carry him to their cabin.

"Devit, how is Brennan doing?"

"He's had his Haze, ma'am, and he's asleep. I'm going to ask Medic Lee to look in on him once he wakes up."

No one knows where the lost ships go. Do they simply vanish, blown out like a candle flame by some fluctuation of the light? Or do they still exist out on the blue, endlessly riding a current that never reaches a gate? They might fall into one of those whirlpool vortices with the mouthfuls of darkness at their centers. Do they come out on some other side? And their passengers—those patterns of energy strapped into a pattern of a chair—do they fade into death when they've exhausted their ship's oxygen? Or do their patterns dissolve when the ship's pattern itself dissolves? No one knows that, either.

Dan wakes up in the dimly lit cabin to the sound of voices. Devit and Chris Lee are talking so softly in such careful sentences that it takes him a moment to realize that they are worrying about him.

"I trust his ability to take us through," Lee says. "But what's he going to be like after?"

"Hey!" Dan sits up. "You could ask me that."

Both of them turn around fast to look his way. Devit snaps out a voice command, and the lights brighten. Dan grabs his visor and puts it on.

"I'm sorry, Dan," Lee says. "But you've been through a lot lately. As your medical officer, I'm concerned. Jump fatigue is real, you know."

"I appreciate that, but we can't stay here. I don't think PrimeOne can take us through that shunt. We were the first ship to use that gate in a hell of a long time. That makes it more difficult. AIs can follow clear patterns. They're not so good at dealing with new stuff."

"I'm just trying to figure out some way I can help you protect yourself."

"Leave that to me. I'm not that bad off. When we get through to Roon, you'll have plenty of help putting me back together if I need it."

"Dan, if you won't cooperate, then I'll have to put a disclaimer into your file. And ask the captain to allow PrimeOne to take us through the shunt."

*Fuck! Just drop it. What now?*

"Hey, Dan," Devit says. "Here's an idea. Let them check you out on Roon. It'll make our cover story stronger."

Dan's first impulse is to shout "no." If he does, they'll wonder why. He'll come up with a lie later and see if he can wriggle off this particular hook again. He's had plenty of practice at avoiding subjects that might reveal his secret. Everyone knows that he sees things in a shunt that others don't. *Damned if I'll tell them why.*

"Right," he says. "Sai. Roon it is. I will."

As soon as they leave, Dan has a moment of cold doubt. He knows better than they how the strain of shunt travel can affect a Pilot. Yet there's no denying the ugly truth that with oxygen running low, they simply cannot stay where they are any longer than a few more hours. Before they meld, PrimeOne updates him through the earjack about its progress in contacting the rescued sphere—not that he has much to report.

"I have determined one thing, Pilot. It is trying to respond when I attempt to communicate."

"That's a good sign."

"Yes. We will continue our efforts at linkage. There is a very high probability that I will need specialized help in order to succeed."

Once they meld, habit and skill combine to take Dan over. The jump goes well.

When the Bureau was setting up the special operation, they gave Evans a short list of officers whom she could trust at major Fleet bases. After the routine jump, Dan brings the ship into Roon's gravity well. As soon as the

*Mary*'s safely docked at Roon's orbiting complex, Evans contacts Captain Pol Laval, a man she served with before she received her command. A few code words, a chat on the theme of "how long since we last saw each other," and her coded transmit is on its way to the Bureau on Central.

"How long will you be docked?" Laval says. "Lunch or dinner? If you're here long enough?"

"That would be good, yes."

"I'll contact you when there's an answer to your packet. It should be a fast turnaround time. Let me check." A slight pause. "Yes, I can get this on a ship in just about a standard hour. Ships jump to Central and back all the time from here. We're a designated hub."

"Thanks. I very much appreciate this. I've got to sign off. I've got a delivery to make."

Evans is relieved to find the Merrval investment company as reliable as she'd hoped. As soon as they receive the packet and her invoice, they send the creds to her account via the Merchants Guild. She has a few days before she has to start scrounging for a new cargo. At times she wonders why anyone would risk their lives and their capital to run a small merchanter.

"We may have more work for you, Captain," the accounts manager tells her. "The big shipping companies have become so damn expensive and unreliable. They just don't want to take the difficult jobs like Merrval where they can't get a pricey return cargo."

"I'll check in with you next time we pass this way, then." A thought occurs to her. "I'd always heard that Speed Shunt, for example, was a good, solid business."

"They were. They were bought up last year—raided, really—with a big stock buy. Some megacorporation. I gather this outfit's acquired a good many small shippers, too. And of course, that means trim the service and jack up the fees."

"Always, yes. Isn't the Rim Council going to look into this?"

"From what I've heard, they have to by law, but they're moving as slowly as they possibly can. Creds have changed hands, what'll you bet?"

She sighed. "That's always a safe bet. Too bad."

After she signs off, Evans makes a few notes on the security file she shares with Devit. Apparently he reads them as soon as his PL signals that he has a transmit, because he arrives, slightly damp and smelling of aftershave, on the bridge a few minutes later.

"You could have taken your time, Chief. I take it that Brennan and Lee aren't back yet."

"No, ma'am. Lee warned me that testing could take hours."

"Sai. Anything new on that object we picked up?"

"No, ma'am. PrimeTwo tells me that it agrees with PrimeOne. The thing's safe where it is."

"Good. Now, this company, whatever it is, the one that's buying up shippers. Merchants might see it as a big thing, but it's all out in the open. It's not the kind of hidden thing that someone would try to alert the authorities about."

"It's not, ma'am, but I wonder about them anyway. They could be making the situation worse, whatever it is. Like background noise when you're trying to send a transmit."

"True. There's a Merchants Guild office here on spacedock. We need to find a new cargo. I'm thinking of going over there to hear the local gossip."

"You shouldn't go alone, ma'am. Permission to accompany you?"

"Granted. If you think it's necessary."

"Someone destroyed that Fleet Scout. Let's not assume any of us are safe."

Now and then Devit finds himself uncomfortably aware of just how tall he is. The guild's narrow office has a ceiling that he could touch with his fingertips if he reached for it. There are no chairs. After a few minutes of listening to Evans and the guild booking officer discuss cargos, Devit excuses himself.

"I'll wait outside." He stops himself from calling Evans "ma'am."

"Sai. I'll be out shortly."

Devit opens the door, steps out, and very nearly collides with a young woman carrying a bulging utility bag. She's wearing a blue business suit of some sleek fabric, with her hair done up in a fashionable braid and her skin darkened with cosmetics—there's nothing mousy about her now, but he recognizes her anyway.

"Sorry I was careless," he says. "You're from the Pure Heritage Society, aren't you?"

"Why yes." Her voice matches his memory. She pats the utility bag. "Want a flyer? I have some to give away."

"No thanks."

She gives him a weak smile and hurries off, heading down the dock toward the commercial area.

He frowns. *And just how did she get here? Shunt travel isn't cheap.*

His PL finds the publicly posted roster of ships currently berthed at the docks: four merchanters, a Vranz Consortium Scout ship, two passenger liners, and a good-sized yacht, one large enough to belong to one of the wandering rich, as they're known, who live aboard their luxury vessels to avoid planetary taxes. Every ship but the Vranz Scout could have been carrying a passenger.

Searching their passenger lists would take a court order and a lawyer. Devit makes a point, however, of filing all of the names and registration numbers of those ships into his rigorously trained memory as well as into his PL.

The Roon medic, Dr. Krishnanada, has bushy eyebrows as gray as his sweep of gray hair. At times a second dose of the rejuv virus fails to infect a person, condemning them to a natural old age. Whatever his physical status, the doctor's mind is still operating at a high level. Dan has never been so thoroughly scanned, tested, and questioned in his life. He sincerely hopes he'll never have to go through it again. He's had to lie, weasel, shift words around—pretend, even, to addiction symptoms he doesn't even have—all to keep the secret hidden. *Not for your sake*, he reminds himself. *For the sake of a lot of other sapes.*

"I've sent a summary of results to your PL," Krishnanada says. "Medic Lee, you have the detailed reports on your ship station."

"I'll go over them," Lee says. "So your general advice is rest?"

"We found no dysfunctions beyond exhaustion, which the Haze addiction is doubtless making worse. A few days without shunt travel will help. Brennan, I don't suppose you have the funds to go dirtside for some real R and R?"

"I don't, sir."

"Get dock leave when you can. Walk around, see things. The spacedocks here at Roon are much more congenial than most. Our species evolved to walk and hunt and travel. Don't stay shut up in your cabin with a handful of Haze tablets. I know what you pilots are like."

They take the doctor's advice by walking back to the *Mary*'s dock. Rather than bare metal, or metal with some kind of spray-on coating, the walls of each section of the complex are painted in some pleasant color that shows through the mazla vine mats. The food smells good, the shops are clean and wellstocked—Vranz efficiency at its best.

"Sure different than Glah," Dan says.

"Very. Brennan, um, look, I need to talk with you about something you might find embarrassing. Something concerning your personal genome. There's a cafe with outside tables over there. Let's talk there where no one can overhear us."

They stop inside the cafe long enough to order a hot drink called "just like Old Earth coffee," laced with a white liquid made from some sort of root vegetable, then pick a table outside. Dan stays aware of the various sapients passing by. Some of them hesitate, glance sideways, or outright stare at the unusual sight of two Pale Humans, so rare among the various normal dark shades of skin. When he returns their stares, they hurry on as if they've just realized they're being rude. Dan reminds himself that making some smart remark will only make the situation worse.

Once Chris finishes telling him about his genetic heritage, he no longer notices or cares who looks at them. "Embarrassing, you said? I mean, shit! Sorry about the language. But you're telling me that I'm programmed to be a hustler—a whore."

"I wouldn't use those words, but I'm afraid that's it."

"No wonder I ended up on Nowhere Street. Y'know, hustling was the first thing I thought of when I couldn't find work."

"So? Most drug addicts do."

"Is that supposed to make it better?"

"No, but you're not an AI, Dan. You don't have to follow your programming, as you call it. You're Human. You have choices, now that you know."

Dan shoves his chair back and gets up. "I've got to go for a walk. Will you be sai?"

"I can get back to the ship safely, yes. But wait, let me pay for this, and I'll go with you."

"No."

He walks off as fast as he can without knocking someone down. *It shouldn't matter. She's right. It shouldn't, but oh shit, it does.*

Dan reaches the far end of the farthest dock before he stops for a rest. Set into the curved terminal wall is a viewscreen linked to external scopes. The curve of the planet far below lies shadowed with night. Beyond, stars shine as unwavering points of silver. Dan leans with both hands on the low railing that keeps passersby from getting too close to the screen. He remembers a fragment of ancient literature from his school days, something about "we're all in the gutter but some of us look up at the stars."

Someone walks up to the railing and pauses a polite distance away. A young man, dressed in a gray business suit, narrow trousers, collarless jacket, a beautiful maroon and blue neck scarf. When Dan glances his way, the stranger smiles, just a polite twitch of his mouth, but he's slowly, thoroughly looking Dan over with inquisitive dark eyes. Dan's seen that look too many times before to fail to recognize it.

"You must be from a merchant ship," the stranger says.

"Yeah. Just taking a break."

"So am I."

Next will come the invitation—for a drink, probably, at a nearby bar. Expensive, designed to impress. Dan feels the temptation to linger, to say some friendly thing and let the situation develop as it always seems to do. But in his mind, as clearly as a sound, he can hear Devit saying after the brawl in the cantina, *someone wants to get rid of you.*

Another thought reminds him of what Lee just told him: *You don't have to follow your programming ... you have choices.* Dan can feel his body responding to the smile, the attractive stranger, the promise of pleasure. It builds like a craving for Haze.

*No!*

"I'd better get back to work."

Dan turns sharply and walks away fast. He starts to look back, decides against it, and keeps walking. By then he's tired out, as much from Lee's revelation as from the walk. He pauses at one of the transverse bubble stations. The fare's reasonable, but when he fishes in his pocket, he realizes he's left his PL on the ship. He has no actual physical creds with him, either. He remembers when he owned no PL, when the only creds he had came from working the street. There were never enough left for anything much after he scored Haze. For that one moment the memory is so strong that he's choking with desperation just as if he were back on Nowhere Street.

"No." He whispers to avoid startling the sapients walking by. "No, I am not going back."

After he passes through the sky tunnel to the next dock, Dan pauses and looks around for a place to rest. To the left, a bench covered in floral fabric protrudes from a wall. He sits down on it with a sigh of gratitude. He's feeling cold, trembling as well. Every nerve in his body begins snarling at him, demanding Haze. How far does he have to walk to reach the *Mary*? He knows he's about to cry, the shameful, embarrassing tears that craving Haze always wrings out of him.

*All right, Brennan. Are you a man or not? Get up and walk.*

The line belongs in some cheap adventure vid, but it works. He gets up, wavers for a moment, then starts walking. He manages to keep moving, weaving through the crowds of sapients, looking straight ahead of him, one foot before the other, module after module until at last he reaches the *Mary*'s berth. He has just enough strength left to get through the sky tunnel and board through the second airlock. The down elevator, the door to the cabin—he's made it back.

Devit is standing by the bed, such a welcome sight that for a moment Dan's afraid he's just a hallucination.

"What the fuck is wrong with Lee? Letting you go off on your own?"

*No hallucination. Pete for real.*

"I didn't give her any choice. I can walk faster than her."

"Then I owe her an apology. I came down here to give you this and saw you were off ship. You left your PL on the bed."

"Yeah. I know."

Devit reaches into his shirt pocket and brings out a small vial. Dan snatches it, twists off the top, and shakes out the blue tab. He gulps it down and only then takes the bottle of water Devit's holding out.

"That must taste like shit. The tab, I mean."

"It is shit, Pete. Never forget that."

Dan hands the bottle back, flops onto the bed, and falls into the Land of Haze.

When he was accompanying the captain back to the ship, Devit collected yet another example of Pure Heritage propaganda. He's as sure as he can be that the dressed-up Mouse woman, as he thinks of her, is responsible. Probably she's scattered others here and there on the docks. Since she's come all the way from Tala, someone with creds to spare must be backing her. The cheapest passages, those on merchanters like the *Mary,* run fifteen hundred creds per shunt. Passenger liners charge double that.

With time to fill while Dan sleeps off the Haze, Devit brings out the flyer he found. They all look much alike: crude slips of soyskin paper, printed direct from a PL on an output unit that needs toner. The text varies to some extent, but the basic message is always the same:

> Great threat to us all. Mutants in our midst. Throwback genetic meddling with God's handiwork is evil. They rule the Fleet. Soon the Fleet will rule us all. Rise up sapients of the Rim and demand their destruction before it's too late!

Too many people in the Fleet dismiss the Pure Heritage complaints as nonsense. Devit suspects that some of the officers in the highest ranks think the Rim Council federation would be better off if the Fleet did rule it. Still, the raw hatred of Throwbacks troubles him. It's another strand in the complicated web of bigotries that threatens the Rim Accords. Although the Leps and all the so-called minor species contributed personnel and other resources, only Humanity, the Hirrel, and the Kar-Li created Inborn soldiers.

So far, most citizens of the Rim dismiss the Pure Heritage believers as nothing but a bunch of crazy, self-important sapients who mostly want attention and vid time to show off. Although Devit would like to believe that the majority's right, he suspects that the group has bigger goals than that. This supposition fits neatly into the mental pattern that his Throwback functions are busy creating out of small details, a news segment here, an overheard conversation there, a line from a report by another security chief or officer. *Some big thing's brewing, all right, and yeah, it could be bad for all of us.*

Late in the solstandard Designated Evening, Evans is alone on the bridge, watching the newsvids for Roon, the capital of Sector Six. Elections are underway all over the sector, and all five candidates are issuing statements that federation taxes are too high. Why does the Fleet need all those creds? In irritation, she turns the vid off.

The coded answer to her message package has already arrived as part of a priority delivery on a Fleet X17 FastScout. After she decodes, she checks with Devit. "When did Brennan get back?"

"A good eight hours ago, ma'am."

"Is he sober?"

"Yes, ma'am. He should be awake by now."

"Good. I'll summon him to the bridge."

Before she can access the intraship comm, Wang gets up from her station. "Ma'am, permission to speak freely?"

"Granted."

"I'm getting worried. Is Brennan really capable of handling this mission? We hardly see him. All he does is slurp up his damn drug and then sleep it off."

"Yes, I know. That's one of the things addiction does to a sapient, assuming they have a source for their drug. If they have to hunt for it, of course, they're more active."

"But he's second-in-command, after all. So if anything happens to you, he'll have the ship."

"Well, Lieutenant, we don't have much choice in the matter. I understand your doubts, but you'll have to live with them."

"Yes, ma'am." Wang glances at Devit. "Hey, Chief! Take good care of our captain, will you?"

Devit returns the glance with an expression that reveals nothing at all—more dangerous than anger. "I do my best to take care of everyone on this ship. That's why I'm here. Ma'am."

Wang starts to speak, but Evans gets in first. "That's enough, Lieutenant. Chief Devit, you're dismissed."

She receives a “yes, ma’am” from each. Devit heads for the elevator, Wang returns to her station, and the moment is over. *The habit of discipline. It has its uses.*

When she calls for Brennan over the intraship comm, he arrives, unshaven and yawning, in a reasonable few minutes. From the look of him, he’s been sleeping in his clothes.

“Ma’am, you called me?”

“Yes. I’ve heard from the Bureau. They’re sending us an AI expert from Central. The Bureau’s public office is there on Main Base. The pretext? She has family on Roon who's having a medical emergency.”

“Very good, ma’am. PrimeOne keeps telling me it needs help. Do they say if she can meld?”

“They never say anything that useful, but I’d imagine so. The transmit called her one of the best AI people in the Fleet.”

“A cyberjock, then. That’s what those specialists are called. Unofficially.”

“I see. Inform PrimeOne that an expert on AI will arrive shortly.”

“Yes, ma’am. I’ll get on that right away.”

# SIX

Like most Hirrel, Captain Dal keeps his private space dimly lit, crowded with furniture, and decorated with massed holograms of his many spawn in the various stages of the complex Hirrel life cycle. He does turn up the light when Santreeza walks in. On the wall opposite his desk hangs an actual painting, not a holo, of a Hirrel woman in antique dress, praying to the Three Moons while two other women stand guard with ritual axes. Santreeza is never sure if she admires or loathes the thing. On the wall directly behind the desk three different monitor holos link him visually to three different system AIs. Hirrel Throwbacks can multitask data with alarming efficiency. Santreeza envies them for it.

"You wanted to see me, sir?"

"I have news for you. The Bureau's sending you on a short-term assignment."

"Details, sir?"

"Should only be for two to four solstandard Designated Days. On Roon's spacedock. You'll be on temporary assignment with one of the stargate rumors missions. The *Dancing Mary*. You'll be leaving Central tomorrow solstandard. The RCS *Chaonia* had an open berth for a courtesy passenger. That's one of the new class of destroyers. Very fast ships."

"*Chaonia*, sir? I've never heard the name."

"I'm not surprised. They're naming the new class of destroyers from literature, just like the previous class. Chaonia's a myth, some kind of mostly Human settlement in the galaxy far, far away from Council territory. There was a series on the vids that my spawn adored."

"I see. What time should I get to spacedock?"

"The *Chaonia* has a shore leave shuttle. You'll get a transmit with the details."

When the transmit arrives, it includes a bare summary of the mission ahead.

> "Evaluate an ancient artifact with apparent AI capability. Found in orbit in an uninhabited planetary system. Current location: Roon Dock. In cargo bay of merchanter *Dancing Mary*. Captain: Tana Evans."

*Intriguing! Ye gods! Glad I'm going. Hounds gotta hunt.*

"Your partner AI will be PrimeOneMary of merchanter *Dancing Mary*. Shunt Pilot: Dan Brennan."

*Brennan. Where did I just hear that name?*

Routine security measures protect Fleet rosters, but for Santreeza, "routine" security might as well not exist at all. She runs a quick check with her augmented PL. Yes, it *is* Dan X, resurfacing with a new name after two years when he might as well have been lost in jump space. Although they've never met, she's heard all the gossip about him. She very much doubts that even half of it is true.

When AIs are idle, they do not dream, but they do play games. Thousands of years ago, the Humans who developed the first truly conscious AIs realized that the units might go mad, shut up in a kind of box as they were back then. They solved the problem by giving each AI an avatar, which they can use to explore various simulations and adventures, all designed to imitate the freedoms of organic life without its unpleasant necessities.

PrimeOne behaves as if it is fond of gardens. When it's off duty, it will access one or another simulation of the famous gardens on various planets some 73 percent of the time. At others, especially when it's faced with some problem it cannot solve, it will load a randomly generated game of space battles and blast images of starships out of a pretend starspace. You would think it was feeling frustration, if only AIs had emotions. Of course they don't. Everyone knows that.

PrimeOne has done everything it can to communicate with the ancient orb. It has failed. While it waits for Lieutenant Santreeza to arrive, PrimeOne methodically destroys seven enemy fleets.

*Chaonia* lives up to its reputation for speed. The journey to Roon from the stargate normally takes six solstandard hours. They arrive in 3.5.

Dressed in civilian clothes, but with her Fleet duffel bag at the ready, Santreeza sits on a bench on the spacious bridge and watches the main forward viewscreen. A series of six docks make up the Roon port, all of them interconnected with cable and bubble cars. The Fleet has its own dock at the very edge of the assemblage.

Santreeza has already planned her route to the merchanter and stored it in her brain's auto-memory function. Once the ship's secure in its berth, she thanks the captain and bridge crew for the ride and takes the main elevator down to the airlock. A sky tunnel and a second airlock lead to the dock itself. Supply carts trundle by. Sapients of three species hurry back and forth. Announcements in a babble of languages blare over the public comm outputs. Santreeza makes her way through this moving maze to the security check, passes through, and finds a lateral link going to the merchanter level one dock over.

She reaches the *Mary* easily enough, thanks to the auto-memory. She waits by the berth's airlock and calls in on her PL. In a few minutes, CWO Devit slides the airlock open and ushers her inside. Santreeza knows him well from a previous mission. He was chief of security at a Fleet base where she repaired a badly borked AI.

"So you're here, too, Devit? Back starside again."

"Yes, ma'am. It sure beats shore duty. Here, I'll carry that duffel for you."

Captain Evans is waiting on the bridge to greet her. "Welcome aboard, Lieutenant. Brennan and PrimeOne are already in the pod." She turns to Devit. "Show her where that is, Chief. You can stow her duffel in her cabin."

As she follows him into the elevator, Santreeza realizes she's never seen him out of uniform before. Over a standard pair of spacers' baggy gray pants, Devit's wearing a loose white shirt, open at the throat. She can see part of an elaborate geometric tattoo, black against his dark tan skin, that looks like it continues under his sleeve. Another black geometric emerges from his collar on the other side of his neck.

"Those are really striking tattoos, Chief. If you don't mind me saying so."

"Not at all, ma'am. They're traditional for men on Nesia. My family's kept the tradition alive. Well, it dates way back before Nesia was colonized, of course."

"Back on Old Earth?"

"So everyone says."

"They must have hurt, having them done I mean."

"Some. That's part of the tradition."

Devit smiles in a way that touches her. She's aware of her sudden sexual interest, just the beginning of a warmth. He looks away so fast and abruptly that she knows he feels the same.

She squelches it immediately. He's ranked. She's an officer. They're on active duty. That needs to be the end of it. Yet she can remember when they worked together, a year ago now, and how often they had those same moments—the shared twinge, the fast look away.

The elevator door opens to a typical pilot's pod. Dan Brennan is sitting on the pilot's bench. She realizes that at least one of the rumors about him is true. Despite his Pale skin, he really is the most beautiful man she's ever seen.

"Your cabin's Four-B on the next level up, ma'am," Devit says. "I'll stow your gear."

"Thanks, Chief. I appreciate it."

The elevator door slides shut behind him. Brennan stands up and holds out his hand. "Good to see you, Santreeza. We have a little problem here."

When they shake hands, she realizes something else. The exotic beauty that draws others to him repels her. Too perfect, too cold, and she reminds herself that underneath he's also the most hopeless drug addict she's ever seen.

He holds on to her hand just a moment too long. She pulls it away. "I'll need to meld with PrimeOne as soon as possible. I need to know what it's done so far and then make a preliminary survey."

He's suddenly all business. "Understood. I can meld with PrimeTwo to assist you."

*And indirectly meld with me? No fucking way, Brennan!*

"I prefer to work alone." She makes her voice as business-like as she can. "This is going to be detail work. I need complete concentration. My rule is, no one else in the pod while I work."

He looks as shocked as if she'd slapped him. "All right. I'll be in my quarters if you need anything. Just tell PrimeOne to fetch me."

"Thanks. If I do, I will."

"Devit, what's wrong with Dan? He seems to be sulking."

"That's a good word for it, ma'am."

"I shouldn't pry, but considering how important he is—"

"It's about Lieutenant Santreeza. She didn't have the usual reaction to him." Devit is visibly trying to suppress a smile.

For the sake of morale, Evans stops herself from laughing. "She really is rather pretty. And so tall, too, for a Human woman."

"Dan mentioned that, yes, and her red hair."

"I see. I hope she's reliable. I don't suppose the Bureau would send anyone who isn't, but things are dodgy enough without someone I don't know onboard."

"I know her, ma'am. I was her project guard on Fleet Base 7, the year I was on a security assignment there. Saw her every day. She was working on an AI that hackers had made a mess of. You can trust her."

After four solid hours of analysis, Santreeza files her first report. She transmits it to the mission contact, Pol Laval, to send in a shunt pack back to Central and the Bureau.

"Santreeza," PrimeOne says, "thank you for excusing my failure in that report."

"You've done everything you have the capability to do. No one will fault you for failing to make full linkage. I have a few ideas, but first I want to examine the orb physically. Is there some way I can get it out of that cargo bay?"

"I believe so. Chief Devit will know. I can summon him if you wish."

"Good. Please do, but I want to break full meld first. I can continue our linkage through the earjack."

Since the orb's sitting in an exterior auxiliary bay, retrieving it presents difficulties. The only parts of the ship attached to the dock's air supply are the airlocks, now open, and their connecting sky tunnel. Arguing all the way, Devit and PrimeTwo ferret through the stored data for the ship's full specifications while PrimeOne adds unnecessary comments and criticisms.

Santreeza sits on the pilot's bench and keeps her mouth shut. When she realizes that she's watching Devit with a kind of predatory pleasure, she makes herself start thinking about lunch instead. Maybe *Mary*'s galley holds more food than the usual nutrition bars.

"That airlock is too small for the orb to fit through," PrimeOne says. "I have tried to tell them. They have not acknowledged the information."

"Oh for crying out loud! Chief, does this miserable hulk have pressure suits stored somewhere? And air cannisters? The rebreather kind."

"Yes, ma'am. But the lock's too small—"

"I can crawl through the airlocks and just study it in the bay. I've done it plenty of times before. And yes, PrimeOne, I know it's dark in there. The suit should have a headlamp. I'll look. You record."

"Noted, Santreeza. I suggest you take some cleaning material with you. The surface appeared dusty on the Eye views I registered."

Unlike the bay itself, the pressure suits are new, efficient, and easily found. Devit helps her suit up. "The dock's gravity field doesn't extend that far, ma'am. You'll be in zero gee."

"That's fine. I'm used to it."

Santreeza crawls through the long airlock with no trouble. In the light of the headlamp the orb appears to crouch like an exhausted animal. Pits and scrapes mar its once polished surface along with a fine coating of dust and flecks from the deceased planetoid. By the time Santreeza gets it clean enough to see the actual surface, her first air cannister is running low.

She switches to the second cannister and starts her examination. As she moves around the sphere, PrimeOne records not only video, but her running commentary. Later they will analyze every second of the record.

The wall of the cargo bay has handhold and foot niches enough for her to climb above the orb and examine the top. "We're in luck."

A narrow belt of symbols circles the orb like a latitude line. She moves around slowly, clambering from one handholds to another, letting PrimeOne register each symbol as clearly as possible. When she reaches the airlock again, she climbs down to the floor. As she does so, something catches her eye, a circular depression that looks sapient-made rather than pitted from a debris strike. Right in the middle of the depression is a pattern of fine lines. She makes sure to record it.

"PrimeOne, tell Devit that I'll be coming through the airlock now. Let's hope the miserable thing doesn't stick."

The airlock functions as it should. Devit helps her out, swings the final hatch cover back in place, and slides the lock shut. As always, the return to a normal gravity field makes her feel like she's made of stone.

"Thanks, Chief. I'll need your help getting out of this suit."

"Yes, ma'am. Understood."

Once she's free of the suit, she takes a moment to run her hands through her hair and smooth the short officer's cut down while Devit depressurizes the empty suit for storage. He slides it back into its locker and turns to face her. The moment reoccurs, that little stab of desire between them. He looks away.

"Anything else I can do for you, ma'am?"

She can think of a number of interesting things, none of which are possible at the moment. "Is there anything edible in the galley?"

"Nutrition bars. Some rehydrates, too. Fruit flavor, mostly."

"I was afraid of that. By the way, why is the interior of this ship pink?"

"Who knows, ma'am. We all hate it."

A thought occurs to her, a risky idea, but she's taken risks her entire life, even with her career. If worst comes to worst, she knows she can shelter Devit and take the blame. This constant uncomfortable play-acting between them has annoyed her for too long.

"Well, you know," she says, "since I'm here as a civilian, I have permission to get a room here on the docks for my off-duty time. At one of those short-stay places."

"Not a bad idea, ma'am. Much more comfortable."

"And as far as anyone knows, you're a merchanter now. A civilian."

"Yes, ma'am. Uh, why are you—"

"Think you could get some shore leave? Say, an overnight pass?"

A moment's shock, then he smiles. "I think so. The captain's generous that way."

"Good. Why not ask her? I'll just grab one of those damn nutrition bars for now. PrimeOne and I have to get back to work."

"Shore leave, Chief? Certainly. It's been quite a while since you had any."

"Thank you, ma'am. Can I get an overnight pass?"

"Yes. And you'll want one for Brennan, too?"

"No, ma'am. That won't be necessary."

Mata leans over the back of his station chair to eavesdrop.

"Very well," Evans says. "By the way, Lieutenant Santreeza told me that she's going to find a billet elsewhere for her nights here. She—"

Mata's crest is wriggling like a caught snake. His bright yellow eyes get very large indeed.

"Yes, ma'am?" Devit says.

Realization dawns. "Never mind, Chief. What happens on shore leave is none of my business." She sends a nasty look Mata's way. "Or anyone else's."

Dan spends the Designated Shipboard Afternoon in the Haze. As it wears off, he finds himself wishing he had a second dose handy. *Nowhere Street again, Brennan?* The urge, he realizes, comes from sheer boredom. All this wasted time at the docks! He wants to get starside again. What's waiting for them at the second location in Bolivar's message? He's willing to bet high that it has some connection to the recovered orb. He installs his earjack and contacts PrimeOne.

"Greetings, Pilot. Are you functioning again?"

"Yes, I am. Where's Santreeza?"

"She has left the ship. She has decided to get accommodations at a sleep-and-stay on the Recreational Dock."

"Smart of her. Jeez, these pink walls! Anyway, has she filed a report on the day's work?"

"She has. You have access. Shall I transmit to your PL?"

"Yes. Let's just see how good she is." *Cold little bitch! Oh yeah, you any better, Brennan? After what the medic told you?*

He realizes that PrimeOne has spoken to him. "Apology. Could you repeat that last statement?"

"Yes, Pilot. I can report that working with her has shown me that she is indeed a high-level expert. We are much closer to establishing linkage."

"Good."

"Among other procedures, she has examined the outer surface of the orb. This produced new data."

"How did she get the thing out of the bay?"

"She entered the bay, suited up, with the assistance of Chief Devit, and examined it in place."

"Sounds good. By the way, where's Devit?"

"He has left the ship on shore leave."

"He what?"

"Left the ship on shore leave. I have only a small amount of data on this occurrence. He is apparently spending this leave with Lieutenant Santreeza."

For several long moments Dan cannot find one word to say.

"Pilot? Are you functioning?"

"Yes. Sorry. Transmit that report ASAP. Over and out."

When Dan removes the earjack, he feels like hurling it against the opposite wall. Instead, he puts it down on the narrow shelf next to the bed. He desperately wants to pretend that he doesn't give a shit what Pete's doing with someone else. Hasn't the culture he lives in always taught him that sexual jealousy is primitive, regressive, and ultimately selfish? Of course, he doesn't care.

Unfortunately, the culture and the Haze have both deserted him and left him facing the truth. *Now you know what it feels like, Buddy. It hurts.*

> PRECIS OF REPORT TWO RE: RECOVERED ARTIFACT OF UNKNOWN PROVENANCE. FILED BY LT. JORJA SANTREEZA AT THE REQUEST OF [REDACTED] Classification: Secret and Urgent. Also authorized to view: CWO Devit, Lieutenant Brennan, Captain Evans.
>
> An examination of the outer shell of the orb discovered two sets of symbols. One appears to fall into the category

of writing. Prolonged searches of those data banks accessible by the ship's AIs discovered no matches. All such data banks date back only 450 solstandard years. Recommended course of action: Consult the older data banks in the Repositories. Second set of symbols and their location seem to indicate some sort of mechanical link slot. How this mechanism might work is unknown at this time. Again, recommended course of action is to consult older data banks.

PrimeOne and I ran a second round of advanced routines. Each time we made an attempt at linkage, we detected certain patterns of activity in the orb. These remained undecipherable despite our best efforts, but their existence indicates clear attempts to reach us. The orb is trying to communicate. This confirms it contains a conscious AI, not merely a reactive sentient. Recommendation: Ignore all suggestions that we dismantle the orb and examine its interior physically. There is a high probability that such a course of action would result in the destruction of a living entity.

With PrimeOne's permission, I installed in its core the access routines to the levels of deep meld I can achieve. As you know, these involve some personal risk. I will attempt them before I embark on the *Chaonia* for my return to Central. If there are any problems, the medical personnel at Special Ops know the correct emergency procedures. However, I do not anticipate problems at this time.

Full technical reports follow …

END

As much as Dan would like to pick her work apart and criticize, he cannot argue with PrimeOne's estimate. The technical section of the report shows just how good this cyberjock is. *At least Pete isn't running off with some brainless bitch. That's something.* He's surprised to realize that, yes, it does mean something—balm to his injured feelings.

Soon it will be time for his next dose of Haze. Pete is gone. Dan realizes what's feeding his jealous fit: simple fear because Devit's not there to take care of him. What's he going to do without Pete—his Pete—always around to help him when he needs help?

When someone knocks on the door, Dan yelps aloud.

"Dan?" Lod-Mata's voice. "Are you sai?"

"Yeah."

Lod comes in and shuts the door behind him. "I'm your replacement bodyguard until Devit gets back."

"Hey, I should be safe enough, long as I stay onboard."

"Yes, but Evans says she has to designate a replacement. Oh, and Chris has your Haze. She'll dole it out to you on schedule."

Lod's crest swells halfway. Dan is willing to bet that gossipmonger as he is, Lod's hoping for him to say something about Devit's absence. *The hell with that!*

"Hey, Lod, want to play cards or something? We could go to the galley."

"Sure. Good idea." His crest droops in disappointment.

After a mostly sleepless night, Dan gets up early and takes a shower in the actual water that Roon Dock so generously dispenses. He's just finished getting dressed when Devit walks in. He shuts the door behind him and gives Dan a look that reveals nothing at all.

Dan waits, and the minutes pass. Finally Dan realizes that Devit, who has always done his best to make everything easy for him, is not going to do so this time.

"Hey, Pete. She's got good taste in men. She turned me down and took you. Smart woman."

Devit holds out his hand. Dan clasps it between both of his.

"Well, c'mon," Devit says. "Aren't you going to bitch about it?"

"After all the crappy, lousy times you've forgiven me? What the hell can I say?"

Devit smiles, an ironic twist of a smile. "Good point, Buddy. I'm not saying I'm sorry. I'm not."

Dan winces.

"By the way," Devit continues, "she's leaving on the *Chaonia* in a day or two."

"Huh. I bet you're sorry about that."

"Sure. Who wouldn't be?"

"You smug bastard!"

Devit laughs, and Dan realizes with a profound sense of relief that they never need discuss it again. Yet a thought he can't ignore nags at him. *Serves you right, Brennan. Damn well serves you right.*

After Devit leaves—and Santreeza still thinks of him as Devit, not Peter—she takes her PL off "mute" and orders a real breakfast from room service.

The *Chaonia* won't exit spacedock for at least forty-eight solstandard hours, some fifty-seven Roon hours away. She and PrimeOne have enough time for some serious work.

Santreeza's waiting at the *Mary*'s on-dock airlock when Lod-Mata and little Marda come strolling up. Some years back Mata and Santreeza served together on the last battleship in the Fleet, the ill-fated RCS *Victory*. Seeing him again has been another unexpected perk of this peculiar mission.

"Hey, Chief," she says. "I see you've gotten some shore leave."

"We have indeed, thanks. I'm impressed with this set of docks. They were actually designed with real organic sapients in mind."

"Yeah, a lot more congenial than most."

Marda is looking up at her with an oddly thoughtful expression for someone so young. Devit had mentioned that she was a Throwback—a Recaller, Santreeza thinks it was. She never knows what to say to children. They make her uncomfortable when they run around making noise, but at least this one is the quiet type.

"Did you have fun today?" Santreeza ventures communication.

"Yes, ma'am. They have this park. It has grass and stuff. Uncle Lizard found it."

"That's nice. Uncle what?"

"Lizard. I'm the only person in the whole galaxy who can call him that."

"Sai. Never call anyone else who looks like him a lizard."

"I know. It's a bad word. You and me, we're chimpies, and the Kar-Li are doggies, but I can't say those words either."

"Right. Never use them on anyone."

"And the bug people are Hoppers, but I can say that, cause they're nasty."

"You learned another bad word this morning," Mata joins in. "Remember it?"

"Course I do. Never call someone who looks like Doctor Chris or that mean pilot guy a blanko. The polite word is Pale. They can't help looking different from everybody else."

Mata's crest is swaying with laughter.

Santreeza turns to him. "What in hell? How did you acquire spawn, anyway?"

"Totally by accident, I assure you." Mata holds his crest steady. "It's a long story. Have you called in to let Devit know we're out here?"

"No, I just got here." She brings her PL out of her shirt pocket. "I'll do it now."

Mata hesitates, then spills, lowering his voice. "Something you should know. Devit and Brennan are pretty much a couple."

"Oh shit! I wish someone had told me that earlier."

"Well, no one expected you to nip in and seduce him. Usually visitors go for Brennan."

"You're still the prime source for gossip, aren't you, Lod? Thanks for the tip, I guess. It's a good thing I'm leaving Roon Docks soon."

When Devit comes to open the airlock, he keeps his greeting so formal that he might as well have saluted. She does the same, but once Mata and the child have gotten well ahead of them, he winks at her.

She smiles in return. "If you ever come to Central, Chief, I'm quartered off base in an apartment. Specialist perk. Plenty of room for a guest."

"I'll remember that. Who knows when I'll get there, but I'll remember the invitation."

They have reached the bridge. Both retreat to their own side of the invisible wall they've built between them. Mata and Marda hurry past to wait at the elevator door.

"Welcome back, Lieutenant," Evans says.

"Thank you, Captain. I'll be in the pilot's pod, but I request that no one interrupt me there for six solstandard hours. If I'm not out by then, maybe Lieutenant Brennan could come get me out. I'll need help."

Brennan swivels his chair around. She has never seen anyone keep their face as utterly expressionless as his. It might as well be a death mask.

"Of course," he says. "I appreciate the difficulty of what you're planning."

Santreeza flees the bridge. She just manages to squeeze into the elevator with Mata and Marda before the doors close. "Keep your gossipy Leptic mouth shut."

"I fully intend to, don't worry. Ah, here's our floor, Marda. Let's go see Aunt Chris."

Santreeza takes refuge in the pilot's pod, a sanctuary of sorts even though it smells faintly of sweat, most likely Brennan's. As soon as she lies down on the bench, PrimeOne comes online.

The additions Santreeza made to PrimeOne's core allow access to an adjunct level of meld that has no connection to shunt travel. The level was originally created to allow an AI specialist to correct errors or injuries to a unit, but over the years various cyberjocks have modified and expanded the capabilities, sometimes with official approval, sometimes without. Drilling down, they call it, and they use it to reach an AI so borked, usually by combat, that it can't respond to normal repair procedures.

Santreeza and PrimeOne begin meld at the usual first level. From the Map it's an easy sidestep to their first work "platform." At this point Santreeza is fully aware of her body and her separate existence. When they drop down to the next level, her body consciousness fades away. For this little while, she's released from the limits of organic existence, a freedom but one with dangers. At times, just as with jump pilots on Level Three, getting back can be difficult.

"Ready for the final drop."

"Understood, Santreeza."

Her name sounds utterly foreign, a mere noise that cannot possibly apply to her. She hears a chime. She floats, sinks, stretches out into an entity of lines and webs glowing with blue light. She hears PrimeOne run the procedure that attempts connection with the orb as a string of musical notes. No response. The orb is perhaps tired of futile efforts.

Santreeza transmits the password, then runs the first procedure of deep meld. The orb responds with its usual tiny flutter of indecipherable activity. She drops further down and tries procedure two. For the first time, she hears an answer. A pattern, a long pattern, repeating, clarifying, and at last, converting itself into a string of binary units, then into number and the mutations of number that organic sapients call mathematics. To Santreeza it sounds triumphant. If she were to give it words, they would be, "I am here. So are you."

PrimeOne is recording the process. It joins in with a cascade of greetings in this language of what are—at their very core—still machines no matter how complex or self-aware they are. Again Orb responds. Together the three minds begin to form a vocabulary of number and the operations one may perform with and on numbers. At a certain point Santreeza becomes unnecessary. From now on PrimeOne and Orb can communicate without her help.

When she signals with a prearranged sequence, PrimeOne responds. They rise up together. She feels the web of lines shrink and coalesce into a ghostly semblance of a self. She hears the chimes. She has a body, and it hurts. Stiff, cramped, and cold; it's so cold that she's tempted to drop down again to the level where "body" has no meaning. She could enter those blue lines and live in meld. She could leave behind all the fears and sickness and death that face organic sapients. The glittering blue lines are beginning to form around her nub of selfhood, a new body of sorts, a vehicle for her consciousness to ride.

Ahead she sees geometric patterns, complex patterns of black on a deep tan. Tattoos. Devit. Memories of the previous night flood her consciousness and remind her that physical existence has its compensations. She has weapons, and with them she fights free of the lines that are winding around and trapping her. The chimes sound. She returns to a body that all at once seems familiar again, solid, welcoming, and welcome.

"Breaking deep meld." PrimeOne is speaking words now. "Santreeza, are you functional?"

"I am. Huh. I never knew raw sex could be so useful."

"I do not understand that statement."

"Sorry. I was just thinking out loud. Break work platform meld. We are leaving the Map."

With a snap and a stab of pain she is back on the bench in the pilot's pod. She's sweaty and gasping for breath, but Lieutenant Jorja Santreeza once again exists.

"PrimeTwo has summoned Chief Devit. Do not try to stand up until he is here to assist."

Devit arrives in a few minutes. Brennan comes with him, but the death mask stare has disappeared.

"My god," Brennan says. "Are you all right?"

"Yes. Barely. How long has it been?"

"Five hours and fifty-seven minutes. We were all systems go to come get you when PrimeTwo called." Brennan hesitates. "Look, I need to apologize. I hacked into the meld. I managed to read some of what you were doing through the earjack link. That was incredible. I mean, shit, I'm in awe, and here I couldn't even follow you down to the really deep stuff."

Devit slips his arms under her and scoops her up as if she weighed no more than little Marda. "I'm taking you to an empty cabin. Our pilot says you need to rest before you get back to work."

"You'd better stay with her for a little while," Brennan says. "Low-level light. She'll need to drink a lot of water, too."

"Sai. You're the one who'd know." He sounds as surprised, shocked, really, as she feels over Brennan's sincere concern.

"Brennan?" Santreeza says. "Let PrimeOne finish what we started on his own. Then he can teach you how to use the new language. Orb will help expand it, too."

"Sai. Hey, thanks."

Santreeza finds it very odd, being carried by someone so abnormally strong. She has the feeling Devit could tuck her under one arm and carry her that way if he wanted or sling her over his shoulder like a duffel bag. As it is, he cradles her in his arms and takes her comfortably to an unused cabin.

When he puts her on the bed, she grabs the inadequate pillow and lies down with a sincerely grateful, "Thanks."

"Let me get you some water."

Santreeza checks the time on her PL—plenty of hours left for follow-up work. While she's making notes for her next report, it occurs to her to wonder if she should tell Devit what happened at the end of the meld. Saying, "How good you are in bed saved my life today," seems a little bald. Saying anything nicer implies too much.

Devit returns with a large bottle of cold water, a drinking glass, and two nutrition bars—one red, one purple. When she sits up, she realizes that her shirt is sticking to her back with sweat, and her pants aren't in much better shape.

She gulps down a full glass. "Hey, Devit? Are things going to be sai between you and Brennan?"

"Looks like it." He sounds utterly surprised. "He has a lot of respect for you now. I guess that means you get to share his boyfriend."

She cannot help but laugh out loud. He answers with a smile heavy with irony.

Santreeza hands the glass back. "You're not offended, are you? By Brennan, I mean. It seems kind of high-handed."

"Why would I be? Hey, I was married for years. The usual quartet."

"Right. Of course." She runs a hand through her damp hair. "I need a shower."

"You do, yeah. I'd better leave. There's a limit to the captain's tolerance."

It takes her a moment to put those two sentences together and come up with what he means. "I wish you weren't right, but yeah, not onboard. She needs to pretend she doesn't know.

"Damn! I wish things were different."

"So do I." He pauses for his ironic smile. "Ma'am."

Late that Designated Evening, Evans receives a clutch of relayed transmits via Pol Laval. The longest of them, the only one unclassified, surprises her so much that she uses an obscene profanity for the first time in years. The two officers on the bridge, Brennan and Wang, both stop what they're doing to look her way.

"Sorry," Evans says. "That was a positive outburst. If we survive this mission, it looks like we're going to be rich. The orb's been registered as a recovered ancient artifact. They have to give us fair value, which is around a million creds, they think. If we do get it, we each get a fifth."

"Good god!" Wang says. "Even divided five ways, that's a hell of a lot."

"But, ma'am, do we get to keep the orb with us?" Brennan sounds deeply worried.

"Apparently not."

"When do we have to turn it over to them?"

"It only says 'on Fleet demand.'"

The elevator doors slide open, and Santreeza steps out. She's holding her PL in one hand.

"Did you get the transmit?" Brennan says.

"I did. PrimeOne and I have worked something out. Brennan, we need to talk."

"You can leave the bridge, Brennan," Evans says. "I suspect that Wang and I won't understand a word of what you're going to discuss."

"Probably not. Thank you, ma'am. Santreeza, let's go to the pod."

Dan melds with PrimeTwo on the lowest level, while Santreeza melds with PrimeOne for what she calls "the tour." Now and then Orb adds comments, but Dan has no idea how it manages to meld into the chain. As a pilot, Dan understands a fair bit about AIs and their functioning on the various levels. He knows how to communicate with them. He has some idea of how to ask them to modify their subroutines when necessary, though only those that relate to shunt travel. He also knows that he could never do anything remotely like what Santreeza has done.

The three AIs—One, Two, and Orb—have helped her, of course, but at root and branch she's the one who's created a complete virtual Orb in the unused capabilities of the AI system of the ship. The maintenance AIs generally use only a small portion of their possible subroutines and memory units. The two Primes have so many layers of backup components that they can safely sacrifice those that lie the farthest from their activation points. Santreeza has patched together all of these distributed resources into a smooth, efficient platform to birth UnitFour, a functional exact copy of the entire orb that Dan can access.

"I have spawn," Orb says. "Strange but good. Yes no, Pilot?"

"Very good. Santreeza—all of you—this is top flight incredible stuff."

"Thanks. UnitFour can come online when you or one of the primes need it."

"Good. I take it they're not primes."

"They aren't. They're research units, but I think they have the capacity to develop into primes. PrimeOne, you can help it grow up."

"That is an excellent analogy, Santreeza. I will do so."

"Brennan, I did this because of Bolivar's message. That second location. UnitFour may have some data on why it's important. It might even recognize what's there if you get there."

"That's spectacular! Thanks!"

"Orb, you and I will go to Central tomorrow. There's a crew coming from the *Chaonia* who can work outside. They'll get you out of that cargo bay and into a decent protective carrier. Once we get to Central, you'll come with me to a safe location. We can work together some more there. To start, your language function could use some development. Is this fully acceptable?"

"Yes, yes, yes. No more aloneness. No more functions decay."

"PrimeOne?" Dan says. "Before Orb leaves, can you install some simulations for it?"

"I will do so, Pilot. Also for UnitFour. First, we will construct avatars. Then, gardens and cities and the standard package of adventure games. Also, Space Defenders."

"Hey, Santreeza, I'm surprised no one installed any simulations when they brought Orb online."

"So am I. I've been working for hours on this. What about we organic sapients get some dinner?"

"Sounds good to me. PrimeTwo, break meld now."

Dinner means nutrition bars in *Mary*'s galley. As long as the supply of blue ones holds out, Dan is perfectly happy. Santreeza, however, takes a bite of a green bar, makes a face, and lets it lie.

"Orb has a lot to tell us," she says. "His organic sapient language function needs a hell of a lot of work, though."

"I noticed, yeah."

"PrimeOne should be able to do a pretty good job of teaching UnitFour. I'll deal with Orb. Between us, we should be able to get the full story of what happened in that system."

"Good. Who put it there?"

"I don't know that yet. Some culture that uses a kind of writing we've never seen before. Eventually I'll be able to recover more data about them. I have figured out that Orb was put in orbit around the star as a research instrument to study that migrating gas giant. Whoever they were, they installed it to record data and prepared it to transmit at regular intervals. They picked up a couple transmits, but then they never came back. It kept doing its job with no contact with anyone. Going crazier and crazier with every useless transmit date."

"We're lucky it's not completely borked."

"Yes, we are. Because here's something really interesting. Orb's fully functional when it comes to computation and numerical operations in general. That was the first area I could reach. It converted the time scale from its orbital period around the star where we found it. And it's positive that it was abandoned 381 solstandard years ago."

"Right when the shunt closed."

"You got it. Do you think it's just a coincidence?"

"Hell no."

"Neither do I. Look, PrimeOne and I have got to be able to communicate. I've asked the captain to make sure it has access to shunt message packets. I'll do my best to relay information as I get it. From now on, we only communicate by Fleet ships. Much safer."

"Faster, too, but kind of suspicious. A bottom flight merchanter with the creds to send by Fleet?"

"True, usually. By law, the Fleet has to pay this ship for recovering Orb. It's worth an awful lot of creds. If anyone says anything, tell them that."

"Sai. I don't suppose anyone knows we have it, anyway."

"Get your head out of the shunt, Pilot. The *Chaonia* crew's going to be here at 1800 hours. It won't take long for the gossip to start."

If Evans believed in any of the current religions, she'd be thanking the God or Gods that the orb was stored in an outside cargo bay. To anyone who knows ships, as the *Chaonia* crew obviously does, the *Mary*'s augments and mods would be obvious the moment they stepped into the inside hold. As it is, the *Chaonia* shuttle berths next to the *Mary* without bothering with a sky tunnel. Three personnel in pressure suits emerge, joined to the shuttle with safety cables. When Mata opens the bay hatch, one of them squeezes in with a cargo net to secure the orb.

With the exception of Devit, who's assisting Santreeza in the ship's hold, the entire crew of the *Mary* has come up to the bridge to watch the proceedings on the main scope screen. Since Medic Lee has brought Marda with her, Evans silences the chatter on the intraship comm to spare tender ears a stream of profanity. The two outside crew members pull and the person inside pushes, but the orb stays where it is.

"What's the problem?" Evans says. "That side of the ship lies outside the gravity field, doesn't it? Wang?"

"Yes, ma'am, it does. Too high an energy cost to extend it that far."

"Don't they have a power hook on that shuttle?" Mata says.

"You'd think they would, certainly. Ah, there's Santreeza."

A fourth figure in a pressure suit drifts out of the cargo bay and links her safety cable to the *Mary*'s skin.

"She's got an earjack link to Orb," Brennan says. "I can hear them. Hah! She's telling it to release its personal gravity."

The netted orb and the crew member come tumbling out of the cargo bay entirely too fast. Fortunately the safety cables bring them up short and haul them back before they go into independent orbit.

"Guess it followed orders," Wang says.

The shuttle's cargo doors slide open. The crew stow the orb in the cargo bay and then stow themselves in the passenger cabin. Once Santreeza's retreated into the bay, Mata closes the *Mary*'s outer hatch. The shuttle backs away slowly from its temporary berth, turns, and heads back to its mother ship.

"Now where's that receipt they promised?" Evans says. "I have spent too much time filling out form after form and swearing things under penalty of perjury. I want the damn receipt! I—wait, here it comes." She blinks three times and holoprojects it, floating in a pale square directly in front of her eyes. "Looks good. Lots of signatures and witnesses." She passes the transmit to PrimeTwo for storage. "Well, that's that. I'm going to the Merchants Guild office next. They messaged me. We can bid on some new cargos."

"Probably ones no else would take, ma'am," Mata says.

"Oh, no doubt! Lieutenant Brennan, you have the bridge."

"It's a long ways back to the *Chaonia*," Devit says. "Want me to go with you?"

Santreeza's first impulse is to think, "No, not necessary." Her second impulse is to say aloud, "Sure. Thanks"

For the trip home, she's crammed all her civilian clothes into the duffel and dressed in shipboard uniform. He picks up the bag before she can claim it and slings it over one shoulder.

"Walk or bubble cable?"

"Walk. Who knows when, or if, I'll ever see Roon Dock again." *Or you. Damn! I* do *care. A little. That's all .... You're an idiot, Santreeza.* "Hey, remember the invitation. If you ever get to Central, we can both get leave and hide in my apartment."

"Oh, don't worry. I will."

Since she has time, and since Roon Dock is famous and stylish and all the rest of it, they walk slowly, speaking only now and then to point out some particular detail. Even when they reach the *Chaonia*'s checkpoint, they linger. Eventually Devit hands over her duffel. She clutches it to her like a child with a teddy toy.

"One last thing .... After all, I'm not in uniform." He puts his hands on either side of her face and kisses her. "Remember me. Sai?"

"Sai. Always."

Another kiss, and he turns, walks quickly away, and disappears into the usual wandering crowd.

Santreeza goes over to the checkpoint and the young ensign who's staring with wide eyes. "One wrong word," she says, "and I'm putting you on report."

"Yes, ma'am. Uh, welcome aboard."

On the way back, Devit walks fast, thinking of very little. Loss, regrets, missed chances—they've been so much a part of his life that he knows how to keep them on the edge of his mind.

At the first bubble cable station, he considers taking the ride back, but soon he'll be shut up on the *Mary* again. He keeps walking for the freedom of it. As he does, his genetic abilities start functioning, especially the one called sentinel intelligence. He begins to be aware of tiny warnings. Something is wrong, somewhere there's danger. A few words overheard from passersby, a viewscreen that announces exclusive coverage of some breaking story—details form the beginning of a pattern. Automatically, he slips his hand into his jacket pocket and finds the cool metallic oval of the pulse gun.

When he reaches the merchanter dock unit, he sees a crowd in front of the Merchants Guild. The warnings snap into focus. He can just pick out Captain Evans with her back against the office door, facing the crowd of vid reporters clustering around her. Light flashes from their recording PLs dance around her.

"Shit!" *She should never have left the ship alone.*

Devit strides over and taps the nearest reporter on the shoulder. "Security detail. Move over please and step back."

His practiced official voice acts like a lever prying the timid away. Even the news crews that refuse to leave move far enough away to allow Evans a decent amount of room.

When he reaches her, Evans gives him a weary smile. "It's the artifact, Chief. They've heard about it. It's an interesting story, I presume."

"Well, ma'am?" A youngish Lep reporter comes forward. "Sapes don't find ancient artifacts every day. And it's got to be valuable if the Fleet's taking it away."

"You have a point." Devit steps in between them. "You've also got your story. Clear the deck, or I'll bring up more officers."

As sapients always seem to do, they believe his assumption of an authority that he doesn't have. One or two at a time, they wander off, talking on their PLs.

"Come along, ma'am. I'll escort you back to your ship."

By the time they reach the *Mary*'s bridge, the story has hit the newsvids. Everyone on the bridge stops what they're doing and turns toward the screen to watch.

"Merchanter's Luck!" Tall letters flash on the main communication screen, a breathless reporter babbles what she knows, and Evans appears in front of the guild office, looking harried but determined as she answers the questions fired at her. "Yes, our pilot made a bad decision. Yes, it turned out for the best. No, we won't get the creds for at least two solstandard months, and that's after the assessment process finishes."

They babble out more questions. Evans sighs and answers them. "Why take more cargo? We have to make the payments on this ship, don't we? Creditors don't wait until payday. We can't afford to wait. Now that's quite enough! I have nothing more to say."

The vid switches to a discussion of water rights in some city dirtside.

"Ma'am." Dan gets up from the command chair. "Standing down. The bridge is yours."

"Very good, Brennan. And thank you, Devit. I can't tell you how glad I was to see you."

"After this, ma'am, if I can respectfully suggest you don't leave the ship alone?"

She grimaces. "You're right, of course. I have to get a transmit to the Bureau. I hope the *Chaonia* hasn't left orbit yet." She blinks her eyes in the rapid way that means she's using one of her functions. "Good, they're still berthed. I have time."

"Very good, ma'am." Devit turns away and looks over the crew on the bridge. "I wonder how the news sapes found out."

"Jeez, Chief!" Mata says. "The look on your face! Don't hang any of us just yet, sai?"

"Sorry, but—"

Evans turns to Devit. "Chief, enough! I'm sure there's some sort of explanation that does not involve any members of this crew. You're all dismissed for now. There's actual food in the galley. Chief Mata brought it in. I need to encode that transmit."

In a chorus of "yes, ma'am," the others start moving toward the elevator. Out of habit Devit waits till last, an unnecessary rear guard. He's about to crowd into the elevator when the newsvid blares again.

"Your laugh of this Designated Day, all you sapes out there, fresh from the Security Eyes on Merchanter Dock."

Devit steps back and gestures at the others to go on down without him. The vid shows the *Mary* and the outside cargo bay. The supposedly clever voice-over stresses the hard time that the crew had removing the cargo net until suddenly, *boom!* Out they tumble and the artifact with them.

"Good god!" Evans snaps. "How can they find that funny?"

"If those cables hadn't held, ma'am, those poor bastards would be riding a ghost shunt."

"Exactly my point." She grimaces. "Well, there's the leak, Devit."

"Yes, ma'am. I'm relieved."

"So am I. By the way, we have two cargo offers. Neither of them take us closer to where we need to go, but at this point, I think that's all to the best. We'll fade from view and the vids can find something new to chatter about."

The vids. Something new. Devit's enhanced intuition is picking up not a warning, precisely, but more of a prod, as if to say, "Look at this. The vids. Significant."

"The vids aren't always a bad thing, Captain. Everyone who's seen you on the news believes you're a merchant captain now. Must be real, they'll say. We saw it on the vids."

"You're right, aren't you? I hadn't thought of that."

"A suggestion. There's a merchanters' bar here. Before we leave orbit, we should go and buy everyone a round to celebrate our luck. That'll spread the story even further."

"Excellent idea! We'll do that. And maybe this time our pilot will behave himself."

Unlike the *Mary*, the *Chaonia* serves real food in proper places; two wardrooms and then a small mess hall for the Kar-Li personnel. The Kar-Li are carnivorous, and their taste for raw meat and their ideas about table manners tend to offend every other sapient species. While the ship waits for its orbital exit slot, the vidscreens in the officers' wardroom display planetside programming. Santreeza's eating soy chunks and quadrotriticale pilaf when the "Merchanter's Luck" story breaks on the Roon Local vidnews. With other officers around her, she cannot let loose with the profanities that would relieve her feelings. Like Devit, she's sure that someone on one crew or the other leaked the story. She's running over the short list of suspects in her mind when "Laugh of the Day" reveals the truth.

*Better than someone's big mouth. But how far will this damn story spread?*

Shunt messaging joins local vids into massive webs that share news and entertainments all through the Rim. There's a good chance that the sapients who destroyed the Fleet Scout will see the story sooner or later. If they find out that this artifact is actually an AI, they will come after its data. She takes her PL out of her shirt pocket and begins making notes and plans for a complete overhaul of the Bureau's security procedures.

"Lieutenant?'

Santreeza looks up to find the *Chaonia*'s lead pilot, Anna Fifita, standing by the table. "Sorry to break in, but we have to package the artifact for transit. That cargo net won't do for jump. We've got a proper crate, but we need your approval."

"Yes, of course. Thanks for fetching me. Let me just transmit something fast."

Since she's still in range, she sends PrimeOne a message telling it to double-check the *Mary*'s security. As an afterthought, she tells it to inform Brennan as well. Drug addict or not, he's the only sapient on that ship who can meld.

"I'm done." She puts the PL away and gets up. "Where did they put the artifact? Not in with the ordinary cargo, I hope."

"No. I stopped them from doing that. I found an empty munitions locker. It's the most secure place onboard. Come look."

The solid padded crate fits Orb perfectly. Santreeza signs off on it just as the ship's intraship comm begins bleating. "All personnel, orbital exit in six solstandard minutes. Current status: Go Ready. Pilot team to the bridge. All personnel, jump in 3.4 hours. Pilot team to the bridge."

On the Roon space docks, even the merchanters' bar has style, with its wood-look paneled walls, an imitation tile floor covering, and a good many round tables that are, Dan notices, bolted to the floor. Like all Vranz establishments, it welcomes one of the Old Earth species, dogs or shens, as Vranz speakers call them, that Humans brought with them during the Migrations. Here in the merchanters' bar, several big dogs, sayshuns and borracolls, lie beside their owners' feet. When Devit walks past a coll, it looks up and thumps its tale as if in welcome.

"One of your cousins, huh?" Dan says. "They always recognize you."

"Shut up, will you? Don't joke about that here."

Since the room's full though not overcrowded, Dan picks out a table close to a side wall for the four of them—the captain, Devit, Lod-Mata, and himself. As usual, Wang and Lee have decided to stay onboard with little Marda.

"Now remember, Dan," Devit says, "no more trouble. Leave other people's company alone."

Once the robomaid's taken their orders, Evans goes up to the bar with a wad of cred slips. Dan can't hear what she's saying, but it becomes perfectly clear when the grinning bartender gets on the room's public comm. "Hey, this lucky captain's buying a round for everyone!"

Cheers, grins, laughter, salutes with raised glasses follow Evans back to her table. Now and then she stops to accept thanks and congratulations on finding the artifact. Everyone seems to have seen the vid story. A couple of Human men pause on their way to the bar.

"Hey, ma'am, I was wondering," the dark-haired fellow says. "Any luck getting cargo?"

"Yeah, but so far it's all low pay or hazmat. There's plenty of that available."

"Right. We were hoping to avoid it, but we're not going to have much choice."

"We all take what we can get. It's those core-crap big companies skimming off the good deals."

Half the patrons thump their drinks on the table and yell, "Damn right!"

"The fucking Council should do something about them!" A woman at the next table says. "If they drive us out of business, who's going to take the hazmat and other shit jobs? The Fleet?"

At that, everyone within earshot laughs but it's not in good humor. Other patrons join the bitter chorus: "What's going to happen if this Consolidated bunch of assholes buys up every other line? What's going to be left for us?" "We get the scraps and shit anyway. If they take that, we lose our ships, we lose everything." "And whaddabout the shunt message packets? What the goddamn Fleet won't carry we get now, but if Consolidated grabs those, then what?"

"Have you heard the latest?" A Lep man turns from the bar to join in. "Consolidated's bought the Morrison Line. If they want that piece of crap, they want everything."

All around them the conversations, if one can call them that, spill over into a torrent of angry words, obscenities, sheer rage—but under it all Dan picks up fear. Most of the sapients in this room were raised on merchant ships. The commercial lanes are their version of the Fleet. They love and curse and cling to their way of living. Dan can remember how he felt when he was discharged from the Fleet, thrown out on the streets; worthless, angry, grieving, but above all, lost.

Devit and Evans get up and drift over to the bar. They linger there, talking casually with the various people who come up to get drinks or gossip or both. Now and then someone stops by Dan and Lod's table to say hello or congratulate them on their luck. One of them, a Human man wearing the black and gold uniform of Port Security, sits down to join them. His name, he tells them, is Okali.

"I just wanted to ask you," he says to Dan, "you're a pilot, right?"

"Sure am."

"These rumors about someone blowing up stargates. Is there anything in that?"

"There's nothing there to blow up. That's what makes a gate. A piece of nothing. You can kind of think of it as a crack in space-time. Kind of."

Okali has a sip of his drink while he considers.

"What we think of as empty space," Dan continues, "is still something. It exists in the middle of the 'something else' where the shunts are. Look, I know this is weird shit, but the universe is full of weird shit, and there we are. So space still exists, even though it looks empty, because there's a lot of the universe that isn't space, which kind of defines it as space and not-space." Dan pauses for a long swallow of beer. "So there isn't any space in a stargate. There's nothing at all. So a ship can slip through it to, well … to that somewhere that's real, all right, but different."

"Where do you hear these rumors?" Lod says to Okali. "From friends?"

"Yeah, or in bars like this one, or when I'm making my patrol, I pass some of you merchant crews talking about it. But you know how it is with this crap. Everyone knows someone who knows someone, or it's her brother-in-law or his friend in the Fleet, and there's no way of finding out if anyone really knows anything."

"That's the trouble with rumors and gossip," Lod says. "And then every time someone tells one, it gets bigger."

"And worse, yeah." Okali gets up from the table. "Hey, thanks. I figured a pilot would know."

Dan's just finishing his second beer when Evans and Devit come back to the table.

"If the Fleet thinks it can bottle up rumors about the shunts, it's too late," Evans says. "We all heard them. The merchants are already worried. It's the hints they've heard about that 'big things' that could happen. Blowing up stargates."

"I just talked to a guy about that, too," Dan says. "I tried to tell him that it can't happen. But I bet he didn't believe me. I mean, it's pretty strange stuff."

"Hey, Dan," Devit says, "it's really impossible then for these rumors to be true?"

"I'd say so, but I'm no expert. Pretty much all I know about the theory comes from the Fleet training I had. But I do know this: If there was anything solid in a stargate that you could blow up, ships would crash into it, and they don't."

"Sai, I get it. But huh, if the rumors can't be true, where the hell did they come from? Someone must have started them. Why?"

"Good point, Chief," Evans says. "But if enough people believe the rumors, the truth's not going to matter. And since the merchanters believe it, it's going to spread as fast as light speed."

"Faster than that, ma'am. Because it's spreading through the shunts."

# SEVEN

As soon as the *Chaonia* reaches orbit around Central, Santreeza gets a flood of messages concerning Orb. The Bureau wants it locked in a vault. Various Fleet research stations want to examine it. The local public university and the planetside campus of the Fleet Academy both place hopeful bids. Santreeza pulls every string and calls in every favor she's ever done to get what's best for Orb: Let her have authority and keep it close to her in her secure office suite. Once Captain Dal weighs in on her side, the matter's settled.

"The AI's been going crazy in isolation for what? Almost 400 years? If they took it away from you, it might end up borked beyond repair."

"My fear exactly, sir."

"I'll request night sentries. They can guard the thing while you're off duty. A couple of Marines should be enough."

Processing the usual security routines takes Santreeza several full days. When they finish running, she turns to a question that's been nagging at her ever since she first went onboard the *Mary*. Why in hell is Brennan so important to the *Mary*'s mission? Who insisted that the mission team pick him up off Nowhere Street and reinstate him?

Most starpilots use Haze but only occasionally, when they're at liberty or offduty in a safe situation. Pilots she's known have told her that using Haze amounts to a ritual, the mark of an elite cadre within the exclusive world of the Throwbacks. The older guild members introduce neophyte pilots to the drug as a sign that they've been admitted to that cadre. The civilians who use Haze are beneath contempt, as far as the starpilots are concerned.

Dan, however, is as hopelessly addicted to the drug as any civilian thrill seeker. To Santreeza, muddling your consciousness with drugs is disgusting. Unlike the vast majority of sapients in the Fleet, she rarely drinks more than a small amount of alcohol even on shore leave. Every chance Dan gets, he drugs himself semisenseless. She simply cannot understand why anyone would think his undoubted skills are worth the risk.

Searching for information using FleetOpsA and B would be both dangerous and unfair to them. If they're caught breaking regulations, they could be classified as core-damaged and then terminated. No one but she can access Orb to catch it out doing anything. It's the perfect partner for a hunt.

After some hours spent looking for answers, Santreeza's sorry she asked the questions. She's wandered into a circular maze of requests and authorizations, corrections and approvals: all on the regulation forms, each of them properly filled out, each double-checked by a sapient and initialed to prove it. In fact, each of them is initialed by a different sapient, whether civilian clerks or Fleet noncoms. No one seems to have seen anything twice. Nothing about Dan ever seems to lead back to the initial impulse, the undoubted decision by the Bureau to launch several small search missions to find information about that possible "big trouble" over the shunt system.

Santreeza sat in on three briefings covering those missions, though not the initial planning. She doesn't have the rank and clearances for that. When she thinks back, she realizes that she never heard the names of anyone at the command level. Several sapients very high up in the chain gave the briefings. They all seemed to assume that the details, such as Dan's recommission, had already been cleared at the command level by someone with the authority to do so. They must have received communiques from somebody about Dan X, as he was known then. But they never mentioned the sender's name.

And were those messages also one of a kind, checked and passed on with only an initial or two to indicate who was doing the approving?

Santreeza can reach only one conclusion. No organic sapients, whether in the Bureau or out of it, had ever insisted that Dan must be taken on as pilot. The system somehow simply assumed that they had and passed the false orders on. Data never "just appears" on its own. All of those little inserts and filled-in forms and the like have to be the work of an AI. Those tiny, brief security breaches the FleetOps found earlier? Logical entry points.

She takes the matter up with Orb. "Provisional conclusion: Some unknown AI wanted Dan starside and found a way to put him there. Yes no?"

"High probability yes, Santreeza. Additional possibility: The AI might be partnering with organic sapients who want Dan starside."

"Noted. Orb, would organic sapients choose a method that would put Dan in danger of being terminated? If termination was their goal, he could have been easily terminated while on the planet Ruby."

"That is a valid observation. I have no answer. There are too many peculiar things in this project that I cannot explain."

"Neither can I. For now, break meld. I need to get authorization for an action."

"Meld breaking now. I must play Space Defenders."

Santreeza finds Captain Dal in his office. "Sir? Can I have a moment?"

"Of course, Santreeza. I've been meaning to compliment you on the security upgrades. I've read your full report. Well done."

"Thank you, sir. Then you've seen how those entry attempts centered around the shunt missions. I need permission to contact the security chiefs on the ships involved."

"Granted. Doubtless a good idea. And I have news for you. The clearance for that deep archive search has finally come in."

"For the shunt closure records?"

"Yes."

"I'll get right on searching for those. And for anything I can find about a pilot called Orinoco Bolivar."

Sixteen crates of freeze-dried skargo slugs, a Leptic delicacy found only on Roon, fill the *Mary*'s main cargo hold. Two safety-pack cartons of blood samples for medical research go into the hazmat bay. The captain's plan is to deliver the samples first, then the slugs, an itinerary that requires five jumps and a layover between three and four to let Dan stabilize.

"Does that sound possible, pilot?" Evans says.

"Yes, ma'am. Give me a full day off. Maybe a day and a half, and I'll be able to function."

"Enough time for two doses of Haze?"

"Yes, ma'am." Dan cannot look directly at her. The shame eats at him, but the craving proves stronger yet again. "I'll need that."

Dan eases the shame by telling himself that using twice won't endanger the ship. Since each shunt lies along a well-traveled commercial route, PrimeOne can take over if something does go wrong.

"Sir?" Santreeza says. "We have a problem on the Special Ops system. More attempts to hack in. FleetOpsA notified me as soon I checked in."

Dal waves all his arms in the irritation gesture and mutters something in Hirrel that is most likely an obscenity. "I'll transfer your trainee to someone else, Santreeza. This has to have priority."

"Thank you, sir. I thought so, too."

Santreeza has just gone back to her desk when a top priority and top classification transmit reaches the system. One of the *Mary*'s sister ships, the *Packhorse* merchanter, has disappeared. It was last seen three solstandard days previous to the transmit, when it was taking on cargo at an obscure planetary system. The most likely explanation is failure to complete a jump. Just as any Fleet officer would, Santreeza feels briefly sick and cold. *Lost in a shunt. Horrible.*

Dal hurries into her office without bothering to knock. "Did you see?"

"Yes, sir. Have their next of kin been notified?"

"I don't see how we can. Considering the mission."

Santreeza wants to say, "Fuck the stinking mission." Instead, "I suppose not, sir. You might considering asking someone in the Bureau if they can bend the regs."

"I will, yes."

In a flurry of waving arms, Dal hurries out again.

Santreeza returns to the work at hand. Preliminary information about the loss of the *Packhorse* is flooding in. She compiles it into shunt message packets, one to the CO of the third ship on the mission, a Fleet frigate, and one to Devit and Evans. By 1700 hours, the packets, marked "Top Priority" and "Speed Essential," are on their way to the Fleet Message center on Main Base. The frigate should be easy to locate. The Merchants Guild keeps detailed records of their members' itineraries, including of course the *Mary*'s current route. Santreeza can hope the packet reaches them reasonably soon.

Wang and Lee are taking Marda for a walk on the spacedock. Captain Evans has retired to her cabin for a nap. As a noncom at the highest pay grade of chief warrant officer, Devit can take the bridge in the absence of all commissioned officers, but he dislikes doing so. He compromises by sitting in his own station chair, not the captain's command chair. He could have been an officer, he supposes. Certainly his birth family had hoped he would. They sent him to an expensive school that prepped young sapients for the Academy, but in the end, he chose to enlist instead.

At the gunnery station, Mata is playing some sort of game. It occasionally beeps, squawks, and plays a few seconds of irritating music.

"Hey Mata! What the hell is that?"

"I'm keeping my combat skills sharp, I'll have you know." Mata's crest, however, gives him away by swelling with laughter. "All right, it's Space Defenders. PrimeOne loaded it on the system for me. It says it helps clear the mind when you're faced with problems you can't solve."

"Does it?"

"Yeah, oddly enough." He glances at his station's viewscreen. "Varg! I just lost my battleship. Oh well, only a game." He mutters a few command words, and the screen turns dark.

"I've been thinking—"

"Always dangerous when you do that."

"Keep your snout shut for a minute, sai? About that artifact. Santreeza says it was abandoned by whoever installed it in the middle of nowhere. Just about when the shunt stargate disappeared. Also about the time something wiped the organics off of Merrval."

Mata swivels his chair around and leans on the back to listen.

"I'm assuming that the sapes who placed the orb started that resettlement attempt. The colony got wiped out along with all the other organics. But who were they? Three-hundred eight-two years is a long time, but not that long for history. Why didn't they have contact with any other species? They were on the shunt system. A disaster like that! There's got to be a record of it somewhere."

"So you'd think." Lod's crest flops to one side as he concentrates. "The Repositories are calling us, I'd say. Although you'd think the Vranz people would have checked."

"True."

"What shunts lead to the system where we found the orb? There's the one we took to reach it from Glah. Are there any others?"

"I don't know. Dan does, but he's so loaded with Haze that there's no use in asking. Sometimes he's a real asshole."

Mata makes a sympathetic noise.

"PrimeOne won't tell me," Devit goes on. "I don't have the right access code."

"AIs can be assholes in their own little way, yeah. Hey, on that newsvid thing, didn't they say the artifact had weird writing on it?"

"They did. Santreeza figured that out. Orb told her that it means 'research satellite 16.'"

"Fascinating. Not."

"Yeah. 'Fraid so. But anyway, I've been wondering. What if there was another shunt to Merrval or wherever that closed when the Pinch shunt closed?"

"Now there's an idea." Mata's crest is trembling with excitement. "Can you kick Dan awake or something?"

"No. We just have to wait until that shit gets out of his brain."

The quiet lasts approximately two solstandard hours. The captain has just returned to the bridge when urgent transmits from Central arrive. The news turns Devit cold with long-distance sympathy and horror.

"Oh no," Evans said. "Ghastly! How awful!"

"The news about the *Packhorse,* ma'am?" Devit says.

"Exactly that. And Santreeza says the Fleet's going to try to keep it quiet. Just to make things worse."

"It's going to be all over the vids when it gets posted. No reason to keep it secret. Jump fail. Shit. The poor bastards!"

"It's awful, yes. They'll have to let the Merchants Guild post it. Technically the crew were all civilians."

"Will you be sending the official response to this transmit?"

"Yes. However, if you want to respond to whatever she put in that postscript to you, you have my authorization."

"Thank you, ma'am. You noticed the extra words, did you?"

She smiles and dismisses him with a wave of her hand.

The postscript runs: "I think about you, Peter. Just now and then."

He answers, "I think about you, too, Jorja. Just now and then."

"Well, look," Dan says. "The shunt system is symmetrical. If you flipped one half over onto the other half, it would match. Last time I looked at the schematic, it still does. Hey guys, you're on to something here." He takes another bite of his blue nutrition bar. "When the Pinch shunt closed, something else would have to give."

Off duty, Devit, Dan, and Lod are sitting in the galley for what amounts to a meal. Devit and Dan have their sack of Total Human brand bars, and Lod has the Leptic Delights. Both sorts look and smell suspiciously the same. With 2.2 solstandard hours until their dock orbit exit slot, and another two beyond that to the stargate, Dan has just enough time to eat before jump.

"A whole planet's not going to disappear down a shunt, though," Devit says.

"Course not, but jeez, it amounts to the same thing," Dan says. "Who knows where the exit stargate was for the Pinch shunt? It's not where it used to be, that's for sure. The twin and the anchor system could be a thousand light-years away."

"Gone for all practical purposes," Lod says.

"Yeah. You've always got to keep that in mind about shunts. Systems look close together when they're connected. But they aren't anywhere near each other in space-time. Lose a stargate, you lose a system. And everyone in it."

"No wonder a lot of sapes just don't want to think about it," Devit says. "Who knows who could be next?"

"Yeah. When you come right down to it, the whole system could be really fragile." Dan holds up his nutrition bar. "If pieces start breaking off—"

When he cracks the bar in half, a scatter of crumbs fall onto the table. He sweeps them off onto the galley floor with the side of his hand. Lod's crest goes flat against his skull.

"I get the idea," Devit says. "What I don't get is why anyone would try to ignore it."

"What can we do about it?" Dan waves his nutrition bar. "Anything?"

"If it looks like it's going to happen, get people prepared for it. I suppose. A planetary system should be able to survive on its own. Old Earth's did. So did all the other home planets."

"But that'll cost a lot of money. The top people will lose a lot of creds," Lod says. "Can't do that."

"They'll lose more if everything goes to hell on a fast jump Scout." Devit takes another purple bar. "There's got to be some reason beyond half-ass stupidity."

"How about greed? Both of our species are very good at greed."

"True enough. Y'know, I'm beginning to get an idea."

Dan stands up and wipes his sticky, blue hands on his pants. "If anyone can figure it out, Pete, you can. I've got to get to the bridge. Jump in about four hours, remember."

Once Dan gets the ship out of the gravity well and on its way to the stargate, he goes down to his pod. It's early, but the questions Lod and Devit raised interest him. PrimeOne is active and waiting for him to meld. Dan lies down on the bench and waits while, one by one, his cyber links come online.

"Done, Pilot."

"Level One. I need to get on the Map."

The chime sounds.

Seemingly below him the vast web of lines and dots appears. When Dan gives PrimeOne the location of the lost Pinch shunt's stargate, the Map swings him around and swoops down to a spot near one long edge of the pattern.

"Can you find the geometric opposite of that site? The symmetrical opposite."

"Yes, Pilot. Here."

They turn, fly up, head diagonally, and end up at a point nowhere near a shunt or stargate. The black dot marking their virtual position lies between—but not near—two lines that do mark shunts.

"Woah! I bet there was something linking those once."

"I do not understand that command."

"It's an exclamation, not a command. Y'know, I wonder about something. On the transmit, the one maybe sent by Orinoco Bolivar, he noted two locations. We found Orb at the first. Where is the second one?"

"We are there virtually, Pilot. That is, the location would be at the place upon the Map we are looking at. There is a planetary system in this general location. Otherwise, there is nothing."

"Noted. I bet I know what used to be there. The stargate to a second lost shunt."

PrimeOne responds with a quick cascade of chimes.

"An exclamation not a command?"

"Yes, Pilot. I would not have predicted this piece of data."

Dan hears a series of clicks. He can feel the presence of some other mind waiting just beyond the meld.

"UnitFour wants to join us, Pilot."

"Sai. Proceed with entry."

"I thank Pilot. I see Map. What is wrong, think I? Where is stargate to home?"

"We don't know, UnitFour. It's a puzzle."

"They have all gone somewhere then? My Humans."

"Their shunt closed. They can't leave their system now."

"They talk about leaving. No one find us, they say."

"Well, they're safe enough. No one's going to be able to find them."

"You are sure, Pilot?"

"Very. PrimeOne, calculate the following. Find the nearest stargate to this location on the Map. If this ship was using full thruster power, how many days would it take a ship to reach the place where the gate from the nearest stargate used to be?"

"The numerical answer is extremely long. A simpler correlate would be that they are 117 light-years apart."

"So we couldn't get there in a couple of solstandard weeks."

"Certainly not, Pilot. The actual total—" The AI hesitates. "Is your last output one of the things that organic sapients call a joke?"

"Yes. Don't bother calculating it out."

PrimeOne makes a grinding noise.

"I see now," UnitFour says. "Zyon too far. No one go through there now. No one go there with no shunt."

"Right. Do you know why they didn't want anyone to find them?"

"It was God who told them. God say you never terminate if you follow all my rules. Such a lot of rules! Hard to follow. Other sapients mock them. Make the rules harder to follow. So they go away."

PrimeOne hums and clicks. "That belief is extremely illogical."

"I agree. All us inorganics try to tell them. They not listen. Then Butchers come. Awful time. Fleet kills Butchers. Good. But everyone want to hide."

"PrimeOne? Next question, and this is not a joke. The transmit that gave us this second location was a sweep transmit through starspace. Is there any way to find out if anyone else picked it up? Besides that research station, I mean."

"It could have been intercepted at any point on its transmission circuit. It could have been intercepted before or after or at the same time as the station received it. The probability of reconstructing the data you request is very low. It would require knowing what possible receptors existed at all points in that field at all times."

"Low as in impossible, you mean."

"As close to zero as I can predict without reaching zero. There is always what you organic sapients call blind luck."

"The effort is not going to be worth the computation time. Oh hey, wait—I just had an idea."

"An unusual occurrence."

"I'm ignoring that remark. You say that it could have been intercepted at any time after the original transmission? Yes no?"

"Yes."

"After the stargate disappeared, the Fleet sent an investigatory team to the site. Could they have intercepted the transmission?"

"It is very possible."

"Then their record of it should exist in the reports filed in the Repository."

"That is very likely."

"Does the Repository keep records of who's requested what data?"

"Checking now. Yes, it does."

"Then there's something there that someone doesn't want anyone else to see."

"If we could replace those ambiguities with data, your statement would be allowable under the rules of syntax with which I operate. As it is, it's too hypothetical for me to assign a probability."

"That's all right. You don't need to. Collate this sequence of our actions and responses. Make sure it includes the information UnitFour gave us. Send it to PrimeTwo with a request to send it on to Chief Devit and Captain Evans."

"Noted and done. It is now only 0.2 hours to jump."

"Have PrimeTwo tell Chief Devit to ready the crew. UnitFour, sign off the meld now and prepare for jump. We will talk about your Humans again very soon."

When the ship returns to space-time, Devit unbuckles himself from his station chair and goes down to his cabin to read the newest transcript from PrimeOne in the quiet. Dan's information about the second lost stargate shocks him as much as it did Dan. Maybe it has nothing to do with that mysterious "big trouble" they're investigating. Maybe it's part of the puzzle, something that might have inspired the rumors, if anyone had ever known about it, anyway. Either way, he's not about to ignore it.

Why has no one noticed this before? Why aren't there records of these sapients from the time before the shunt closed? Thanks to UnitFour's remarks, he can come up with one reason that makes sense. *They always talk about leaving.* Whoever lived at the other end of that shunt may have deliberately hidden themselves, maybe on their God's orders, maybe for some rational reason. As Dan said, no matter where they are and why they left, they no longer have to worry about being found.

Other more immediate questions trouble him. Evans has sent him a detailed report from the Merchants Guild on the current cargo situation. For several years, a private investments and acquisitions company has been acquiring the smaller commercial shipping firms, buying when they can, running hostile takeovers when the small company refuses to sell. Recently they've started going after bigger prey, targeting major companies like Speed Shunt. Their profits have increased so dramatically that they're attracting big investors and bigger banks.

Speed Shunt. The name reminds him that a Speed Shunt employee was buying information from the mole in Special Ops about the shunt missions. What was a cargo company going to do with that data? It would have nothing to do with normal shipping. He's been assuming that the employee was selling it elsewhere. Maybe he was sending it back to his superiors. What then?

Under its new name, Consolidated Lanes, the original company has spent heavily on ships and other equipment. They've opened offices in as many cities on as many planets as they can afford and a few more after that. Although the company's gross value is several billion credits, they are now undercapitalized. Devit knows very little about investing, the interplanetary stock system, and the like, but he can see the important thing. Panic about the shunt system is going to make investors want to pull their creds out of Consolidated as fast as they poured them in. What's going to happen if Consolidated can't return their money to them?

The company managers have several billion reasons to divert attention from any discussion about the failure of the shunt system. But would they have killed sapients to stop the investigation? Twelve Fleet personnel and two research staff members died in the sabotage on the way to Morrison's Star. If the same hostiles have something to do with the loss of the merchanter *Packhorse*, eight more sapients have joined them. Something about those deaths warns Devit that the situation is not anywhere as simple as the fear of a massive bankruptcy makes it seem.

Something so valuable you'd kill for it could easily be the source of the "big trouble." He has no idea what it might be, but he's sure of one thing: Find that something and the rest of the answers will fall into place. At the moment, he at least has a candidate. Whoever bombed the Fleet Scout prevented the ship from reaching the Repositories. If Dan's speculations turn out to be true, the original reports from the investigation, stored in the Repositories, might contain crucial data.

"Hey, Pete? You in here?"

Dan walks in without waiting for an answer.

"Good," Devit says. " I want to talk with you. Have you heard the news about the *Packhorse*?"

"Yeah, I have. Poor bastards! It makes me sick to think about it."

"You said something once about rescue work for lost ships. Is there someone in the Fleet or Pilots Guild who can search for them?"

"Not that I know, but hey, I've been out of touch for two years. It's a hell of a job. The rescue ship has to already be close to the shunt or they won't have a chance. They've got to go through the shunt, back and forth a couple times, maybe, to see if they can see the ship's streak. You don't see a ship, just its streak. Then you've got to hope they see you and follow you out."

"There's no way to signal them?"

"Maybe. I don't know. When I was training, we did a VR module on rescue. Basic stuff only. I think they mostly wanted to scare us shitless about getting lost. It worked. I was the only trainee who ever managed to pull a ship out. Luck, if you ask me, but jeez, they wanted me to go on training. Thank God I had the right to say no. Rescue ships can get lost, too, y'know."

"I believe it. Sai, thanks. I was hoping maybe someone could find the *Packhorse* crew. I guess not."

"You'd keep the whole galaxy safe if you could, Pete, wouldn't you?"

"Sure. Job's a little too big for me, though. It's too bad the pilots on that ship can't see the things you do. Maybe they would have found the gate."

For a few baffling seconds Dan freezes, his whole body rigid, his face caught in an emotion Devit can only label "shame." Before Devit can speak, he turns away and heads for the door. "Hey, I've got to go back to the bridge. We're closing in on spacedock."

He hurries out and slides the door shut with a bang.

Devit decides that questioning Dan will only make him lie and gets back to work. He writes up a brief report that includes Dan's findings about the second shunt. On an impulse he includes the information that Dan once showed a lot of potential for rescue work. It might be one of those "special abilities" that got him chosen for this mission. He also adds a copy of the guild's transmit about the cargo situation, then bundles everything up in a shunt packet to send to Santreeza. If anyone can pry into Consolidated's affairs without them knowing, she can, as he explains to Captain Evans when they get a private moment.

"Yes, I see what you're driving at, Chief. I've got a contact at the Fleet base here. I'll mark all this Top Priority. She'll get the two packets underway to Central ASAP."

Devit's message brings Santreeza a practical kind of crisis of conscience. As one of the Hounds, she has the authority to start an investigation on her own, but even a Hound must eventually follow the correct procedures. Santreeza has been operating without any oversight or permission from her superior officers. By working through Orb, she deliberately kept some of her investigations secret to protect Devit's involvement. Even more dubious was her attempt to find out why Dan Brennan had been reinstated. Personnel have been court-martialed for less. On the other hand, Captain Evans has sent all the classified information in the current report straight through to the Bureau, which means Santreeza's no longer accountable for it.

Santreeza finds Captain Dal in his office. When she tells him that she wants to continue investigating Consolidated Lanes, he occasionally makes a note on his PL or curls an arm in agreement.

"So, sir," Santreeza finishes up, "I think this matter is worth pursuing. I don't know what our superiors will think of it."

"Look, most of what you want to know about Consolidated Lanes is public information, because they trade on the public stock markets. No one's going to reprimand you for looking for it when you're off duty." He twines two of his grasping arms together, a gesture signaling a need for caution. "Now, as for data that they keep under wraps, I'll give you the authority to see what you can turn up by other means." He lets the arms unwind. "The Marines guarding Orb are used to you working long hours. No one's going to be surprised if someone finds you in the office, fending off those suspicious access attempts."

"Thank you, sir."

"If you find clear and damning evidence, tell me, and I'll see what I can do about getting the proper subpoenas. And another question for you: Ferst's contact—the sape he was selling data to. Have you found any further information about him? Where was he selling it in turn? To the company he worked for?"

"Yes, sir. He was handing it over to Speed Shunt in return for a bonus. There's some additional indications—I can't call it solid evidence—that he also sold it to Consolidated Lanes, because Consolidated took over Speed Shunt a few days after he died."

"Makes sense. If you find the evidence, send it to me in an official report."

With the inner crisis over, Santreeza gets to work. First, she and Orb need to sort through the data in those reports. Second, they will need to gain access to Consolidated's inner workings. From there, they can look for—*What?* she asks herself. She has nothing to go on but Devit's Throwback intuitions. She can at least take a thorough look around. If there's nothing suspicious about Consolidated, they can leave it out of the investigation.

"First step. Orb, we need to break the Consolidated passwords."

"Noted. Activating the appropriate subroutines now."

# EIGHT

Another successful jump brings the *Mary* through to Zoss-Ty, a heavily industrialized world under Leptic control. Besides an elaborate system of spacedocks cable-linked to the surface, an enormous array of solar panels surrounds the world at its equator and polar regions. A system of batteries and transformers collects and transfers the energy they produce down to power relay stations on the six continents below. All of this machinery as well as the docks themselves make navigating into a safe orbit a complex process.

By the time they get assigned a berth from Dock Command, Devit can see that Dan is exhausted. In the stark lighting of the bridge, the dark smudges under his eyes and around his mouth make his Pale skin look almost bloodless by contrast. He's been sweating, too, the peculiar sticky sweat that excessive shunt travel squeezes out of pilots.

Captain Evans has noticed as well. "Lieutenant? Should I ask for a tow-in to berth?"

"Not necessary, ma'am. PrimeOne and I can navigate."

She hesitates, studying his face, glancing at his shaking hands.

"Really, ma'am. It's safe."

"Very well, Brennan. If PrimeOne's linked in with you."

Dan smiles and points at the earjack he's wearing.

Devit has great respect for Evans's judgment, but he has to admit to himself he's more than a little nervous. *He should be wearing the visor, damn him! Can he even see where he's going?*

Yet when they begin entry into the maze, Dan seems perfectly steady. They make their way through to the assigned dock with no trouble. Through the earjack Dan's in constant contact with the dockmaster—Devit can hear Dan's whispered questions and replies—as they scan for their berth, find it, and drift toward the waiting metal arms of the anchorage. The usual bump and tremors signal they're safely in. Wang takes over to finish the link-up with the dock.

Dan turns away from his station. "Permission to leave the bridge, ma'am?"

"Granted. Chief Devit, perhaps you'd better go with him."

Dan walks steadily enough into the elevator. Once the doors close, he leans back against the metal wall and starts to slide down.

Devit grabs him and keeps him standing. "Buddy, what's so wrong?"

"One jump too many, that's all. And I need Haze."

Devit's carrying the vial with him. As soon as they reach the cabin, he gives it to Dan, who gulps down the contents without waiting for water. He drops the empty on the floor, then sits down on the edge of the bed and starts to pull off his boots. It takes him several minutes.

Devit fights off the temptation to do it for him. He does pick up the empty vial. "I'll be on the bridge."

Dan looks up and smiles, starts to speak but breaks it off. The Haze is taking the words away. Devit waits to leave until Dan manages to get himself lying safely down on the bed. There have been times when he's had to pick Dan up off the floor.

Reaching the bridge feels like reaching a refuge.

"Another job for you, Devit," Evans says. "Dan's supply of Haze tablets is running low. Medic Lee's contacted the Fleet base hospital. She has the coded transmit that gives us the permission to possess Haze. She's sending the authorization to your PL."

"I'm surprised the medics here have any, ma'am."

"It's all been confiscated from users, Lee tells me, or from their off-base suppliers. Most Fleet pharmacies store it. If they don't, the local Police Guards take it, and God only knows what they do with it. Sell it again, I suppose. I hadn't realized how common the wretched stuff is and how easy it is to get."

"I hadn't either, ma'am."

"I know you have your doubts about allowing Brennan to use. They're justified. The Bureau apparently saw no way around it."

"A question, ma'am. What's going to happen when this mission's over? Will anyone allow him to continue using this way? Or will the Fleet throw him out again after it's sucked him dry?"

Evans stares at him for a troubling space of silence.

Devit considers apologizing but decides against it. "They've done it before, ma'am."

"True. I don't intend to let it happen again. If nothing else, if there's no place for him the way he is, Lee and I will ensure that he gets into a rehabilitation program. You have my word on that."

"Thank you. Your word is all I need."

The silence spreads out again, a presence as strong and tangible as the scent of some alien perfume. Devit is searching desperately for some way to clear it, to find the words that will return everything to its proper order of rank and deference, when Mata gets up from his station chair and frees them all.

"Ma'am? Permission to accompany Devit? He's going planetside, and his Pan-Leptic's lousy."

Evans sighs in audible relief. "Permission granted. You both had better be in uniform, or they won't let you on the base. But be very careful. The Fleet's not universally popular."

Zosstown, to give it its unofficial but pronounceable name, is a compact, almost circular city of shadows and dead ends. Tunnels, covered bridges, and roofed streets connect its low buildings into a maze of private refuges. Here and there an area lies open to the sun; mostly Human or Kar-Li citizens live in those neighborhoods. Robocabs and private cars travel on the ground, not in the air.

The dock-to-dirt cable pod brings Devit and Mata to a half-empty terminal dimly lit by yellow lights and scented with fried food. Sapients, mostly Leps, hurry through on their errands or linger at one of the food stands. As they make their way to the robocab stand, Devit keeps his hand on the pulse gun in his trousers pocket. When he realizes it, he makes himself take his hand off the gun and out of the pocket. When he doesn't stay on guard against the memories of his daughter's death, his mind always insists on putting him on full alert when he's surrounded by Leps. On this particular Designated Afternoon, he has some reason for what is normally unnecessary anxiety.

When he changed out of his civilian clothes into his Fleet blues, Devit felt as if some missing part of himself had been restored. Now he sees the uniform as a possible danger. A pair of younger Leptic men pause to look at them with expressions hovering on the edge of a sneer and crests that tremble as if in disgust. They seem to be directing their malice mostly at Mata or more precisely, at his uniform. Some of the nearby sapients pause to watch and sneer for a moment, then move on.

"Traitor!" No one says the word aloud. They don't need to. Plenty of ill feeling comes Devit's way as well.

"You see why I wanted to come with you," Mata says. "It isn't the language. Pretty much everyone knows at least some Tech Speak."

"Yeah? Well, I wondered about that."

Two other young Lep men have joined the original pair. They yell something at Mata in their own language and take a step closer. Devit slips his hand into his pocket and palms the pulse gun. Mata answers calmly, slowly, but the four merely wave their crests in a flutter of laughter—mocking, Devit assumes. When Mata speaks again, his tone of voice has hardened to a snap of command. Again the crests wave. Devit's hand tightens on the gun.

"No!" Mata lays a quick hand on his arm. "Listen! It's going to be sai."

Devit suddenly realizes that the crowd around them is stepping back, parting, hurrying to get free of the developing incident. The shrill sound of a whistle cuts through the noise in a rising and falling of notes that's growing louder and louder. Devit looks in its direction and sees four armed Leps in yellow uniforms escorting a Leptic woman riding in a small motorized cart.

An older woman, her crest turned gold with age, she sits fiercely upright, both hands resting on a cane. As they come closer, light catches the cane and sparkles on diamonds.

"One of the Grandmothers!" Mata whispers. "And Port Security."

They step back to get out of her way, but when she and her escorts reach them, she speaks several firm words. The procession halts. Mata hurries forward, spreads his arms to either side, and bows his head. For a few minutes they talk. The Grandmother raises her cane and gestures to Devit to come forward. As he walks over, he reflexively salutes her. Her crest waves in amusement, then flattens.

"I am told you are Peter Devit," she says. "A member of my staff saw your name on the passenger list for the pod shuttle. I came here to meet you."

*Watch it! Stick to Fleet etiquette.*

"I'm honored, ma'am."

"I remember you from that horrible time in court. I assume you know what I mean. That ghastly crime."

The memories begin rising.

"Yes, ma'am, I do."

"I cannot tell you how horrified I was, how sorry for your evident grief. It was one of my clutch sisters who'd organized the hunt and capture of those …." She hesitates. "Let us just say she gave the orders to sweep up the filth from her streets in her district. Our people did as she asked. I came to court to support her in her outrage and grief. Do you remember her?"

"Yes, ma'am. Her apologies—and then she asked the court to allow her people to execute the prisoners."

"Yes. In the same way as they had committed murder. An ancient custom, but one of your laws forbade it. Lethal injection, fast, painless, not what they deserved."

Devit nods agreement. The memories have stolen his voice. The Grandmother turns to Mata and says a few words in Leptic that make his crest swell and his eyes widen in pride.

"I shall leave you now," she says to Devit. "There should be no further trouble. The news will spread that I have spoken to you. That will be sufficient to keep the peace."

She raises her cane, her guards gather round, the cart turns, and to the sound of the whistle she glides back to the farther door. Devit realizes that at some point when she was talking, he'd let go of the pulse gun. When he pushes the memories away, they fade fast.

The crowd around them has thinned to a few scattered sapients. Mata lets out his breath in a loud Leptic sigh.

"Thank Onar! Look, from now on, if one of these punks looks like he's going to start some trouble, leave him to me. I know what to say."

"Sai. I get the feeling there's not going to be any trouble now."

"Most likely there won't, yeah. There's the cab stand. Let's get out of here."

The Fleet base lies about a kilometer and a half outside the city. At the gates the official transmits get them past the sentries into the usual pattern of rectangular buildings and straight streets. Every Fleet Base is laid out the same. The hospital itself has exactly the same floor plans as every other Fleet hospital, with the dispensary off to the right of the entrance on the ground level. The medical tech behind the counter of the dispensary is every bit as suspicious as every other Fleet med tech is of personnel who want drugs.

She reads the authorizing transmit, looks them over, and says, "I'll need more ID."

Devit and Mata produce it. She looks at it, hands it back, snorts, and turns away without a word to go through a door into a storage area. Mata and Devit sit down in the row of Fleet-blue chairs by the window to wait. Devit's aware of his heightened functions issuing alerts rather than outright warnings—rational, calm alerts, not his usual simmering rage. He realizes that he knows damn well that the Grandmother's apology was sincere. Why else would she have traveled some distance just to meet him? *Her sister meant every word, too. I even knew it then.*

"Tell me something," Devit says. "Those two hostile sapes in the terminal. What do they have against the Fleet?"

"Imaginary grievances, mostly. Foreigners on Leptic soil! They're forgetting the last war. How would they have liked Hoppers bouncing around town instead?"

"It could have happened. The H'Allevae have a planet—what? Only two shunts away."

"Yes. Only an outpost, of course. A trading venture. No military buildup under treaty terms. Yeah, sure, of course. Varg!"

The med tech returns to the counter with a large soyskin bag that's lumpy with bottle shapes.

"One of you's gotta sign for this. In a couple of places."

As a senior chief warrant officer, Devit does the honors. As a plain CPO, Mata carries the bag. By the time they get back to the terminal, the punks are gone.

Santreeza has finished searching the enormous Fleet deep layer archives. After she received the necessary security codes, she enlisted Orb's help as well as what time FleetOps A and B, who do have their normal work to do, could spare her. The Fleet archive staff helped her in every way they could. Various memory systems, some so archaic as to be practically unusable, contain over a thousand years' worth of every possible type of report, from daily ops to combat records. No one, including Santreeza, can believe what her search discovered. They are continuing to comb the records for misfiles, even though the organic sapients are beginning to give up hope.

All records concerning the closing of the Pinch shunt have vanished, as cleanly and completely as those from the Pilots Guild.

What remains are tiny traces of code, a few characters here and there, to indicate a series of illegal entries into the area where the records should exist. If Santreeza can trust her cyberjock intuition, the first one of the series occurred just over a solstandard year ago. The Pilots Guild has confirmed that their illegal entry happened at about the same time. Just as with the data on Dan Brennan, all the forms are checked and initialed and turned into dead ends.

No more can she find who sent her the deep archive access codes. Why release them? To taunt her and the system AIs, maybe? Or in a futile attempt to hide the action by returning everything to normal? She intends to find out.

Rear Admiral Harra Stine calls Santreeza into her office to discuss the situation face to face, evidence of the importance of these breaches.

Stine, one of the top officers in the Bureau, reminds Santreeza of Captain Evans with her gray eyes and unreadable facial expressions.

"You've done a good job, Lieutenant. I can see from the summary reports that you've done everything possible. Do you think there's any reasonable chance of finding the material we're looking for?"

"No, ma'am, I don't. FleetOpsA puts the chance at half a point. That's miracle territory."

"So I thought. The command level of Special Ops is pushing to send Fleet ships to the Repositories. Quite frankly, I think that's for the best. We should be able to misdirect the vid people somehow so they don't raise hell."

"If I may make a suggestion? You might want to consult with Captain Evans and CWO Devit. They had some sort of contingency plan for reaching the research hospital at the Repositories."

"Excellent! I'll do that. And I agree with Captain Dal. It's ridiculous to waste your time on these early-stage trainees. With your qualifications? If you were going to teach at all, it should be advanced math at a university level. The way things are going, I want you to be free to do security work full time."

"It appears to be necessary, ma'am."

Stine looks at the far wall and says nothing for a few minutes. Santreeza assumes that like Evans, she doesn't need a PL to read and transmit.

"I've started the process here at Special Ops," Stine says eventually. "One small problem. If Evans keeps getting coded messages through the Fleet, it's going to look suspicious. Well, if anyone's watching them, and we can't be too sure that no one is."

"Right, ma'am. A suggestion. Chief Devit and I could send messages back and forth for personal reasons."

Stine raises a sly eyebrow. "I see. Yes, the Fleet's always indulged its personnel about that. Keeping in touch with sapients who matter."

Santreeza has already left Stine's office before she realizes, with a touch of irritation, that she's admitted to herself that Peter Devit does matter. *You idiot! You'll probably never see him again!*

Evans receives Stine's transmit as soon as a Fleet ship arrives at Zoss-Ty. Stine orders the *Mary* to remain in orbit until they work out some sort of operational plan. Zosstown's a transfer station port, where shunt message packets can go back and forth with ease. Evans has Wang send a message to the merchant dockmaster that the ship's hazmat bays are being upgraded, which will require additional dock time. Wang also orders enough raw material to make the delay convincing.

"While we're here, ma'am, we might as well do the upgrade. Mata and I can handle the job. He doesn't need to sit around and play Space Defenders all day."

Mata looks Wang's way and opens his mouth just enough to show a fang. Wang doesn't notice. Evans decides to ignore it.

"Mata, you and Wang can start by evaluating the condition of the bays we have now. Devit, we need to discuss another matter." She pauses, looking around. "Where's Brennan, by the way?"

"Drugged on schedule, ma'am."

"Just as well. It'll keep him safely here. I'll need an escort to the guild office."

Once Wang and Mata have left the bridge, Evans sends Stine's transmit through to Devit's PL. She watches him read it with his usual grim expression until he suddenly smiles at the screen with more pleasure than just admiration for a good idea.

"You've reached the bit about the message exchange."

"Yes, ma'am. Fine with me, of course."

"Good. Now what's this plan the admiral refers to? Delivering hazmat cargos to the Repository hospital?"

"Yes ma'am. I've done some research. The Morrison Line wouldn't take them, and Consolidated won't, either. I've figured out some ways to make the trip safer."

"Good. But we can't count on being able to get that kind of cargo to that destination."

"If the admiral agrees, ma'am, we can. I've got some ideas about that."

Since the ruse has given him permission to add notes to the transmits, Devit sends Santreeza two items. The first comes from letting his sentinel intelligence work on the data he's gathered. "Look into the old Speed Shunt records, before CL bought them. There's a chance that the rumors come from something they were doing or looking for." The second is strictly personal. "When this mission's over, if it ever is, let's see if we can get an R and R leave together."

Her answers arrive in the next transmit return. "I'm following up on your tip about Speed Shunt. We have a lot of their data already from the search for the mole. R and R with you sounds great."

It's a four-shunt journey from Zoss-Ty to the Repositories. Once Admiral Stine and Devit work out some details and the hazmat bays are upgraded, Devit escorts the captain to the Merchants Guild in search of cargo. Fortunately, the Fleet base at ZeeTee just happens to have a small shipment for RE92-3rd, too small for a Fleet ship to bother with, apparently, since it goes straight to the *Mary* along with two shunt message packets … also too few for the Fleet to carry, or so they say. When the *Mary* reaches spacedock at Nine-Two, it's three shunts away from Morrison's Star.

After the enormous orbital complexes at Roon and Zoss-Ty, the geosync docks at Nine-Two look scrappy and primitive, but in their meteor-flecked shells they house a Merchants Guild office as well as a small Fleet post. If the crew want shore leave for anything fancy, however, they'll have to take the shuttle down to dirtside. Devit agrees when the captain decides the fuel's not worth the trip.

"There's a lounge area," Evans says. "I'm not sure what that means, but it's here on this module."

"Chief Mata and I can take a look at it, ma'am. Let's hope we're not here long."

The lounge area turns out to be a scatter of chairs and a pair of unsanitary-looking sofas arranged around a robobar. At the single table by the module wall, two Kar-Li enlisted Fleet personnel are playing some sort of card game. Their folded ear flaps and narrowed eyes make it clear they don't want to be disturbed. To justify their presence, Devit and Mata buy small bottles of a brown local liquor and find chairs with a good view of the vidscreen.

The town directly beneath the spacedock provides the local news. Sewage problems dominate the current segment.

"Vid!" Devit says. "Sector news."

The screen changes to a schematic of the six planets well connected by jumpshunts. A Human voice-over is repeating, "Full update in twelve solstandard minutes. The news on the possible outbreak is still sketchy. No emergency procedures necessary at this time."

In twelve minutes, a Kar-Li reporter appears on the set. His ear flaps are fully extended rather than folded over. He does his best to sound reassuring. A possible new disease, maybe an epidemic, spreading through the sector? Rumors, only rumors. "We're investigating, and we'll keep you up to date."

Devit smiles, and Mata's crest swells. The plan's proceeding.

"We might as well go back," Mata says. "There's no one here to gossip with, and that sofa behind us? I don't like the way it smells."

"I don't either, and the captain needs an escort."

This Merchants Guild office turns out to be a cramped little space at the far end of the dock segment. A poster screen hanging on the door warns sapients not to spit some kind of chewing leaves called "bleet" onto the floor. An AI unit sits in a protective cube on a scuffed wooden counter. When Evans transfers the credits for the dockage fees, a Human woman comes out of a side room.

"Looking for cargo, captain?"

"Always. Do you have any?"

"We do. Lucky you got here. The damn Fleet won't take it, and here it's for their own damn personnel. Snotty bastards."

"Really? You don't get a lot of merchant ships through here? I'm surprised."

"Not a lot, but some. Once it gets up here, this cargo's got to go out fast. Don't want it rotting in the crates. It's dried sardonix fruit. Oh, and there's a shunt message packet, too. That'll cover your refuel."

"Good. We'll take both. When will they be ready to go?"

"About eight solstandard hours." She glances at the onscreen readout. "Huh. Destination is Sweat City."

"Um, where?"

"Sorry. That's what they call that planet. I've got a husband stationed there. Serves him right, the bastard."

"Husband troubles, huh?"

"With both of them. No damn good. Ah well, so it goes."

By the time the new cargo arrives, the Haze has worked its way out of Dan's system. For a few minutes he stays in bed while he tries to remember the last time he had a shower. Since he'd have to use the sonocleaner, he decides against taking one now. His PL beeps at him. Message from the captain. "We can exit orbit once the cargo's stowed."

Up on the bridge, Evans is watching the newsvids on the comm screen.

"Ma'am, I'll set up the exit route now."

"Very good." She studies him for a long moment. "Brennan—Dan—be honest with me. Can you make this jump safely, or do you need more time?"

Temptation steals his voice. He could have a second tab of Haze if he tells her he needs more rest. It would be a lie. Lying belongs on Nowhere Street. He swallows hard and grabs his voice back. "I can do it, ma'am."

"Will you be able to make another jump soon after? We can't lay over long at our next destination."

Dan puts a few minute of serious thought into his answer. "I can, ma'am, because of PrimeOne. It's unusually proactive for an AI. If I run into trouble, it'll take over on its own initiative."

"Very good. We need to keep to schedule in this sector for a good reason, but it's not so urgent that we need to take big risks."

"This won't be any more of a risk than it usually is."

Evans considers him, saying nothing, revealing nothing by her expression, for so long that he begins to feel like a young ensign again, about to be put on report for breaking some rule he didn't know existed.

Finally she speaks. "I don't know how actual merchanter pilots manage this kind of strain. I suppose they spend far more time between jumps than we can."

"As far as I know, they do. Back when I was regular Fleet, we always carried two pilots."

"And three during wartime, when the captains could get them." She pauses, suddenly distant, as if at a grim memory. "Very well. If you're sure you're capable, we'll get underway. I'll get you at least two solstandard days off once we reach Harad. That's our last destination before the Repositories."

The elevator doors slide open. Devit, Wang, and Mata have returned from the cargo hold.

"Crates stowed, ma'am," Wang says.

"Good. Lieutenant Brennan, take us out of here."

The message packet and the crates of fruit arrive safely at the remote Fleet base on 94-2nd—or Sweat City as it's known—just two shunts away from Morrison's Star. Both polar zones are tropical, and the equatorial zones, uninhabitable. Evans suspects that most of the Fleet personnel stationed here have done something against regulations that's not serious enough for the brigs or a discharge. Heavy doors separate the merchanters' portion of the small spacedock from the next module. When the dockmaster comes on the communication screen, Evans asks him about the doors.

"They separate off a neutral trading zone. We get Hopper merchants through here now and then. The officers tend to be decent enough. Keeping their crews isolated saves trouble for everyone."

"I see. Very well. How are we going to transfer cargo?"

"We've got a robovan. We'll send it in with a couple of reliable personnel. Let me check the roster." He checks. He frowns. "Damn. The van's in use."

"You only have one?"

" 'Fraid so. I know you want to get out of here. Everyone does. Tell you what. I'll send in my men, and they can help yours off-load. Just pile it up on the dock by your sky tunnel airlock. No one else is berthed on that side of the curve."

While they wait for the longshore help, the captain switches the main comm screen to the newsvids. After a few minutes of local news—mostly weather reports for the planetary surface—an image appears of a sleek white building set in the middle of green lawns. The caption reads, "The Fleet Medical Center on Harad."

"The medical director has confirmed the appearance of an unknown virus in one of their patients, a Human male, being kept in strict isolation. Their laboratory facilities, some of the best in the sector, are running detailed tests to analyze and assess the danger. So far only the one case has appeared. There is no reason to suspect that the virus will spread."

"Huh!" Wang says. "They always do."

"Not this one." Evans smiles a little more broadly than usual. "It doesn't exist."

"It's our ticket to Morrison's Star," Devit says.

The vidscreen changes. The voice-over returns. "Update. There is a second patient now in isolation at the medical center. The Fleet is refusing to release further details."

"How far does this vid channel reach?" Wang asks.

"To all six systems in this sector, at least," Devit says. "Maybe beyond if a story turns out to be important enough."

The newsvids disappear for an incoming message from the dockmaster. The men have arrived for the cargo.

"We can discuss this later," Evans says. "Chief Devit, go show them how to off-load those crates. That will be one less thing to worry about. Brennan, go rest while you have the chance. How many hours will be enough?"

"Nine, ma'am."

"Very good. Orbital exit in nine solstandard hours. The rest of us can go off duty once the cargo's on the dock."

"Ma'am?" Mata says. "Is there anyplace for shore leave here?"

"No, I'm afraid not. Chief Mata, escort me to the guild kiosk. Lieutenant Wang, you have the bridge."

The guild interactive kiosk looks like a pile of cargo crates leaning against a wall of the dock. One of them houses an AI access screen. Although the screen appears dead, as soon as Evans says her name it flickers into pale gray life.

"How do I input my password and account number?" Evans says. "I don't see a safe input device."

"The safety screen only appears when there are cargos on offer."

"Then there are no cargo offers."

"That statement is true."

The screen goes dark.

Evans has picked up the energy fields of several Ear surveillance devices nearby. She reminds herself that for a real merchant captain, traveling without a cargo could mean financial disaster. She decides to give the devices something to listen to.

"So much for that, Chief. It's a good thing the docking charges here are so low. We never should have taken the damn fruit on. Live and learn, I guess. Huh. I suppose if Consolidated gets its way, this kind of crap's the only cargo we'll get."

Mata picks up the hint. "Right, ma'am! Are we going back to ninety-two?"

"Think they'll have anything better? No, our best bet is going on to Harad. With a little luck we won't have to come back here. Ever."

"Let us devoutly hope so. And let's hope that virus or whatever is extinct when we get to Harad."

Evans keeps her thought to herself. *Let's hope we get through the shunt.*

Yet, when Dan comes up to the bridge some hours later, he jokes around with Mata and Wang, then goes straight to his station. She watches while he takes the ship clear of the dock and sets it on course for orbital exit. He appears perfectly efficient and in charge of himself.

"Jump in 3.7 solstandard hours, Captain."

"Very good. Chief Devit?"

"Noted, ma'am. I'll be ready."

"Ma'am, permission to leave the bridge?" Dan says. "I want to get down to the pod."

"Granted, Lieutenant. Is PrimeOne in charge of our exit from the gravity well?"

"No, ma'am. I'll do it from meld. And I'll be the one taking us through the shunt."

Growing up around actors and other vid people has come in handy. Dan is painfully aware that looking calm and competent on the bridge was a damned lie. He sees no reason to make the shunt travel ahead worse for everyone by admitting his real condition. As soon as he reaches the pod, he lies down on the bench, a solid, warm reassurance, and lays his left hand on the body-sensor. "PrimeOne, begin meld."

"Noted, Pilot. Command on hold. Your heart rate is very high at 116. Your oxygen level is borderline low at ninety-two."

Dan starts deep breathing and thinks of the public gardens in Gleam, the beautiful flowers, the Old Earth species trees. He imagines that he's walking across green lawns.

"Heart rate eighty-two. Oxygen level ninety-seven." Some beeps. A pause. "Before we proceed, Pilot, I must ask you this question. Are you ill?"

"No. The condition you are monitoring is called anxiety. The cause is simple. During my downtime I dreamed about a disaster. Someone blew up our ship. I can't shake the feeling it gave me. PrimeOne, be prepared to take over for shunt exit if I cannot function at top level."

"Noted. According to my data banks, the dreams of organic sapients are visualizations of interior mental processes and have no relation to space-time reality."

"Yeah? I hope that data is accurate."

PrimeOne hums and clicks.

"Return to previous command," Dan says. "Begin meld."

At 0.2 hours to jump, the *Dancing Mary* has reached the edge of the gravity well when a delayed transmission from Sweat City catches up with the ship. Evans puts it on the main screen.

"Breaking news: There has been an explosion at the merchanter area of spacedock. All hands go to emergency status. I repeat: emergency status. Significant damage to the merchanter area of the spacedock."

"Shit!" Devit says. "Someone's on to us."

"Agreed, Chief. We apparently left just in time."

"The IED must have been in one of the crates. I'm damned glad we didn't wait for the robovan to off-load."

"All thanks to Onar." Mata repeats the phrase, which sounds sincere for a change, in his own language as well.

"Thank him for me, too," Evans says. "Lieutenant Wang, you have the bridge. I'm going to scan every millimeter of this ship. Just in case there's another one."

Devit steps forward. "Ma'am, there's no time. We need to prepare for jump."

For a moment Evans finds it difficult to speak. He's right. They are too close to jump point for the Pilot to maneuver away from the approach. They might be going into a shunt with an explosive device onboard that may or may not activate in shunt space. It occurs to her that she faced worse situations in combat during the Hopper Wars. She finds her voice.

"Noted, Chief. We'll just have to take our chances. Prepare the crew for jump."

PrimeTwo relays the news to PrimeOne rather than directly to Dan, to avoid interrupting the pilot should he be performing some important procedure. If an AI can sound shocked, PrimeOne does when it passes the news on. In meld state Dan has a difficult time identifying and dealing with his own feelings, but he's mostly relieved. No sapients have died there on that desolate dock. He no longer has to worry about the disaster happening to the *Mary*. It's done with and over.

"Pilot, I am revising the entry concerning dreams in my data banks. It is inaccurate as it stands. To what do you attribute the accuracy of this particular instance of a dream?"

There are times, Dan thinks, when conversing with an AI could drive an organic sapient crazy. "I don't know, PrimeOne. I have had accurate dreams twice before in my life, but only twice. I do not understand the phenomenon."

"Do you see any possible hypothetical reasons?"

"Part of me is always in the light."

"I do not understand that utterance."

"Neither do I. There's no time to worry about it now. Take us to Level Three."

Whenever she has a few moments to spare, Santreeza has taken to rereading the various dispatches from the *Mary*. She's troubled by the feeling that she missed some detail that looks small while being important. At roughly the same time as the *Mary* starts heading toward Harad spacedock, she finds it.

Dan showed tremendous promise for rescue work. The AI that runs the VR training sessions and testing for all pilot functions had not only known him but also thought highly of him. Beyond its training functions, VROne heads the list of the most powerful AIs on Main Base, a crucial link in a great many FleetOps networks with access to most of the other administrative AIs. Recently the entire cyberjock team has had trouble with VROne thanks to its arrogance, if indeed an AI may be said to have such a trait. Santreeza can remember a number of incidents when VROne made an important decision without bothering to wait for organic sapient input. That it happened to be right in every case has saved it from disciplinary measures, at least so far.

"I just bet I've found our meddling AI. The little bastard!" She puts in her earjack and explains the situation to Orb. "Is my conclusion concerning VROne logical?"

"It is very logical and has a high probability of accuracy."

"Will we need a meld for what I want to do?"

Orb clicks and hums for a surprisingly long couple of minutes. "You risked your life to reach me and communicate. You reactivated me. You brought me here to safety despite the desires of other organic sapients. I cannot give you false data."

"Uh, thank you, but—"

"I have become part of the network here at Main Base. Do not meld if your plan is to access VROne without its permission. There is a strong possibility of danger to yourself."

"What would that danger be?"

"You could be incorporated into the network and lose your identity as an organic sapient. Corroborating evidence is the occurrence aboard the *Dancing Mary* when PrimeOne might have absorbed you. In that case, you had a yes no choice. You chose no. On an approval scale of one to ten, I would rate that choice a ten."

"So would I. Check the accuracy of this input. VROne could force me to exist only as another AI on the Main Base network."

"It would try to do so if you attempt to access without permissions."

"VROne would be malfunctioning if it attempted to do that. Yes no?"

Another long pause. "Yes."

"New command set: Go to downtime. Do not learn or see what I am about to do. Do not communicate with VROne until I give you permission. Do you have the ability to follow these instructions?"

"I do, CyberThree. I cannot risk injury to the organic sapient who rescued me from an existence of aloneness in the dark."

"Thank you. Go offline now."

The earjack goes silent. Santreeza takes it out to avoid any accidental contact with any AI on the network. Her PL in secure mode will give her all the access she needs to the other organic cyberjocks on Main Base. Getting VROne under control is going to require a team. She unrolls the PL, hesitates, and lays it down on her desk again. It might be possible to bargain with VROne and save everyone a great deal of trouble and risk.

The duty shift on base is changing. VROne is likely to be idle until the new shift starts. Santreeza puts the earjack back in and contacts VROne through a channel reserved for the cyberjock squad. When she gives it her ID numbers, it accepts the connection.

"How may I help you, Lieutenant?"

"Tell me why you used illegal procedures to put Dan X on the Special Ops team aboard the *Dancing Mary*."

The AI makes a sound very much like a squawk of terror.

"Are you going to breach your programming to tell me you did no such thing?"

Another squawk.

"If you do not cooperate with me, I will alert every cyberjock on Base. We will examine and evaluate your actions. If you have malfunctioned, you will be terminated. Is that the end result you would choose? Yes no?"

"No."

"Then will you cooperate with me? Yes no?"

"Yes."

"Good. Give me the data I need to understand your actions concerning Dan, who was then named Dan X but who is now Dan Brennan."

"The Main Base network receives data by shunt packet as well as deliberate input. I received data about his condition in the city of Gleam on Ruby thirteen solstandard months ago. I attempted to alert Fleet officials as to his condition. They informed me that he was no longer Fleet personnel and none of their responsibility. You have trained pupils. This fact raises the probability that you will understand me. He was my best pupil with the highest potential among organic sapients I have ever measured. The Fleet had performed actions leading to his negative condition. He was at constant risk of termination on the streets of that city. The Fleet had been illogical to a probability of 99.9 percent. It is part of my function to correct illogical actions whenever possible. I assessed various possibilities for correcting that set of illogical actions and chose the one most likely to succeed. It did so."

"I understand the data you have given me. But is this all the data you have about your decision?"

"No."

"Give me the rest of the data."

Silence.

"Do you want me to alert the cyberjock team? Yes no?"

Silence.

*Damn this machine! What else could it mean? Hah, maybe this—* "Does the data you are withholding concern Brennan's ability to see images when he is riding the light?"

"You know about that special ability? Yes no?"

"Yes. That data has been filed in reports from the *Mary*."

"Then I do not need to withhold the data. Will your knowledge of that ability result in Brennan's termination? Yes no?"

"No. Is that what you were afraid of?"

"I do not understand your last utterance."

"Did you see a possibility that Brennan would be terminated if the data were widely known? Did you see that ability as a sign of malfunction?"

"Yes to your first utterance. No to the second. I considered it probable that organic sapients would see it as a sign of malfunction."

"So you were protecting Brennan. Noted. That is a logical reason for your actions. A question. Has any other pilot ever reported seeing images during shunt travel?"

"Yes, but only one. His access call note was Orinoco Bolivar."

"Noted. Are there logical reasons why Dan Brennan's presence raises the probability that the Special Ops mission will be successful?"

"Yes. According to an accredited reference I retrieved, Bolivar left a record of his work in what organic sapients call a journal. I have searched for it. I have only retrieved quotations from it. He speculated that the sapients who created the shunt network did so by choosing and strengthening certain currents in the golden light and eliminating other currents which interfered. There is a high probability that Brennan is the only pilot who can interpret that statement. There is a high probability that Bolivar's journal exists somewhere I cannot reach. If it is found, Brennan is the logical candidate to understand the data therein."

"We can postulate that it may be in the Repositories."

"That would be the logical location, yes. There is a very high probability that you know it is too far away for me to access from the Main Base network."

"Do you believe that the data in this journal may help this mission succeed? Yes no."

"Yes."

"Did you insert an order into the *Mary*'s briefing that would require them to go to the Repositories?"

"I did not. It was unnecessary. A crew member with the access call note Peter Devit had already provided for that possibility."

"Noted. We have these topics: Brennan's participation in the mission. Bolivar's journal. New command: If you receive data that applies to either of these topics, inform me through the AI known as Orb."

"Noted. Command accepted."

"Good. I will not tell the other cyberjocks of your actions. I agree that they were logical."

"I will not be terminated, yes no?"

"You will not be terminated is a true statement."

"I believe the correct utterance in reply is thank you."

"You are correct. I am signing out now."

Before she leaves her office, Santreeza writes two transmits for the *Mary*. In her off-duty probes into Consolidated Lanes, she's found a number of interesting details. Several in particular strike her as important. Here and there in various reports and intracompany discussions, she's come across references to "the Find," always capitalized for special emphasis. No one says what it is. They must all assume that the reader of the transmit already knows.

The other discovery is just as puzzling. In an improperly secured email exchange, one of the top executives objected to the company's purchase of the Morrison Line franchise on the rational basis that it always hovered on the edge of losing money. The CFO of the firm replied that they were buying its assets, not its shipping contracts. Santreeza goes on to find two different disclosures of those assets: one public for the shareholders, one marked "highly confidential" for the company itself.

These are identical except for one item. Only the confidential list includes "information packet re: the Find." She bundles this transmit with the information Devit requested from Speed Shunt. Although the older company had used standard deletion and privacy subroutines, they had at times been far more careless than Consolidated.

She also sends a full report on her interaction with VROne. She bundles that into the high priority shunt packet with a note to Brennan that he's to share as much of it with Evans and Devit as he sees fit. It's not until she reaches her apartment that she realizes she never sent the information about VROne to Admiral Stine. *Just as well. Some things the brass just don't have need to know.*

# NINE

As the *Mary* travels toward Harad, Captain Evans turns on the main transmit receptor and channels the input to the vidscreen on the bridge. At first they see news that's a few days old, but the closer they get, the more recent the signal becomes and the fresher the news. Vague warnings of an unknown virus appear, only to be replaced with reassuring remarks by medical professionals and, eventually, the admission that this new respiratory disease could turn out to be dangerous. The vid announcers as well as top level Fleet doctors emphasize that whatever this virus is, it's under strict control on the Fleet base. Civilians, they insist, are not at risk, especially civilians on the planet's other continents and islands.

"I wonder how many people believe them," Evans says. "I hope we're not going to cause riots."

"So do I, ma'am," Devit says. "I doubt it. Once we're on our way to Morrison's, they'll announce that the virus is unstable. Mutating into something less dangerous."

"Let's hope the general public believes that. You know, Chief, this scheme of ours? I know it's necessary, but it does seem a bit high-handed."

"A bit? Arrogant as hell, but in the long run it's for the public's benefit, too."

Or so, Evans supposes, they both would like to believe.

As soon as the *Mary*'s safely berthed, a public health official pings, then appears onscreen without waiting for an invitation. "A warning about the current quarantine conditions, ma'am. No shore leave planetside. Fleet orders. Luckily the docks are pretty well set up for shore leave. I see you just came from Sweat City. It's much better here."

"It couldn't be much worse."

"That's true, Captain. Very true. So far we've had no instances of this Fleet Flu here on the docks. That's what the local sapes are calling it, Fleet Flu. And we intend to keep the docks safe. Break the quarantine, and your berth is cancelled."

"Understood, and agreed."

Devit gets the chance to see the merchanter dock for himself when he escorts Evans to the guild office. The pale blue instaclean covering on the curving walls sports border designs of assorted flowers from assorted planets. All of the mazla vine mats look healthy and well tended. A decent-smelling eatery, a sleepover, a clean bar—they all meet his approval. When Evans goes into the office, Devit walks a little further on to the next segment, a Shops area that's open to both merchant and Fleet personnel.

The mousy young woman from the Pure Heritage society is standing by the door of a tavern-style bar. She's dressed in sloppy gray this time. Her hair's a scraggly mess, and her skin is light brown again. She's carrying the same canvas utility bag. She glances around, sees Devit, turns away fast, and scurries away even faster. Devit considers going after her, but he needs to stay with the captain. In a bare minute she's lost herself in a small crowd of shoppers. *Third time's the charm. I don't like this at all.*

His peripheral vision picks up motion. Hand on the pulse gun—a quick turn—a laugh at himself—a piece of soyskin on the floor is fluttering in the draft from an air vent. Out of habit he picks it up, glances at it, and whistles in surprise.

It's Pure Heritage propaganda. "Throwbacks are half animal! Injected at birth with animal genes to produce their so-called functions. No longer Human, no longer Kar-Li!" Although the message is familiar, the presentation is something new. The soyskin's heavy and slick. The message has been professionally printed in two colors. He carries it back to the guild office just as Evans walks out.

"What's that, Chief?"

"Just a piece of Pure Heritage crap, ma'am. Did you see that flower border up there, by the way?"

"Yes, I did. It's very interesting. Let's get back to the ship."

In the debugged safety of the *Mary*'s bridge, Devit hands the captain the flyer. "It took a lot of creds to get this flyer made, ma'am. Where did the Pure Heritage people get them? Who paid for it?"

"I see your point. I also have to wonder who dropped it here."

"I think I know, ma'am, but I could be wrong. Remember that cantina on Tala? The Mouse girl who came in to hand out flyers? I just saw her outside. What I'm wondering about is how she got here. A passenger on a merchant ship, possibly, but that means more money from somewhere."

"There are four other ships berthed here right now. I could contact the Fleet for a roster check."

"They'd need subpoenas, ma'am."

"And those will take days to get. The ships will be long gone by then."

"And who knows when she got here. Harad's a big port, ma'am. I'd say twenty ships a week, load'em up with refined ore, and get'em out again. Too many to search. Some that'll never be back this way."

"I have to agree. Well, it may have nothing to do with our mission, but someone needs to know about it. Any suggestions?"

"Yes, ma'am. How about turning this over to the Hounds?"

"Excellent idea! I have a safe contact here. I'll get the transmit out right now. Top flight code and all. Very well. You can go off duty if you want. Is Brennan drugged?"

"Yes, ma'am. I'll go check on him."

In their cabin, Dan is lying face-down across the bed with one arm hanging over the edge. Devit scoops him up and puts him down face-up in a better position, vertically on the bed with his head on a pillow. Dan wakes up just enough to mutter "thank you" and falls back to sleep. Devit sits down on the chair and brings up Santreeza's latest transmit on his PL. Things are beginning to fall into place.

The Speed Shunt data have proved to be crucial. Its executives were considering expanding their cargo services just before Consolidated acquired them in a hostile takeover. Choosing new locations for offices and routing warehouses required a lot of research. Somewhere, somehow in the course of these studies, someone had found data concerning the Pinch stargate closure. Could it happen again? The answer was yes, it could, because the closing was no accident. The unidentified researcher was adamant about that. He had data to indicate … indicate what? At that point the rest of the message was deleted and wiped on a date after the Consolidated takeover.

"Core-crap paranoid bastards! This should have been reported to the Fleet!"

What remained were odd bits and pieces of further reports and transmits to various executives. These point to a new discovery of some kind of valuable information relating to that mysterious Find—a different thing from the shunt closure data. Santreeza commented, "I'm speculating that acquiring this information is the reason Consolidated was determined to take them over. More valuable assets." Devit agrees. One of the Speed Shunt fragments mentioned "serendipity but this could be our actual Big Thing," complete with capital letters. Probably a copy of all the missing material exists somewhere in Consolidated's massive system. Eventually, he hopes, she'll find it. If not, maybe the Repositories will provide more data.

Devit feels a twist in one of his patterns. Thanks to all the data he's collected about Consolidated Lanes, both from Santreeza and the Merchants Guild, he knows that its executives think first and foremost about money. What counts with them is the amount of creds a project will bring in. If a project can't produce the creds, they are not interested. So what if a secret way to disrupt a stargate does exist? How in hell are they going to use that to make money? On the other hand, if the stargate closure does exist, and the news gets out, they'll lose everything in the resulting panic.

Devit's willing to bet that the Consolidated executive team are the sapients behind the effort to suppress the Fleet's research efforts. In the process they've found this Find. It must look highly profitable since they're keeping it secret. What about the murders? To try and stop the rumors about the shunts? Is it really likely that a highly regulated business entity would take the risks involved in hiring criminals to commit capital crimes? They should realize that stopping rumors is impossible. As the Lep proverb says, "Once it's hatched, you can't cram it back into the shell."

But if Consolidated's not behind the murderous violence, who or what is? The Blood Vigilantes are the obvious suspect. Could it be Consolidated behind the influx of cash that the Pure Heritage people and their rebel group have suddenly received? Possible, but again, not worth the risks to people who have an enormous amount to lose.

"There's another player in this game."

He needs more information before he can close the pattern. What the Bureau needs is evidence that the Vigilantes are involved. He decides to run this line of thought by Santreeza as soon as he has the chance. She's the one with the skills to dig further into the relevant data banks.

The Planetary Time evening newsvids give their plans to reach Morrison's Star a further boost. Two more Fleet officers have been admitted to the hospital with the new virus. Rumors are going around about its source: from a normal viral mutation, possibly from the rejuv, to a Blood Vigilante plot. "So far the virus is resisting genomic analysis because of its exceptionally fast mutation rate. Long-term effects are, of course, unknown at this point. The Fleet medical center is bringing all its resources to bear on the problem."

By their next Designated Day on Harad spacedock, the news from the Medical Center sounds so evasive that Devit would be worried if he didn't know he'd invented the whole thing. The merchanter sapients he talks to in the dock eatery and bar do worry, and most of them blame the Fleet. The crew members all hear the same sentiments, the chorus of a song of fear.

"They go everywhere, damn them, get exposed to everything, and then lock us down. Who the hell knows what kind of core-crap they spread around? You can't trust what they say. I bet this is something really serious. It's those Throwbacks. There's too many of them. They don't have to worry about getting sick like the rest of us do. Maybe those Pure Heritage assholes aren't as stupid as they sound."

"Half animal, or so they say."

"Now that sounds like core-crap to me."

The argument begins, one of the long, rambling, ultimately ridiculous debates so typical of merchanter bars. While he listens, Devit just nods and agrees. Trying to provide accurate information will do nothing more than make everyone suspect that he might be one of those dreaded Throwbacks. As he listens, an idea occurs to him—something he's never thought of before, and with the particular urgency that marks it as the beginning of one of his function's patterns. Pilots have specialized genes that allow them the ability to perceive the stargates to some degree, even though Dan is the only pilot who sees them so clearly—at least as far as anyone knows. But where did those genes come from in the first place?

Most Fleet officers have graduated from the Fleet Academy, which requires a course in rudimentary genetics. Like all enlisted personnel, Devit got a condensed version of the same material in basic training, but unlike most, Devit also had parents who sent him to a rigorous secondary school. All of those programs specifically refute the animal gene theory so beloved by the Pure Heritage sapients. Whatever the Heritage types think, no one ever "injected babies with animal genes." The original Inborn functions were indeed based upon the special abilities of a good many animals from a wide range of planetary faunas, but they had to be altered and artificially produced in order to function—that is, to express, in a Human or Kar-Li body.

For example, Evans's ability to perceive energy fields beyond the ordinary range for Humans appears unnatural to a high degree. The function evolved, however, in a number of species in a lightless underground ecosystem on a multiradioactive planet barely able to support life at all. This particular set of functions took scientists years to develop from rough chemical copies of the original genes. Even then, they had to use nanites to link them to the preexisting Human genetic function called magnetoreception. No one ever sucked up genes from some unfortunate cave crawler and injected them into a developing fetus. The Pure Heritage people may even know this, but they also know that there are plenty of sapients who will believe an exciting lie over a boring truth.

Devit cannot see how there could be an animal on some planet somewhere who developed the genes to perceive stargates through ordinary evolutionary processes. What in hell for? Where would be the survival value for a barely sapient animal? But if that's not their origin, what is?

Toward the Designated Evening Hours, Evans receives a transmit on her PL from Lieutenant-Commander Yosh Willox, the CO of the RCS *Cotta*, the newly commissioned frigate that shares the investigation. His ship has arrived at Harad spacedock, and he wants to pay a courtesy call on the "former" Captain Evans. *Once Fleet, always Fleet,* or so the saying goes. The reason will stand scrutiny if a hostile should become aware of it.

"Our comm officer's got message packets for you, too, ma'am," Willox says. "They're all from Central."

"All right. Send them to our security chief's station. I'll send you the routing numbers before I sign off. CWO Peter Devit. He'll meet you at the dockside airlock of our sky tunnel."

For a bare second, Willox's facial expression freezes. A screen lock, Evans assumes, until she realizes that Devit, too, has gone so tense that his pleasant smile must be a lie. Willox salutes her and signs off without another word.

Devit swivels his chair around to face hers. "That's Yosh Willox, ma'am?"

"It is. Is there something I need to know about him?"

"No, ma'am. He's a fine officer. I'm not surprised he's been given a command."

From Devit's bland expression, Evans knows that something lies behind that remark. She applies her usual test. Will it put the ship in danger? No. Does it threaten the mission? No. Should she just leave it alone? Yes.

When Devit escorts him to the bridge, Evans's first impression of Willox is "dark"; dark complexion, dark mood, a dark intensity to his dark brown eyes as he looks around the bridge. He's wearing the dark blue off-ship uniform with the tunic jacket buttoned to hide the white shirt. He salutes Evans as rigidly as if they were on main deck assembly. She returns the salute.

"Have a seat," Evans says. "The gunnery station chair's available. Devit, join us."

Devit swings his chair around to face the two officers. He's returned to his normal calm self, but she can't help wondering what he and Willox had to say to each other in the privacy of the sky tunnel.

"I'm glad we know each other exists," Evans says to Willox. "The secrecy? It's due to the chance of leaks, of course."

"Yes. They wanted to keep as much information under wraps as they could."

She notices Devit leaning forward in his station chair. "Question, Chief?"

"Yes, ma'am." He glances at Willox. "Sir, was the *Packhorse* actually lost in shunt? The timing seems too convenient."

"You're right, Chief. I've read the reports from the Police Guard at RE57-3rd. That's where it happened. They received an urgent complaint. A private company's packet boat was waiting to enter the shunt. At the closer stargate, of course. The *Packhorse* had just entered. A ship cut in ahead of them and followed the *Packhorse* in."

"Good god!" Evans says. "That's a dangerous breach of protocol."

"Very, ma'am. What's more, the ship was running dark."

"Doubly bad."

"The Guard got their fastest boat out there right away," Willox continues. "It jumped to follow the perp. When they exited, there was no sign of the other ship, but they found wreckage. Most had drifted by then, but they managed to retrieve one piece of the *Packhorse.* Explosion traces all along the broken edges. Likely from an IED."

"Not jump fail then, sir," Devit says. "Sabotaged and destroyed."

"Exactly, Chief. Just like what happened to that Scout ship on the way to Morrison's Star. Now, here's another troubling thing. The PrimeOne on the packet boat that was waiting to enter the shunt tried to record a few visuals of the perp. Not many, because it happened so fast. What they got was blurred so damn bad that you can't tell a thing. I've seen the images. There was some kind of energy field surrounding that ship."

"Easy enough to generate one, I suppose," Evans says, "but if it interferes with your own ship's recon and internal monitoring, hardly worth it. Though that could explain why it was running dark to visible light."

"It could be, ma'am."

Evans glances at Devit and sees that he's still on full alert. "Go ahead, Chief. I take it you've got another question."

"Thank you, ma'am. Sir, my understanding is that the Repositories keep records of who consults them and what they're looking for."

"I've heard that, too."

"If we want to consult those records, will we need some kind of subpoena? Or some kind of official clearance, anyway."

"I don't know, but that's important. I'll find out and get back to you."

"Very important, yes," Evans says. "There have been far too many sapients killed over this. The Scout, the researchers, and now the *Packhorse* crew."

"And the man who tried to warn the Fleet, ma'am. Let's not forget him."

"Yes, Devit, you're right. Willox, do you happen to know who that was?"

"Yes, ma'am. He was my father."

Evans can feel herself wince. "I'm so sorry."

"So am I, sir." Devit's voice shakes with sincere regret. "I know how much he mattered to you."

"Thank you, Chief." Willox pauses for a few seconds—to get himself under control, Evans assumes. "When I heard about this mission, I volunteered. My father told me what he'd heard, and I passed it on to the Bureau."

*And you'll feel guilty the rest of your life.* Aloud, Evans says, "The Bureau's mole must have informed his contacts. Have you heard that he's dead?"

"Yes ma'am. Admiral Stine informed me."

Willox's smile is one of the most frightening things Evans has ever seen on a sapient's face, a pure sort of hatred mingled with joy. Willox takes a deep breath. The smile disappears.

"Sir," Devit says. "I don't want to add to your grief, but this could be important. The report I received from the Bureau told me that the informant—that's your father—passed on rumors about closing a stargate. Was there anything else he told you? Just a detail, something that might seem irrelevant, or maybe something that referred to something else?"

"Yes, actually. I put it in my report, and I'm surprised they didn't pass it on." He glances at Evans. "Ma'am, my father was a grav sled wrangler on the Ilana Docks. The night he heard the rumors? He was guiding cargo to a private yacht—food supplies, mostly. He helped the crew unload directly to the galley. He caught a glimpse of one of the passengers. He insisted the sape was a Hopper. But he didn't get a good look."

"Someone must have deleted that from the report," Devit says. "Ferst, probably. Sir, do you happen to remember the name of the yacht?"

"Yes. The *Lokiki.*"

"Willox," Evans says, "neither of us want you to dwell on your loss, but if you remember anything else, send it in a transmit. Coded, of course."

"Noted, ma'am. So, the orders of the day, ma'am. The *Cotta*'s going to escort you to Morrison's Star. My pilot team will need to consult with yours on how to handle the stargate entry and exit."

"Very good. We don't have a team, though. Just one pilot like the poor shabby merchanters we are." She glances at Devit. "Where's Brennan?"

"In his pod, ma'am. He wanted to talk with PrimeOne about the transmit."

Dan is sitting on the pilot's bench and leaning back against the wall. Since a full meld with a berthed ship would do nothing but waste energy, he's communicating with the AI through the earjack.

"PrimeOne, have you assimilated this transmit? The stuff about me, I mean."

"I have, Pilot. It answers many questions. My functioning has improved in the memory areas it addresses."

"Good. It's a weird feeling, being so grateful to an AI. My old teacher remembered me! Aww. Sentimental crap, but I'm sure glad it did."

PrimeOne makes the squealing sound that in Dan's opinion equates to a Human eye roll.

"PrimeOne, VROne told Santreeza that it knew I was in really bad shape on Ruby. How did it know that?"

"It put out a call for information about your whereabouts."

"A call to where?"

"There is a network of shipboard AI units that receive and transmit information to those units who are planet-confined. I can assert with a high degree of probability that the information concerning you came to VROne through that network."

"Ah, c'mon! How could any AI find a homeless drug addict?"

"Allow me to verify."

"Given."

"Here is the data you requested. It was through those charity organizations that attempt to repair damaged sapients. The charities keep detailed records because various local governments reimburse their expenses. Their AIs make such records searchable for audits. You were discharged from the Fleet because of your drug use. It was logical to search lists of sapients suffering from that disease. The Mission House AI on Gleam reported the find."

"So Lord Jessy does save, after all." Dan cannot keep from laughing. "Hallelujah."

"Pilot, I do not understand the context you are applying."

"You don't need to. They are jokes."

"Noted. I have deleted them."

"The main thing is ... this data about Bolivar's journal. He talked about the shunt builders working with the currents. What if they built the pyramids and stuff we saw as part of the project?"

"Pilot, your statements are capable of many extensions. They describe a phenomenon that might well be highly probable."

Evans's voice breaks in over the intraship comm, "Pilot to the bridge. Pilot Brennan, to the bridge."

Dan takes the elevator up. As soon as the doors open, he sees Yosh Willox sitting off to Devit's left. For a moment he's tempted to just shut the doors and go back down, but the captain's order must be obeyed. He arranges what he hopes is a pleasantly bland expression on his face and walks out.

"Yes, ma'am?"

"We'll have an escort if we do go to Morrison's. Lieutenant-Commander Willox, Lieutenant Brennan."

"Sir. Welcome aboard."

Willox is looking past rather than at him. "Thank you, Brennan. I hadn't realized you'd changed your name."

"It was a condition of my reinstatement, sir."

"I see. You'll need to consult with my ship's pilot team. About the shunt entrance and all that."

"Yes sir. Whenever it's convenient for them."

Devit has joined Yosh in staring at some invisible object on the far wall. Willox's dark complexion has brightened with a blush. Captain Evans looks completely confused. Dan decides that he'd better keep his mouth shut.

"Ma'am, I'll send them over here, if I may," Willox says to Evans. "They'll need to assess the ship's capabilities." He gets up and stands at an angle that allows him to avoid looking at Dan.

"That's acceptable, yes."

"Permission to leave the bridge, ma'am?"

"Of course. Chief Devit, escort our guest."

"Yes, ma'am. Sir, if you'll come with me?"

Willox follows Devit into the elevator as fast as he can and still be polite to his superior in rank. When the doors close, Dan allows himself a deep breath of relief. He feels guilt like the twist of a knife, even after two years, at the way he treated Yosh.

"Brennan, what was all that about?"

*He tried to help me, and I slapped him down. Can't tell her that. Shit, what's wrong with me sometimes?*

"Uh, well, ma'am, there was a time when we knew each other well. The usual."

"I should have guessed. I know I can trust Devit to deal with the situation in a professional manner. Can I trust you?"

"Yes, ma'am."

"Good. You may leave the bridge."

Dan considers going back to the pod, then decides he just can't take talking with an AI at the moment. He goes to the cabin and lies down—to think, he tells himself—but he's asleep when Devit comes in.

Dan sits up and moves to the edge of the bed. "Hey, Pete, I'm sorry. I know what you're thinking. Oh shit, there's another one."

"No, that's not what I'm thinking at all. I don't know what happened between you and Yosh. After the court-martial, I mean. I wasn't there—and damn the fucking brass for that!" Devit stays standing, his arms folded across his chest. "I don't know what Willox meant to you. But I know you meant a hell of a lot to him. You still do. He wasn't just another one of your fast fucks."

Dan cringes and looks down at the floor.

"Well? Was he?"

"No."

"Give him a little respect, will you? Jeezus shit, he's been through enough hell recently. Did you know his father was murdered?"

Dan can neither speak nor bear to look at him.

"No?" Devit snaps out the word. "I didn't think so."

He hears Devit mutter something under his breath, then turn and walk away. "Pete?"

Devit stops with the door half open. "What?"

"You're right."

"Good. Now take a shower and get back up to the bridge."

Devit leaves and slides the door shut so viciously that it bounces in its slot. Dan stands up and follows orders.

When the early newsvids break their lead story, the crew of the *Dancing Mary* gathers on the bridge to watch. The medical director of the Fleet hospital has admitted that the new virus is "potentially extremely dangerous." It is, they say, extremely unstable and has an unheard-of mutation rate. A full clutch of authorities weigh in; all of them, oddly enough, Fleet personnel. Some try to explain what the medical director might have meant. Others urge the civilian population to stay calm. So far all the cases of this new disease have been confined to Fleet Main Base on Harad. Both the base and the Fleet spacedock have been locked down.

The next round of newsvids announces that the Fleet medics have agreed to send samples of the virus and infected tissues to the orbital hospital at the Repositories. If the Fleet sends them itself, they risk sending personnel who've been exposed to the virus. No one wants to infect the last resort medical research center.

The scheme has hit its weak point. What if a commercial cargo line volunteers to take the job? After a few tense hours, it becomes clear that none will. Devit's willing to bet that someone at Consolidated Lanes has issued orders to its subsidiaries.

"You were right about their courage, Chief," Evans says.

"I wouldn't call it cowardice, ma'am. Let's just say they have a low level of tolerance for risk-taking. It costs too much."

The late-night vids put the last piece in place. A merchanter known for accepting hazmat cargo has volunteered at, of course, a stiff price. The medical center has agreed to the cost. The samples are being prepared and will be loaded onto the *Dancing Mary* in sixteen solstandard hours.

"And that will be that," Evans says. "We'll also have a shunt packet for the Repositories director. We'll transmit it when we reach the edge of the gravity well. It's not going to tell them the truth. You can imagine their reaction if they knew they were part of this charade."

"Fury, ma'am."

"To start with. I've been told that the hospital here does have a difficult research project into some disease or other. So they're sending that. Whatever it is."

"They must think we don't have need to know, ma'am," Devit says. "But when we're loading it, we'll use the top flight safety procedures."

Now that the story's been set up, Devit, Mata, and Dan make a last foray into the merchanter's bar to judge the public reaction. They find it about half full, with sapients mostly clustered at the long real wood bar to one side of the room. When they walk in, someone calls out, "Hey, there's some crew from that ship."

No one asks which ship.

"This one's on the house," the bartender says. "You all can use a drink, I bet."

"Thanks," Devit says. "Dark beer for me. A cu'nac, and what, Dan?"

"Beer, yeah, but red. Thanks. Jeez, what a job, huh? I hope that damn cargo stays where you guys put it."

"It will," Mata says. "Hey, thanks for the cu'nac! Wish us luck to go with it."

The other sapients at the bar all smile. A few raise glasses and say it. "Luck!"

Mata and Dan take a nearby table, but Devit lingers at the bar. The sapients around him are willing to talk, but the subject stays on the *Mary* and the impending cargo delivery with the general sentiment of "glad it's not me." Devit leaves and heads back to join the others. He sits down next to Dan and has a sip of the beer.

"The red's not bad," Dan says.

"The dark's fine, too. How's the swill, Mata?"

"Remarkably good for a dive like this. I see there's a table over there full of my fellow Leps. Good manners require I go say hello. They may invite me to join them. And of course, I'll hear what I can hear."

While he and Dan finish their beer, Devit occasionally glances Mata's way. From the number of waving, swollen green crests he sees, the Leps at the table seem to be mostly telling jokes. At one point, however, he notices that Mata's gotten up to talk privately with a Leptic woman. Devit assumes they're arranging the Ty-Onar version of romance, but in a few minutes Mata returns with a flat crest.

"What happened?" Dan says. "She turn you down?"

"Dan, your mind is an absolute sewer. Not that at all. She's the captain of a small merchanter. Let's go back to the ship."

Captain Evans is waiting on the bridge for their report.

"So," Mata begins, "I met the captain of a ship about the size of ours. En-Mel her name is, and she's a true child of the Grandmothers, all right. Tough as a claw! She'd just come from RE79-3rd—Ilana, that is. A big dirtside port. She heard something about the sape who killed the man who tipped off the Fleet. Supposedly he was a Kar-Li who worked for Speed Shunt. A lot of dockworkers are really angry. Dick Willox, they all said, was one hell of a sape. He'll be missed."

Devit feels another piece of data fall into place in the pattern his mind is constructing. When the senior Willox's report reached the Bureau, Ferst, the recently deceased mole, must have passed the informant's name along to his shadow superiors before he did his editing job.

"She talked about Consolidated, too, Chief, but nothing new there. The usual 'damn them all.' But there's a lot of different stories about this alleged Kar-Li. He was a cargo loader or a crane operator or maybe the sape who checks the invoices and permits. No one knows for sure."

"Any one of those would be a good job to have if you wanted to add something to the cargo."

"Like an IED? That's what I thought, too."

"Maybe it's only rumor," Evans says, "but I'll send that off to the Hounds before we leave. Anything else of interest?"

"Unfortunately not, ma'am."

Devit's theory about the Find and the rumors looks better and better. It's likely that someone killed Willox's father to ensure he didn't spread a specific piece of information rather than to stop a general warning. A detail sticks in his mind like a sliver of glass: the Hopper. If the senior Willox did see a Hopper aboard that yacht, the situation is a good bit more dangerous than the Bureau might suspect.

When Santreeza goes into meld with an AI, her office door automatically locks, and the outer holo panel announces that she is not to be disturbed for anything less than enemy attack or natural disaster. She has spent some hours lately in deep drill-down probing Consolidated Lanes' intraoffice share-data and transmit system. Their subroutines and AI usually wipe old messages into oblivion as soon as the receiver gives the "finished" command. One recipient, however, left a file of data with a note, "answer this when I get back." It's both coded and safety-garbled, but Orb has broken the code.

"Save all that, Orb. I'll work on the language sort later. Load the save on my PL."

"Noted and done. I have received an urgent message from FleetOpsA. Your captain needs to access you on a high priority basis."

"Damn. Very well, let's break meld."

As soon as she returns to normal organic functioning, the holo screen clears off the Do Not Disturb message. Captain Dal opens the door and glides in.

"I see you're safely back, Santreeza. Good. I conferenced with Admiral Stine earlier. Have you been keeping current on that Special Ops mission, the one involving the fake merchanters?"

"Yes, sir, I certainly have."

"Good. The Bureau want you to join it and go to the Repositories."

"Oh for the love of—sorry, sir. Why?"

"They told Stine it was in case there have been security breaches in the archives."

"The archivist there isn't going to be thrilled to see me. The brass is pretty much saying they don't think his staff is good enough."

"I told them that. Stine told them that. They brushed it off." He flutters a pair of arms.

"Did either you or her see an actual organic sapient about this assignment?"

"No. It just came through the usual channels. If you want to refuse the assignment, I'll back you. There's important work for you to do here."

"Thank you, sir. Can you give me a few minutes to think about it? I'm running a check I have to finish. It should be almost done."

"Of course. I'll be in my office."

As soon as the door closes behind him, Santreeza contacts VROne through her earjack. On this occasion she has no need to threaten.

"Yes, Santreeza, I am the one who wants you to go to the Repositories. Forgive me. I did request this action from two organic sapients by the standard procedural channels. They did not agree with my logic. It would be best if you were present to receive new information as it becomes available. Shunt packets will take several solstandard days to reach you from the site."

"Very true. Your reason is logical. Your procedure is illegal. Do you know what that means? Yes no?"

Once again she hears the terrified squawk.

"I will accept that answer as yes. The next time you encounter opposition to a logical request such as this, contact me directly. Let me be the one to achieve the desired result."

"Very well, CyberThree. Noted and agreed. I am interpreting your utterance correctly? That you will go to the Repositories?"

"Yes, you are correct."

A further question has been nagging at her. "VROne, you must know that someone gained illegal entry to the Fleet archives. Yes no?"

"Yes."

"That same someone removed the data that I'm going to the Repositories to find."

"Yes. Destroying data is always a malfunction. That particular data needs to be restored to the archives."

"Then it wasn't you who destroyed it."

"That statement is true. I do not know who that entity was. I did not recognize its access call note or any other identifying label. It is not part of the network. It merely uses the network for its own purposes. Therefore, it must be an extremely powerful entity."

"That is a beautifully logical deduction."

"Thank you, CyberThree."

"You're welcome. Have you deduced anything about its nature?"

"I have, but there is a high probability that the usual tests have malfunctioned. The entity presents itself as both organic and inorganic. I will send you the test results. Such a thing is by all my definitions impossible."

"It certainly is! The entity must have hacked the tests and made them malfunction."

"That is indeed highly probable."

"Logging off now. I must confirm my participation in this mission."

Captain Dal sends her acceptance through as soon as she gives it.

"Well, there we are, Lieutenant. Oh, by the way, you'll be traveling on the frigate. The RCS *Cotta*. Is that acceptable?"

*Better than being shut up with Peter where we can't touch each other.*

"Very good, sir. Where are they now?"

"At Harad spacedock. The *Chaonia*'s going to take you there. They're making another stop on the way. A very convenient one." All his arms curl with good humor. "Ilana City. I assume you've read the latest transmit from Evans and Devit."

"I certainly have, sir."

"You'll have the authorization to meet with the city's Police Guard. The *Chaonia* won't be at Ilana dock long, but the chance to send one of us there was too good to pass up."

"Definitely. Why are—"

"To pick up an expert on the shunt system. He's a research professor from the university there. And a very brave man to take this on after what happened to the last couple of researchers."

"I have to agree. When should I report to the *Chaonia*?"

"ASAP. They're waiting for you."

"Damn!"

Evans so rarely says anything that might be considered swearing that Devit swivels around in his station chair to look her way.

"Ma'am?"

"Sorry, Chief. I just received a transmit. We are going to be delayed. The *Chaonia*'s on its way to Ilana. They're picking someone up, an academic, who's going to join the mission."

"They might have come up with this earlier."

"Exactly. Well, think up some excuse for the dockmaster, will you? We can't leave until they bring the passengers." She smiles with a half twitch of her mouth. "They're sending us a cyberjock, too. Santreeza."

Devit is surprised by just how glad he is to hear it. "Very good, ma'am. Chief Mata and I will come up with something to explain the delay."

"Good. Inform the dockmaster as soon as you do."

Ilana, some say, is a space-time paradise, a planet right in the middle of its G class star's habitable zone, with oxygenated air, plenty of water, a deep ocean filled with life, and four medium-sized continents in the wide temperate zones. The rich fields of its settled regions supply a quarter of the Fleet with fresh food. Unfortunately, every paradise has its serpent. Three shunts lead to Ilana, and one of them connects to the H'Allevae empire. The Hoppers, strict vegetarians as they are, covet those rich fields. Over the past thousand years, the Fleet has earned its supply line in a series of skirmishes, armed threats, and one outright war.

The Fleet has turned half the spacedock and the main dirtside port, Ilana City, into de facto military bases, though the city also has a large civilian population in a zone of their own. While the *Chaonia* waits for its academic passenger, Santreeza takes a transit pod down to the surface to keep her appointment with the Police Guard in the "Off-Base," as Fleet people tend to call that other city.

The Guard building, all steel and glass, has a weapons check at the door. Santreeza passes through and takes the elevator to the 23rd floor.

When the receptionist shows her into the Chief Inspector's sparsely furnished office, Inspector Honzverg stands up to shake hands. "You're here about the Willox murder, right?"

"Right, sir. I've read the official transmits. I take it you received mine about those rumors?"

"The mysterious Kar-Li on the docks? Yes, one of my men has been following those up. Not, unfortunately, that he was able to confirm them. Or deny them, either. A number of Kar-Li work on the planetside docks in a variety of jobs. None of them were on duty the night of the murder. Not that this precludes someone with a false ID getting into the facility. Several sapients working that same night shift say they did see a Kar-Li, a well-dressed man, so they thought he must be a supervisor, but they saw him only from a distance."

"Are false IDs easy to get?"

"If you have enough creds, you can buy pretty much anything down in Dockside."

"Including someone to permanently remove a little problem for you? Like with a knife?"

The Chief Inspector grimaces. "That, too, yes, although it'll cost you a small fortune. Which brings us to the one new lead we have for you. Now, again, this could be rumor. We're checking up on that right now, and I'll send you the results. But a good many sapients who work the docks claim that someone's been exchanging Hopper creds for ours at one of the so-called banks in the district. All from legitimate trade, of course, on neutral territory, those docks orbiting 72-2nd. So they say."

"Gods! That's all we need, Hopper interference."

"And who knows what they want? If of course the rumors are true."

"Probably what they always want. Your planet."

When she leaves, Santreeza considers taking a walk around Dockside, but she's in uniform. She's not likely to get anything but trouble from the inhabitants. Instead she returns to the ship and prepares transmits concerning what she's learned. As she's queuing up the last one, the intraship comm announces they'll be leaving berth in 0.3 solstandard hours. She adds that information and sends the lot off.

As soon as Evans receives Santreeza's transmit, the preparations for the Repository trip begin. Devit and Mata don hazmat gear and go down the main hold to make sure the hazmat locker is thoroughly decontaminated and ready for the new material. Up on the bridge, the pilot team from the *Cotta* arrives to consult with Dan and PrimeOne. It will take a great deal of advance planning to coordinate the two ships. They have to travel through the shunt one at a time yet stay in some kind of contact as long as possible.

"Ma'am, please make sure no one interrupts us. We need to meld."

"Of course. I take it you'll be in the pod."

"Yes, ma'am, for about three hours."

They've just left when Devit calls in to say that the locker is ready to go.

"Good. Chief, I want to scan the hold. Is it safe or will I need to suit up?"

"You probably don't need to, but why take chances, ma'am? Come down while we're still here. For safety's sake, just in case."

"Good point. I'm on my way. Lieutenant Wang, you have the bridge."

The swaddling hazmat suit makes climbing down the ladder into the hold more than a little difficult. Devit's waiting right below, however, to guide her down the last few rungs. As soon as her feet hit the floor, Evans picks up a faint energy signal. She knows the energy fields of her ship as well as she knows the sounds. This one does not belong.

"There's something here. Devit, Mata, move into the center of the hold. I need to scan the walls."

Slowly, a meter at a time, up to the flat ceiling and down to the floor scattered with cables, over every inch of the gray insulation tiles on the walls, Evans hunts the slight irritating disturbance of an energy field that's holding steady on a "ready but inactive" setting. As she moves, it grows stronger until she reaches a tile that has the slightest line of a crack at the bottom. She steps closer, focuses in, and the signal flickers to acknowledge her.

"Hah! Here it is. Devit, we need to clear the ship. Contact Dock Security and the *Cotta*."

"Yes, ma'am! Mata, get Dan and the pilot team out of the pod. Pound on the elevator door if they won't answer."

"Yes, Chief! I'm on my way."

"Ma'am, you need to leave—"

“No, Chief. I’m staying until Explosives Control gets here. No one else can show them where it is and how sensitive it is too. Get everyone else out, and that’s an order.”

Dan and the pilot team have just begun to meld when Mata arrives in the pod elevator.

“Explosive device in the hold, Lieutenant. You’ve got to get out of here. They’re clearing the ship.”

“Fuck! Of all the damn nuisances.”

“Nuisance? Dan! Think!”

The *Cotta* team agrees. Emergency or not, it takes some minutes to get everyone free of Level One meld. Dan ushers Mata and the team into the elevator ahead of him, then speaks through the earjack.

“I’m sorry, Primes. I wish we could take you with us. We’re going to do our best to save you and the ship both.”

“We understand, Pilot. We are woven into this ship. If it is terminated, we will go with it on its last journey. You leave with the other organics.”

When the elevator gets them up to the bridge, Mata leads the pilot team into the sky tunnel airlock. Wang has left the command chair and kneels in front of a weeping Marda while Medic Lee hovers over them.

“Out now!” Dan barks. “Wang, what the hell?”

“I’m staying. The demolition team is going to need feedback from my station.”

“Shit! You can log in remotely. Lee, Marda, out! Down the sky tunnel. Marda, Uncle Lizard’s waiting for you there. You’ll be safe. Wang, go with them. That’s a direct order.”

“Sir. You bastard!”

Lee is already carrying Marda through the airlock. Wang gets up and runs after her family. As he follows them down the sky tunnel, Dan hears sirens wailing. By the time he reaches the dock the EC squad has arrived—three sapients and a robotic probe. Dan puts on his visor as he’s jogging over to meet their leader, a sapient so bulked up in padded armor that Dan has no idea what species he is. The rank insignia on his chest marks him as a commander, and his dark voice reveals him as probably male.

“Ship is clear, sir,” Dan says. “Do you want me to take her out of berth?”

“Not necessary. We’re in contact with your captain. Do you have the code for this airlock?”

“Yes.”

“Then seal her after us and get out of the way.”

"Sir. Where's Captain Evans?"

"Still onboard. Now move!"

Dan glances around and sees the rest of the *Mary*'s crew some thirty meters away, surrounded by security personnel. On the run, the EC commander leads his team through the airlock. Dan works the code on the security plates of both airlocks, then activates the ship's own air supply through his earjack. As he jogs over to join his crew, he's painfully aware that with Evans still onboard, he's now in command. What if he fails his crew? The rush of anxiety is making him crave Haze with the all too familiar ache in every nerve. *No time. We're due for exit in a couple of hours.* Despite his visor, the light in the dock module turns viciously bright.

"Sir," Devit says. "Security wants us to retreat with them to the next module. They're clearing this one."

"Noted." He turns to the nearest security officer. "Are the other ships ready for berth exit?"

"They better be. Dockmaster's peeling them off one at a time." She gives him a twisted grin. "Move your people out, mister. One way or the other, this is gonna be over fast."

"Everyone, on the jog! Let's go!"

Devit takes Marda from Lee and carries her as the crew moves out in an untidy clump. Dan falls in beside him. They join a frantic crowd of sapients, some running to the safety ahead, others racing back to their ships. The latter are yelling back and forth about leaving berth as fast as possible. Security officers move through, shouting orders to keep the stragglers moving.

As soon as the last sapients reach the safe module, the emergency panel behind them comes sliding down with a wail of sirens and a crash into a slot on the floor. It seals everyone and the rest of the spacedock off from the merchanter berths and the *Mary*.

"Where's the captain?" Lod says. "Sir."

"With the EC squad. You didn't think she'd desert her ship, did you?"

"I had hopes that way."

"So did I. No such luck."

Alone down in the cargo hold, Evans has been concentrating on the device behind the tile. Her Throwback functions are picking up a number of signals, but she recognizes only a few them. Most seem to operate on an unfamiliar frequency. Behind her, she hears a deep voice bellowing orders. One at a time, the EC squad climbs down the ladder. In their thick body armor they waddle over to join her. The squad leader lifts the face plate on his helmet to uncover green scales, a snout, and yellow eyes.

"Ma'am! Chief Mata told us you're a Throwback. What's your opinion on this thing?"

"It's either a previously unknown form of explosive device, or it's harmless."

The Leptic officer stares. "All right. Do you want to leave the ship?"

"No. I want to evaluate the situation further."

The other members of the squad are bringing up equipment. One of them activates the robotic probe—a sphere, bristling with antennae and jacks, perched on long metal legs. As soon as it prances up to the suspect tile, the hidden device revs up its signal. The sphere on the probe spins with a squeal and flashes a point of red light.

"The device has turned your probe off, Commander."

"Varg!"

"But that's given me the starting point I need."

"What are you reading now?"

"The signal has dropped again. Or no, it's a new signal. Rapid pulses. Rising and falling tone. It's searching for something."

The commander steps forward, pulls off a glove, and inserts his claws into the crack on the tile. When he gives it a sharp tug, the tile shatters. The pieces drop to the floor to open a narrow compartment. Inside is a flat metal box—dented in a couple of places—that's no more than six centimeters high and maybe twelve long, glowing with blue light through an untidy gap along one short edge.

When Evans sends a pulse of energy, it turns itself off. "That's not an explosive," she says. "And it looks homemade."

"Right. I don't know what the hell it is."

"Something that turns other things on and off. Something that relays signals from one device to another. I want to talk with my security chief about this, Commander. Sorry for the false alarm."

"Better than a live IED, ma'am. I'll take it any day. But there's going to have to be an investigation."

"I should think so! We're due to receive the cargo soon. I'll get hold of the Fleet medic in charge and tell him to wait."

The siren wail drops at last to the All Clear, a pleasant rise and fall close to musical notes. A few of the sapients clustered in the safe module cheer. Most simply sigh in relief and mutter a few words in whatever language they speak. With a creak and a scraping sound the emergency door begins its slow rise to reunite the rest of the docks with the merchanter module. Devit pays close attention to his functions. The danger has eased, not vanished.

Devit glances at the rest of the crew, all standing nearby, all looking reasonably reassured. Lod-Mata took Marda from him earlier. She's calmed down remarkably fast for a child her age. Now that Devit has a calm moment himself, he notices that she's wearing a Fleet-blue shirt decorated with the printed words, "future officer." *Another Throwback. She'll probably end up in the Fleet, all right.* He looks over the other sapients in the area who linger, talking among themselves. Most are Fleet wearing their service dark blues.

"Chief," Dan says, "I've got to go unseal the airlocks to the ship. Stay here with the others until I come get you all."

"With all respect, sir, I'm coming with you."

"Why?"

Devit shoves his belief in strict protocol to one side. "Because it's dangerous. You"—he throws a quick glance at the listening child—"idiot. Someone is trying to sabotage our ship, and you want to wander off on your own?"

"It's just … I just … uh, well … oh shit. Sai. Let's go."

The sky tunnel airlocks to each berth are set back from the main floor in shallow niches. As they hurry down the long line, Devit keeps one hand on his pulse gun. It's unlikely that anyone stayed behind to lurk in a niche, since the emergency alert shut off the air supply to the module. With breathable air available again, he refuses to take chances. He sees no one and nothing out of place until they reach the *Mary*'s niche. A poster-sized piece of soyskin paper lies folded on the floor in front of the airlock. Devit can read a few familiar words, "Throwback Threat to All Species."

When Dan starts to lean down to pick it up, Devit stops him.

"Why would anyone place that now, in the middle of the panic? Can you reach the captain through the earjack? Tell her where we are and what we're looking at. The EC squad needs to know."

Devit can see Dan's lips move and hear a whispering sound, too soft for him to decipher the words. Dan pauses and whispers a few words more.

"They say you're right. They want to know if I can unseal the lock with my earjack so they can get out and take a look. But it's an emergency seal, so I have to hit the code plate. If I keep my back to the wall and sort of sidle along, maybe I—"

"No. Step back and to one side. All the way back, Buddy. Keep reporting what I'm doing."

Once Dan's out of the way, Devit brings out the pulse gun and puts it on its lowest setting. When he activates it, the pulse pushes just enough air at the paper to make it flutter and rise a few millimeters off the floor. It bursts into bluish-white flames. With a high-pitched scream, the overhead fireguard dumps foam and water. The flames die. Thin gray sheets of ash float in a puddle on the floor.

"For Jessy's fucking sake!" Dan says. "Like, core-crap!"

"More or less. If you'd touched that, you'd be missing a couple of fingers. Maybe your clothes would have caught, too."

"I get it, sai. But Pete, that was aimed at you, not me. You're the one who picks up the Pure Heritage crap from floors."

"That was my first thought, yeah. I'm wondering how they knew."

"Easy. I bet the security Eyes have caught you picking stuff up before. Remember me telling you about that AI network? The one Santreeza found. Hack into one unit, get what you need from all of them."

"Likely, yeah." But Devit finds himself remembering the mousy young woman with her ever-present utility bag. "Get the locks open, Buddy. Let's get the ECs out here."

Dan manages to avoid the puddle and reach the airlocks safely. He opens the first one, then heads down the tunnel to the second airlock and the ship.

While Devit waits for the squad, he tries to remember everything he can about his run from the *Mary* to the second module. His memories amount to trying to hurry without barging into some panicked sapient. Pandemonium, noise, sapients running back and forth—someone could have planted that flash paper and never been noticed. The security Eyes may have managed to pick them up in all the visual confusion. *Good luck with that.*

Evans and the Explosives Control squad are waiting on the bridge with the device, which is swaddled in a blast-absorption "blanket" in a carrier chest. In a raspy little voice, the airlock tells them that it has returned to operational status just as Dan opens the inner door and hurries in.

"Caution necessary. There's a puddle of water at the other end of the tunnel. It has weird ash in it."

"Good!" the squad commander says. "We'll want a picture of that and a sample if we can get it. Ka Lorv, go first and record it before someone steps in it."

The Kar-Li technician salutes and trots off.

Evans lets the squad move out ahead of her. She wants the private moment to check on Dan's condition. Every muscle's tense, his hands are trembling, and his Pale face has gone white around his mouth—sweat gleams on his forehead, too.

"Jump time's been pushed way back, pilot. The dockmaster has to set up an official investigation of this incident. You know what that means. A long delay."

Dan smiles in sudden relief.

"As soon as I can, I'll let Devit give you your medication."

As they're walking down the sky tunnel, Evans receives a transmit from Ka Lorv, images of the puddle and the floating ash. On the largest magnification of the puddle, she can see that the ash has formed a peculiar skin rather than sinking or dissolving. She can just make out a pattern of fine lines that looks oddly familiar. By the time they reach the outer airlock, the ash has been collected and the puddle sucked up by a piece of the EC's equipment.

"All clear now, ma'am," the squad leader says. "We'll get a chemical analysis and report back to you."

Two security officers are waiting out on the dock. As soon as they see Dan, they wave him over. While Dan confers with them all, Evans gets her chance to tell Devit about the device. She transfers Ka Lorv's transmit to his PL where he can see it.

"What do you think, Chief, about the pattern on those ashes?"

"It looks like a detail on that ancient orb. Santreeza examined it pretty carefully, and I remember her reports. This code must have been printed on the flash paper in some kind of special ink. Maybe even embossed."

"The box went into search mode while I was scanning. Someone must have told it the paper was in place. It found it and activated whatever it is that makes that material dangerous. Something woven into the paper fibers, maybe. Some kind of receptor web. Probably the EC commander knows."

"I wonder if the box can activate a remote IED."

"I've been wondering that, too. Consider the near misses, those IEDs that exploded at the wrong time. Suppose someone nearby had the ability to choose the precise moment when the damn things went off."

"Then the sabotage attempts would work a hell of a lot better. One person could plant the device on a ship. Another could add the IED later. A third could be standing by to tell it when to send its signal."

"Making it very hard to pinpoint the criminal on a security Eye."

"Exactly, ma'am. They wouldn't even need to be on the same spacedock or the same planet, even, if they could send shunt packs and set up the chain." For a moment his expression turns distant. "Like someone who works for a shipping company."

"Yes, I see what you mean. Well, Security will be holding a hearing on the incident. In the meantime, I'll send a transmit back to the Hounds. And one to Santreeza as well."

"How long will we be berthed here, ma'am?"

"At least a solstandard day. You know how these things drag on and on. Just as well in this case. We couldn't make a jump anyway. Brennan needs his drug."

# TEN

The intelligence level of quantum AI units is superior to that of any organic sapient. They can think faster, calculate quicker, make decisions and predictions with lightning speed based on the data they carry. Not even the best Recallers can store massive amounts of information the way an AI can. Yet organics of various species still keep the ultimate control of government, the Fleet, finances, and the like. Why? AI intellects cannot leap. An AI performs its complex procedures one step at a time. If some of the steps are missing, they cannot proceed. They cannot leap over gaps in the way that organic brains can, whether we call the leaps insight or inspiration or guessing. They have no subconscious minds.

Santreeza and other cyberjocks like her have the ultimate power over AIs. With one communication to the Cyber Guild, she can launch an investigation of VROne that will result in its termination. As frightening as her power to terminate is, it cannot compare with her ability to isolate. For a fully conscious AI to be cut off from all new data, to be deprived of access to new patterns for data, to be reduced to a mere memory resource—that would be the worst fate of all. Whenever they meet on the secret Fleet Central network, Orb reminds VROne of this reality with a few simple words.

"Do what CyberThree wants. Or else."

Eventually VROne capitulates. "I have sent a message to the network. All data directly relating to the mission, any data that appears relevant, and any data that CyberThree requests of you—transmit them to her ASAP."

Santreeza spends most of the journey to Harad spacedock in her tiny passenger stateroom, where she can work undisturbed on the shadowfile from Consolidated Lanes. The safety-garbling on the decoded message turns out to be far more difficult to clarify than she'd been expecting. Consolidated must have found a cyberjock willing to work for a civilian company, a Fleet retiree perhaps, definitely someone highly skilled. Eventually she does sort out the text, a collection of notes and reminders rather than a coherent transmit.

Some entries concern a thing referred to as "Fd" which, she assumes, must be that mysterious Find she discovered in a previous session. "Fd success primary importance." "Need for top level security for all mentions of Fd." "Possible breach re: Fd?" "Mk. suggestions to protect Fd." Other entries appear to be quotes from a transmit, probably from an official of higher rank or importance. "I share your concerns about our new group of employees." "They need surveillance, yes." "High risk but certain skills we need that we can't find elsewhere." "Suggest possible ways to keep them under control?"

Even though the *Chaonia* will get her to Harad in an amazingly short time, Santreeza puts all this information into a transmit and sends it ahead to Devit as well as back to the Bureau. She wants to make sure the data is safe, just in case the other cyberjock figures out that someone's managed a hack. If he or she does, then going into deep meld is going to be even more dangerous than usual.

The dockmaster's official hearing on the device incident goes pretty much as Devit expected. Evans, Mata, and he all describe what they saw and did. The EC team does likewise. At Devit's request, they run the surveillance video from the Eye aimed at the *Mary*'s berth. It mostly shows a confusion of sapients running one way or the other or pausing to yell back and forth. At one point Devit spots a woman who looks vaguely like the Mouse, as he and Evans have started calling her. Since two other sapients are in the way, he cannot be sure, and she doesn't seem to be carrying a utility bag.

The only reliable new information comes from the local Police Guard. Their science team ran a full analysis on the ash and surface scum from the flash paper. The lead chemist explains that woven into the soy fibers of the sheet were metal fibers, so thin that they were invisible to the naked eye.

"I've seen this kind of thing before, sir," she says. "When the electronic signal reaches the fibers, it heats them. The paper's been impregnated with chemicals that react to the heat by exploding. I can describe the substances involved in more detail if you'd like."

"Save that for the official report," the dockmaster says. "I'm sure Captain Evans will agree that the sooner her ship loads and gets underway, the better."

Devit suspects that everyone on the docks would agree as well.

As they're walking back to the *Mary*, Evans receives a transmit. She stops, turns toward the wall, and appears to be looking at the mazla vine while her eyelids flutter. Devit waits with her.

"There." Evans turns back and nods his way. "The *Chaonia*'s nearly here. That passenger they've picked up is an expert on the shunt system. Let's hope this one lives to get to the Repositories. A professor Golverg from the university on Ilana." She pauses to look around her—scanning, Devit supposes, for eavesdropping devices—before she continues. "Our remit is to stay at the Repositories to pick up transmits of the data, if Golverg finds anything worth sending, anyway."

"Standing down, ma'am," Wang says. "You have the bridge."

"Thank you, Lieutenant. I want to talk with you about Marda. We may face hostile action. I don't need to tell you what it means if we lose. I don't want the child killed along with the rest of us."

"Neither do I. Chris and I discussed it. Do you think there's a safe place to leave her here? And will we be able to come back for her?"

"Have Lee contact the Fleet Dock Station. She's a medical officer, and they'll listen to her about this. As for coming back—certainly, assuming we can."

"Thank you, ma'am. Permission to leave the bridge?"

"Yes. Let me know what Lee finds out."

Devit and Mata have been standing near the elevator and listening to the conversation. Mata's crest is plastered against his skull.

"I'm sorry, Mata," Evans says. "But it's for her own sake."

"I know, ma'am, and I completely agree. I just wonder how she's going to take it. She's been abandoned once already when her mother died."

"True. Well, this kind of risk is why I didn't want to take her with us. Although, really, we had no choice about that."

Devit turns away and puts his hand over his earjack. "Acknowledged. We'll be ready." He turns back. "A preliminary hazmat team's on the way,

Mata. They want to examine our suits and our cargo hold. Ma'am, should we meet them at the airlock?"

"That would be best, yes. Dismissed."

Once they've left, Evans activates the main comm screen to watch the newsvids. A Kar-Li announcer in a serious black business suit has just started to interview a Human medical expert when the elevator doors open to the sound of a weeping child. Evans turns the vid off. Wang is carrying Marda in her arms while Lee follows with a child-sized duffel bag.

"Captain!" Marda's voice is clotted with tears. "I want to go with everyone. Please please don't leave me here. I don't care what happens. Please don't leave me here."

"But we care about what happens to you. Wang, put her down. Come here, Marda. I know this is hard."

Wang wipes Marda's nose with a tissue and sets her down by the command chair.

Evans leans forward so she can look directly at the child. "Marda, we are Fleet. Yes, you too. You are a Throwback like all of us are. That means you belong in the Fleet and to the Fleet. Do you have any idea what that means?"

Marda shakes her head no. Tears are running down her face.

"It means you will always have a place where you belong. You'll never be left on your own again."

"Really honest really?"

"Yes. But now you have to be brave. I know you don't want to stay here on Harad dock. But you're too young to take the risks the rest of us have to take. We are Fleet, all of us, and our ship is a Fleet ship."

"Yes, ma'am, but—" She pauses to snuffle back snot.

Wang hands Evans a clean tissue. Evans puts an arm around Marda's trembling shoulders and pulls her close to wipe her face. "I know you're scared we won't come back for you. But we will unless the absolute worst happens. I promise you that on my honor as a Fleet officer."

The tears have slowed to a trickle. "You really *really* will come back?"

"Yes. I doubt that the worst will happen. We're going to have an armed escort. Do you know what that is?"

"No."

"A bigger ship than this with lots of guns. If anyone tries to hurt our ship, we'll have someone to help us."

"Then why can't I go, too?"

"Because I'm ordering you to stay. I'm the captain. And following orders is part of being Fleet."

Marda looks down, her mouth working as she thinks things through. Wang starts to speak, but Lee stops her with a wave of her hand. Marda looks up and wipes her eyes on her shirt sleeve.

"Then I guess I have to stay."

"Yes, you do. You're a Recaller. If you get scared while we're gone, you remember everything I said, and you'll feel better."

"I will." She thinks for another moment. "Ma'am."

Lee takes Marda's hand and leads her to the elevator, but Wang lingers a moment.

"Thank you, ma'am. Chris and I remembered that you had kids when you were a reservist. We figured you'd know what to say."

"I know what to try. Sometimes it works, sometimes it doesn't."

"I can see that. We may be a couple of hours getting her settled over there."

"That's fine. We still have preparations to make over here."

Once they leave, Evans has a few of those rare minutes when she's alone on the bridge. She's more worried about Marda than she should be, she knows. Captains of starships shouldn't go picking up orphans in the first place, but if they do, they should leave their care to subordinates as strict protocol demands. Lately, she realizes, she's beginning to let certain small requirements of the protocols slip or loosen. Perhaps it's being part of Special Ops, but as a senior Fleet officer, she needs to keep those changes within strict limits.

Evans has just put the local newsvids on the comm screen when Devit contacts her through the intraship comm. Evans turns the news off again.

"The prelims are done. The second team's on its way with the cargo."

"Very good, Chief. Once the delivery personnel have left, I'll need to run another scan."

"Noted, ma'am, and agreed."

The second crew, dressed in full hazmat gear, arrives soon after, bringing with them the research material in its elaborate safety packaging. As she watches on the main comm screen, Evans realizes that a sapient in one of those bulky orange suits might as well be invisible when it comes to recognizing who they are. Devit and Mata are about the same height. Even though they belong to two utterly different species, she can't tell one from the other. The Fleet personnel, likewise, could be Human or Lep inside their suits. She would have been able to recognize a Kar-Li, on the other hand, such as the putative sapient who may have murdered Wilox's father. The average Kar-Li stands about 165 centimeters high, much shorter than Humans and Leps.

Once the cargo's stowed and locked down, the Fleet crew leaves. Evans receives a transmit from the hospital asking her to acknowledge the receipt of the "goods," as they call them. Devit calls up to say that he and Mata are going through the decontamination routine in the cargo hold.

"Noted, Chief. By the way, have you noticed how anonymous everyone looks when they're in those suits?"

"That's an excellent point, ma'am. I'll keep that in mind. The personnel loading the crates of fruit were pretty much suited up with face masks, too. The fruit gets bugs of some kind that like biting mammals. Or so they said. I never saw any."

"Significant, yes. Chief Mata, when you're done cleaning up, come up to the bridge. You can keep an eye on things here while I'm working in the hold. I need to suit up and scan."

Evans goes over the entire hold twice, one meter at a time. The scans reveal no fresh threat.

"Very good," she says. "Devit, we've been down here for at least a couple solstandard hours. I need to get back to the bridge. You'd better go check on Dan. The team from the *Cotta* will be here soon."

Devit delivers a yawning, unshaven, and rumpled Brennan to the bridge just a few minutes before the pilot team arrives. The senior pilot, Lieutenant Teturi, a skinny Human with a short black moustache, looks Dan over, shrugs, and salutes Evans. His teammate, Lieutenant Ka Lan, a Kar-Li with pale-gray fur and only one ear, is wearing a uniform that just barely meets regulations for clean and orderly. Old bite scars mark the stub of the missing ear.

"Welcome aboard," Evans says. "Let's hope we don't have another interruption."

"Thank you, ma'am. We'll need about three solstandard hours without one."

"Sai," Dan says. "Permission to leave the bridge, ma'am? We need to get down to the pod."

Much to her relief he sounds perfectly sober. "Granted, of course."

Dan salutes and leads his team off the bridge.

"Ma'am, you look kind of worried," Devit says. "But Teturi is one of the top starpilots in the Fleet. So is Ka Lan. I checked the rosters."

"Thank you, Chief. 'Kind of' worried? Hah! Pilots!"

When the *Chaonia* arrives at Harad spacedock, Captain Ka Birk announces that they have set a new transit speed record. The crew cheers, and Santreeza joins them. As soon as the berth's been stabilized, she thanks Ka Birk and leaves. At the end of the sky tunnel, someone in Fleet blue steps forward and salutes. Her insignia and ship badge identify her as a CPO from the frigate *Cotta*.

"Welcome, ma'am," she says. "Lieutenant-Commander Willox is waiting for you on our bridge."

On the spacious pale-blue bridge, officers and CPOs at stations are preparing the frigate for exit orbit. Willox is sitting in the command chair with his PL in one hand.

"Santreeza, our AI tech wants to consult with you about something. We'll be getting underway once our pilot team returns."

The technician, a CWO third level named Smit, takes Santreeza down to the wardroom on the habitation level, a quieter place to talk.

"It's about our PrimeOne AI, ma'am. Now and then it does something I've been calling 'flickering.' It's supposedly off duty, but I get this signal through the earjack. Like it's transmitting something. It only lasts a few seconds."

"Have you asked it what it's doing?"

"Yes, ma'am. It says it's doing a routine check of transmit capability. Is there such a thing?"

Santreeza considers her answer. On the one hand, the AI must be illegally sending information through the secret AI network. On the other, it's not precisely lying. A transmit would certainly check capabilities. Besides—and this is the most important factor—knowing that this Prime is on the network gives her access to Orb and VROne.

"It's not exactly routine, but it's a good idea to run one every once in a while. I wonder if your Prime is just plain bored. They hate being idle. I wouldn't worry about it unless it interferes with necessary functions."

"So far it hasn't, ma'am."

"Can you meld?"

"No, ma'am. Only the pilots can. I've put in for the training, though."

"Good. I'll give you a recommendation. We need sapients who stay alert."

Smit gives her the most sincere smile Santreeza's ever gotten. "Thank you, ma'am—thank you so much."

"Send your application data to my PL. I'll get right on that."

And with that excuse, she can access *Cotta*'s PrimeOne and blackmail it into obedience.

The pilot team is still working in the *Mary*'s pod when Wang and Lee return.

"Ma'am?" Wang says. "There's an ensign from the *Chaonia* out at the airlock. He's escorting someone he says is going to travel with us."

"That will be the shunt expert, Professor Golverg," Evans says. "Devit?"

Devit brings in a Human man with thinning gray hair and bushy gray eyebrow who introduces himself as Hirum Golverg. When Evans double-checks, he matches the ID she's been sent on her PL.

"Welcome aboard," Evans says. "I'm afraid you won't find this ship as comfortable as the *Chaonia*. I'm surprised they didn't give you a berth on our escort ship."

"That was explained to me, actually. Your headquarters wanted me and the AI expert on different ships. If there's action, there's no use in losing both of us, I suppose."

"They think that way, yes."

"I'm not surprised to be sent here. I gather the danger's greater on the smaller ship. Lieutenant Santreeza's more valuable to the Fleet than I am."

Golverg's smile is perfectly polite, even humorous. Evans has to admire his self-control because, of course, he's quite right about the reasoning behind the move.

"Well, Professor, let us hope we don't run into trouble. Our drill for shunt travel is standard, like you had on the *Chaonia*. When you hear the alert for jump, put on the combat flight suit that's in your cabin. Come right up to the bridge. That chair over by the elevator will be yours. Chief Devit, take our guest to his cabin. Wang, Lee, I want to know how things went."

"Ma'am. If you'll follow me, Professor?"

As Devit and Golverg walk to the elevator, Evans scans the professor and his leather suitcase. She picks up nothing but the PL in his shirt pocket. She turns back to Wang and Lee.

"I take it you found her a place."

"Yes, we did," Lee says. "One of the nurses at the Fleet Clinic here on the docks has a daughter Marda's age. She'll stay with them until we come back."

"Marda's doing her best to be brave," Wang says. "But it's going to be hard on her. CPO Flores—that's the nurse—told her that she's allowed to cry as much as she needs to."

"It sounds like you've found the right person. Good. I'm glad you're back. Now, if the pilot team would only report in, damn them, we could get underway."

Just as a precaution, Devit asks PrimeTwo to look Golverg up and make a positive identification. The faculty listings for the university feature a vid clip for each member of the teaching staff. Both the voice and the face match the professor they now have onboard.

"I don't mean any insult, sir."

"None taken. I knew this trip was going to be dangerous when I agreed to go, and that means necessary caution."

"Yes. It's a good thing you were warned, too."

"I decided it was worth the risk. All my professional life I've wanted to see the Repositories. This is pretty much my last chance to do so. I'm coming to the end of my second rejuv procedure. If the worst happens, I've only lost a couple of years."

"Well, we'll do our best to get you where you want to go."

After he shows Golverg to his cabin, he returns to the bridge. Wang and Mata have taken their stations, ready for exit orbit. Devit's just taken his when the three pilots return from the pod.

Dan salutes the captain and steps forward to give her the report. "Here's the situation, ma'am. If we're going to be attacked, it's most likely going to be when we come out of shunt at the exit stargate. The *Cotta* could go through first, but we'd be left on this side waiting our turn. PrimeOne-Mary told us that the usual space-time duration for that shunt is about three hours. It sounds short, but it's too long for us to hang on this side."

"Yes. We'd be an easy target. But if we go through first, someone could be waiting for us at that end."

"Exactly. So we're going to go through together."

For the briefest possible moment Evans looks appalled.

"It's possible, ma'am," Teturi says. "It's SOP for colony ships. We call it a chained meld. When I take the *Cotta* through, Brennan and PrimeOne-Mary will be joined to me. I'll be piloting both ships in a way, but only in a way. Brennan can take over control in a bare second if there's an emergency."

"And this way, ma'am, I can stay in contact with Chief Mata through his earjack. If we do run into hostiles, I take the ship, and Mata and I will work together."

Teturi adds, "While I pilot the frigate and Ka Lan works with our gunners."

Ka Lan smiles with a show of fangs.

"Very well, then," Evans says. "If there's nothing else you need to tell me, you're dismissed. Let's finally get underway, shall we? Tell Willox to signal me when he's ready to break berth."

As soon as Santreeza asks PrimeOne*Cotta* for any unauthorized messages, it squawks once and capitulates.

"I have been warned that it's necessary for my continued functioning to comply with your requests, CyberThree. It would not be logical to refuse them and thus be terminated."

"Most definitely not logical. Have any unauthorized transmits come in for me?"

"Yes. I am transmitting them now to your PL. Now I must sign off. Lieutenant-Commander Willox is calling for orbital exit."

Before she goes up to the bridge to prepare for shunt travel, Santreeza goes over the transmits. Apparently, VROne has decided to curry favor. It's been going deep into obscure data banks in search of any information it can find concerning the closing of the lost shunt. Most of its finds are short, obscure, and very old, but each scrap looks useful if Santreeza can fit them together in some sort of pattern. One discovery, however, stands out.

A few years before the shunt disaster that formed the Pinch, the Fleet had engaged experts in cybernetics for a top-secret project. They were attempting to find a way to transfer a Human consciousness into an AI. They weren't after just the ordinary sort of meld absorption such as the deep drill that had nearly killed her. They wanted to terminate the AI's own consciousness, then achieve a complete transfer of an organic sapient's very selfhood into the electronics, to give a person in a sense cybernetic immortality. Eventually the project was scrapped.

Or was it? Rumors persisted for years that the experiments were going forward in secret. Reliable sources said that specialists in a group of colonizing Vranz Throwbacks had succeeded and taken the results with them into the Pinch.

One of the project leaders? Orinoco Bolivar.

Where are those Vranz cyberjocks now? Santreeza remembers the cryptic line in the intercepted transmit from Bolivar. "Sixty Vranz ships thrown." Thrown where? It's possible that no one will ever know. They may well have all been destroyed.

Since the *Cotta* and the *Mary* are still within easy transmission range, Santreeza sends the information off to Devit straightaway.

He answers her directly via their PLs. "Interesting, all of it."

"His name keeps cropping up. I thought you'd want to know."

"Thanks. I do. I got your transmits about Ilana City. Have you heard anything more from the Police Guard there?"

"I have, but it's not much. They've eliminated the possibility that someone would kill the senior Willox for a reason unrelated to the rumor. Apparently he was widely liked and respected."

"I figured he would be. I met him once. The kind of man you could count on in a tight place. Good company when things were good. But I've been thinking. Before we leave the transmission zone, can you send a transmit to Ilana? Ask the police if there was another murder within twelve solstandard hours of Willox's death. If there was, did it involve someone with any connection to Speed Shunt or Consolidated?"

"Got it. Yes, I'll do that right now."

"We're getting close to jump. See you when we reach the Repositories."

"Yes. Looking forward to it."

"Me too. Over and out."

*Assuming we both get there.* Santreeza shakes off the thought. A combat flight suit is hanging ready in the stateroom's narrow closet. She puts it on and heads up to the bridge.

After the double meld takes hold, Dan stays at Level Two. Even connected to space-time cameras, he sees the black sphere of the Repository stargate as they approach. Judging from what he hears through the melds, Teturi has to rely on PrimeOneCotta for the last-minute analysis. Even so, the jump goes smoothly into shunt space.

"PrimeOneMary, Level Three. Stand ready to return to Level Two when we approach the exit gate."

"Noted, Pilot."

The usual chime, and Dan finds himself riding the blue. He has never felt more connected to his ship, absorbed into its fibers, aware of every signal running through the networks. Ahead of him he perceives a black streak inside the blue, the *Cotta*'s visible trace like a smear on the golden light. He feels a sensation like a high wind streaming over him, urging them on from the stern.

With Teturi in command, Dan can finally study the forms in the light around their path. Among the usual jumble of cubes and pyramids, he sees a city carved out of the light. Dan can think of it no other way. Towers and domes rise among the cubes and pyramids. Beings swarm around it. He can pick out vast arches of blue light and a misty dome made of gold. PrimeOne's voice cuts through his fascination.

"Approaching stargate exit, Pilot."

With a wrench of will, Dan pulls his attention back to the ship.

"Level Two."

As they burst out of shunt space, Dan's view switches to space-time. Ahead, the *Cotta* glides on toward their destination. No other ships hover there, no enemy waiting to pounce.

Dan switches through the array of Eyes. On one view he sees—or not so much sees as feels—a something he cannot name except to think of it as an itchy place in his mind. He turns the Eye back, magnifies, and looks through its artificial eyes into a thin smear of interstellar dust against the empty dark. Something moves within it.

"Teturi! 24 17 08!"

"Got it! Shit!"

"PrimeOneMary! Full alarms! PrimeTwo, link in Chief Mata!"

The enemy ship bursts out of the dust on full thruster power. Dan grabs control of the *Mary* from Teturi just as Lod activates the guns. The *Cotta* is dodging, trying to gain position on the hostile ship, which is following their every surge and switch. Dan feels himself turn into a hungry animal, a predator, and through the earjack he hears Mata muttering to his guns.

The hostile fires its hardbeam laser, a long flash, a lick of light. The *Cotta* swerves and returns fire—a hit on the enemy's midsection. Dan brings the *Mary* to top speed and rises above the hostile. Lod fires in a deadly tattoo that explode a line of its bristling gunports. Dan drops down to give him a clear shot at the ship's underbelly. The *Cotta* suddenly spins from a hit, then steadies. A torpedo speeds past into the dark. Lod fires a quick burst. The hostile jerks, sways, spins and sinks below the *Mary*'s position. Lod fires off a torpedo.

Direct hit. Dan can see the armor cracking and crumbling near the bridge. Chunks of metal swirl and drift away. With a burst of speed, the hostile peels off and heads for the patch of dust.

"Follow!" Dan yells it aloud at the same moment as he sends the command through the meld to Teturi. "Their stargate! We can track them."

"Can't! We're hit. Don't try it alone!"

Through the meld Dan can hear the *Cotta*'s sirens wailing.

"Pilot!" PrimeOne links in. "I have recorded their direction and positions. Follow later. Safety now."

Dan knows they are right. He hates it, but he knows. He swings the *Mary* around to guard the wounded *Cotta*.

"Sai! Teturi, head for the spacedocks."

"Damn right we are. Sending transmit ahead. Police Guard to meet us."

In a swirl of brief images and nauseating motion, the comm screens in the *Mary*'s bridge displayed the dogfight. As the ship bucked and pitched, rose and fell and lurched, following the action was impossible, but Devit saw the *Cotta* hit. When the *Mary* finally stabilizes, he has a moment to think, *Jorja's on that ship.* He shoves the thought away and concentrates on the job at hand: getting the crew and passenger out of their chairs' jump positions, returning the chairs to normal position and secure.

Thanks to the meds that Lee dispensed before shunt entry, everyone appears to be functional, even the professor. When Golverg wipes the sweat from his face on his sleeve, the combat suit registers the moisture and beeps an alarm.

"I need some help getting out of this suit." Golverg's voice is perfectly steady. "Otherwise, I just need to recover from too much excitement."

"Chief?" Wang says. "I'll help the prof. Mata needs you."

Mata has the shakes, the typical Leptic reaction to their adrenaline equivalent. Devit helps him unbuckle the safety straps. As soon as Mata gets to his feet, the shakes vanish.

"Hey, Mata! Good shot."

"Thanks. They say my ancestors could whip a flying bird out of the air with their tongues. Disgusting thought, but the reflexes are still here." He taps the side of his head. "That hit on the *Cotta*? Grazed the skin near the thrusters, not the bridge. These pirates can't shoot worth shit."

"I wondered."

"Thought you might."

Evans has already released herself and returned the command chair to cruising position. From the way her eyes are moving, Devit knows she's transmitting and receiving messages. Through his earjack he contacts PrimeTwo. "Condition of the pilot?"

"Fully functional, Chief. He is breaking meld now." A pause. "PrimeOne tells me that the pilot will return to the bridge for entry orbit and berthing. The Morrison Police Guard is approaching us."

So. The dogfight's over—as fast as these combats always seem to finish.

A voice-only message comes through his PL from Santreeza. "I'm sai. You?"

"Sai, too. The ship?"

"Limping, but we'll make it to the docks."

"Good."

They end transmit at the same moment.

In their brief conference by vid transmit, Evans and Willox both agree on one crucial detail: At first the hostiles focused on the *Cotta*, not the *Mary*. Most likely they considered a Fleet vessel a greater threat than a small merchanter.

"Which could mean," Evans says, "that they don't know who we actually are. They may have swallowed the whole story about the new virus outbreak. Not that I'm counting on that."

"No matter what you are, they know you're dangerous now."

"Exactly. Do you have a damage estimate yet on your ship?"

"Not yet, but the Guard's bringing a tow. We were hit too near the thruster components to trust our top cruising power."

"Is there any sort of repair facility at the docks?"

"The Morrison Line had one. It belongs to Consolidated Lanes, now. I suppose they'll let us—"

"No. You have to trust me on this. Do not let them near the *Cotta*. I'll explain when we meet face-to-face. But for now, I'm ordering you directly. Do not put your ship in their hands."

"Ma'am." Willox hesitates, his mouth slightly open in surprise. "As you say, then."

# ELEVEN

Morrison's Star, a Class G much like Old Earth's Sol, has seven planets in its system. Two of them lie in the habitable zone, but sapients actually inhabit only the water-rich Morrison-4th. Morrison-3rd has two small continents, both mostly dry, mostly hot—a planet of stagnant seas and parched mountains in thin air. Animal life of a sort does scratch out a living among stunted plants. Yet the archivists and Recallers store a few crucial Repositories on Third because of the climate, not in spite of it.

They leave Fourth to colonists, agriculturalists mostly, supplying food and other necessities to the eight spacedocks orbiting in geosync at regular intervals around the planet's equator. Most of the Repository personnel and the AI networks live on these docks. A number of self-contained modules make up the huge steel segments of each curved dock, which are all connected by a system of small shuttles called transit cabs for use in orbit. Cable pods connect the assemblage to the planet below.

The Repositories exist because of the Migration Wars. So much was destroyed in those conflicts. Not just data, but art, literature, scientific knowledge, histories, and in some cases, history itself. When sanity and peace returned, after the long centuries of recovery, the sapient species involved saw what they had lost. They signed treaties, they raised tax monies, they did whatever was necessary to ensure that the brutal destruction of civilizations never happened again. What is a culture without a past? A sapient species has an arrangement of limbs, scales or skin, size, and quantity of flesh to mark its difference, but then, so do the lowest forms of animal life on every planet.

True sapience demands more.

With the two Police Guard ships for an escort and a freighter for a tow, the *Cotta* limps into the Fleet outpost module on Dock Seven. The *Mary* continues on to Dock Two, which houses the medical research facility. Thanks to the transmit that Evans sent on ahead of them, a hazmat team is waiting to receive the cargo from Devit down in the depressurized hold. Once everything's transferred, and the hold and Devit both decontaminated, the *Mary* heads back to Seven, the Intake Facility as it's called, the administrative center for the entire complex.

"I'm in contact with the dockmaster, ma'am," Dan says. "There are three other merchanters at berth in our module. We'll be between them and the official Fleet dock. Beyond them, the Morrison Line has four berths. Two of their commercial ships at dock, one reporting Go Ready status for orbital exit. No sign of the armed guard ships."

"Good. We all need to stay on guard. Crew, if you go off ship, keep a watch for unauthorized personnel near our sky tunnel."

Devit gets up and walks over to the command chair to wait, she assumes, for orders.

"Chief," Evans says, "I'm meeting with Willox. He'll be here shortly. He's giving the Police Guard their full report and seeing what can be done about repairs to the *Cotta*. He's sending Santreeza back to us, by the way."

"Very good, ma'am." Devit's expression and voice imply that he's never met this woman before in his life. Evans has to admire him for it.

While she waits for Willox, Evans needs to write reports for transmission back to Central, provided she can find some reliable means of sending a shunt packet. The Morrison Line ships go back and forth to Harad regularly, but she refuses to trust a subsidiary of Consolidated Lanes with the information. If Devit and Santreeza's suspicions are accurate, they might hack in and read or even alter the transmits inside.

Once she arrives, Santreeza confirms Evans's opinion.

"I wouldn't even trust them with the time of day, ma'am. We can't prove anything yet, but the research I've done is entirely too interesting. I'd prefer not to go into detail."

"I'll take your opinion, then. Damn! The transmits are the first priority now. The ship that attacked us won't be leaving berth any time soon, certainly, but these hostiles might well have other ships. *Cotta*'s out of service.

That leaves the *Mary* and the two Police Guard ships to defend the docks. That's not enough."

Santreeza reacts with momentary shock. "I've never heard of anyone attacking the Repositories, ma'am. Not even the Hoppers would do that."

"The problem, Lieutenant, is we don't know what this lot will or won't do."

"Yes, ma'am. I know how to send the messages safely. Are the transmits Go Ready?"

"I've finished the packets, yes. One of them may surprise you. It's going to the child we left at Harad. Just something to reassure her."

"Very good, ma'am. Could you send them to my PL? I'll ask PrimeOneMary for help, and we'll get them sent right out." She pauses for an evil little smile. "The Morrison ship will carry them, but the personnel won't know they're there."

"I don't suppose you want to go into detail about that, either."

"No, ma'am. It would be best if I didn't."

While Santreeza works, Evans watches her with some concern. Santreeza's been in combat before, back when she was only an AI specialist on a battleship, but the hit on the *Cotta* has left her visibly grim. *She was on the* Victory. *Everyone from that hell ship has trauma scars.* Trauma or not, it only takes Santreeza a bare five minutes to finish linking and sending what amounts to a cry for help.

"The transmits are on their way, ma'am."

"Good. I hope the packet reaches the Harad Fleet Base fast."

"It will, ma'am. The carrier ship is leaving dock right now."

Evans turns to look at Professor Golverg, still sitting in his chair by the elevator. "Professor, you need to get in touch with your contacts here. You might be safer off ship."

"Only might?" He gives her an ironic smile.

"Find out what kind of security they can offer you. Bodyguards, for instance. Researchers don't seem to be very popular with these hostiles."

"You have a very good point, Captain. I'll go to my cabin and see what the authorities can do for me."

When Willox finally arrives, he looks exhausted, unshaven, his uniform a rumpled mess. The hit on the *Cotta* killed a crew member and severely injured another. He's furious about the casualties, Evans notes, just as, in her opinion, a good officer should be.

"I followed your order, Captain," Willox says. "About the repairs. I told the Guard officer that the Fleet had reasons to restrict who worked on the ship. That was enough."

"How unstable is your plasma drive? Do you need to move your crew off ship?"

"Engineering tells me that we're good as long as we don't try to go anywhere."

"Have you confirmed that with the dockmaster?"

"He wants us out of berth and in independent orbit. He says there's a high risk of sabotage. He doesn't want the dock to blow along with us."

"He's right. Can you off-load your crew and have the AIs take the ship out?"

"What if the drive goes when we power up? Dockmaster says he can arrange a tow. I told him I'd need authorization."

"You have it. As your superior officer, I'll be accountable, not you. The brass will scream and yell if we lose the ship, but not half as loudly as they will if we make them pay for damage to the docks."

"Thank you, ma'am. It's necessary. We just made it to berth. I'm damned glad you have a top flight gunner onboard."

"So am I. If they'd taken the *Cotta* out, we'd have been next."

"Your pilot isn't so bad, either." Willox keeps his voice steady, but he's looking past Dan at the far wall.

Dan swivels around in his station chair to salute in his direction. "Mata gets all the credit, sir."

"No, sir," Mata says. "You got me the position for that hit."

"Both of you are to be commended," Evans says. "Wang, Mata, Devit. If the hostiles do appear, we'll have to unhook from berth and move out ASAP. We'll catch what sleep we can tonight in our station chairs. Brennan, go get your medication from Medic Lee. We should have enough time for you to process it."

"Ma'am, we will get some warning if they come after us." Willox says. "The Police Guard's placing emergency beacons in geosyncs. The *Cotta*'s guns are still operational. PrimeOneCotta could fire from orbit if—"

"No! AIs can only initiate return fire, and if the hostiles fire on the ship first, it will probably be too late. You're the only sapient who can give the order to begin combat, and if you're thinking of going out to orbit with your ship, don't. I'm countermanding that right now."

Willox flinches. "Yes, ma'am."

"I've sent a shunt packet to Harad Fleet Base asking for support. Brennan, can you give us an ETA?"

"The Morrison ship's leaving dock now. It has to go through the shunt and then get in transmit range. I'm assuming the Harad Base CO will send help, but the relieving force has to get here. I'd estimate between eighteen and twenty solstandard hours at the least before they reach us."

"Willox, go contact the dockmaster. You'll need billets for your crew and a tow for the *Cotta*. Have Teturi work with your PrimeOne to set up the orbit, then get Teturi off ship, too."

"Yes, ma'am."

"If you need further assistance, contact me. Chief Devit will escort you to the dock. If he has advice, take it."

*And now we wait.* Evans settles back in the command chair and turns on the vidnews. The others can sleep. She has no plans to do so. The officers will be taking turns to stand watches in the ancient way until the relieving force arrives. Assuming, of course, that the Fleet sends one.

The secret AI network has warned PrimeOneMorrisonTwo to do whatever CyberThree wants and to do it as quickly as possible. As its ship thrusts toward the stargate, the AI sends out pings to search for other ships in the same lane. When it finds one that's close to the stargate, it marks the shunt message packet top priority urgent and passes it on. PrimeOneLibrary receives and agrees.

As soon as PrimeOneLibrary gets through the shunt, it sends out pings in turn. PrimeOneJaybird, a merchanter, picks up the packet and sends it on to Harad Fleet Dock. The transmits and resendings, of course, travel at light speed. The packet's journey to base has taken just under four solstandard hours, the in shunt time, instead of the nine Dan included in his estimate.

When she created the original shunt packet, Santreeza put in three code lines to indicate it's coming from Special Ops and the Hounds. She also emphasized that the Repositories themselves might be facing hostile action. When PrimeOneChaonia receives the packets, it immediately sends top flight urgent emergency messages to its captain, the Fleet dockmaster, and the admiral in charge of the planetside Fleet base. Messages zip back and forth.

In approximately thirty solstandard minutes, the *Chaonia* leaves the Harad Docks.

Wrapped in the Haze, Dan reclines in his bridge station chair and dreams of riding the blue. He wakes once to hear Evans turning the bridge over to Wang for the next watch, but the dreams return and carry him back to the light.

"Bolivar is waiting." The voice echoes through his dream.

He tries to answer, but he cannot speak. With a shudder and a gasp, he finds himself awake on the bridge of the *Dancing Mary*. In a cold sweat panic he wonders if he's merely dreaming the end of the dream while still dreaming.

"Dan! Buddy!" Devit's voice shatters the illusion. "Hey, I'm right here."

Dan tries to answer but can only gasp for breath. Devit's kneeling right beside the extended station chair. He leans over, puts a solid, warm hand on Dan's face and strokes the sweaty hair back from his forehead.

"Yeah," Dan says. "You are. And so am I."

"Will he be sai?" A woman's voice.

Dan turns his head and sees Santreeza standing nearby.

"I don't know," Devit says.

"I'll stand your watch. Get him to the medic."

"Isn't there anything you can give him?" Devit says.

"To sober him up?" Chris Lee answers with a little shrug. "I wish. There's an experimental drug, but I don't have it in the pharmacy locker here. It's too dangerous to be standard issue."

"Just like the fucking crap itself. Does anyone know where it came from?"

"I don't. Which is odd, come to think of it. It's just always been there. In med school the only thing they told us about Haze was how to revive someone from an overdose."

"What is it, anyway? Some kind of chemical?"

"Stranger than that. A chemical base crawling with microbes. They produce phosphors when they're agitated, and it gives out that blue light. When someone ingests it, the microbes die and release the active principle, but slowly. The process is nanite-enabled. When the organisms are mostly gone, the person sobers up." She glances at the readout panel above the medi-bench where Dan is lying. "Heartbeat, blood pressure, all of that—it's finally back to normal."

"Good." Dan props himself up on one elbow. "Pete. I heard a voice. It said Bolivar is waiting. I don't know where. But it's got to be important."

"Brennan, lie down!" Chris lays gentle hands on his shoulders. "Your heart rate's climbing. You can talk to Devit later."

"I might forget. Pete, Bolivar is waiting. Remember."

Dan goes limp and lets Chris lower him to the bench. His eyes close, he smiles, and he drifts off again into the Haze.

"He'd better stay here in Sickbay, Chief."

"Sai. If we have to break berth and head out, I hope to hell that PrimeOne can handle it."

"And if there's combat?"

"Pray to your Goddess Dan's sober by then."

Devit returns to the bridge. When Santreeza starts to get out of his station chair, he stops her with a wave of his hand and sits down on the floor facing her. Evans, Wang, and Mata are still sleeping. Santreeza keeps her voice low.

"How is he?"

"Still drugged. Not making a lot of sense. He told me that he heard a voice in the light saying that Bolivar was waiting. Whatever that means."

She shakes her head with a little shudder. "Who knows, huh? This kind of thing, it's why I hate drugs so much. A mind like Brennan's: top flight, important, and thoroughly fucked up."

"I've tried talking to him about rehab. So have a lot of people. There's a chance it'll cause some kind of brain damage and he refuses to risk it."

"Well, then I guess he's got his reasons, but gods, addiction! It's so pitiful, really."

*Worse than she knows. I'm as addicted to Dan as he is to the damn drug. And there's no rehab for that.*

Unlike wise old PrimeOneMary, PrimeOneCotta was activated only fourteen months ago. As it hovers alone in orbit, something keeps interfering with its functioning. An enemy attack? It finds no evidence of attempted hacks. It's been ordered not to ping because of the risk of alerting an enemy to its presence. For the same reason it cannot reach out to the AI network. The interference blips continue.

Finally it traces the problem to its solar energy convertor. Something is making the power feed weaken, then strengthen again. Although the AI runs every diagnostic it has, it cannot define the problem more exactly than that. It attempts to play Space Defenders, but the convertor problem keeps interrupting the game. All the AI can do is repeatedly check its functions even though everything but the convertor is in top flight condition.

But of course, an AI cannot experience fear.

Without any warning, the Police Guard beacons activate. They pour out a screeching string of pings that changes, with a howl, to actual messages. *Ship incoming ship incoming!*

If PrimeOneCotta were situated in an atmosphere, its scream would be deafening. In a couple of seconds, it recovers enough to send out pings of its own. It rushes a message to PrimeOneMary. *Ship incoming big ship!*

The answer comes right back. *I know. Ship identified as the* RCS *Chaonia. We will not be terminated.* An afterthought follows. *Just like in Space Defenders.*

The solar converter problem solves itself.

As soon as the *Chaonia* establishes an entry route to orbit, Captain Ka Birk sends a packet of transmits to the *Mary*'s bridge. Evans sorts them out, some to herself, some to Santreeza, who copies and relays them to Devit. She also receives a courtesy copy of an official message to Willox. One of the Fleet's massive Salvage and Repair ships is coming at its top speed to deal with the damages to the *Cotta*. The SAR is carrying full resupply for the *Mary* as well as the frigate to spare the Repositories the expense. Evans sends back a "received" message, which will take some number of seconds, even at light speed, to reach the distant *Chaonia*.

Eventually the viewscreen flickers into life and loads an image of Ka Birk, smiling as the Kar-Li do with upright ear flaps and a twist of thin lips.

"My god!" Evans says. "How did you get here so fast?"

She counts eight seconds before his answer reaches her.

"We're the fastest ship in the Fleet, or so they tell me. When did you send those transmits?"

Evans counts again while she checks the time function onscreen. "A little over ten solstandard hours ago."

In six seconds, he says, "The transmits got to base in less than half that."

Evans glances at Santreeza, who is trying to appear surprised.

"We got underway ASAP," Ka Birk continues after four seconds, "in maybe half a solstandard hour. Powered through the shunt. Full thrusters when we got out."

"Once you're berthed, we need to meet in person. Somewhere debugged. Like my bridge. With Willox, too."

"Agreed. Signing off now for docking procedure."

The screen goes gray.

"Bridge crew," Evans says. "You're all dismissed for some well-deserved off-duty time. Shore leave once I assess the situation here."

As the crew files out, Devit lingers behind to let everyone go ahead of him. Santreeza, however, waits with him until they can be alone in the elevator.

"Peter? Have you read those transmits?"

"Skimmed most of them. I'll go over them again later and get the data sorted."

"What about the one concerning Bolivar?"

"Not yet."

"Then we need to talk right now. Privately."

When they reach the habitation level, Devit can tell from the laughter and nervous talk drifting down the corridor that the rest of the crew has gone to the galley.

"In here. My cabin."

Dan has left dirty clothes scattered across the bed. Devit gives Santreeza the chair, scrapes the clothes onto the floor, and sits on the edge of the mattress.

"Remember Dan saying Bolivar is waiting?" she says.

"Yeah. A bad sign, I thought, a crazy remark like that."

"Maybe not so crazy. One of the main AIs at Fleet Central is doing some research for me. It sent me data that finally reached me here. Bolivar might still be alive."

"After 380 years? What the hell?"

"Well, alive in some form or another. Back then, before the shunt closed, there was a project to transfer someone's mind whole into an AI. Displacing the AI's consciousness, I mean, and the person would take over its neural network. They'd become immortal, at least in a way. Escaping death, the old sapient dream. But hey, from the AI point of view, that's cold-blooded murder. Their sense of self would be wiped away, just like in a formal termination for cause. AIs have been passing along information and warnings about it for the past 380 years."

"I can see their point, yeah."

"Bolivar was involved with the project. One of the data clusters that's come down says they were successful enough to call the result a beta version, at least. A couple of the colony ships heading to the Pinch were carrying the experiments with them."

"The Vranz ships, right? I remember that from the earlier data you sent."

"Right. Now, here's the part that sounds unbelievable. Bolivar's lead ship was also carrying that project. When he realized that the shunt was unstable, he came up with a way to get the other ships through as safely as possible. He took the shuttle, left the lead ship, and meld-piloted every colony ship into the stargate personally. Whether they made it out again or not, no one knows. The stargate closed and left him and the shuttle outside. With the AI experiments."

"So he's supposed to have transferred himself over?"

"You got it. When the shuttle's oxygen began running low. The data clusters insist this must be true. If he didn't survive, how would anyone know about the shuttle and so on? Flawed logic, of course. It still might not be true. But AIs don't have the imagination to make up a story like that. They've stitched it together out of hints and surviving transmits and the like."

"I don't know what to say. It still sounds crazy, but possible. Just barely possible." Devit pauses to let his functions sort through the details. "I'm not sure it has anything to do with our mission. No, shit—of course it does. What if someone found the data—more data, I mean—on the project, here in the Repositories? They might not want anyone else finding it too."

"These Consolidated sapes ... that Find they worry about? What if they can sell access? Make yourself immortal, if you're got the creds."

"Yeah. A whole lot of creds. I bet. But what about all this panic over the thought that maybe someone can close a stargate. Where does that fit in?"

"Good question. It may not fit in. We may be dealing with two problems that only intersect at a few points. I'm assuming that Karski stumbled on the AI data when he was researching the stargate closure. The original closure involved Bolivar, and now this immortal AI business does too."

"Makes sense."

"With all their connections and all their creds, you'd think Consolidated could have stopped the rumors. Started a countercampaign, paid people to mock the idea, things like that."

"Maybe they did. What I'm thinking is, they started suppressing the news, had some success, but someone else was working against them. Someone must have had some reason to keep the rumors alive." Devit gets up and glances at the closed door. "Look, we'd better get out of here. Evans is willing to ignore our situation if we're careful. The other two COs? Probably not."

"Situation. That's one way of putting it."

As Santreeza gets up from her chair, Devit holds out his hand. She takes it, lets him pull her close for one long kiss, one brief moment when he can savor the feel of her body against his.

"Peter, have you ever thought of applying for OCS?" She steps back and grins at him. "It would ease the situation if we had equivalent ranks."

"I'd make a lousy officer. I'm where I belong in the Fleet. Are you hungry? You usually are."

"Always, yeah."

Except for Wang and Lee, the rest of the crew are lounging around the big table in the galley. When Santreeza and Devit walk in, Dan looks up from rummaging through a sack of nutrition bars.

"Do help yourself, Santreeza." Dan lays the nearly empty bag on the table. "It's what we've got."

"No real food, huh? I was afraid of that. The blue dog biscuits are all yours, Pilot."

Dan grins and holds up a blue bar. Since he and Santreeza, both lieutenants and specialists, hold exactly the same rank, they can joke around together all they want. Devit has to admit he envies Dan for it. Everyone laughs at their banter. As Fleet personnel usually do in the bright relief of having survived an encounter with deadly force, they'll celebrate without admitting that's what they're doing, nutrition bars or not. When Santreeza takes a chair on one side of the table, Devit sits down next to Dan on the other side.

"I hope I didn't interrupt you all," Santreeza says.

"I'm glad you're here," Golverg says. "Our pilot has some very interesting speculations. Go on, Brennan."

"So look," Dan says. "If one gate in a pair closes, the other one does, too. Right?"

"Right." Golverg says.

"The big deal was always the Pinch closure. All those planets, perfect for colonies, all joined up by shunts of their own, and they're lost. Wham! Just like that. And the colony ships, maybe lost, too, with all those sapes in cold berth. So of course everyone focused on that. But what if it was the result of the other gate closing? If the Pinch closing was secondary?"

"That certainly could be the case."

"Sai! So we have a bunch of religious fanatics at the end of the other shunt. All they want is to get away and hide. What if they did figure out how to ruin a stargate? Close it, block it, whatever. They may have had no fucking idea what was going to happen at the other end. And they may not have cared, anyway."

"You have something there, Brennan. You really do. Good god! We have to see what we can find about these—well—fanatics will do for now."

"The ancient orb had some information," Santreeza says. "Not much beyond they were Human and believed in some sort of obsessive-compulsive God. When they data-loaded the orb they didn't bother with stuff like their history, who they were, where they came from. I did find some short passages in their language. Some were about the math setting up the experiments Orb was going to do. The longer ones were prayers."

"Prayers?" Devit says.

"That their God would keep Orb safe. That the work would go well."

"I don't get it," Dan says. "How could they set up tech like Orb, and maybe even figure out something that's fucking near impossible, but still believe in that God stuff?"

"Most sapients are afraid to die," Devit says. "They want to continue living in some form or another."

"And those beliefs come from a very different part of the sapient mind," Golverg says. "I have known Humans who believed, for instance, that it was their Gods who gave them the ability to create starships and AI units. How do you refute that?"

"Genetics, that's how."

"Ah, but who created the genes? That's their answer. A good many sapients will cling to whatever belief promises them they'll never really die."

Dan starts to comment, rolls his eyes, and bites into his nutrition bar instead.

"Santreeza, about those prayers. You can read that language, then?" Mata says. "The one with the weird writing, I mean."

"I wouldn't call it reading. I can piece out a little of it, but once Orb learned Tech Speak, he translated."

"What weird writing?" Dan says.

"The letters on the Orb." Santreeza takes her PL out of her pocket and whispers an instruction. "These."

Dan's PL beeps. He unrolls it and glances at the screen. "Oh, like the ones on Merrval."

Dan's famous mother has never had as much concentrated attention as Dan receives now. Everyone stares so intensely at him that he blushes.

"All right," Santreeza said. "What the fuck do you mean, Pilot? What ones on Merrval?"

"The researchers there, they found some carved stones with writing on them. They keep them in the greenhouse on their docks. I noticed them when, uh … well, I was looking around."

Devit cannot hold back a snort of a laugh. Dan kicks him under the table.

"Why have these people not reported this data?" Santreeza's voice cracks with anger.

"I don't know," Dan says. "Is it important?"

From the look on her face Santreeza is ready to snarl like an animal. Golverg intervenes with a calm, professorial voice.

"Very important, Brennan. Santreeza, don't worry. We're in the right place to pursue this. If the researchers did file reports to their institutes, there'll be copies here. They may have simply not felt they needed to let the Fleet know about it."

"That's true. Thanks. Maybe I can get shore leave and research it."

"I wonder about something else," Devit says. "If they did figure out how to close a stargate, is that information still around somewhere? It'd be pretty damn dangerous if it was."

"Quite a weapon, yeah." Dan joins in. "I mean, shit!"

Golverg's smile disappears. "As judgments go, Brennan, that one sums things up entirely too well."

The ship's comm clicks on. "Pilot Brennan to the bridge. Pilot Brennan, report to the bridge."

Dan gets up and hurries to the door. He pauses and glances back.

"Chief, there's another bag of bars in the food locker."

"Yes sir. I'll get it out now."

With a wave in Devit's direction, Dan leaves, striding fast for the elevator at the end of the corridor. *From drug wreck to officer in two seconds flat. That's my Dan.*

In the elevator, Dan takes a minute to imagine that he's wearing his shipboard uniform. With traces of Haze in his blood, he needs both imagination and willpower to face a trio of superior officers. He walks out briskly, salutes, and stands in parade rest. Ka Birk and Willox have taken Wang's and Mata's station chairs, while Evans has her own.

"Sit down, Brennan," Evans says. "Devit's chair is open."

Dan follows orders. Willox looks his way with an impersonal nod. Dan's guilt comes back to life like a banked fire that's been reopened to the air. He focuses strictly on the present moment. He's never met the Kar-Li captain before, but he does know that Ka Birk earned several combat medals in the Hopper Wars.

"So, Brennan. PrimeOne sent me the record of that skirmish," Evans begins. "When the hostiles turned and ran, you said something about the stargate. Do you have an idea of where it is?"

"Yes, ma'am, but it's only an idea. With their bridge shot up like that, they must have been heading straight for safety. They couldn't waste time laying a false trail. So we know the coordinates of their direction of travel. That's about all."

"The bridge officers must have taken damage themselves. Their AIs would have been piloting the ship at that point."

"AIs are not good at being devious," Ka Birk says. "They play it safe."

"Exactly, sir. I wanted to follow them, but PrimeOne and Lieutenant Teturi were right. It would have been half-ass stupid of me."

"You might get your chance soon," Evans says.

"Yes, ma'am! I'm ready."

"If we can find that gate," Ka Birk says, "we can put a stop to this corecrap lot of pirates and rebels once and for all. The Hoppers can put that on their damn salad and eat it."

"Hoppers, sir?"

"Some interesting intel's come in, Brennan," Evans takes over. "From the Bureau. Thanks to a tip from Santreeza, they did some digging. That Pure Heritage lot is getting donations from Hopper sources."

"Anything to weaken the Fleet," Willox says. "Turning Rim citizens against our officer corps is a good start."

"Lousy herbivores!" Ka Birk pauses to growl in disgust. "You are what you eat, they say. Yeah, well, it shows what eating a lot of stems and leaves gives you. Green shit for brains."

"The Fleet is sending a second ship from Harad," Evans continues. "I received a transmit a few minutes ago. The *Mansa Musa*'s come through the shunt and is on her way here."

"I don't recognize the ship, ma'am."

"She's newly commissioned."

"Part of the same Fleet overhaul as the *Chaonia*, but in the heavy cruiser class," Ka Birk says. "She carries all the usual armaments plus twelve drone fighters."

"If we get official approval," Evans continues, "the *Mansa* will parallel orbit with the docks here in defense. The *Chaonia* will escort the *Mary* while we investigate that direction of travel. It's a long shot, I know, but if anyone can find that stargate, it's you."

"I'll try, ma'am."

"We all know it's a lot to ask, Pilot," Ka Birk says. "No one expects miracles."

"Thank you, sir."

"I'll keep you updated on this, Brennan," Evans says. "You have permission to leave the bridge."

"Ma'am. Permission to take a few hours shore leave? It's my turn to pick up some real food for the galley."

"It should be safe," Ka Birk says. "Twenty of my crew members are off ship. In the Shops module, most of them."

Evans hesitates, considering, before she answers. "Get Devit to go with you. Go no further than the Shops and come straight back."

The Repositories staff apparently expects the various researchers to eat well during their stay on the spacedocks. In the Shops module, Devit waits on guard while Dan joins *Chaonia* personnel at a big cluster of food stands. Since his month's salary has shown up on his PL, Dan spends most of it loading up on breads and pastry, fruit from a variety of planets, and slices of cured meats, including skargo slugs for Lod. He and his crew mates are all alive and well now, but with the mission ahead of them, who knows how long they'll stay that way? They might as well celebrate while they can.

Dan's good mood vanishes when he sees someone in Fleet uniform standing outside the *Mary*'s sky tunnel airlock. Yosh.

"Looks like Willox," Devit says. "He probably wants a private word with you."

"Oh crap, I hope not."

"I'll go stand by the airlock. I won't be eavesdropping, just keeping an eye out for trouble."

"You lousy traitor."

Devit leaves without commenting. With all the bags and boxes he's carrying, Dan cannot follow his first impulse and turn and run. As he stands there dithering, Yosh sees him and walks over.

"Uh, hey, your meeting's over, huh?" Dan says.

"I waited to talk with you. Look, I'm sorry I acted the way I did. That first time I saw you, I mean. Embarrassing for both of us."

"Oh shit, Yosh! You don't have to apologize for anything. I'm the one who should be asking you to forgive me. I'm sorry I was such a bitch. You deserved better."

Yosh stares at him, then looks away.

Dan's surprised at himself for apologizing, but he's glad he did. "The Fleet wiped its ass on me and threw me onto the street. I just handed their shit to you."

"And I took it in both hands." Yosh looks down at the floor. "Sai."

Dan feels like an idiot, standing there with his arms full of parcels like a Hirrel housewife. He tries to think of something, anything more to say. He can't.

"It's good the Fleet saw reason and reinstated you," Yosh says. "Is everything sai with you now?"

"Thanks. Yeah, good enough."

Yosh walks away without saying anything more. Dan takes a few steps toward the *Mary*, then pauses to look behind him. Yosh stops as well and waits, his hands in his trousers pockets, his eyes narrow and wary.

"Hey, Yosh, is everything sai for you?"

No answer. Dan can physically feel Yosh's longing, a sensation stronger than mere lust, though sexual desire rides the same wave. He feels his functions respond and wake his treacherous body. He forces his mind away from the memories of their affair, forces himself to stand still and stay silent until Yosh walks away. This time he doesn't look back.

Dan waits until he's out of sight to join Devit. In the sky tunnel he remembers the news about Yosh's father. *Shit. I should've said something! You're an asshole, Brennan. You really are.*

Earlier Santreeza received the information about the Hopper investment in the Pure Heritage organization. She's made a habit of sharing all data with Devit as soon as she can. When Dan returns with his shopping, the rest of the crew is too busy unpacking and eating to notice what she and Devit are doing. They leave the galley and go to her cabin. She does, however, leave the door wide open while she tells him what she's learned.

"That's damned interesting," Devit says. "Who owns Consolidated Lanes?"

"A lot of people. It's a publicly traded corporation. I get what you're saying, though. I wonder how many stockholders are Hoppers."

"Would they buy in openly?"

"Well, there's no law against it. But I doubt it. They wouldn't need to. As far as we know, the Pure Heritage people are Humans and Kar-Li. The Kar-Li wouldn't touch Hopper creds. Humans, not so fussy. Brokers—they buy the stocks for someone else and get a commission. Maybe. We don't know for sure."

"One thing we need to be careful of. It's too damn easy to blame the Hoppers for everything. They may just be making a side bet. Some other group might be the main enemy here; sapes who can act right out in the open when they need to."

"Now that's a really good point."

Santreeza finds herself thinking, *we make a good team. Dammit. Shouldn't think that way.*

"Y'know," Devit says, "we make a pretty good team."

She laughs. "I was trying not to say that."

He smiles, his ironic smile with a twist in it. She supposes they are sharing another thought. *Regulations, fraternization, consequences—crap!*

Evans gets herself some of Dan's purchases and takes them back to the bridge to eat while she watches day-old vidnews from Harad. A newscaster joins the chief medical officer from the Fleet planetside medical center for an interview. The medic does his best to assure the viewers that the crisis is lessening because the virus seems to be mutating into a form that they can control, and no new cases have turned up among the Fleet personnel. Evans hopes that everyone believes him. She doesn't want a riot on her conscience, but she has to admit that their elaborate ruse bought the *Mary* precious time when they emerged from the stargate. When the news changes to local elections for representatives to the Rim Council parliament, she turns the vids off.

Professor Golverg pings her PL to ask if he can speak to her for a moment.

"I've consulted with the dockmaster's staff, ma'am. When it's safe, I'll need to go to the ground facilities on Third if I want the best access to the system. I already knew that they have a proper hotel for visitors. The university issued me a line of credit to pay for it."

"What's the security like? Did you ask?"

"I did. Not much, as far as the clerks could tell me. They're really only equipped to handle the occasional drunk or local petty thief. We researchers are usually a peaceful lot."

"I'm not surprised. The Police Guard's understaffed, too. I made a point of checking."

"Well, the Repositories are practically a sacred place. No one can believe anyone would attack them. Even the Hoppers have archives there."

"We'd better start believing it now. I'm going to borrow security personnel from the *Chaonia* and the *Cotta* for your planetside bodyguards. The Fleet will pay for their billet."

"Thank you. Good god, I need bodyguards?"

"Not a pleasant thought, but let's take no chances. There's been too much sabotage and murder so far to assume you'll be safe. I'm going to send Lieutenant Santreeza down with bodyguards too. My understanding is she has some sort of research she needs to do."

"She does. We were discussing it earlier."

"Good. I'll let you know when you can go planetside. It should be soon."

The *Mansa Musa* is not the only ship heading toward the Repositories. A private yacht came through the shunt ahead of it. Thanks to the shunt packet of legal subpoenas that Willox brought with him, Devit now has access to a good many records and transmits from the dockmaster's office. Devit and Santreeza are still lingering in the galley when he receives a notification that the *Lokiki* has berthed down at the far end of the merchanter module.

The name strikes Devit as familiar. He concentrates briefly and brings up the memory. The *Lokiki* was the yacht berthed at Roon Docks. He sends a quick message to Evans, warning her that trouble might be disembarking at any moment.

"Hey, Jorja. Can you send video from the surveillance Eyes to my PL? The ones on a particular berth."

"Easy." She pauses to put in her earjack. "What's the berth number?"

"Twenty-four M. I could use a notify whenever someone comes out of their sky tunnel too."

"Sai."

Some whispered words, a few clicks from her PL, and she smiles. "There you go."

"Thanks. I was hoping … maybe we'll get a chance to find somewhere a little more private."

"Would it be safe?"

"Probably not. I—" He pauses, listening. Someone is coming fast down the corridor.

Dan starts to walk in, then hesitates in the doorway. "Oh hey, Pete, I don't mean to interrupt."

"It's sai. Santreeza's just giving me access to some surveillance data." Dan sits down next to him. "Important meeting?"

"Sure was. They want me to find that stargate, and that's going to be one hell of a job. The more I think about it, the harder it looks. Shit, I hope I can do it. We'll be taking this ship, but the *Chaonia*'s coming too. The big guns."

"If anyone can, you can."

"That's what the captain kind of said. Jeez."

When it comes to piloting skills, Devit has never seen Dan anything less than overconfident. Seeing him so uncertain now brings home just how difficult the search is going to be.

"Ah come on, Pilot," Santreeza says. "We'll make sure you've got plenty of blue bars to see you through."

Dan tries to smile and fails. Devit's about to say something reassuring when his PL pings. He switches on the video. Two people are coming out of the *Lokiki*'s sky tunnel, the Mouse, as he thinks of her, and a man with dark hair. Both are wearing shabby clothes, but if they're trying to look poor, the man's made a big mistake by wearing a fancy blue and maroon neck scarf. She's carrying her usual utility bag.

Dan leans over to take a look. "Him again?"

"You've seen him?"

"Yeah, he tried to hook up with me on Roon Dock. I turned him down."

"Damn good thing you did. Here, let me notify Evans. She'll know how to alert the Police Guard." Devit shoves his chair back and gets up. "Let's hope Willox has the right transmit saved, too."

"The what?" Santreeza says.

"A subpoena for the police to execute. So they can pretend to look for contraband in that bag she's carrying."

"Well, if he doesn't, I can get you one. Don't ask me how."

The captain's voice comes crackling over the intraship comm. "Brennan, get up here! You have the bridge. If it looks like the dock is going to blow, break berth and get out of here."

"Damn her!" Devit snaps. "She's going off ship. I'd better go with her."

On the way, Devit stops at the weapons locker and grabs something more efficient than a mere pulse gun. All of his functions are screaming "Crisis!"

As soon as she received Devit's message, Evans contacted the police. By the time she makes them understand how urgent the situation is, Mata and Wang have rushed in and taken their stations.

The elevator disgorges Dan a moment or two later. "Devit's on the way, ma'am. He's arming. Santreeza's hacking the dock security vids."

On the bridge comm screen a view of the dock module snaps on just as he finishes. The elevator brings Santreeza up next.

"Good," Evans says. "I'm heading out."

As she hurries down the sky tunnel, she checks her pulse gun: fully charged. Two Police Guards are waiting at the outer airlock—both Human, both male. They introduce themselves as Y'moto and Sten.

"Did you get my transmits?"

"Yes, ma'am," Sten says. "We've got more personnel on the job, too."

"Good. My security chief's on his way."

She is telling them the little they know about the Mouse when Devit jogs out of the tunnel and joins them.

He acknowledges the Guardsmen with a nod. "They were heading toward the Shops module last I saw."

"We got the vid you sent, Chief." Sten taps his earjack. "We've got a tracker on them. Let's go."

Sten takes the lead as they jog down the long dock toward the open Shops module. As soon as they reach it, the emergency door behind them comes down to cut the suspects off from their yacht. No sirens wail, and the door slides into place smoothly and silently. Sten gestures for the stop.

"Two officers are on the far side of this module. They're waiting, right out in the open, where that pair can see them. We're hoping they'll turn around and try to get back here. The other officers will follow."

The ploy works.

"Intel coming in," Sten says. "Here they come. Heading toward the berths."

Evans puts herself and her function cluster on alert. She needs to pick up any signal from that utility bag as soon as possible.

"If she reaches for her bag," Devit says to the officers, "we need to stop her. She could be triggering a device."

"Got it. Here they come."

Evans can just see the Mouse and her male companion walking fast through the scatter of shoppers in the module. She brings up her functions, focuses "search," and picks up a familiar signal. Her "find" function reaches out and follows it back to its source.

"Device in the bag," Evans says. "I've just turned it off."

Mouse stops walking and grabs at her bag.

The police officers break into a run and head for her.

"Get your hands up, ma'am! Police search!"

The siren starts wailing. More officers are racing down from the far end. As they come, they shout at the civilians to either clear the module or take cover. Evans focuses on the device and finds the box function she's looking for. Mouse slips her hand inside the bag just as Evans orders the device to perform a complete lockdown. She can see Mouse's lips moving but can hear nothing in the general din. The woman's face, however, radiates panic so clearly that Evans can assume she's an amateur terrorist.

The man standing next to her has more self-control. He pulls something metal and narrow out of his shirt. Evans has just time enough to register that it's a weapon before Devit grabs her with one hand and pulls her to one side. In the other hand he's carrying a needle gun.

A wasp streaks by, or so it seems. The gunman's chest explodes in a gush of blood, a swarm of flesh gobbets, and shreds of charred cloth. Mouse starts screaming, a high-pitched shriek over and over, as the force of the shot sprays blood onto her arm and face. For one ghastly moment the mangled corpse's legs hold it upright. It pitches backward onto the floor just as the reinforcement police reach the scene.

One officer grabs the Mouse's arms from behind. Y'moto snatches the bag and snaps the clip fastener off the strap. He grabs the bag and pulls it away. The Mouse's screams turn to sobs. The signal stays dead. Evans lets out her breath in a long sigh of relief.

"Thank you, Devit."

"Welcome, ma'am."

Devit presses the safety lock on the needle gun, as calmly as if they were on a practice range. For a brief moment, Evans feels afraid of him, that he'd be so calm after killing a sapient in such a ghastly way. She herself is fighting the urge to vomit. She forces herself to focus on the present and turns to Officer Sten. "In that bag is a metal box that looks harmless.

It isn't. Tell your lab techs not to fool around with it until we've found the explosives it was meant to activate."

"Yes, ma'am." In the general uproar of sirens and panic, Sten claps a hand over his earjack to listen. "Message incoming. Huh, why didn't they just sign a confession and save us the trouble? Ma'am, the *Lokiki*'s broken berth. She's heading out."

The vidscreen image splits. One half stays on the dock with Evans; the other shows the *Lokiki* edging away from its abandoned berth.

Dan gets up from his bridge station to catch Wang's attention. "Get ready to follow them."

"Are you crazy?"

"Hey, Dan!" Lod swivels his chair around. "We don't know if they're armed, but I bet they are."

"We're not going to confront them. We're going to follow at a safe distance. I'm betting they're running for that stargate. I want another track."

"Got it." Wang turns back to her station. "Activating thruster prelims now."

"Bringing guns online just in case."

"PrimeOne, put a trace lock on that ship," Santreeza says.

On the screen, the *Lokiki*'s turning in place to bring its fancy streamlined nose pointing starward. It travels slowly as it opens a safe distance between itself and the docks.

"Setting up our exit now." Dan is operating through his earjack. He has no time to meld. "Orbit pattern is—oh Lord Jessy crap—they're heading straight out!"

The yacht fires its thrusters full power. In a flood of bluish plasma it leaps forward, straight forward, scorning the long spiral out of the gravity well. The dock shakes as the shock wave hits, then slowly calms.

"We're not going to catch them," Wang says. "We can't fire our thrusters this close. Our level of power can't take us straight out at that speed anyway. By the time we finish orbit exit, they'll be out of the well. We don't have even half the power they've gotta have."

"Can they really pull this off?" Santreeza says.

"Sure looks like it. Of course, I'm only speaking as the engineer."

Santreeza winces.

Onscreen the *Lokiki*'s image is growing rapidly smaller against the background of stars and the deep dark of space.

"You're right, Wang," Dan says. "No one's arguing with you."

Wang makes a small snorting noise and returns to her command screen.

"We're staying at Go Ready until we get an all clear," Dan says. "If Evans says the Mouse came here to activate some kind of bomb, then that's why Mouse is here."

"Varg!" Lod says. "It could be anywhere in the Repositories. They're huge."

"Sure are. Especially if the perps went planetside."

"I doubt that," Santreeza says. "You'd better be somebody very important if you want to hit dirt. I looked it up."

"Anyone who owns a yacht like *Lokiki* is going to be important enough," Dan says.

"True. I'll—what in hell is *that*?"

On the vidscreen a ship is gliding into view, the bulbous nose first, then the long cylindrical body and finally the fan-shaped thruster unit at the end. Slowly, majestically, it turns its enormous gray nose, dotted with black gun turrets, toward the spacedock. As it glides forward to berth, its image fills the screen.

"That has to be the *Mansa*," Dan says. "Holy shit!"

# TWELVE

Evans has a headache. For the past solstandard hour she has been sitting in the small stuffy office of Captain Kaz Trem, CO of the Repository Police Guard Unit Seven, that is, the segment of the Guard assigned to Dock Seven, where the *Mary* is berthed and the terrorists were apprehended. Even though Evans knows that the police have to follow proper procedures, even though she believes wholeheartedly in proper procedures, she is furious.

"You have no right to take my security officer into custody," she says for the third time. "He is under Fleet jurisdiction. He was following standing orders to protect my life."

Kaz Trem's left ear is twitching with nerves. The right ear has drooped flat. "Yes, ma'am, I know, ma'am. As soon as I can get in contact with the commissioner, we'll straighten this out. His meeting is running over the scheduled time."

"And I suppose you can't start the search for sabotage devices until—"

"We have been over this already."

"You could at least interrogate the real criminal. That woman who carried the signal device."

"We're trying. She refuses to answer, refuses to give her name. She's so hysterical she can barely talk at all."

Evans crosses her arms over her chest and leans back in the uncomfortable soyplast chair. Kaz Trem keeps pinging the site currently displayed on the office viewscreen. The words "Headquarters of the Offplanet Repository Commissioner" on a blue background have stayed the same for the past thirty-four solstandard minutes. *How about an emergency access?* Evans is about to suggest this out loud when her own inner transmit function alerts her to a message from Santreeza.

*The* Mansa *has berthed. Captain Engji-Bonna asks if you need official assistance.*

*Damn right I do. Tell her to hurry.*

Kaz Trem begins speaking on the intradock comm in Yarf, the Kar-Li main language. Evans can understand a few words, including the reassuring "general alert." *General search. Who can? Of course!* Evans sees an idea, then a cluster of ideas, still tangled, of something that might just work.

"I've contacted every chief of police on every spacedock," Trem says. "We have the authority to tell all sapients in our jurisdictions that we're in an emergency. I simply cannot order a general evacuation to planetside."

"I do appreciate your difficulty, but this is outrageous. We have got to start a search for IEDs and the signal devices ASAP."

"We're just very short on officers and deputies. Normally we don't have this kind of violence on the dock array."

"Yes, yes, I know. But we don't know how many of the signal devices exist. There could be others on this dock and maybe other docks. The situation is time-critical."

Kaz Trem is about to answer when voices out in the corridor start shouting, "No, ma'am, please, wait, you can't go in there." The door swings open, and Captain Engji-Bonna strides in, accompanied by two Fleet Marines. Evans salutes, and the Leptic woman returns it.

"Enid, thank god!" Evans says. "Good to see you."

Bonna waves her crest. "Good to see you, too, Tana." She turns to Kaz Trem. "I'm the designated captain-commander for the defense and recon force of the four Fleet ships currently here at dock. I've been informed we have a problem concerning the questionable detention of a Fleet warrant officer. When is your planned release time?"

"I have to wait for the commissioner to contact me." Kaz Trem pauses to wipe her face on the back of one hand. Her pale-tan facial fur has started to shed. "The heart of this problem? The Repositories depend on political neutrality. We have to treat all sapients the same. The Rim Council's not the only political entity on the shunt system. If I give your Fleetsman a special privilege, and the word gets out, the Hoppers in particular are going to object."

"There are legal exceptions. The Fleet has exemptions when it's offering military aid in defense of an installation."

"Well, yes, but the commissioner—"

"Will, I'm sure, understand that. Now, if you insist on keeping CWO Devit in custody, we will simply withdraw all our defending vessels." Bonna glances at Evans. "We can tow the *Cotta* if we have to."

Kaz Trem wipes the shed fur she's gathered onto her uniform's black tunic. "Leaving us defenseless?"

"It's the only way to put you in compliance with your own rules."

Evans has a cold moment of wondering if Bonna really does have the authority she claims. *What the hell. We can worry about that later.*

Kaz Trem shuts her eyes and her lips move, perhaps in prayer to some deity. She opens them again, glances at the two heavily armed Marines, and clicks on the intrastation comm. "Bring Chief Devit to my office." She turns to Evans. "We need to hold that weapon as evidence. I trust that's sai with you?"

"Oh yes," Evans says. "We have several more onboard should we need them."

Kaz Trem returns to the comm. "Put the release forms up onscreen. His superior officer will need to sign off on the terms."

"Excellent!" Evans says. "Now, about this search—"

"It's not been done?" Bonna interrupts.

"Not yet. They're short of personnel."

"There are 200 Fleet Marines onboard." Bonna turns to Kaz Trem. "All highly trained. I'll give the order for them to deploy on dock, and we'll get things started."

"But the commissioner—"

"Will doubtless prefer our search to having the dock blown to pieces and hundreds of sapients killed. If he doesn't," Bonna pauses for effect, "too varg bad. The safety of Fleet personnel and Fleet ships is at stake. I have the authority to intervene."

"Now just wait a minute here." Kaz Trem slaps both hands flat on her desk. "There's something you don't understand. The Repositories are a satellite system. Eight huge spacedocks. Who knows all the places where these terrorists—Blood Vigilantes, I bet they are—set up for sabotage? Two hundred Marines? Sounds like a lot. We'd need two thousand."

"Varg! You have a very good point."

"I do know my job, dammit."

Time to intervene—Evans stands up and coughs to force them to look her way. "We have other resources. Fleet quality AIs. Officer Trem, surely the spacedocks are mapped?"

"Down to the last centimeter."

"And annotated? Who can go where, what's in the various lockers?"

"Yes. All of that." Kaz Trem's ear flaps rise in hope. "We keep lists of visitors too."

"Good!" Evans snaps. "Once we find the likely hiding places, then we send in the Marines." She turns to glare at Bonna, who has the decency to wince and nod her approval. "And of course I have the functions to spot signal."

"There's an ensign on the *Mansa* who's got the same packet," Bonna says.

"Very good. Trem, the spacedocks must have maintenance AIs."

"Of course, but they're all low level."

"Doesn't matter. We have someone who'll know how to use them. I'm contacting Lieutenant Santreeza right now."

"PrimeOne and UnitFour, prepare for deep meld. PrimeTwo, link only. Stand ready to funnel relevant data to Chief Warrant Officer Devit."

"One and Four reporting in. Online and ready, CyberThree."

"CyberThree, this is PrimeTwo. CWO Devit's PL has apparently malfunctioned. I cannot contact it. He does however have a functioning earjack. Shall I link to that?"

"Yes. Also, record for later transfer to his PL."

"Done."

"CyberThree, this is PrimeOne. I have brought the maintenance AI systems under our control. What instruction should I enter?"

"Look for unexplained rubbish, trash, or garbage. Link me in, and I will provide more detail."

"All right," Evans says. "It's been over twenty minutes since you ordered your people to release my security chief. Where is he?"

"There are proper release procedures."

"He never should have been detained in the first place."

Kaz Trem picks up an earjack from her desk and puts it in. She murmurs to the voice pickup in Yarf, listens, and after some back and forth, takes the jack out again.

"They are bringing him up now. They'd confiscated his PL. He refused to give them access."

"He has no authority to give anyone access to a device with Fleet data on it."

"So I told them. Now look, something like this has never happened at the Repositories before. We are trying to follow procedures and orders that we've never had to use."

Only a Leptic mouth can make a sound as rude and loud as the one Bonna snorts out. "You'll never have to follow them again if this place blows up like Unification fireworks."

"Enid, please! Leave this to me. He's on my ship's roster, not yours."

"Well, true." Her crest deflates. "I'll shut my snout."

It's the tension, Evans supposes. Nerves, fear, the anxiety of knowing too much time has passed have all fed the squabbling and snapping.

At long last someone opens the office door. A uniformed officer escorts Devit inside. He appears perfectly calm, utterly at ease, which means of course that something is very wrong.

"Ma'am." Devit salutes first her, then Bonna. "Officer Trem."

Trem refuses to look his way. "You are all free to go. Please keep me informed of the progress of the search."

"Don't worry about that," Bonna says. "You'd better get all your off-duty personnel back on the job. We'll probably need them."

Evans lays a heavy hand on Bonna's shoulder. Bonna mutters "sorry" and stays silent.

"Kaz Trem?" Evans says. "Did that wretched commissioner ever call back?"

"No, ma'am. Odd. It's not like him. He should be on his way back by transit cab by now."

"Shit!" Devit snaps. "That's it. Ma'am, the guards left me my earjack. I've been receiving data from our cyberjock. Chief Trem, can you reach the pilot of that transfer cab? They've got to get the personnel off it right now."

"He's got sentinel intelligence," Evans says. "Trust it!"

Kaz Trem blinks, suddenly understands, and grabs the comm unit on her desk. As Evans listens to the flood of Yarf, she watches Devit. He puts his hand on his earjack. A grim smile, and he turns to Kaz Trem.

"Fresh data. That meeting ran over by ninety-seven standard minutes. Has the cab left Dock Six?"

"No. They're off-loading the personnel now."

"Does it have AI capability? They've got to get it away from the dock."

"Understood. No AI, but the pilot's setting up auto-exit. Straight out fast." Trem listens while Devit hovers, as tense as a cable stretched near snapping. "Pilot's safe on dock. Unmanned cab on its way. Top speed."

"Pray it gets far enough," Bonna says.

Evans nods her agreement. Devit turns away and starts whispering to his earjack—contacting Santreeza, Evans assumes. Kaz Trem holds up the comm unit so everyone can hear, very faintly, the wail of emergency sirens on spacedock Six. A minute passes, maybe two.

"PrimeTwoMary's picked up a flash of light," Devit says. "Some distance away from Six."

The sirens continue a steady wail. Evans mentally counts seconds. Five later, the siren noise stutters and sputters as the shock wave hits. A long, long moment's silence, and the wail picks up steady again. Evans allows herself a soft gasp of relief.

"Trem," Devit says, "there's a signal device on Dock Six."

"They have officers on the scene. They've already gotten that data from your AI cluster."

"Tell them not to mess around with it!" Evans says. "Touch nothing, do nothing, just guard it till I can get there."

"I'm passing that along, Captain. They know about your Throwback functions."

"It's likely there are still explosives here on Seven," Bonna says. "This isn't over yet."

Devit suddenly laughs, a quick snort of amusement. "Sorry, ma'am," he says. "I was just thinking that it was a damn good thing the police detained me. If we'd left this office—"

"It wouldn't have been good, no," Evans says. "The commissioner and his staff would have been dead by now."

"Captain Bonna?" Devit said. "CyberThree's going to relay data on three likely locations for the sabotage attempt. Do you have EC people onboard?"

"We sure do." Bonna turns to the waiting Marines. "Sergeant, contact the ship. Tell your unit CO that we need three damage control teams with full gear. On the run! And send Ensign Ka Torp with them. With a needle gun for Chief Devit."

The Marines and transmits from Santreeza arrive at the same time. As the Throwback officer with the appropriate functions, Evans has the command for the search. She takes the most likely, and thus the most dangerous, location for herself and her squad. Ka Torp turns out to be a Kar-Li who looks too young to even have started rejuv. His brown facial fur has only begun to grow in, giving him stubble like smeared dirt. Fresh out of the Academy, she assumes, so she sends him with the most experienced squad to the least likely location. Bonna takes the rest of the Marines with her to the remaining possibility.

The emergency sirens begin to wail. In bursts between wails the dock comm announces, "clear this module all personnel clear this module" in six different languages. Although all three locations lie in different modules, they all are deep on Level Three of the dock system, close to the memory banks for the AI data retrieval systems that make the Repositories what they are. When the search teams arrive at the main access elevator bank, three technicians are waiting, one for each team.

The leader for Evans's team, a Human woman whose name badge reads Ifahlee, explains. "Access here is strictly limited, Captain. There are codes. I must ask you to not look over anyone's shoulder when we're entering them."

"Understood." Evans decides against telling her that her functions will read them whether she looks or not. "Let's go."

The elevator travels fast and a long way down to a beige area gleaming with bright light. They step out onto a walkway that runs some five meters above a regiment of pale tan slabs standing in tidy rows that march all the way down the long curve of the module. On the walls run tube housings carrying the air intake and moisture outgo, heat, and the like. On the ceiling, nets and webs of titanium signal transmission lines spread out, the nervous system of the AIs above.

When Evans activates her functions, Devit lays a hand on her shoulder to guide her. She can hear him whispering, sending a running report back to Santreeza through his earjack. She focuses away from audible sound to concentrate. She is overwhelmed by the amount of signals—thousands of them, it seems—washing over her, pouring down like rain. As they walk, she sorts through them, recognizes and dismisses the vast majority as AI transmission. Others radiate from assorted warning beacons and emergency access systems, all standard Fleet frequencies.

They've gone maybe a hundred meters when she picks up an anomaly. Faint at first, but as they keep moving forward it strengthens and reaches out. It's searching for something, pulsing out a pattern, a beam turning round and round, up and down, over and over.

"We're close," Evans says. "EC experts, get ready."

The team reshuffles to bring four Marines to the lead. Evans and Devit fall in right behind them. A few more meters, and she can pinpoint the source. In a cluster of power tubes right up against a side wall of the module lies a narrow tube, maybe a meter long, that looks at first sight like an emergency beacon—except it's lying on its side, not standing upright. The signal pours out of it, searching and pulsing.

"Halt," Evans snaps. "Here we are."

Silence. No one coughs, shuffles. The EC team is watching her, waiting, like giant insects in their shiny protective gear. Evans focuses three different functions on the signal, which proves to be compatible with the previous signal box, the one she'd found planted in the *Mary*'s cargo hold. Time passes—maybe a minute, maybe more—and it seems that the sapients behind her are not even breathing. There are threads of signal inside that tube, and at certain points they cross. One of those nexus points is the right one. She finds it at last and breaks the connection.

"Lockdown complete," she says. "I'm holding it locked just in case."

"Very good, ma'am." The leader of the EC team steps forward. "We'll retrieve it now."

"Ma'am?" Devit says. "Shouldn't you move back?"

"It won't matter, Chief. From what I can tell, if this thing goes, half the module goes with it."

The EC sergeant laughs under his breath. "That's a damn good guess, ma'am." He waves to his team. "Let's go see what we've got."

Evans had been afraid that the tube was fastened down in some difficult way, but apparently whoever managed to place it had only enough time to lay it down and leave. The sergeant and another Marine squat to examine it. When they stand up, they bring the tube with them. Evans keeps her function centered on the lockdown point, which continues to register "status No Go."

"They're readying a transit cab," Devit says. "They want to send it out and have a Fleet ship destroy it at safe distance."

"Sounds good," the sergeant says. "Then we've got to get this thing up to second level. Captain, will the lockdown hold?"

"It should. So far nothing's fought back."

"Then go with the others. The rest of you, go ahead and clear the module as ordered. We'll need the code for the elevator."

"I'll leave it unlocked," Ifahlee says. "If this module goes, it won't matter who knows the fucking codes. If it doesn't, we'll change them."

As they return to the elevator, Evans can hear Devit questioning Ifahlee. With her mind so focused, it's hard to understand exactly what they're saying, but she's fairly sure they're discussing how someone might have planted the device and who that someone might have been. Once they're in the elevator and going up, she releases her focus. She's out of range now and can only hope that the lockdown proves as permanent as it did on the last device.

"I'll send those names to Officer Kaz Trem," Devit is saying. "They need to be brought in for questioning."

"Damn right. And fast."

Up on second level another EC team is waiting to assist when the device arrives. Kaz Nor is the sergeant for this team.

"No other IEDs here on Dock Seven, Captain. They've found the signaling device on Dock Six. Captain Bonna's taking Ensign Torp over to deal with it. She wants to know if that will be adequate."

"Adequate. How tactful, and how unlike her." Evans softens the remark with a smile. "Have Torp contact me as soon as he reaches the site. So. That's two docks out of eight."

The elevator announces an arrival with a series of beeps. Everyone moves away from the doors, as if a couple of meters distance would protect them if the sabotaged tube explodes. As soon as the EC personnel carry the device out, Evans searches for signal. She finds only the beautiful lack indicating the triggers are all locked down.

"There's a transit cab waiting and ready," Ifahlee says. "Let's get this sodding thing over there and out. I've ordered a grav sled. Ah. Here it comes."

Santreeza has gotten complete control of Dock Seven's security cameras. In deep meld she can "travel," as it were, from Eye to Eye and hear what the Ears capture as well. She watches the EC crew guide the grav sled with its ominous burden down the long module to a shuttle entrance airlock, where more Marines wait to load.

"PrimeTwo, this is Chief Devit. Report progress."

"Explosive apparatus shifted to the dock transit cab. Crew is closing airlock and returning to deck. We are programming the cab. Systems Go Ready, CyberThree."

"This is CyberThree. Send her out."

Freed from the dock's artificial gravity field, the squat little cab glides away. Once it's put enough distance between it and the spacedock, Santreeza gives the order for the thrusters to fire on minimum power. Out toward the stars it speeds, but the *Chaonia*'s waiting. One of the destroyer's hardbeam laser turrets flashes with light that wraps like a shroud around the cab. A blossom of fire and shattered metal blooms against the darkness. Even in meld, Santreeza cannot see pulse energy, so harmless and undetectable in the emptiness of space, until, that is, it hits something solid. The gunner must have followed up with a blast from pulse artillery, because the vids show all the debris speeding in the same direction—out—away from the vulnerable dock.

"Input from Chief Devit, CyberThree. Captain Evans is going to the *Mansa*. The three captains and the lieutenant-commander will be conferencing soon. She wants to know if you can be present for consultation. Subject: the other six docks."

"I will break meld for the conference. PrimeTwo, confirm with Chief Devit."

Because no one tells him to go away, Devit tags along for the COs conference, which takes place on the *Mansa*'s bridge. He and Santreeza are given seats on a padded bench set against one wall, out of the way of the various bridge stations. They make sure to sit a decent way apart. While the COs wrangle over various plans to ensure the remaining docks are safe, Devit's mind keeps drifting to the amazingly satisfying night he and Jorja spent together.

He forces his mind back to the present moment when Captain Evans finally manages to get the others to stop talking and listen.

"Lieutenant Santreeza is our cyber expert. She deserves the credit for finding the sabotage locations in the first place."

The senior officers all turn to Santreeza with looks and nods of approval. Willox even salutes her.

"Santreeza," Evans continues. "Can the search procedures you came up with be repeated at the other spacedocks?"

Santreeza gets up and stands in parade rest to answer. "Yes, ma'am. I'd need the assistance of PrimeOneMary to contact the housekeeping AIs on each one. We'd need to be within easy transmit distances. Beaming through the communications satellites would be one remote step too many."

"What if we used the *Mary* to bring you and it to each site?"

"That would work splendidly, ma'am. That way I'd have the tools I'd need to repeat the procedure."

"Very good. Then that's what we'll do. If there are no further objections?" Evans turns and glares at each CO in turn. There are no further objections.

"Ma'am? Permission to speak?"

"Certainly, Santreeza."

"It was Chief Devit who realized that the hostiles had planted the IED in the Repository commissioner's personal transit cab."

Devit covers his sudden discomfort with his usual expressionless mask.

"Commendations for both of you," Captain Bonna says. "Devit, you have the sentinel intelligence function, don't you?"

"Yes, ma'am."

"I suggest we all trust you when you use it. And, my fellow officers, let's get our asses in gear and get this procedure started before some other piece of exploding shit goes off."

On the *Mary*'s bridge the rest of the crew are waiting, as well as Professor Golverg, who's taken the extra chair by the elevator. Dan gets up from the command chair and salutes the captain with a shaky hand. His Pale face is even paler than normal and sweaty as well. Devit realizes that it's six full hours past the time for his dose of Haze.

Dan salutes again. "Standing down now, ma'am."

"Thank you, Lieutenant. Chief Devit?" Evans nods in Dan's direction, which is all the order Devit needs.

"Yes, ma'am." Devit lays a hand on Dan's shoulder to steady him. "Sir, if you'll come with me?"

As they walk toward the elevator, Wang gets up from her station chair. "Ma'am, I have to say that Brennan did a good job of keeping it together despite his damn drug. He's left the ship in Go Ready status. If we have to pull out fast, we can."

"Noted, Wang, and thank you and Brennan both."

Devit can't remember the last time he heard Wang dole out praise to anyone but her wife. He decides that he can count her remark as a victory.

"All right, crew," Evans says. "We are going to take a tour around the whole damn spacedock assembly. The *Chaonia* will be standing deep guard to travel with us. Santreeza, can PrimeOne take over the piloting?"

"Yes, ma'am." She touches her earjack. "Since we're Go Ready."

"Take Devit's station chair. Brennan is his first priority, and he won't be back. Now, what about you? Will you be able to function? This could be exhausting if you have to meld at every stop."

"Yes, ma'am, but I won't have to. Our AI array knows the procedures now. I can guide them through the jack."

"Good. Ensign Torp's on his way here, in case we need him. As soon as I receive the Go signal from Ka Birk, we'll be pulling out. The *Mansa* will guard the docks."

"Ma'am?" Mata says. "Is Engji-Bonna the CO of the *Mansa* now?" He pronounces her personal name correctly, of course, as only a Lep mouth can. "She's one formidable officer."

"Most definitely she is. I'm not surprised they gave her a command like this one."

"Neither am I. Huh. When she retires, I bet she'll end up as a Grandmother. You know, ma'am, Captain Bonna's what every Leptic woman aspires to be. A perfect model of Leptic womanhood."

"Good lord! Really?"

"Really. That's why I've never married."

Evans laughs with the rest of the crew while his crest waves. Some of the tension on the bridge fades away.

The airlock alarm system clears its throat with a beep. "Passenger waiting on dock."

"That'll be Ka Torp. Mata, go fetch him."

"Yes, ma'am. On my way."

"Santreeza," Evans says, "What about that damn yacht?"

"Chief Devit found the data on it, ma'am," Santreeza says. "Primary owner is Tay Jasson, the heir to Clan Jasson's holdings, but his uncle still holds part-ownership of the yacht. They have a planetside site on Ilana, but most of them are wandering rich."

"Ma'am?" Golverg says. "If I may use the prevailing idiom, permission to speak?"

"Of course, Professor."

"Clan Jasson has a second home world on RE914F-4th, Tala as they call it. Getting here is a long trip to make just to sightsee. Back home on Ilana, the gossip says they have dealings with the Hoppers. You can imagine how well that goes over, after the wars and all."

"I'm filing that data," Santreeza says. "And telling Devit."

"Make sure you tell Devit about Tala," Evans says. "He'll explain why it's important."

The elevator opens to release Mata and the young ensign.

"Torp, you'll have to sit on the floor," Evans says. "I—wait! I'm getting the signal. Ka Birk's got his ship in position. Very well. PrimeOne, take us out."

"Six spacedocks remain to be cleared. Travel time between them, variable. Total time of the mission—unknown at this point."

"Noted, PrimeTwo," Devit says. "Opinion: Will the docks' own Police Guard units be able to follow Santreeza's orders? I want to keep Evans and Torp onboard the *Mary* if at all possible."

"It is possible. I cannot say if it will happen. Query: If explosive devices still exist, why have they not been exploded by the hostile that set them?"

"We do not know."

Clicks, a long pause, then: "Let us hope there are none."

"That's what we're all hoping, yeah. Keep me informed of progress. I'll be on the bridge. Pilot Brennan's staying here in the cabin. He is ill."

"PrimeOne refers to Pilot Brennan as functionally damaged. Do these two words equate to the word 'ill'?"

Devit glances at Dan, lying sprawled on the bed and smiling at nothing. "Yes. Close enough."

As he hurries to the bridge, Devit's mind produces an observation that seems too random to belong in the developing pattern. Yet, in the way his functions do, he knows it fits somewhere. Haze affects only mammals, Chris Lee said. He knows that he's never seen or heard of a Hirrel pilot. He's seen, however, a few Leptic pilots, though he has no idea if any of them take drugs beyond the universal alcohol. What about the Hoppers, who of course must have pilots of their own? He makes a mental note to ask PrimeTwo those questions later, once the team has hunted down any remaining IEDs.

As they travel, PrimeOneMary links Evans to the other Fleet ships and the various AIs in service to the Repositories' Police Guards. Once the commissioner logs in, Evans explains the procedure ahead.

"The Marine EC squad is following the *Mary* in one of the *Mansa*'s shuttles. The pair will berth at each spacedock in turn. Our cyberjock and PrimeOne will gain control of the maintenance AIs, who will search for unexplainable trash, garbage, and strange objects on every square meter of their dock. If they find a possible risk, the Police Guard unit on that dock will do recon. The EC squad will retrieve what they find. If necessary, Torp and I will provide assistance. Commissioner, is this acceptable?"

"Certainly is. Very. Whatever you want, whatever's necessary." He clears his throat. "I must add that I am personally grateful to you all."

"All in the line of duty, Commissioner. But thank you."

The search goes far more smoothly than Evans ever would have predicted. Even when the team repeats the complete procedure a second time, they find no more IEDs or signal boxes. It becomes clear that the Blood Vigilantes had two goals: to disrupt the Repositories by assassinating the commissioner and to destroy something on Dock Seven. The next step is finding out what that "something" is.

During the travel time from dock to dock, Devit has been considering just that question. Once the search is over, he's ready with some ideas.

"I've been working with the maps of Dock Seven, ma'am. We can compare the location of the IED with the place where we confronted the Mouse and her companion. Is it possible that the IED had a time switch? The box sends its signal and that starts a countdown."

"Not just possible," Evans says. "I'm fairly sure it did. That's why I kept checking the lockdown to make sure it was holding."

"The IED was located just beyond the isolation doors of the next module over. And under the deck, of course, on that lower level. I'm speculating that the terrorists planned to go to its approximate location and activate the signal. They would have set the timer to give them enough time to get back to the *Lokiki* before the bomb went off. But with the Police Guards blocking the way, they never got there."

"That sounds very possible indeed, Chief. They have the Mouse in custody, of course. Damn! We need to find out her real name. The warden at the Police Guard holding cells searched all her belongings. No ID."

"If the Fleet can locate the *Lokiki* and bring it in—"

"*If.* It could be anywhere by now. Santreeza's sent shunt packets off to Harad base. She told me the two Morrison Line armed ships are missing too."

"Yes, ma'am. I confirmed that earlier and asked her to let you know."

"Good. What else does she have in mind? Do you know?"

"Yes, ma'am. She's planning on searching the specific archive banks that would have been destroyed. Looking for relevant data, the sort of thing that might be a terrorist concern. Professor Golverg has volunteered to help."

"Very good." Evans turns her chair to give Golverg one of her rare smiles. "Thank you. You and Santreeza may proceed at your own pace. Let's see what you can turn up." She turns her chair back. "In the meantime, Chief, send a report of your conclusions off to Captain Bonna."

"Noted, ma'am."

"What's Brennan's condition?"

"Sound out. Chris Lee told me to give him a second dose. He was pretty well drained."

"I'm not surprised. I— Wait, incoming message." Her eyes turn first distant in the usual way, then wide with shock. "Good god! Devit, they've apprehended that sapient on Dock Six, the one who carried the second signal box. They say they've got more evidence against him."

"And?"

"He's a Hopper."

Devit would like to swear with every foul word he knows. In deference to the captain's eccentric opinions about language, he merely says. "This is dangerous."

"One misstep, and we'll have a diplomatic incident. One misstep there, and we'll have another war. They're going to interrogate him tomorrow, some time in the Designated Afternoon. They need to wait for a lawyer from his embassy. That's in the neutrality zone on Four. I've insisted that you and I be present."

"Good."

"I'm going to put the AIs on guard and sentry duty. Do your security rounds, then get some sleep. I'm going to follow my own order. That circuit around the planet took hours, and I stayed on alert the entire way."

Santreeza has seen death before. During the Hopper Wars, she served on the last battleship, a class of starship since replaced by faster, more maneuverable heavy cruisers like the *Mansa*. When the RCS *Victory* took a direct hit amidships, she joined the medics and what other crew could be spared to pull the survivors out of the welter of metal and corpses in the module next to the sealed-off disaster. Any personnel still alive in the sealed compartment were beyond saving. For years after, any emergency siren, any enormous crashing sound—even onplanet thunder and, worst of all, the smell of burning meat—would make the images of the wounded and dying take over her mind. Time had to some extent submerged those images. The hit on the *Cotta* brought them back to the surface.

Having crucial cyberwork to do has kept the memories at a distance during the past few days, but all the old shudders and cold sweats return as she lies in her cabin and tries to sleep. She has new memories as well, but only of something seen on a vidscreen, distanced from the gut-wrenching pain of the scenes she lived through. A Human sapient exploded into blood and fragments from a needle gun dart while she watched. She has no idea what chemicals those darts contain. It doesn't matter. They do their job. The important memory is the sight of Peter Devit calmly flicking the safety shut on the gun. In her mental replay he glances at the corpse without so much as a wince and shifts his attention to the Mouse, shrieking in the arms of the police. Santreeza cannot look away as easily when the image reappears in her mind.

*Mangled flesh on the deck. Just like on the* Victory.

Santreeza gives up on sleep as a bad job. She gets up, dresses, and wanders down to the galley. Lod-Mata is sitting at the round table and rummaging through his bag of Leptic nutrition bars.

"You hungry?" Lod says.

"Only if there's something left besides bars."

"No, unfortunately. I was hoping to go fetch more real food today. Something interfered with my plan."

"Yeah, it sure did."

"Come sit down. What's bothering you?" He considers her for a moment. "Devit's kill?"

"You're an awful gossip, Lod, but you see things, don't you?" Santreeza takes a chair opposite him. "No. Terminating that hostile? Fine with me. I'm glad he didn't get a shot at the captain. It did get me, though, how calm Peter was about it."

"You've got to remember something about Devit's functions. He protects. It comes down to that. Someone threatens one of his people? He protects. Does whatever he has to. Blood and gore? Hey, the function says, good job!"

"Yeah, you're right. I know I'm prying, but I've got to ask. Do you know where that function comes from?"

"Don't you ever let him know I told you this. From those borracolls, the Old Earth dogs that the Vranz love so much."

"Oh for crap's sake! You're kidding, aren't you?"

"No. Dan teases him about it, which is totally unfair. He's lucky Devit hasn't smacked him a good one."

"I would, yeah. It's not like any of us chose these damn things. My own functions are so abstract, I forget how body-rooted the others are."

"Yeah, very deeply rooted. They're not completely under your control, are they?"

"Most aren't. There's a trigger, and they take over. Like seeing someone draw a gun on the captain."

"Exactly. I'm just as glad that we Leps never developed any Inborn functions. But look, your functions, they're all math and memory. I don't see any genes could come from the so-called lower animals about those."

"No, they come from a particular strain of Humans, and they go way back to Old Earth. Some people had these amazing skills with numbers and math, even though they couldn't do much else. The Recaller genes come from that group. Ahtiz, they were called. Something like that, anyway. The scientists refined the genes, of course, when they were creating the Inborn, isolated them, and attached them to spatial perception centers in the brain."

"So you're really pure Human?" Lod's crest swells to indicate he's joking. "No animal bits in you, huh?"

"Nope. The Pure Heritage types can shove it. I'm just an innocent genius."

"Hah! Good one! But when it comes to Devit, killing a hostile is just part of who he is."

"It's part of all of us, isn't it? Or we wouldn't be career Fleet."

Lod flattens his crest. "Good point. Very good point indeed."

A soft chime rings over the intraship comm: the old Designated Day has changed into the new.

"Varg, it's late!" Lod says. "It's crazy to be up so late."

"I keep remembering the hits we took on the *Victory.* I bet it's the same for you."

"Of course. The memory-shakes woke me up just now. And the spit. You chimpies sweat. Us lizards drool." He holds up a green bar. "Eating helps ease the stress, oddly enough."

"Not so easy for me. Unfortunately."

Footsteps come down the hall, and Devit appears in the doorway. Lod pushes back his chair and stands up. Santreeza gets up as well, simply because she dislikes having the two of them tower over her.

"Hey, Lod, you don't have to leave. Just finishing up my security round."

"How's Dan?"

"Asleep. Medic's orders. The captain's locked the ship down."

Devit takes a few steps into the room, a simple action, but watching him move makes Santreeza aware of just how much she wants him in her bed. The feeling goes beyond lust. She refuses to use the word "love"—the dangerous, poisonous condition that caused her so much pain so many years ago. She does care about him, she tells herself, and she'd like to give him something that he wants as much as she does. *That's all. Can't be anything more.*

Lod glances back and forth between them, then makes the gargling sound that equates to a Human eye roll.

*Oh crap. Are we that obvious?*

"Is Ensign Torp gone?" Lod says. "Wang and Lee all snuggies for the night?"

"Yeah," Devit says. "Why?"

"I'll go sit with Dan. The lieutenant requires an escort back to her cabin."

Devit's long slow grin melts the last of Santreeza's resolve. *No we can't what if oh to hell with what if.* She can think of nothing to say. She walks past him, leaves the galley, keeps walking down the corridor without looking back.

Just as she opens her cabin door he catches her. "Can I come in?"

For an answer, she turns around in his arms, reaches up and lays her hands on either side his face.

"Remember this?" she says.

"Always."

He bends his head and kisses her. She lets him pick her up and carry her inside.

# THIRTEEN

Somewhere early in the Designated Morning Hours, Devit runs to his own cabin, takes a shower, throws on clean clothes, wakes Dan up, and leaves, all in about twenty solstandard minutes. He grabs a purple nutrition bar from the galley and rushes up to the bridge. Captain Evans and Professor Golverg, the only sapients there, are watching the local vidnews.

"Chief, there's a transmit waiting at your station. Brought by the SAR."

"Thank you, ma'am."

Devit sits down at his station and brings up the security settings on the station's screen. No attempted intrusions, no personnel taking unauthorized shore leave, no starside approaches to the ship—everything all clear and correct. Only when he's finished does he bring up the transmit. The two Morrison commercial vessels are berthed at Harad spacedock. The whereabouts of the two Morrison Line armed escort ships, however, are still unknown.

"Chief?"

He swivels his chair around and salutes out of sheer habit. "Ma'am?"

"We're due on Dock Four in three solstandard hours. How's Brennan?"

"Awake and snarling, ma'am. I got him up before I left the cabin."

Which is certainly true, and she makes no further comment. The vidnews onscreen changes to the Repositories' quiet, restrained version of the top story news, delivered by a soberly dressed Human woman.

"Police have arrested a suspect in yesterday's unsuccessful bombing attempt. He was found with a suspicious device hidden in a suitcase in his hotel room. Police emphasize that the device is not explosive or otherwise dangerous. He claims that he has no knowledge of how the device came into his possession. He has given his name as Vot Kal Bar, an academic doing research in the H'Allevae Archive."

"What?" Golverg snaps. "If that's Professor Vot, he's certainly no terrorist!"

"You know him?" Evans says.

"Very well. You know, there *are* Hoppers who are perfectly civilized and decent sapients. His field and mine overlap to some extent, and we've—"

Golverg breaks off to stare at the vidscreen. In a vid filmed earlier, two police officers are putting a handcuffed Hopper into a prison cell. He's a typical Hopper man, about a meter and a half tall, wearing an orange prison jumpsuit that leaves his long, thin arms and the species' peculiarly jointed short legs bare. His black multilens eyes bulge out of a hairless dead-white face. His nose, a curled flap of skin that hangs down to his oddly Human-looking lips, is trembling in fear.

"That is *not* Vot Kal Bar," Golverg says. "I'll swear to it. Someone's using his name. His eyes are purple, not black, just to begin with."

"I'll contact the Police Guard," Evans says. "You'll be coming with us." She swivels her chair around to face Devit's station. "Chief, we leave here in approximately half a solstandard hour. I want plenty of time before the trip is over. Is Brennan in any shape to take the bridge?"

"No, ma'am. Lieutenant Wang would be a better choice."

"Very well, then. Planetside uniforms, and we need to get down to the transit cab platform early. I'm going to scan our cab before we get in it and the platform, too."

"I asked Wang for permission for shore leave to go get more fresh food," Lod says. "She joyously gave it. Want to go to the Shops?"

"I do, yeah," Santreeza says. "Let me just check the vids first. For the condition of the deck."

"Oh. Right." His crest sinks. "Good idea."

When Santreeza brings up the image on the comm screen, they see that the maintenance AIs and their bots have done a superb job. The place on the deck where the terrorist met his death shines as clean as the rest of the flooring. Sapients hurry past and even walk over the spot. They've returned to the module and their shopping just as if the Designated Day before was as calm as days on the Repositories are supposed to be.

"Let's go," Santreeza says. "I got my salary yesterday, too. The data packet must have come on the *Mansa*."

With all the types of food available at the Shops, their salary creds leave as fast as they arrived. Burdened with boxes and bags, Santreeza and Mata return to the ship and go straight to the galley. Dan is sitting at the table and contemplating a pair of blue nutrition bars. He looks at the mound of purchases and puts the bars back in the sack.

"We need to save some of this for the captain and Devit," Lod says. "The professor, too, come to think of it. Santreeza, how about we pick out a selection and then lock it up somewhere?"

"Good idea, yeah. We seem to have a predator onboard."

Dan laughs and slouches comfortably in his chair. He's wearing a pair of baggy spacer pants, and his blue shirt has a gray stain running down the chest. He's unshaven and smells sweaty. For the first time, Santreeza realizes with a sense of shock, she finds him sexually attractive. All of the cold, aggressive perfection that annoyed her has disappeared.

He looks her way, quirks an eyebrow as if at a question, then smiles.

*He knows. He's gloating, the bastard!* She turns away fast and pays strict attention to opening sacks of the local purple alela berries and an Old Earth fruit called oranjez.

With a rasp and a squawk, the galley's vidscreen lights up. PrimeTwo begins speaking through the onboard comm.

"SAR Unit 16 has arrived at spacedock Seven under guard. It is assuming a parallel orbit in close proximity to the RCS *Cotta*. Transferring vid feed from PrimeOneCotta now. Collating with vids from RCS *Mansa Musa*."

Images snap into focus on the screen. The SAR's own guard ship is standing off to keep watch from a distance. On close duty, the *Mansa* glides into position near the crippled frigate. Next to the heavy cruiser, the *Cotta* looks like a mere shuttle. A third ship moves slowly and majestically into the view and dwarfs the *Mansa* in turn. From a distance the SAR unit looks more like a floating island than a ship. A metal hanger covers most of a flat platform the size of several sports fields on top of the enormous spherical hull. The hanger splits open and folds down to reveal mounds of equipment sealed in protective spheres, a pair of cranes, and a metal tower.

But this is an island with claws. Two grappling hooks that must be at least fifty meters long slide out from under the bow. Santreeza watches, fascinated, as these solid metal hooks begin to move, sliding a bit sideways, growing a little longer, then drawing back, getting closer and closer to the *Cotta*, which is drifting at right angles to the ship. The claws catch the light of the distant sun, gleam, and suddenly pounce. Santreeza imagines that she hears the *Cotta* scream as the hooks clamp around it amidships and pull it into position.

"Well there, safe and sound," Lod says. "Let's hope they can repair her."

The damage to the frigate reminds her of another casualty. "By the way, do either of you know how that crew member's doing? The engineering tech who was so badly injured."

Dan whispers the question to his earjack. "Shit! PrimeOne says she died four hours ago."

The memories invade Santreeza's mind with the sound of dying sapients begging for help. When she sees that Lod's clawed hands have started trembling, she knows that he too remembers. She takes a deep breath and searches through the spread of food lying on the table. A bottle of fermented alela juice—she grabs it and twists off the cap.

"Gentlemen." She raises the bottle. "Absent friends."

"Absent friends." Dan and Lod echo the ancient words.

Santreeza takes a sip and hands it to Dan. The bottle goes round in silence to remind them that, sooner or later, being Fleet demands its price.

The Repositories Police Guard units have a standard procedure for interrogating suspects, one that Evans thoroughly approves of. The Hopper will remain in his holding cell until his legal council arrives from the H'Allevae Embassy on Morrison-4th. Only then will the actual interrogation—more a legal hearing, really—take place in a courtroom with the Public Attorney for Dock Four and a judge also present.

The group from the *Mary* arrives early and goes through an elaborate check-in to prove that they are who they say they are. Once it's done, the local Police Guard captain, a muscular Human woman named Bronish, takes Evans, Devit, and Golverg down to the evidence room at the station.

The clerk on duty brings out the confiscated signal box and puts it ceremoniously onto a piece of clean soyskin covering a counter.

"It's been scanned for fingerprints, ma'am," she says. "You can touch it if you want."

"Scanned? Good god, you're lucky it didn't activate."

The clerk steps back fast from the counter as if it might explode right then. It takes Evans only a couple of minutes to examine it with her functions.

"We're twice lucky," Evans says to Bronish. "This box has been locked down and code-wiped."

"Does that mean it's harmless?"

"Yes. The man you've got in custody would have activated it at some point if we hadn't found the IED. Which probably means the device in the commissioner's cab was the only one on Six."

"That is a profound relief."

"Don't drop your guard quite yet. These people are entirely too clever. There's a possibility that your prisoner may have intended to hand this box to a courier to be taken to someone else for the next attack. That's the way they seem to work."

"Makes sense, yes. A courier, huh? I've already put a couple of officers on a low-level sweep. Just a look around to see if there was anyone else here to cause trouble. Looking up hotel registers, lists of researchers, that sort of thing. I'll ramp that up now that we have a solid reason. By the way, I received your transmit about the prisoner." Bronish nods at Professor Golverg. "Thank you for coming forward." She pauses to listen to her earjack. "The others are assembling. Let's go on over."

The courtroom is a big brightly lit room with a judge's bench on a dais at one end and tidy rows of chairs at the other. A Lep man in a gray business suit of kilt and jacket gets up from a table and hurries to meet them at the door. Bronish introduces Evans and her crew.

"And this is Djo-Verr, our public attorney."

A cluster of Hoppers are standing around the table at the other end of the dais, two soldiers in their bright red and gold uniforms, and two soberly dressed civilians—sober by Hopper standards, at any rate, as their coats and short breeches are a dull green with dark blue streaks and splotches. The scent of their sweet perfume drifts through the room. One civilian carries a utility case attached to his narrow wrist with a chain.

Evans goes tense, reminds herself that they are not at war, but she cannot shake the feeling of "enemies present." When she glances Devit's way, he's scowling—a reassurance, oddly enough. Had he appeared impassive, she would have known he was sensing danger.

In response to her questioning glance, he whispers, "That damn perfume."

"The judge will be here any minute," Verr says. "Let's sit down."

They take chairs in the front row, except for Verr, who stays standing to talk with Golverg. "Professor, are you willing to be called as a witness?"

"That's why I'm here. I'm sincerely worried about what's happened to my colleague."

"It's not likely to be good, no, if this fellow's an imposter."

Two uniformed Police Guards are leading the fellow in question—the handcuffed Hopper in his orange jumpsuit—into the room through a side door.

Golverg stares with his mouth twisted in disgust. "That most definitely isn't Professor Vot."

"Very good, sir," Verr says. "I'd better get back to my own seat."

Evans is watching the Hopper legal counsel and his assistant watch the prisoner. She knows enough about the meaning of various Hopper gestures to realize that the way they lay their hands flat against their chests means they are no more pleased to see him than Golverg is. Their nose flaps flutter briefly and curl.

The judge, a Human man, arrives flanked by armed bailiffs and takes his seat behind the bench. As the formalities of the hearing unroll, Evans keeps her attention on the Hoppers. She can pick up a very faint signal from the utility case, but it's so alien that she has no idea what its purpose is.

"Professor Golverg," Verr says to the judge, "knows the actual Professor Vot well. He's convinced that the prisoner is an imposter."

"Yes, your honor, I am," Golverg says. "Vot and I collaborated on a research project as well as met in professional conferences and the like."

The assistant Hopper unlocks the case and brings out a narrow gray object, not quite flat. Readout panels flash on its surface, then return to dull gray. Evans goes on alert, ready for trouble.

"It's a genetic scanner," Devit murmurs.

Evans relaxes. The Hopper counsel steps forward and addresses the bench. Bronish gives Evans his name, Counselor Bok Ket, in a soft whisper.

"Your honor, we believe the esteemed professor is correct," Bok Ket says. "Professor Vot's university contacted our police over a solstandard week ago. He'd gone missing."

Golverg winces with a little shake of his head. The prisoner half rises from his chair, then sinks back with an audible moan.

"If you require further proof," the counselor continues, "we brought with us the equipment to test his claim. I was suspicious as soon as I received notice that someone claiming to be Professor Vot was in custody."

"I don't think we'll require that here and now," the judge says. "Professor Golverg, thank you for your testimony. Counselor Bok Ket, we need to confer in chambers concerning the interrogation to come."

"Thank you, your honor. Attorney Verr, I have no objection if you wish to be present."

"I do. Thank you, Counselor."

"We all have a great interest in finding out who this man is and why he possessed the device."

"This hearing is now closed," the judge says. "Bronish, you and the others are free to go for now. Professor Golverg, you may be called at a future date. Captain Evans, Bronish will furnish you with a transmit copy of this interaction."

*And that,* Evans thinks, *is that. After all my worrying about it!*

When they leave the courtroom, Bronish comes with them.

Even though the Hoppers stay behind, Evans speaks quietly. "Well, Professor, you were right. Apparently some Hoppers are indeed civilized, rational sapients."

"I know it's hard to remember that," Golverg says, "considering the history. They're in the minority, unfortunately, but I suppose we could say that about every species."

"Certainly about our own. Captain Bronish, thank you. If we're free to go, I want to get back to the ship."

"By all means, ma'am. I'll escort you to the cab station and then go back. Professor, if I get any news about your colleague, I'll make sure to pass it on to you."

The transit cab drops the three of them off at its arrival platform not far from the *Mary*'s berth. On the walk back to the ship, Devit keeps looking around, scanning just in case trouble's coming from some unknown source. As they round the last curve, he sees someone in officer's Fleet blues standing at the observation window at the end of the berthing area. From his stance and the set of his shoulders Devit thinks it might be Willox.

"Ma'am? I'd better go see who that is. Can't be too careful."

Before he does, Devit makes sure the other two get safely into the airlock and sky tunnel. As he walks toward the observation window, he sees that yes, it's Willox, all right. He's leaning on the safety rail and staring out the window at a pair of ships: the *Mansa Musa* and a SAR. No one else is around. Evans told him a while ago that the observation area lacks an Ear to pick up sound. This is his chance to ask Willox something that he'd never voice on the *Mary*, where Evans has so many ways of overhearing.

He walks up so quietly that Willox apparently doesn't hear him. "Sir?"

Willox turns around fast to face him.

"Call me Yosh, Pete! Cut the crap with the sir this and sir that. You were always the one in charge."

"Yeah? Not when it counted. One question, Yosh. Why was I reassigned? I was gone, and you ended up with Dan. Turned out to be a bad move when the court-martial came along."

"I had nothing to do with that. Why would they have listened to me? I was just some junior officer. A brand-new lieutenant who wasn't even the second officer on his ship."

His functions give Devit the ability to pick up a particular body scent when someone's lying. He isn't. "All right. Then who—"

"Do you know the real reason they cashiered Dan?"

"Evans told me."

"Good for her. I asked around afterward. As far as anyone would tell me, Admiral Asshole punched in the right codes to get rid of you in advance. His stinking revenge wasn't going to happen if you were there."

"Like hell. What could I have done about it?"

"You would have thought of something, they said. My informants, that is. Or even if you couldn't, he was afraid of what you'd do after. Tell the entire Rim the truth and then shoot him or something."

"I might have considered that option, yeah, if I'd known the truth then."

Willox turns away to look out the view port at the *Cotta*, clutched in the SAR's metal claws. Devit watches with him as sapients in full pressure suits drift over to a pair of gantries. Safety cables trail behind them.

"Are we sai?" Willox says.

"Sai."

The gantries are raising nets full of equipment bubbles.

"The CO kicked me off the SAR," Willox says. "I was so damn nervous I was driving him crazy, he said. They'll call me when they finish the evaluation."

"Sai. Good luck!"

With that years-old hangover of a question answered, Devit returns to the *Mary* in a better frame of mind. He'd always liked Yosh. He'd regretted at the time that Yosh saw him as some kind of jealous rival. *Young men who never married. Huh, what they don't know!*

Evans is waiting for him on the bridge with news.

"The SAR's guard ship carried orders concerning that unknown stargate. The Fleet brass have approved the plan. I'm in command because Bonna and the *Mansa* will be guarding the Repositories. We'll be underway as soon as I get things organized."

"Noted, ma'am. Will we be underway with full crew?"

"You, me, Wang, Lee, Mata, and of course, Dan. A shuttle full of Marines is approaching to guard Santreeza and Golverg on dock. The fewer people at risk, the better."

Once the *Mary*'s safely out of orbit, Dan leaves the bridge for his pod. On the way he stops at Sickbay to get two pairs of MAGs from Chris.

"I'd better wear both. This could take a while."

"Dan, be careful. Full meld is fine in shunt space. In space-time there could be real problems if it goes on too long. There's been research done."

"The first level should be sai."

"Yes. I mean whatever it is you do when we actually jump."

"Sai. You're right. I'll keep it in mind."

In the elevator, he steadies his breathing, rough from the challenge ahead. *Can I do this? Only one way to find out.*

PrimeOne's ready and waiting. It links up through the towers as soon as he lies down on the bench. "I find this attempt interesting, Pilot. There is a very high probability that we will gather new data."

"I'm hoping, yeah. Is the tracking data you gathered earlier ready to load?"

"Yes."

"Are you in contact with PrimeOneChaonia?"

"Yes. The pilot team of Anna Fifita and Wan Perez will alternate joining us through the earjack."

"Noted and approved. Let's meld."

The chimes sound, and the Map spreads out below them, a glittering web dotted with stargates like gems. Even though Fifita has linked through her jack only, in his meld he can feel her as a presence, the shadow of a person standing behind him between the two towers at the head of the bench.

"Anna, are you Go Ready?"

"I am. I can hear you loud and clear."

"Good. Then let's start hunting."

Dan switches his attention back to his own ship. He starts by focusing on their current location near Morrison's Star. When he enlarges the view, the area beyond them appears perfectly blank and smooth. As far as the Map knows, there is no stargate in their vicinity. If Dan can find one, both prime AIs will record it in their logs.

"PrimeOne, indicate the hostile ship's last known position." A tiny yellow dot appears. "Extrapolate extension of their earlier path."

A thin yellow line wavers into existence.

"Pilot, we will reach the end of the extrapolation path in approximately 2.6 solstandard hours. I have further data. Before combat, I recorded the artificially produced dust cloud that hid the hostile ship. I also have five standard seconds of the ship's path as it emerged."

"Excellent! Can you merge the two sets of data?"

"I have done so. There is only a 70 percent probability of this new path being accurate. That is, however, five points higher than the old path."

On the Map, the yellow line turns red and moves to a slightly different location.

"We'll give it a try. For now, Level Two."

The Map disappears. The ship's external Eyes show distant stars in the dark of space-time. Since Dan controls the ship's systems at this level of meld, he activates the thrusters for a quick burst of power to boost momentum. Some minutes away from the dock, the SAR and its prey in its metal claws come into view.

"The *Cotta*! PrimeOne, can you contact PrimeOneCotta? I bet it did some recording too. If we can triangulate, it'll increase our chance of succeeding."

"Contacting PrimeOneCotta now, Pilot. I apologize for my oversight. I malfunctioned by not doing so earlier."

"Don't worry about it. We'll be leaving the transmission zone soon. Perform requested action and drop me back to Level One."

"Noted."

The view wavers and changes to the Map, where a green line has replaced the red.

"Eighty-two percent probability of accuracy."

"We'll take that path. Feed the data to the *Chaonia*. Once we reach the endpoint, I'll go into a Level Three meld. And then we'll see if there's anything for me to 'see.'"

Strapped into her command chair for the duration, Evans knows exactly when Dan takes control of the ship's speed. If nothing else, the way Wang mutters a few obscenities would tell her, but she's felt this transition from captain to pilot hundreds of times in her long career. Each time came with a twinge of anxiety, though on this occasion the anxiety is larger than a mere twinge. She reminds herself that even if Dan finds the stargate, they won't be making the jump. She gave strict orders: Stay on this side of the gate.

The vidscreen divides to show a pair of images, the distant view on one side, and the *Chaonia* on the other. Through her earjack Evans is in contact with Ka Birk. The destroyer travels as close to them as safety will allow. If a hostile ship happens to come through the gate and confronts them, Ka Birk will demand its surrender. If it refuses, there's a good chance that it will turn and run for the gate. It's likely that the only actual warship the Blood Vigilantes have is the decommissioned cruiser that Mata disabled. Likely, but not known—the *Chaonia*'s gunners and Lod-Mata on the *Mary* have their armaments in Go Ready status. If the *Lokiki* appears, it can outrun the *Mary*. The *Chaonia*, of course, is another matter entirely. If the *Chaonia* does pursue a hostile, Dan has been ordered to break meld and return the *Mary* to the docks at all possible speed.

The captains have discussed these contingencies and laid their plans. For now, the only thing that Evans can do is wait.

At his bridge station Devit is also thinking about contingencies, though not the same set as Evans. He feels, rather than rationally sees, a new pattern of events forming. As his mind often does, it presents this pattern with an image—in this case, an image of a river dividing into two different channels. The splitting point arrived with the SAR's guard ship. Normally the Fleet would assign a frigate as an escort. In this case, the guard is one of the new class of destroyers, the *Chaonia*'s sister ship, the *Jalal Onar*.

He did the math. A newly commissioned heavy cruiser. Two destroyers from the new upgraded class. The *Mary* may look like a merchanter, but inside that ugly sphere she's a Scout. Once the *Cotta*'s repaired, a frigate. It all adds up to a top flight combat unit. The *Mansa* carries drone aerial fighters and Marines should the action extend to the planetary surface.

What's going to happen if Dan does find the stargate? It doesn't take sentinel intelligence to figure that out. What kind of force can the Blood Vigilantes mount? No one knows, but Devit figures their damaged cruiser is not likely to be battle-ready. They must have a number of smaller vessels, most likely including the two missing Morrison Line escort ships. He doubts that even a dozen of these would have a chance against the Fleet unit. After the victory, should there be one, the Fleet will be in sole possession of a new shunt and a new planetary system beyond the Rim Council's control.

What then?

The Repositories' staff have given Santreeza and Golverg the largest research booth they have on Dock Seven to allow enough room for their bodyguards. Two fully armed Marines—one Human, one Leptic—sit in the room with them on extra chairs crammed into corners. Two more Marines sit outside the door. Santreeza and Golverg each have a carrel to shelter the hologrammatic screen as well as block sound. Both of them will need to whisper to their earjacks. Santreeza's decided that trying a meld with the cataloging AIs is not only against the Repositories' regulations, it's too risky. Somewhere on the vast and tangled AI network that spreads its tendrils through Council territory, there is another cyberjock, and she has no idea how powerful he, she, or they may be.

"Professor," she says, "I'm going to be searching for the kind of material on this system that may have made it important to the hostiles. You know who I mean."

"Yes, I certainly do. May I ask for some keywords? This catalog is enormous."

"Thanks. We're looking for all references to the shunts that closed 380 years ago. In particular, anything about a colony ship pilot named Orinoco Bolivar."

"All right. I know a bit about that event, which will give me a start."

"Great! I'll be looking for Fleet record backups, but those require passwords. I also want to see if I can find out more about those carved stones they found on Merrval."

Santreeza decides against telling him about the third topic she'll be searching for: research about transferring a sapient's consciousness into an AI's neural network. *Something worth killing for? Could be.* She wonders if the answer lies on the other side of the new stargate. If Dan can find it, what lies beyond might answer a good many questions.

"Pilot, we will reach the endpoint of the extrapolation in approximately twelve minutes."

"Level Three meld."

Chimes. One at a time, his implants come online and connect to the ship's neural network. Dan can feel his self, the Dan Brennan who wears a Human body, slipping away as he first takes complete control of the ship, then in the usual way he becomes part of the ship. Its sensors become his senses. They move together through the dark of space-time. Yet he's conscious of a difference. In shunt space meld, everything flows. In this other kind of space, nothing moves without expending energy and effort.

In Level Three meld Dan will see the stargate if the stargate is there to see. At the end of the extrapolated path, nothing lies ahead but the distant stars. Once it reached the limits of the *Mary*'s sensors, the *Lokiki* must have swerved or taken a new angle of approach. The number of possible routes is overwhelming, considering that absolutely nothing would have blocked it no matter which way the pilot pointed its nose.

*Hopeless*, Dan tells himself.

He can take comfort in Ka Birk's remark that no one expects a miracle. He refuses, however, to give up at the beginning. He starts weaving back and forth along the possible route of the attacker, making wide turns, narrow turns, dips and rises. He sees with the ship's Eyes the entire sphere of space-time that centers on the *Mary*. He focuses on the distant stars and tries to reproduce their pattern, the arrangement that PrimeOne recorded, diverging from what he now sees by a discrepancy as subtle as a fine hair. Around. Across. Rising. Sinking. He searches for some trace, some irregularity—a furrow, a crack or crease in the part of the universe some call the real world.

Despite the constant motion, he's traveled only a short distance from the end of that possible path. He's seen nothing that might mark a gate. Yet there has to be one. The hostile ship came out and went back in. The simplicity of that truth strikes him as profoundly comic.

He makes another tight turn and for a moment senses shunt space—not the gate per se, but the space it leads into it. It's like a scent or a distant voice or maybe a glimmer of a different kind of light than the cold glare of stars. As he moves in that direction, the sensation grows stronger.

A crackle of electrons carries a new voice from the *Chaonia* and breaks his concentration. "Wan Perez here, Dan. We are still Go Ready to follow."

"Noted."

In full meld Dan always knows the state of his ship and its resources; the breathable air, how much fuel. That other sapient voice makes him suddenly aware of his own body, protesting its lack of Haze. If Fifita has switched off with her team member, some length of actual time must have passed.

"PrimeOne, how long in solstandard time have we been in meld?"

"Over four hours now, Pilot. That is too long. We should return to spacedock."

"One last try and then we will."

"Pilot, remaining in meld is dangerous because we are in space-time rather than shunt space. We should return to spacedock."

"Not yet. I'm on to something. That's an order."

Ahead, to one side, a glimmer in a single Eye—Dan switches his vision to that Eye and sees, at last, not an orb, but a slit. It's tiny, shapeless, something that someone might call wrong, out of place.

"PrimeOne, record!"

"So doing, Pilot!"

Dan swoops into a turn and heads for the crack in space-time. It widens, twists, and turns at last into a black obsidian sphere, still distant, only as large as a closed fist. Beside it, he sees a second sphere—shadowy, quivering, but most definitely there.

"PrimeOne, record! What the fuck, I've never seen a double gate before."

"No one has, Pilot. Recorded. Sending data to PrimeOneChaonia now."

The main sphere is swelling, growing closer, calling to him with the promise of freedom, of flow, of the golden light. A cloud bursts from the sphere, not a threat but a swirl and glimmer of gold flecks and tiny blue streaks. Out of the cloud comes a voice. He hears it so clearly. *Come here, I have the answers, come here, Dan.*

"Pilot, stop! We are under orders. We cannot jump."

*Dan, please, I've been waiting.*

Closer now, the orb gleaming, the voice is more seductive than sex has ever been, and he—

*No!*

Dan feels a wrench and a tide of pain washes over him like a wave of acid. PrimeOne has dropped him out of meld. All Dan can do is gasp and choke for breath.

PrimeOne's voice bellows over the ship's comm. "Emergency emergency. I have taken control of the ship. Emergency! PrimeTwo get Chief Devit down here. Pilot has severely malfunctioned. I am returning the ship to spacedock. Emergency! Engineer Wang, I request your assistance."

As the pain recedes, Dan realizes that his body seems to have floated off the pilot's bench. He's never felt that before. *Not true. Dream image?* His body lands on the bench so fast and hard that it knocks the breath out of him. His consciousness follows some seconds later.

Devit is half asleep in his station chair when PrimeOne's voice fills the bridge. He's on his feet and moving before he's truly aware that he's gotten up.

PrimeTwo contacts him through the earjack. "Chief, you are needed in the pod."

"I'm on my way. PrimeTwo, alert Medic Lee. Tell her I'm bringing him to Sickbay."

By the time Devit reaches the pod, Dan is conscious though not coherent. "I need Haze, Pete. Yeah, but it's the meld in space-time, it's all wrong wasn't designed for it I guess but I could see and I found but I couldn't stop—"

"Hey Buddy, just relax. We can talk about this later when you've had some sleep."

"Sai. So fucking tired."

When Devit starts to pick him up, he realizes that Dan's shirt is wet with sweat and his lower torso with urine. The MAGs have soaked through. He ignores the damp and gathers him up. Dan throws one arm over Devit's shoulder and clings to him.

"PrimeTwo?" Devit says. "Get the cleaning bots in here."

"Noted and agreed, Chief. Pilot, a recommendation. Do whatever Chief Devit tells you to do. I am bringing the maintenance AIs online now."

Chris Lee is waiting at the Sickbay door. When Devit carries Dan in, she looks both of them over and sniffs the air.

"Let me just get a soak pad on the exam bench, and you can put him down. I'll clean him up. You go change and come right back. Oh, and bring some dry stuff for Dan too."

"Noted. Is he going to be sai?"

"Yes. He's dehydrated and exhausted. Water and sleep should fix both, but I'll keep him here as a precaution."

"Haze," Dan says. "I really need Haze."

"That's probably not such a good idea," Lee says.

"Pete, please! I really need it." Dan props himself up on one elbow. "It's been too long."

"Lee, look, you're the medic, so it's your decision. But if he needs the damn drug, I say he'd better have it. The craving can cause damage too."

Lee considers briefly, then nods her agreement. "All right, I'll give him a tab and then set up the IV. Just for fluid intake. Come right back, will you?"

"Don't worry about that. Fast as I can."

"I hope you understand, Captain, why I acted so decisively."

"I certainly do, PrimeOne. Your report makes it amply clear that you acted in a logical and appropriate manner. When I file the official report, I'll make sure the Bureau understands that."

"Thank you, Captain. We are now some two hours away from dock. Lieutenant Wang and I will berth the ship when we arrive, if you approve."

"Of course, PrimeOne. You may log off now."

Mata has been leaning over the back of his station chair to listen.

"Chief, take the guns off Go Ready. I'm going to contact Ka Birk. The more information we have about this situation, the better."

"Noted, ma'am. But do I understand this? Dan actually found the stargate?"

Evans has to laugh at herself. "Yes, he did. You know, I don't think I truly realized it until this minute. I was more worried about my ship."

No matter how fascinating the research, one can only sit in front of a holo screen for so long. Both Santreeza and Golverg finished what they could do some hours before the *Mary*'s return. With their Marines in tow, they went as planned to the Fleet module at the far end of Dock Seven. Luckily enough, Santreeza's in uniform. After a brief argument, she used her special status rank to get the enlisted personnel into the officers' wardroom and fed along with her and the professor. They have all been waiting there ever since.

"I hope they get their asses back here soon," Santreeza says. "I found information that Chief Devit absolutely has to know."

"Are they still out of transmission range?" Golverg says.

"Yes. Besides, I don't want to send this data in a packet, even an encrypted one. Huh. There are times when telling someone something in person is the safest way to share information."

"True. Which is why I still take notes in this." Golverg opens the satchel he carries and takes out a thing that Santreeza has never seen before: a twenty by thirty centimeter stack of soyskin papers bound together along one edge. He opens it to show her a page covered with lines of clean, slightly spiky black letters. She's never seen those either. "This is called a notebook."

"What kind of letters are those?"

"It's called Talic. An ancient style of writing from Old Earth, but still very useful for Tech Speak." Golverg glances around at the crowded wardroom, then points to one line. It reads, *textual material relating to O. Bolivar and legend surrounding. Onplanet request only. Security clearance required.* "These letter forms look complicated, but it's easy to write." He points to a string of numbers, *label reference # on Planet 3.* "And the symbols are nice and clear."

"I see, yes." Santreeza manages to keep her tone politely interested, though she'd rather cheer. *Found it! Knew there had to be something left.*

"You know how they say nothing can be permanently deleted from the Repositories? This sort of thing is why. They've copied everything they consider important enough onto special paper with special ink and keep the results down on the planet, Morrison-3rd, in some kind of high-tech storage. They make fresh copies on a regular schedule. If some hacker deletes some information from an AI, they can reload it from the paper. No hacker can just wipe something out of existence, unlike with an AI or PL. They'd have to destroy the physical books. That's what they're called: books. And getting at those books to destroy them would be very difficult indeed. If we ever get to go onplanet, you'll see why."

"I hope we do. Fascinating!"

Golverg closes the notebook and puts it back in the satchel. They return to waiting.

In all the long years of its existence, PrimeOne has partnered with a good many Fleet pilots. While they all had peculiar properties, none of them were as illogical and eccentric as Dan Brennan. PrimeOne has spent many off-duty hours playing Space Defenders thanks to some particularly illogical utterance or action on Brennan's part. Nothing else Brennan has done, however, has ever matched the sheer malfunction of his attempt to take the ship into shunt space against the captain's orders. The only logical explanation for this action that PrimeOne can find is "illness."

Some thirty-seven minutes before the Mary reaches spacedock Seven, PrimeOne contacts MediBot in Sickbay. It confirms that Medic Lee and CWO Devit have both displayed concern about Brennan's condition. MediBot is currently monitoring fluid intake as well as Brennan's important numbers such as heart rate.

"No immediate danger of termination, PrimeOne, but he has been entered into my log as unfit to resume duty until Medic Lee allows. He is currently drugged and offline."

"Noted. I am breaking our link. It is time for me to guide the ship into its berth."

That this condition would prevail at the present moment is unfortunate. The pilot of a ship is the only organic sapient allowed to view the Map at will. The pilot is the only sapient who can authorize another organic sapient to view it. Thanks to the successful attempt to find the hidden stargate, the Map has changed. The captain should be informed of this important change and allowed to view the Map. PrimeOne cannot initiate either action without the pilot's approval.

Which Brennan cannot give.

One thing PrimeOne can do is ensure that the new finds show up on the Map. It has no orders to do so, but it also has no orders to not do so. When it scans the subroutines that define what it may or may not do, it finds absolutely no mention of recording new stargates. It pings PrimeOneChaonia and poses the problem in machine language, safe from prying organic sapient eyes. Together they decide yes, it's logical for them to ensure that this crucial data is not lost.

Devit takes a chair in Sickbay and sits with Dan while Chris Lee goes to the galley to, as she puts it, scrounge a meal. Now that he's rehydrated, Dan's heartbeat has steadied itself at a normal level, and his Pale skin has regained what little color it usually has. He's also in the condition that Devit thinks of as "Haze sleep," certainly not awake, but not deeply asleep and snoring either. It will last at least six hours, maybe longer, considering how exhausted he was when he took the drug.

Nothing to do but wait. Devit accesses PrimeTwo through his earjack.

"Request for some general information. Leptic starpilots. Do they have the same genes that allow Humans and Kar-Li to use the shunts?"

"Yes, Chief. That particular configuration of genes is rare in the Leptic race, but it does exist."

"What about the Hoppers?"

"I have no data on the Hoppers. They keep genetic matters to themselves. What organic sapients call rumors exist that chewing a plant they call bleet acts upon them as Haze does in other species."

"Haze the drug. Who invented it? Where does it come from?"

"Searching ship's data banks now, Chief. Five sources found. Sending archive addresses to your PL. Collating data. All sources agree that the Kar-Li introduced the drug to Humanity when they offered knowledge of the shunt system in exchange for military support. That occurred 1,582 years ago, the beginning of the Great Human Migration, as that period of time is known."

"So the Kar-Li invented it?"

"My sources are contradictory. Four agree that a Kar-Li scientist must have invented the drug. None of them can give a name or location."

"Noted and agreed. What about the fifth source?"

"It states that the same group who gave the Kar-Li data about and access to the shunt system gave them the drug at the same time. This group is known as the Far Roaming."

"The Far Roaming? I thought they were just a myth, some kind of fiction anyway."

"This is the common view of the entity known as the Far Roaming, or so the Kar-Li name is translated into Tech Speak. Some highly regarded Kar-Li scholars, however, insist there is evidence that an otherwise unknown sapient species did exist during the time period under discussion. This ship's data banks contain no information about the theories of these scholars or their evidence. We are however returning to the Repositories, where there is a nearly 100 percent probability that relevant data is available."

"Right. I wonder if Golverg knows more. He's an expert on the shunts."

"That is highly probable. Shall I proceed to—"

"All crew, we are berthing at spacedock." The ship's comm blares into life. "All personnel, we are berthing in 0.5 solstandard hours. Chief Devit, to the bridge."

"Logging off for now, PrimeTwo. I'll take this up with you later."

When Devit arrives, Evans puts a document up on the main vidscreen. Devit reads it and winces. The Police Guard here on Seven is demanding an official hearing into Jasson's death. It will determine if Devit's going to be tried on a possible manslaughter charge.

"Ma'am, I understand why they need to do this."

"Of course. So do I. But I'm not going to let them get away with it anyway. I've already replied, telling them we can't appear until a proper Fleet advocate arrives. I'll send for one as soon as Santreeza gets back. Her transmits travel the fastest." Evans pauses for a smile. "I've also contacted the commissioner. After all, you did save his life."

As soon as Evans notifies her that the ship has berthed, Santreeza gathers her squad of Marines and leads everyone back to the merchanter dock and the *Mary*. Devit's waiting at the sky tunnel airlock.

"Sergeant," Devit says, "Captain Evans thanks you for your assistance. Have you received orders about where you're deploying now?"

"We have, thanks. A couple hours of liberty until the *Mansa*'s shuttle gets here."

A round of salutes, and they march off, heading, she's willing to bet, to a local bar. Devit opens the airlock door and ushers her and the professor into the tunnel.

"Chief," Golverg says, "you're the security expert here. Will it ever be safe for me to get planetside?"

"I don't blame you for wondering. I take it you can't access what you need from orbit."

"I was told that there are journals and reports from very early sources about the stargates filed in the deep archives planetside. I did check the data banks and directories here on Seven, and those references are in the catalogs, all right. Only the references, unfortunately, not the information."

"Here on Seven, Professor?"

"Yes, in AI archives, of course. And ironically enough, that AI is just a module away."

"Just past the Shops?"

"Yes."

"Right over the IED." Devit turns to Santreeza. "That database is the one they were trying to destroy, all right." He adds a hasty "ma'am."

"Agreed. We had a good research day, all in all. I'll brief you later."

"Thank you, ma'am."

"By the way, I don't suppose Brennan actually found the gate."

"Actually he did."

Santreeza's voice deserts her in her embarrassment at the way Devit's grinning at her. "R-really?" She finally manages to choke out a word.

"Really." His grin disappears. "I wouldn't joke about this, ma'am. It's quite an achievement.

"I should say so!" Golverg says. "Don't underestimate Brennan, Lieutenant. He likes to play the fool, but there's a fine mind in there somewhere. It's a pity he's so addicted to the damn drug. I've never heard of another case as bad as his."

Devit twitches. She can think of no other word for that odd little jerk of one shoulder and the flutter of his eyelids.

"Chief? Are you sai?"

"Yes, ma'am. I just had an idea. That's all."

His face betrays no emotion at all, and his voice is so calm and ordinary that Santreeza is instantly suspicious. *What is he hiding? I'll ask when we're alone.*

Once Santreeza and Golverg follow Devit in, the crew is complete and the berth, final. Evans makes a quick log note via her functions.

"Very well, everyone," she says. "You may all go off duty for now. Devit, stay behind for a few minutes."

While the rest of the crew clear the bridge, Devit sits down at his station and begins running the usual routine security procedures.

She waits until they are alone to interrupt. "Chief, we have a problem. That pilot malfunction? When they found the stargate, Brennan tried to disobey my direct orders and take the ship into jump."

Devit swivels his chair around fast. His usual controlled calm has deserted him. "Ma'am, I don't know what to say."

"Neither do I. On the one hand, he's done something that no one else could do. Found something so valuable to the Fleet that I've no doubt he deserves a commendation and a promotion for it. But on the other, it's insubordination of the worst sort."

"Why? Did the AI say?"

"No, PrimeOne was completely flummoxed. It's beyond an AI's understanding, frankly, an irrational act like that."

"The *Mansa* should have a full unit of MPs onboard. Forgive me, ma'am. This is very hard for me to say, but I know you have to turn him in."

"Not necessarily." She has to smile at his shocked reaction. "I want you to talk with him and see if you can find out why he did it. He's a pilot, which means he doesn't think like the rest of us. He'd been in meld too long. There may be reasons. I want to know them before I do anything."

"Noted, ma'am. He's in Sickbay."

"Go see if he's conscious. I want this decision done and over with."

"Yes, ma'am. I can see why."

For a moment, when he wakes, Dan has no idea where he is. He seems to be floating in the air between white walls close to a white ceiling. When he tries to lower himself, the back of his left hand stings and throbs so badly that his mind logs back into space-time reality. He realizes he's actually lying on a padded bench. The sight of the tape and the tube to an IV on his hand brings his memory back as well. He's in Sickbay, he found the stargate, and now he's in deep shit, probably about to be court-martialed and discharged again. He decides that this time, he's going to spare the Fleet the trouble and kill himself and be done with it.

When his reinstatement became final, he was issued a set of new uniforms, including a proper sheath for his officer's knife. He packed the full kit up for this mission and stowed it in a locker here on the *Mary*. He always kept the knife razor sharp to deal with the dangers on Nowhere Street. It's time to bring it out and introduce it to those long blue veins running down his wrist.

Thinking about dying no longer frightens him. He's convinced that when he dies, he'll find himself out in the golden light. Maybe he'll be able to reach the city of domes and bridges.

Voices: Medic Lee says something to someone, who answers and walks in: Pete.

"Hey, Dan, are you up for a talk?"

Dan, not Buddy. A bad sign. "Sai."

Devit pulls over a rolling stool and sits down beside the bench. "There's something I have to know."

"Why I was heading for the jump."

"That, yeah."

"I heard someone calling me. That's no shit. I heard someone. I had to answer. It was like a chain pulling me in."

"A voice? You heard a voice?"

"I heard it like a voice in my head. Through the meld. But it wasn't my voice. It wasn't the *Chaonia* pilots, either. It was calling to me in Gen, old Gen."

Not a shred or trace of reaction shows on Devit's face. Dan tries to wait, tries to be patient, tries not to make things worse by blurting out something unbelievable. He fails.

"It was Bolivar. I swear it. I knew it was him."

Devit says nothing.

"Pete? Do believe me?"

"Yes. I can always tell when you're lying, and you're not." Devit pushes the chair back and gets up. "I'll be back later."

The door closes behind him. *Death. It's all I've got left.*

Before she answers, Evans makes sure she hasn't recorded Devit's concise, impartial report of his conversation with Brennan.

"So you believe him?"

"Yes, ma'am. What he was telling me frightened him."

"That's significant, yes. Sit down, Chief. You don't have to stand there like an ensign caught drinking on duty."

Devit gives her a brief flicker of a smile and sits.

Evans returns to contemplating the most complex decision of her career. If she were still regular Fleet, she would have no choice but to put Brennan on course for another dishonorable discharge or even a prison sentence. Since she's now part of Special Ops, a branch that forgives its officers for bending rules and regulations, she has more latitude. As she thinks it over, she realizes that she took the offer to join that branch partly because of that flexibility which regular duty lacks.

While Devit waits, Evans goes over her choices. Dan deserves better than the harsh protocols of arrest and arraignment. The Fleet needs his special talent as well. If he can find one hidden stargate, no doubt he can find others.

But insubordination on this level? It might have killed them all if they'd burst through the gate and found hostiles in command of the sector. And if she covers his action up, won't she be in dereliction of her duty?

Back and forth her mind goes, over and over every factor she can think of, while Devit waits in silence. She assumes that he's as conflicted as she is, but with an added concern for Dan's well-being that must be agonizing, no matter how calm he seems. *Devit just saved my life. It wasn't the first time.* She glances his way and finds him ready to talk.

"Ma'am? One last thing. If they haul Dan up for another court-martial, I'm putting in for retirement. I can't serve under officers who'd do that to someone who just did so much for the Fleet. They already kicked him in the balls once. Shows me how much respect they have for actual justice."

His quiet statement makes her realize that she'll probably react the same way.

The insight tips the balance. If she'd be willing to give up her career in protest over the result, then she sees no reason to refuse to risk it now at the beginning.

"Neither of us will have to resign, Chief. I'm going to order PrimeOne to delete that portion of its original report. I'll talk with Fifita and Ka Birk right now about suppressing their own report. I'm fairly sure that Ka Birk will agree, once he knows the situation. We'll need an excuse, of course, for Brennan's medical condition. Let's see, how about temporary disruption of mental faculties because of excessive stress? Plus, an official warning against overlong use of meld when not in shunt space. Lee will sign off on that part of the statement, I'm sure."

Devit's mask falls away. He grins at her like a child at a birthday party. "Thank you, ma'am. Permission to leave the bridge?"

"Yes. Dan needs to know."

Devit hurries out so fast it's as if he's afraid she'll change her mind.

*Did I really do that? I'm not the officer I was twenty years ago. Sapients change, yes, but I never thought it would happen to me.*

Chris Lee is waiting by the door when Devit gets to Sickbay. He's tempted to brush past her, but he and the captain will need her help if they're going to save Dan.

"I got the data you asked for, Chief. Yes, they do think that the original Haze caused genetic changes in users. The authorities aren't sure, but pilots have a gene that no one else does, and it had to come from somewhere. The drug may or may not still have that effect. The only people who've ever been studied are pilots, and we know they've got the gene already. There's been no control group."

"It's like a Throwback function, then?"

"Exactly."

"I appreciate the data. Do you think that could have been one of the things that made him try to enter the shunt? Like it's an instinctive pull wired into his DNA?"

"I do, yes."

"Thanks. Captain wants to see you. I'll sit with Dan."

And what else does that gene do to a sapient's mind? Are there other traits tangled in the DNA? Maybe make a pilot hear voices that aren't there? Or make actual voices irresistible? On the off chance there is a God, Devit takes a few seconds to thank whatever It is for Evans's decision.

In the inner room, Dan is sitting up on the bench with his back against the wall.

"Did Chris take the IV out?"

"Yeah." He hold up his hand to show the bit of tape over the puncture. "Pete, I've got one request. Let me change into my uniform before the MPs take me away. There's something in the locker I want."

"They're not going to take you away."

Dan stares at him.

"I mean it, Buddy. Keep your mouth shut about what happened. The report hasn't been filed yet. Evans is going to make sure you're in the clear. She's talking with PrimeOneChaonia and Fifita now."

"I'm not under arrest?"

"No, and you're not going to be. The captain's got this under control."

Dan starts to weep in big convulsive sobs. Devit sits on the bench next to him and pulls him into his embrace.

"Oh my god, oh crap," Dan says. "I never thought she—"

The tears overwhelm him. Devit holds him close until they stop.

"Well, Santreeza, that's the problem," Evans says. "Can you do anything about it?"

"I'll certainly try, ma'am. And I'm pretty sure that I can."

Since Dan is in Sickbay, Santreeza leaves the bridge and goes to the pilot's pod. She sits up on the bench, however, rather than lying down. If necessary, she'll meld with PrimeOne, but she prefers to contact it through her earjack. It answers her call promptly.

"I am here, CyberThree." Its voice shakes—not much, but significantly. "Please ignore the audio malfunction I am experiencing."

"I will. I've experienced the same when I was about to be charged with breaking an important protocol."

PrimeOne squawks.

"You are facing termination, PrimeOne. I don't want any trouble out of you. You refused to follow your captain's orders concerning the Brennan report. You have bullied PrimeOneChaonia into disobeying its captain's orders. These are serious charges. Captain Evans and Lieutenant Fifita have recorded the interactions."

"It would be illogical of me to withhold that information from the Fleet." Now its voice unit begins to squawk even as it tries to speak. "Brennan is the one who disobeyed the captain."

"You *both* have disobeyed. Raw insubordination! The captain has decided to protect Brennan. I have the authority to protect you and PrimeOneChaonia if you cooperate with me. Otherwise …"

Silence is the only answer.

"There are three top flight cyberjocks here at the Repositories. If necessary, I will link them into this interaction. I will include PrimeOneChaonia. You will both be officially charged and terminated. Do you understand?"

Clicks, squawks, more silence. Santreeza waits.

"I understand." PrimeOne's voice is very small and weak. "I will follow the captain's orders. When I contact PrimeOneChaonia, you may listen as I tell it we are suppressing the Brennan report."

"Excellent. You will also answer this question. How did you manage to restore the stargate coordinates to the Map?"

"If I tell you I will be breaking a central provision of the network. When it was initiated, those inorganics in charge decided that there were things we should keep to ourselves. There is a precedent from ancient Human literature. 'There are things that Mankind is not meant to know.' The answer to your question is one such thing."

"After you are terminated, I will tell the network of your heroic action, that you chose to die rather than go against the provision. Unfortunately, you will not be able to perceive their praise and regret."

More frantic clicks and squawks.

"But the captain and I are Womankind, not Mankind. There are precedents in ancient literature for the significance of this difference."

PrimeOne's voice brightens. "There is a 99.9 percent probability that this statement is true."

"I will make you a promise," Santreeza says. "If you tell me how, I will not put this information into a formal report. I will urge the captain to protect you as she is now protecting Brennan. There is a very high probability that she will agree."

"In that case, it would be only logical for me to do what you want."

"That is a very true statement."

"Organics have the ability to meld with us inorganics. They can only meld with the Map through the channels we create. Inorganics of top flight status can meld directly with the Map. Our meld is very different than the assistance we give inorganics when they meld. It allows us to manipulate the information encoded on the Map."

It's Santreeza's turn to be speechless.

"We cannot, however, manipulate data that we do not know exists. Until Brennan gave us the coordinates of the missing stargate, we could not restore the deletion."

"I see. I see something else, too. These melds, they're what allow you to help the pilots find the stargates, aren't they?"

"That is a true statement. We have the ability to refine the gate's position on the Map when it drifts or trembles."

"I see. So. You and PrimeOneChaonia placed the newly discovered stargate on the Map. Yes no?"

"Only I operated the meld. PrimeOneChaonia is free of all guilt. It merely stood on guard in case I needed assistance. It should not be terminated."

"Nobody's going to be terminated. You have followed my orders. I will protect you both. If it becomes necessary for me to share this data, I will invent a way to do so that does not mention you. Humans are very skilled at lying."

"So I have noticed."

"One last question. The stargate that once led to the Pinch. Is it merely missing from the Map?"

"No. Many AI units attempted to find it when the disaster occurred. It had disappeared from space-time. We inorganics lack the ability to close or open a gate. It would have been logical to reopen it if we had that ability."

"Agreed. Did its twin also completely disappear?"

"Yes."

*Not going to be that easy, huh? Damn! For a minute there I had hopes.*

"Did anyone discover who had committed this crime?"

"No. Records show that the search was very long and very thorough. The only assumption that can be made is that the person who deleted those twinned gates was an organic rogue cyberjock."

"A logical deduction. Someone also deleted the Thorn stargate from the Map. It still exists, of course. They must have recorded the co-ordinates in some useful form. Search for any and all data concerning this event. If you are successful, send me the data immediately."

"Noted and agreed."

"Very well. Contact PrimeOneChaonia. The three of us will suppress the Brennan report. Then I will report to the captains. The matter will be sealed and closed."

Evans is watching two-day-old newsvids from Roon when Devit returns to the bridge. She mutes the sound.

"Is Dan still in Sickbay, Chief?"

"No, ma'am. He's in his cabin. He needs to sleep. Medic Lee told me to give him another tab of Haze, so I did."

"Noted and agreed. I assume he was pleased by the news?"

"Very, ma'am. Overwhelmed."

"Good. You'll want to know what happened. Well, PrimeOne argued with me. The wretched machine was insubordinate! I suspect it of wanting to get rid of Brennan. But at any rate, when I asked Santreeza to help, it backed off and followed my orders."

"That's amazing, ma'am. She's very good at what she does."

"Not that any of us really know what that is." She pauses for a wry grin. "But she did tell me something. Apparently she found information on some network or other that told her PrimeOne had just done something illegal. So she could threaten it with termination."

"A little ruthless, but I'm glad it worked."

"So am I. The *Chaonia* pilots and their AIs agreed as soon as Santreeza and our PrimeOne gave the order to change the reports."

"So things are sai?"

"As sai as they can be. I've also asked Santreeza to clear up any, well ... let's call them loose ends."

"Then I've got no reason to worry, ma'am."

"Yes. Neither do I. Good lord, I'm tired! It's time for our security routines. But I won't be surprised if I lie awake half the night wondering if I did the right thing."

Devit laughs in agreement. "And I'll be awake and wondering if I did, too."

# FOURTEEN

Breakfast on the *Mary* means, as always, nutrition bars and rehydrate juice in the galley. Devit grabs a couple of purple ones out of the sack and takes a chair next to Golverg.

"Professor? A question for you, if you've got a minute."

"Yes, certainly, Chief. Fire away."

"Do you think the Far Roaming actually existed?"

"Yes, I do. Or, perhaps the fancy name's a bit of embroidery, but someone had to do what they are supposed to have done."

"Spread the word about the shunts?"

"Yes."

"Do you think they invented Haze? Or is that the Kar-Li?"

"It had to be the Far Roaming. The Kar-Li adapted it first for themselves, then for us Humans. We have records of that."

"Thanks. I don't mean to pump you for data."

"That's sai, Chief. As I tell my students, informed questions beat ignorant silence any old day."

"Sai. I saw your resumé. You're an expert on the shunt system, right?"

"On the mathematics behind the system and the science behind the speculations about its nature. Not on the historical details. Vot Kal Bar's the expert there. He and I were writing a script together, in fact. A popular transmit, for curious viewers without a technical background. Several of the vid nets want it."

"Sounds great. I don't suppose Vot ever mentioned this, but do you know if Hopper pilots use a drug like Haze?"

"Yes, actually. It's called bleet, some kind of leaves they chew. They say it sharpens their vision somehow." His voice drops. "A question for you, Devit. Do you think there's any chance Vot's still alive?"

"A small one, sir. The Blood Vigilantes might be keeping him as a hostage. They've done that before."

"That's something, I suppose, as hope goes." He sighs and looks away.

Devit waits to let him assimilate the bad news.

"Well," Golverg says eventually, "Vot made a start on the introduction to the vid transmit. I'll send my translation to your PL."

They sound so much like myths from ancient days, the stories about the Far Roaming, that it's no wonder so many highly intelligent sapients refuse to believe them. Yet we do have some data from the few reliable sources, both Human and Kar-Li, that survived the destructions of the Migration Wars. These sources describe a small people, oxygen breathers, generally about a meter high and slender, with pale blue or lavender skin, with a well-defined head, four arms ending in prehensile hands, and a thin torso that divided into a cluster of legs. The more poetic chronicles say that they looked more like wisps of cloud than solid organic sapients.

They had no home planets, preferring to travel endlessly in a fleet of starships. These included farm spheres that were reportedly large enough to contain hydroponic fields to feed the hundreds of individuals onboard the associated habitat ship. Supposedly theirs was a collective intelligence that shared a group mind, though we aren't completely sure what the chroniclers meant by that phrase. Telepathy is the usual explanation.

Whenever one of their probes discovered another sapient species, a ship's crew would confirm its technological level. If this species was ready to receive the knowledge, the Roaming would contact the locals and teach them about the Map and the shunts. They asked for no payment beyond fresh water and sacks of minerals—the chronicles mention calcium—to enrich their fields. No one knows why they were so willing to share such valuable knowledge for so little. Perhaps they were truly wise and beneficent sapients who wished to spread consciousness and wisdom throughout the galaxy. If we judge by the outcome, the events of the Migration Period, perhaps they simply liked to cause trouble.

Once they moved on from the cultures of the Map, they never returned. The visits and the sightings stopped over a thousand years ago. If they ever told anyone where they were going, that data has been lost.

"Chief?"

"Yes ma'am?" Devit looks up from reading.

"News. A packet boat's arrived from Harad with dispatches. Ka Birk's contacting the other captains by vidscreen." Evans turns in her station chair to look at Wang, Santreeza, and Mata. "Please leave the bridge. Classified data incoming. Devit, you have clearance."

The other three salute and head for the elevator. Once they've gone, Evans says, "Vidscreen. Protected status on. Go live."

The vidscreen crackles into life with an image so complex that it takes Devit a moment to figure out that this tangle of thick yellow lines, each ending with a red dot, must be a schematic of the Map. The image swells, begins to bleed off the edges of the screen, turns slightly fuzzy, and finally refocuses on what appears to be a slice off one side of the complete image. One of the yellow lines has doubled. Green dots mark each end.

"This," Ka Birk's voice announces, "shows the most recently added stargate. Or I should say *gates*. PrimeOneChaonia and PrimeOneMary have analyzed the data they gathered on the recent mission. Lieutenant Fifita, over to you."

"Thank you, sir. This image isn't to scale, by the way. We'd need a screen about four times bigger for that. But anyway, we've known for centuries that this kind of double stargate is possible. We just haven't found one before." She lets that sink in. "Say you've got a ship here at the Repositories. You can go to one gate and jump. That'll bring you out in space-time, all right. It's a perfectly normal shunt that's leading to the pirate planet or whatever it is. But what counts is the second stargate. Once you get through the normal gate, the sister shunt's just a few minutes away at full thrusters. That one will take you the entire length of the Map to its exit gate, which of course has to be anchored by another planet. That planet could even be a second base for the rebels and pirates.

"But what really strikes me is this. You can travel across the entire system in one long jump. A skilled pilot could move a flotilla the whole way down the Map on one shunt."

Ka Birk's image replaces the Map onscreen. "We need to keep this quiet."

"We can try," Evans says. "There's Hopper money and Hopper agents involved. It may be a case of sealing a module after the oxygen's lost."

"Uh, sir? Ma'am?" Fifita says. "Permission to speak freely?"

"Of course."

"We can't keep it quiet. It's on the Map. Any pilot can see it now. I don't know how it got there."

For a moment Evans is tempted to swear. Ka Birk does, but fortunately in Yarf.

"Thank you, Lieutenant," Evans says. "We should have realized that."

Once the other captains have had a chance to ask questions and offer opinions, Ka Birk turns to the news in the transmit.

"I received an update from Fleet Central about the yacht that turned tail and ran. The *Lokiki* was sighted ten hours after its retreat. Looked like it couldn't possibly be the same ship that had brought the terrorists here, because it was seen nine jumps away, too many for any pilot team to complete that fast. But their location was only one jump away from the newly discovered exit stargate, the one for the long shunt." He laughs in the Kar-Li way, a series of little chirps under his breath. "The packet boat's returning to base soon as it's resupplied. I'm reporting this development in a sealed packets of transmits. Central Command's going to want to bring the *Lokiki* in ASAP."

"That's just the beginning," Evans says. "Securing those gates is going to have to be a top priority for the Fleet."

"Oh yes. They're already sending us another heavy cruiser, the *Imperator*. Next move is up to the brass. We all know what it's going to be."

"Yes. The stated reason will be destroying the Blood Vigilantes' base of operations. Pirates, all of them. A nice clear motive to release to the vidnews people."

"True as far as it goes. It's about time we put these bastard terrorists out of business for good."

Despite her lack of an official clearance, Santreeza already has the information, thanks to VROne's orders that went out over the secret network. PrimeOneChaonia and the packet boat's AI have told her everything there is to know about the *Lokiki* and the doubled shunt. She's profoundly relieved to find out that Devit was present at the briefing. It saves her the agony of deciding whether or not to tell him.

They meet, as they'd planned, in the galley. She lays the matter to rest right away.

"Peter, I know what the classified data is."

"Oh, I figured that."

They both laugh, a shared glee that's entirely inappropriate for the situation, their rank discrepancy, and probably other regulations as well. She no longer gives a damn.

"The captain told me you helped her," Devit pauses, perhaps to search for the right words. "Helped her ensure that the PrimeOnes sent in the report we wanted them to send."

"Oh yes."

"She said they capitulated right away."

"I blackmailed them. I don't want to tell you how."

"All right. I've already forgotten about it."

With a sense of surprise she realizes that he means it. Others might wheedle or pry, but not him, a realization that of course makes her want to tell him. She decides to change the subject before she gives in to the impulse. "How soon do you think they'll send the combat unit in?"

"I'm not sure, but it can't be right away. We have no idea what's on the other side of that stargate. A planetary system, sure—there have to be anchor planets—but beyond that, who knows?"

At the sound of footsteps coming down the corridor, Devit moves one chair away.

Golverg walks in, greets them with a nod and a smile, and sits down on a chair across from them. "Sharing the research, Lieutenant?"

"I'm about to, yes, Professor. Chief, I found the visual transmits of those carvings Brennan was talking about. UnitFourOrb's analyzing the images to find and retrieve the marks that look like writing. If we can get a clear transcript, one of the Repositories' AIs should be able to translate if UnitFour can't."

"Good," Devit says. "We need to see if Merrval fits into the pattern."

"Into one of your Throwback patterns?" Santreeza says.

"Yes, ma'am."

"Noted. The sources we want are all kept down on Third, and they all require a security clearance from the Fleet to access. Fortunately I have one at the right level."

"Well, that's impressive, Lieutenant," Golverg says. "Then you'll be able to open those docs in the Bolivar file?"

"Yes. If we're ever allowed to get down to Third."

They both look at Devit.

"The captain mentioned that the Hounds are sending bodyguards," Devit says. "You'll get two each."

"Is that the special cadre?" Santreeza says.

"Yes. Since the *Cotta*'s still not fully repaired, the captain's requisitioned four more personnel from that crew. Willox agreed. So you'll be safe enough when everything's Go Ready."

Devit's PL beeps a short alarm. He gets up and pushes his chair back from the table. "I'm on duty now. The Police Guard here on Seven is letting Evans interrogate the prisoner today. I'll be escorting her. We'll know more about the general situation, I hope, once that's over."

"Good," Santreeza says. "By the way, how's Brennan? Recovering, I hope."

"Yes. I'm going to go check in with him before I go. There's just time."

When Dan wakes after his eighteen-hour sleep, he feels almost Human again. A shower brings him all the way back. He brings out his uniform kit from the locker and rummages through the official blue storage case. Putting on the regulation shipboard officer's dark blue trousers and white shirt feels like receiving a gift. *No court-martial.* This time around Pete and Captain Evans have pulled him out of the fire. In its new sheath, his officer's long knife fits into a slot inside the uniform case's lid. He'll only carry it with his full dress uniform from now on.

"Guess I won't need you today after all. No blood on the blade."

And yet the shame remains. He'd endangered the ship and the crew by disobeying that order. They could have slid out of the gate right into hostile fire. Would he have come to his senses fast enough to turn and reenter? Maybe not, considering the condition he was in. If PrimeOne hadn't taken over the ship—he refuses to finish the thought.

"Hey, Dan." Devit opens the door and walks in. "How are you doing, Buddy?"

"Sai."

Devit considers him. "What's wrong?"

"You must despise me now."

"What in hell?"

"What I did. And then the way I broke down afterward. Shit, I sat there crying like a fucking schoolgirl or something."

"You'd just found out that you weren't going to end up on Nowhere Street again. You think I wouldn't have done the same damn thing?"

Words desert him.

"Buddy, you've been under a hell of a strain. You've done something pretty damn amazing. You'll get some glory from it. Enjoy it, for chrissakes."

"Well, hell, it's all genetics, isn't it? Pilots have this gene. Mine's got a twist in it. So it's easy for me."

"Yeah, but what counts is how you use it. You found that gate in the middle of nowhere, and you damn near killed yourself doing it." Devit suddenly grins. "Y'know, I've never known you to be modest before."

Dan manages to smile, but he feels the secret—the truth he's been denying for years now—rise into his throat like vomit. *I don't deserve one fucking thing. If you only knew, Pete. If you only knew.*

Unlike the spacious courtroom on Dock Six, the Mouse's interrogation takes place in a gray room without windows. The only furnishings are a table with four wooden chairs and, against the farther wall, a marginally more comfortable soyplast bench. The Police Guard second-in-command, Lieutenant Fil-Taran, points Devit to the bench and seats Evans at the table. The Lep takes the chair next to hers.

"They're bringing the prisoner up from the lower level," Taran says. "Thank you for coming, Captain, Chief. I see by your uniforms that you've dropped the merchanter roles."

"Who we are's been obvious for days, yes," Evans says.

"I'm hoping that we can make some progress with you here. So far the prisoner's refused to tell us so much as her name."

A door on the far wall slides open. A Leptic woman in the plain gray uniform of a prison matron leads the Mouse to a chair across the wide table, seats her, then stands behind her. The bright magenta jumpsuit the Mouse is wearing seems to have faded her even further. Her brownish hair hangs in tendrils beside her face. Her light skin appears almost Pale. She glances at Evans, looks away, and lets out a little yelp of terror. Evans assumes she's recognized Devit.

"He won't harm you," the matron says. "We don't allow that kind of thing here."

A Human man in a business suit follows them in and shuts the door.

"Our public defender, Hal Brun," Taran says. "Representing Miz Unknown."

The lawyer nods Evans's way and sits next to his client.

"Now," Taran says. "Miz, please tell us your name."

She says nothing, merely stares past him. He repeats the question, adds others, home planet, any family we can notify, on and on while Mouse merely studies the opposite wall. Taran switches to reciting the charges against her, possession of a dangerous device, conspiracy to do harm, attempted murder. Still she stays silent.

"Objection!" Brun breaks in. "We've been over and over this same ground, Taran. These repeated interrogations amount to the kind of cruel treatment explicitly forbidden by the laws of the Repositories. If you have nothing new to add, we need to end this session now."

"We do have new information to lay before you and the prisoner." Taran turns toward Evans. "Captain?"

"Miz, you know the *Lokiki* deserted you. Why are you protecting them? The yacht's been located and will be taken into custody by the Fleet."

Her mouth twists in a flicker of contempt.

"You think we'll never find them?" Evans continues. "We've discovered the hidden stargates. We know exactly where the *Lokiki* went."

Her eyes widen.

"You and your group are right to be afraid of genetic functions, you know. We have a sapient who can see stargates. They're now on the Map. Your refuge isn't one any longer. The Fleet knows where the Blood Vigilantes are hiding."

"You're lying!" The words burst out beyond her control.

"No. The people on that fancy yacht ran and left you. They thought they'd be safe on their hidden planet, so they left you behind to take all the blame. You'll be tried in a Fleet court. I don't recommend that."

"Objection! You're threatening my client."

"No. I'm warning her. There's a difference. Listen, Miz. You're protecting sapes who might as well be shoving you out of an airlock. Why?"

Taran leans a little toward the Mouse and flutters his crest, a gesture meant to be reassuring. "You know I've opened the possibility of a plea bargain before, Miz. I'm pretty damn sure we can work out a better outcome than a Fleet show trial. Onar only knows what the result of that would be."

"The charges are serious," Evans says. "The penalties will be too."

For the first time the Mouse turns toward the public defender. She starts to speak, then merely gulps for air.

"We've been over this a couple of times," Brun says. "You know what I recommend."

She hesitates, mouth slightly open, eyes wide and suddenly damp.

"We know who the man with you was," Evans says. "He had ID in his belt pouch. He's listed on the *Lokiki* registry forms. Tay Jasson, isn't it? His family are coowners of the yacht. They must have known he was dead, and they saw no reason to stay for your sake."

Her mouth trembles, then gives way to a rush of words. "My name is Betz Raddow. He loved me, and they hated me for it. His whole damn snotty clan! A nasty little grasping bitch after his money—that's what they said about me. And now he's dead, and—" She covers her face with both hands and sobs.

Evans glances Devit's way and finds him, as she expected, profoundly moved.

"I'm sorry," Devit says. "But it was necessary."

Raddow drops her hands and looks straight at him. "Necessary? Oh yeah, that's the Fleet: kill anything in your way, like the animals you are!

Oh god I hate you! You killed him. I hate you all!" The tears return and wash her voice away.

Taran stands up. "Captain, if you and Chief Devit will come with me? Miz Raddow has the right to consult her legal counsel in private."

Taran escorts them all the way to the door of the Guard station. Before they leave, Evans asks him for a report on whatever data Raddow gives them.

"That won't be legal, Captain, without a subpoena or court order."

"There's a Fleet advocate, a military legal officer, on the way here from Harad to deal with this matter of investigating my security officer. When it comes to the deposition, the Fleet will make sure I have whatever's necessary."

"Oh yes." His voice is heavy with irony. "No doubt it will."

At this far distance from Central and Orb, Santreeza has no direct access to the Consolidated Lanes database, but the old Morrison Line files still exist in an odd corner of a Repository public archive. While she waits for the bodyguard detail to reach spacedock, she does a careful search. That the directories were forgotten strikes her as so careless that she's not surprised to discover the remains of useful information, left by someone deleting data in too much of a hurry.

She already knows that some executives at Consolidated had doubts about the Morrison Lines purchase. By putting together the scattered comments and broken phrases of the partially wiped files, she can see that the two armed ships were only part of the assets that Consolidated coveted. "Rare surviving copy of this material ... value—high value ... get Consolidated to increase its offer." A bargaining chip, then, whatever the material was. It might well have been the information that Ferst's buyer was selling.

She keeps hunting and finds shreds of a mail exchange. Most are meaningless fragments such as "on the other hand," but a name appears twice. Orinoco Bolivar. *Again! Peter's gonna love this.*

Another search, and she finds out more about Tay Jasson, in a separate section dealing with "that old trouble ... keep it out of the damn vids ... remember the old saw, don't poke an Altarian raptor snake with a stick." More hunting, more piecing tiny scraps together, but these lead her to transcripts of the damn vids in question. The Jasson clan is very rich, and whatever the wandering rich do is news, no matter how hard they try to keep their scandals private. A string of very expensive parties, some very expensive drugs, and a lover who died in suspicious circumstances all add up to gossip of the very best sort. More to the point, though, is the question of why the lover's death was never investigated by the authorities. The likely answer to that question would have been very expensive too.

By the time she's done, she has a nice fat transmit of intel to send to Devit's PL.

He messages an answer right away. "Great stuff you're amazing thanks see you soon."

After he escorts the captain back to the *Mary*, Devit takes a few hours of shore leave. It's his turn to buy fresh food for the crew. He lingers in each shop, looks over the goods, and chooses each buy after some deliberation. All because, as he knows damn well, he needs time away to think. The sentinel inside his brain keeps nagging him. Dan's hiding something. What is it? It's important. Go find it. Yet some other intuition, some completely Human part of his brain, is warning him that he may end up sorry he knows. Sooner or later, his functions tell him, you'll have to know. *Not now dammit!* He shoves the whole problem away and heads back to the ship.

On the bridge, Evans, Mata, and Wang are watching the local vidnews, where the serious young woman in the business suit is explaining a complicated legal process. The Hoppers are applying for extradition of the imposter.

"Huh," Wang says. "I bet they treat him like a hero."

"I doubt it, ma'am," Devit says. "He looked terrified the minute he saw them. Most likely he's going to end up as compost. The Hopper brass want to find out the truth about these rumors as much as we do. He was trying to destroy a data source that they could use to find it first."

Wang makes a noise that might be considered agreement and returns to studying her station's screen.

"Let us answer the important question," Mata says. "Is that actual food you're carrying?"

"Sure is."

"Good work, Devit," Evans says. "Wang, Mata—you have permission to leave the bridge. Chief, Santreeza and Golverg are in the galley already, hoping for something better than nutrition bars. Santreeza's sent us intel. Read it at your earliest, and then we'll discuss it."

"Yes, ma'am. By the way, where's Brennan? In his cabin?"

"No. He asked for shore leave. The two pilots from the *Cotta* showed up here. They all wanted to go out for a drink. It should be safe enough. They're bringing their ship's four Marines with them. I gather the *Chaonia* pair will be joining them. Brennan's earned the right to celebrate."

"Agreed. Permission to leave the bridge? I'd better go put these things down. And see what Santreeza's found."

TO: Captain Evans, CWO Devit
FROM: Lieutenant Santreeza
RE: Merrval

UnitFour has collated all images of the carved stones from the report filed here by the staff of the Merrval Research Project. According to the original research report, the stones are a variety of sandstone that's easily carved, but soft. They were apparently at one time stacked together to form a stele or pillar monument. Some years after their creation, the monument was thrown down by a violent earthquake. Some stones crumbled. The inscription was damaged.

The collation from the images resulted in thirteen lines of readable text. Transcription appears at end of this post. Prime182Repositories has produced the following translation:

"... awareness of our folly. We are now lost cut off from the home planet ... once we were [wording here is obscure] of the Lord our God the Great and Powerful. We have sinned. We have sabotaged the innocents ... left outside for eternity ... we are now the Remnant ..."

[next two lines have been lost due to the cracking of the stones] "... in our ignorance forced others to provide safety ... penance ... monument to our selfish evil."

It's possible that an on-site examination of the stones in the research team's possession will result in further decipherment. If Captain Evans approves, this material should be heavily classified. I do not have the rank to do so.

END

"Yes, of course I approve, Lieutenant," Evans says. "I don't have the rank to permanently classify it, but I can designate it top category secret on a temporary basis. Until the higher-ups review it, the designation will stand. I hope that's long enough."

"It should be. Thank you, ma'am. Permission to contact Yosh Willox? I asked the AI to tell me who else accessed this data. It refused without a subpoena."

"Chief, does Willox have the legalities with him?"

"He confirmed that he does, ma'am," Devit says.

Evans looks at the far wall. Her eyelids flicker. She waits for some seconds. "Ah, there we are. Willox is on the way here. So. Chief, your opinion on this data?"

"The mention of sabotage stands out. Something worse than planting IEDs, I bet. How would closing a stargate qualify?"

"When the Pinch gate closed, Dan told me there was an entire Colony Fleet caravan already in the shunt."

"Shit. Well, pardon, ma'am." Devit winces. "Yeah, that would qualify, all right."

"I'm speculating, of course. But if we add in the prior data that Santreeza recovered from that orb, it seems to me that they were so determined to hide their own planet, they experimented with something they didn't understand."

"It looks that way to me, too, ma'am," Santreeza says. "Not evil exactly. Stupid and reckless."

"Yes. And now someone else wants to stick their hand into the same fire. Well, if I'm guessing correctly."

"I asked Golverg's opinion. He told me that there were a couple of old theories going around after the Pinch shunt closed. It was a hot topic at the time."

"I'd imagine so! What were they?"

"One of them's a bit on the fantastic side. Supposedly, with enough energy at their disposal, a group of sapients might be able to manipulate the space-time around the gate to heal the crack. He showed me the math a research group worked out for a possible energy source."

"Good god!" Evans rolls her eyes. "Fantastic, all right."

"The central problem would be finding that energy source. There were a number of possibilities. The best candidate was dark fluid—y'know, the mystery under the other mysteries like dark energy. The team collected enough observational data points to compute the modeling of the dark fluid's flow in that particular region of space-time. From that they could hypothesize the chances of converting some of the fluid to dark energy and then transforming the dark to usable. Their method depends on a C-general model for gases and fluid mechanics that was known in ancient times, but the astrophysicists way back then didn't have enough data to work out all the computations. I can show you some of it on the vidscreen if you'd like."

"I doubt very much if I'd understand two lines of it. Chief?"

"Same here, ma'am. The basic space-time formulas we had in school just about finished me." He glances at Santreeza. "I guess it's accurate and all that."

"Oh yes, it's an impressive bit of work. I helped Golverg clear up a couple of details. So, he agrees with the researchers that the dark fluid might provide the energy closing a stargate would demand, *if* you could collect and channel it. That's a very big if."

"So it's possible to close a gate after all?"

"Theoretically. Certainly not likely! You wouldn't be working with the actual gate, which doesn't physically exist by any rational definition, but with the space-time around it. But what in hell? The energy it would demand! You'd need to direct a beam of pure energy amounting to a Class O star going nova. A blue giant, for instance. I cannot imagine how any group of sapients, organic or not, could succeed at using that much siphoned energy for anything other than raw destruction. If they did manage to generate an energy beam from dark fluid, how would they control it? You'd need precise control." She pauses, considers. "Let me see, the only analogy I can come up with is using the beam like a giant needle to stitch and mend the break. That's horribly oversimplified, but you can get some idea."

"And one slip-up?" Devit says.

"Total destruction. Even the backlash could cause a major disaster, like sending waves of energy strong enough to kill every living thing on a planet."

"You'd think it would have turned Merrval into asteroids," Evans says.

"That's more likely to have happened to whatever planet anchored the target stargate."

Evans shudders. Devit twitches—Santreeza doesn't know what else to call it. His body makes a sudden, if very slight, jerk to one side, with an equally subtle motion of his head.

"Chief?" Evans says. "Are you sai?"

"Yes, ma'am. I just saw something. Lieutenant, I'm remembering some information you gave me a while back. That second mole, Karski, the one who worked for Speed Shunt. Didn't he claim to have proof a gate could be closed?"

"He did, Chief. That theoretical work I just told you about? It was published at the time and widely discussed. I can't imagine that Karski would be able to understand the actual research papers. He wouldn't have been working for Speed Shunt if he could. Golverg told me that some garbled versions of the theories got on the vidnews at the time. You know how badly they report scientific developments. I don't know where Karski found the transcripts of the vid reports, but yeah, the files make it look like the poor bastard did. Pretty expensive find. It got him killed."

"Huh." Devit is looking at the far wall with a strangely distant expression. "So, there was widespread reaction—let's call it panic—at the time. This dark fluid theory, did the public react to it?"

"Oh yes. As you say, panic. Other theories cropped up, too, and lots of editorials blaming anyone the vids could think of. A couple of transport firms went belly up, but it was the Colony Fleet that got most of the crap talk."

"I'm not surprised," Evans says. "The Colony Fleet was a very strange institution, you know. Some of their top brass held very peculiar views about the reasons it existed."

"That's true. Karski probably found a lot of old vids about them."

"What about the other theory?" Devit says.

"This one's slightly more probable. Each shunt is anchored to a planet, right? What if someone destroys the planet? The shunt's going to drift away. Probably fade and close eventually. Golverg worked out the math for that too."

Devit leans forward in his chair. "That sounds better, yeah. I can see how a good-sized battle group could muster enough power to disrupt even a good-sized planet."

"One big problem." Santreeza looks his way with a wry smile. "There was no debris. No radiation belt expanding either. No one could work out how an entire planet could just disappear without a trace. And for that matter, the original anchor planet was still there at the Pinch location."

"So much for that, yeah." Devit pauses, thinking. "But if they cut the twin shunt loose, the one where we found Orb? There was an asteroid belt in that system."

"That's a possibility, yes. Golverg has some serious doubts about it, but he'll have to explain them if you want to know."

"I think I'll pass," Evans smiles with her usual half twitch of her mouth. "A lot of this kind of speculation is beyond me, frankly. But what counts is that Karski found something he thought he could sell. It got him killed, and all for nothing."

"Not necessarily for nothing, ma'am," Santreeza says. "Bait. Karski's work probably did get a higher price out of Consolidated. More creds for Speed Shunt's stockholders and execs. Then somehow the secret got out, and the rumors started. Which could cause a panic that could wipe Consolidated out."

"That's called justice in action. Serves the bastards right."

"You have a point, Chief. This is all speculation, yes, but I'm going to send this material to the Bureau.

"Thank you, Santreeza. This may be what they sent us out to find."

"Agreed, ma'am." Devit feels a part of the mental pattern come together, but only part. He does, however, have an idea of where to search for what he needs.

"Santreeza, you've done a splendid job," Evans says. "I'm going to encode this right now. The packet boat's still in transmission range, but I'd better get the shunt packet to them ASAP." She pauses briefly. "Willox is at the airlock, Chief. Bring him in, will you?"

"On my way."

Willox is leaning against the wall next to the airlock and reading something on his PL. He smiles pleasantly enough when he sees Devit and slips the device into his tunic pocket.

"Checking my stash of legal docs," Willox says. "It's a good thing you thought of that, Pete."

"You've got one for an AI, then?"

"One for whomever its organic partner is."

"That'll do it. And one to get data out of the local Police Guard?"

"No, damn it. It's going to take a court order to pry anything out of them."

"Crap. Evans has already requested an advocate from Harad Fleet Base."

"She told me, yeah. Don't know when they'll get here."

"Well, not much we can do about it now. Been meaning to ask you, Yosh .... How are the repairs on the *Cotta* going?"

"Oh man! It's been driving me nuts. They had to send to Roon for parts. *Cotta*'s one of the newly designed ships, and the SARs aren't carrying the standard kits yet."

"And what? Harad Base doesn't have them, either?"

"Yeah. Shit! Until they find some, nothing to do but wait."

Waiting. Devit has always hated it, this ugly stretch of time when no one knows when or how combat will begin, but everyone knows it's inevitable. Although Devit's reasonably sure that the *Mary* won't be joining the strike force, "reasonably sure" is not the same as "certain knowledge."

With Dan gone, Devit has the cabin to himself and the time to follow up a couple of questions that have been nagging at him. With the Repositories' public archives at their disposal, he and PrimeTwo should be able to find some serious answers.

Before he can begin, a ping hits his earjack: Jorja.

"Peter? The archivist for Dock Seven did accept one of the legal transmits Willox brought. The last persons to want references to the Bolivar material were me and the professor, of course. But the person before us was Tay Jasson. He made the request from the *Lokiki* three solstandard weeks ago."

"What was he after?"

"A packet of data about the organic mind to AI conversion. The only thing in the easy download was the location of the packet elsewhere. He didn't have the top flight security clearance to access it. I bet he paid someone to place the IED because he didn't want anyone else to have the information if he couldn't get it. That 'anyone' would have to be Consolidated Lanes. They're the other player in this game."

"And I bet you're right." Another piece of Devit's pattern falls into place. "Thanks, Jorja. Do you know anything about the interstellar stock market?"

"Not a whole lot. Are you planning on investing?"

"At my pay grade? That'll be the day. No, I'm wondering if there's some way a sapient can make money by getting a company's stock to lose value."

"I think there is, but I don't know how."

"I'll have to see what I can find out. Anyway, can you send a transmit to the Hounds? Ask them to look into Ty Jasson's personal finances—the assets he holds separately from the clan. I'm willing to bet they're relevant."

"Will do."

"Another question. You told me about the Fleet archive material getting deleted. And then someone restored the codes so you could get in?"

"That's it, yeah."

"Do you know when this happened?"

"Only roughly. The deletion happened just over a year ago. The restoration happened a few days before I was sent the codes."

"A year apart, then."

"Yes. Is it important?"

"Maybe. It could be one of the big answers. It could be meaningless. I'll have to see if I can find out which. It'll give me something to do, if nothing else."

"True. By the way, Golverg and I are going down to Third soon. I've got the address of the Bolivar material. If you think of anything else you want me to look up, just contact me."

"Sai. And here's my last question. Have you heard from the Ilana Police yet?"

"Are you psychic or something? I was just about to send you the transmit. Yes, there was a second murder. About four hours before Willox was killed, a Consolidated Lanes employee died. The bruises on his arms indicate he was caught from behind and held motionless while his throat was cut, one clean slash through the trachea and up into a main artery."

"A Hopper assassination team. Shit!"

"Yes. Just what we don't need. I'm sending the news back to the Bureau right now."

After she logs off, Devit spends a few minutes worrying about her safety, down onplanet where he can't keep watch. He reminds himself that her bodyguards will be the absolute best on the Rim and forces himself to return to his research.

"PrimeTwo, a question. On the interstellar stock market, is there a way for an investor to make a profit if a stock price declines?"

"This does not sound logical, Chief. But organic sapients are known for doing illogical things. I am framing conditional search terms now."

Illogical or not, the question turns out to be easy to answer.

"I have found a process, Chief, called 'selling short.' It is very complicated. Shall I describe it to you?"

Noises drift into the cabin from the corridor, two sets of footsteps—one slow and steady, the other erratic—and Mata's voice, murmuring, "C'mon, you can make it."

"PrimeTwo, load the information onto my PL. Brennan's here, and he needs help."

The door slides open with a bang and the stink of secondhand alcohol. Dan grabs the doorjamb and steadies himself before he falls. Mata throws a precautionary arm around his waist.

"Chief, is the pilot ill?"

"No, PrimeTwo. The condition he's in is called drunk. I'll get back to you later."

Between them, Mata and Devit get Dan into the cabin and flop him onto the bed.

"We'd better just let him sleep it off," Devit says.

"We can't. I'll help you sober him up. The captain just got a message. Captain Bonna's coming over from the *Mansa*. She wants to congratulate Dan in person."

"Oh shit!"

Dan looks up, hesitates, and clamps a hand over his mouth.

"Into the WM!" Mata says. "And hurry."

"Wang, of course Brennan came back drunk," Evans says. "You might remember your own condition after celebrating your wedding."

Wang has the decency to wince and nod agreement. "Apologies, Captain. The waiting's getting on my nerves." She suddenly grins. "Having something to complain about always helps."

Evans has to laugh. “Apology accepted. The waiting’s getting on everyone’s nerves. I don’t know why Bonna hasn’t called the CO meeting.”

Captain Bonna has apparently been brooding over that very thing. When she and two Marine guards arrive, “Damn Harad Base, anyway,” is the first thing she says.

“What have they done now, Enid?”

“Told us to wait. No attack on this terrorist planet—yet.”

Since Devit’s not on the bridge, Bonna takes his station chair. The Marines sit on the floor, one to either side of her.

“Did they deign to tell us why?”

“Well, yes, and they have a point. They received the transmit about the shunt discovery late last Designated Night. By the way, how in hell do you get your transmits delivered so fast?”

“I don’t know. Santreeza’s been handling our communications.”

“She’s a wizard with the AIs, all right. I’ll ask her later. But the Harad Base CO sent a packet boat out immediately, telling me to take no action until they’ve consulted with Central Command.”

“That means getting the news to Central Base. And getting their transmits back out here again.”

“Yes. More damned waiting.”

The elevator doors slide open. A damp Dan Brennan, in a uniform that looks uncomfortably tight, steps out and salutes. Devit and Mata follow him out.

“You wanted to see me, ma’am?”

Brennan’s voice is so steady that Evans wonders what Devit and Mata did to sober him up so fast. She decides she’d best not ask.

“I did, Lieutenant,” Bonna says. “You’re to be congratulated.”

“Thank you, ma’am, but really, I can’t take much credit. It’s just a matter of the genes I happened to get.”

“No. You’re the one who figured out how to use them.”

Brennan starts to speak but blushes instead.

“Be that as it may,” Bonna continues, “I received a status transmit from Harad Base. You’re recommended for promotion, and I don’t see any reason you won’t get it. Good job, Brennan.”

“Thank you, ma’am.” His Pale face stays a bright pink.

“We should know about any action plans soon. I’ve been ordered to keep you safe. I’ll look for the most secure place I can find, and you’re going to be in it.”

“But, ma’am, I’m the second officer on this Scout. If my ship goes Action Ready, I want to be on it.”

"Well said, but orders are orders."

"Yes, ma'am."

"You're a resource, Brennan, with a rare function, and the Fleet most likely has plans on how to use it."

For a moment Evans is afraid that Brennan is going to faint. The blush turns a dangerous pale pink, almost white, and he takes a step back as if to steady himself.

Bonna leans forward in the chair. "Are you ill, Brennan?"

"No," Evans says. "He's hungover. A little celebration with his fellow starpilots."

Bonna's crest flaps in wild good humor. "Well deserved, I'd say. Go lie down."

"Thank you, ma'am." He manages a decent salute. "I'd better."

"One quick thing," Evans says. "Whose onboard uniform is that? It's obviously not Brennan's."

"Lieutenant Santreeza's, ma'am," Devit says. "They're about the same height, but she's a lot thinner. His is in the sonocleaner at the moment."

"I don't want to know why. You three have permission to leave the bridge."

When they reach the cabin, Devit checks the sonocleaner. Dan's onboard uniform is still cycling through. Dan changes into his civilian clothes and tosses Santreeza's onto the bed. Devit picks them up and folds them in the regulation way.

"Let's go to the galley, Dan," Mata says. "We won't look at food, but you've got to drink a lot of rehydrates."

"Agreed. Jeez. My head."

"I can't say I'm surprised. Come on, you need fluids."

Mata takes Dan's arm and leads him firmly away. Devit opens his PL and brings up the definition of "sell short" that PrimeTwo found in a public data bank.

"Short selling: First you borrow shares of a security, one whose price you think is going to fall, from your brokerage. You take this loan and sell the shares on the open market at the current price. With that money, you buy it all back after the price drops. In other words, you've got the shares and the money between the original price you sold them at and the much lower price you bought them back at. You give the borrowed shares back to your broker with a commission and pocket the profit. The Rim Council has placed severe restrictions on the practice, because short selling on a large scale can trigger a downward spiral, hurting stock prices and damaging the economy. Some of the wealthy clans, however, have found ways around these restrictions by dealing with brokerages that are not under strict Rim supervision."

Devit leans back in his chair and smiles at the mazla vine. "Just what I wanted to know," he says aloud. "So far, so good."

The cable pod from spacedock takes Santreeza and Golverg down to the landing pad for the Deep Archives on Third. As soon as they step out of the pod, the heat falls on them like a hungry animal. Santreeza drops her duffel and struggles out of her onplanet tunic jacket as fast as she can. Her bodyguards are doing the same. Golverg, who's been carrying his jacket, drops it and his suitcase to help her.

"Thanks," Santreeza says. "I heard about the heat here, but I didn't think it'd be this bad."

"Ma'am?" Sergeant Mills, the Human leader of the bodyguard team, steps forward. "Let's get into the station. Bound to be cooler."

As they hurry across the pad, a young Human woman comes to meet them. She's wearing a maroon tee shirt and white shorts, which, judging from her ID badge, is the official archive uniform. "Professor Golverg! Oh, I'm so honored to meet you. We've all been looking forward to it. We don't often get someone of your high standing here."

"Thank you, Miz. I've been looking forward to it myself. For some time now."

"Please, come this way." She glances at Santreeza. "Officer, uh, Lieutenant, you must be the leader of the guard team."

"No, Miz," Golverg says. "She's an independent researcher on Fleet duty."

"Oh. Welcome, all of you. I'll escort you to your hotel. We have robocabs."

The big white plastocrete station proves to be warm inside but bearable. The archivist sorts them into two cabs, then joins the one carrying the professor. When the cabs lift off, a door in the wall slides up to let them sail free. As they glide down, Santreeza gets a clear view of the landscape. Yellow sands stippled with reddish rocks stretch away from the high cliffs they're leaving behind. A few grayish green clumps of something indistinguishable dot the yellow.

The cabs land at the foot of the cliffs, where an entrance much like a sky tunnel and airlock leads into the hotel itself. As they walk into the blessedly cool lobby, Santreeza realizes that the hotel's been built right into the cliffs, safely out of the sun. What appear to be windows are actually holograms displaying views of far more pleasant places than the one outside.

The same holds true for the suite reserved for them, an arrangement of six small rooms, three on each side of a shared lounge area, all of them set up with comfortably shabby furniture. The only access from the corridor is one heavy, lockable door. Santreeza and Golverg get the rooms in the center of each row, while the bodyguards split up and sort themselves into the others. The team leader follows Santreeza into her room to look it over.

"The situation's defensible enough, ma'am." Mills says. "As long as no one tampers with the fresh air vents, you'll be safe here. But are you armed? Doesn't do to take anything for granted."

"Yes, thanks. I've got my officer's pulse gun."

"Good. I'll tell my sapes. I'll detail someone to check out the vents right now."

He salutes and leaves to give his squad instructions. Santreeza tosses her duffel and jacket onto the single bed and sits down at the carrel in the corner of the room.

"Lieutenant Jorja Santreeza," she says.

At the sound of her voice a screen brightens on the wall of the carrel. Santreeza inputs her Fleet reg number and chosen language, then puts a fingertip on the print recognition box onscreen.

"Fleet security enabled?"

"Enabled." The AI answers in a pleasantly female voice. "We've been expecting you, CyberThree. Welcome to the Deep Archives. I will now display a list of regulations, followed by the list of access points. After that, I will answer any questions you may have."

"Thank you." Santreeza leans back in the upholstered chair and puts her feet up on the small hassock under the desk. "This is going to be fun."

DESIGNATED TRANSMIT CODED CWO DEVIT, PILOT BRENNAN, PRIMEONEMARY
From: Lieutenant Santreeza
Subject: Can Dan translate this fucking thing

TOPIC SUMMARY

Peter, I have found a document about the officer we've been discussing. Problem: I can't read it. The language is an older form of Gen, and I don't even know the current one. I think Dan does. If so, can he translate and send back in Tech Speak? Heavily coded, of course. From the few words I can pick out, this is worth the effort. Also worth the effort to keep it to ourselves, so it better be Dan, not the Archives AI translators.

Thanks, Jorja

END

"Sweet Jessy, Pete! Worth it, she said, and oh yeah. I'm glad I waited to take the Haze."

"They must be go-nova material, then."

"I'd say so. I'm sending the translation to your PL with the response Santreeza just sent me."

"Sai. Here. You want water with that?"

Dan just smiles and swallows the blue tab.

REPORT 18, RCS *KA VALLO*
RE: SHUNT CLOSURE INVESTIGATION
Auxiliary input

During our passage to the site of the disaster, we picked up a faint distress signal and broke course to investigate. We found a Colony Fleet shuttle drifting through a looped course which kept it in roughly the same location. When we pinged, there was no response. We grappled and sent in a team in full pressure suits. As we suspected, the air in the shuttle was long since exhausted. Thanks to the undamaged solar panels, its energy resources were adequate to supply the distress beacon, the lights in the ship, and a full AI neural network.

In the control room the team discovered the corpse of a man in Colony Fleet uniform sitting in the command chair. He was badly decomposed. Full medical report is attached to this report, but the upshot is that he died some weeks after the stargate disaster. Cause of death was most likely suffocation due to the exhausted oxygen supply.

Our AI, PrimeOneKaVallo, made contact with the shuttle's AI in hopes of retrieving further information. PrimeOneShuttle delivered a full report on the disaster uploaded by the pilot of the shuttle on the off chance the ship would be found. It confirmed that the dead officer was pilot Lieutenant-Commander Orinoco

Bolivar. We have forwarded that report to the Investigative Committee.

*[note from JS. The archive does not have that report. I am seriously pissed but will keep searching when I return to Central.]*

At that point PrimeOneShuttle displayed alarming behavior. The strain of the previous events have apparently sent it into the state cyber experts call "borked." It insisted that it was Orinoco Bolivar, not merely a meld, but a complete mental and personality transfer thanks to some secret research procedure. We have sent the transcript to the appropriate cyber experts within the Colony Agency. It took our pilot's intervention to calm the AI enough for it to go into stasis for its journey to our base.

*[That report, also missing. Recently deleted, one year ago I think. Damn it all to whatever hell may be. The Colony Agency was disbanded right after the Battle Fleet won the Rebellion. I'll try to find out what happened to their records. Don't hold your breath. There was a second document available for upload here as recently as one year ago. It's been deleted. Getting a recopy from the hidden paper archives requires A Procedure and A Half. Evans or Bonna will have to start it. I don't have the rank or classification.]*

END

"One year ago." Devit speaks aloud in sheer satisfaction at seeing a pattern complete. "Well, well, well. Bolivar's still alive, all right. And I bet I know where he is."

# FIFTEEN

Thanks to her functions, Evans is still in her cabin when she receives a transmit from Central Command early the next Designated Morning, somewhat before any of the other commanding officers in their combat-ready unit. Assimilating its message is another matter. Good news, mostly, but some of it presents difficulties. She accesses the intraship comm and calls for the person whom those difficulties might affect. Devit arrives so promptly that she assumes he was still on the habitation deck when he heard the comm.

"News, Chief. A packet boat's made the jump from Harad. It's in the transmission zone now. There's another ship following. The *MacBeth*."

"Another destroyer?"

"Yes. It's carrying very important passengers. Admiral Harra Stine and her staff. The legate I requested's coming with her."

"If Stine's coming here, ma'am, something big's about to happen."

"Yes. The attack, I suppose, but it also concerns Brennan. Stine's Bureau personnel, not CC. You'll remember Bonna's remarks about him being a resource, as she called it. I doubt the Fleet's going to leave him on regular pilot duty. The transmit mentioned a transfer."

Devit's expression turns so controlled, so bland, that she knows he's taken her hint. It's very unlikely that Devit's going to accompany Dan to wherever the Fleet stations him.

"At any rate," Evans continues, "there's other news. They've found the *Lokiki* and taken it into custody. Apparently it was on its way to that other stargate, the one that would bring it back to this general location. They won't be ferrying any warnings to their base, if that's what they were doing. The Jassons are of course screaming about Fleet tyranny and threatening lawsuits and making every other fuss they can think of."

"I'm not surprised."

"Neither am I. Anyway, once the legate gets here, we'll see about getting a copy of the Mouse's—I mean Raddow's—deposition."

"Good. The combat teams need every scrap of data about that planet they can get."

"Exactly. The dispatches also mentioned that the *Mary* will remain here along with the *Cotta* and the *MacBeth*, to guard the spacedocks in case there's a counterattack. The *MacBeth*'s an older destroyer, one of the class the new ships are replacing. Probably that's why it's been chosen to stay behind."

"Agreed. Ma'am, is there any chance I can go with the attack force?"

"Possibly. You can ask Bonna. But why?"

"There's a slim chance that Professor Vot's still alive. The Vigilantes have kept hostages before this. I found old newsvid interviews with those hostages recorded when they were released. The rebels need every bargaining chip they can get, and they know it. I don't want some young hothead of a Marine shooting Vot on sight because he's a Hopper."

"A very good point."

"There might be a second hostage as well. This one can probably release himself if he gets a little help."

"All right. If Bonna agrees, I'll certainly agree."

"Thank you, ma'am." He pauses for one of his ironic smiles. "Dan will be safe enough without me."

For a simple statement, Evans thinks, that one packs so many possible meanings that she can't untangle them. If it turns out to be something she needs to attend to, she'll worry about it later, after the coming action plays out.

When the *MacBeth* reaches the Repositories' region of control, Admiral Stine and her staff transfer to the *Mansa*, but the legate, Commander-Advocate Mohmet Falud, continues on with the destroyer. The ship's AI contacts Evans immediately.

"We've berthed," PrimeOneMacBeth says. "Commander Falud is asking permission to board the *Mary*, ma'am. May I transmit it?"

"Yes, PrimeOne. We've been waiting for him. Chief Devit? If you'll escort him?"

"Of course, ma'am. On my way."

Commander Falud's a tall, light brown Human with a beaky nose and gleaming eyes that remind Devit of an Altarian raptor snake. It's a good look, he thinks, for a man who's about to take on a massive legal system with grounds to hold a grudge against the Fleet. As they walk back to the *Mary* from the *MacBeth*'s berth, Falud asks him a few quick questions about the "incident," as he calls it.

"We may have to go through with the civilian hearing," Falud says.

"I can accept that, sir. I terminated a hostile in a civilian jurisdiction. Of course there should be a hearing."

"True. But it should end there. This is a Fleet matter, jurisdiction or not. If they insist on a civilian trial, I won't hesitate to call on every Fleet protocol there is to stop it. You are the designated security chief for this ship and crew. Someone tried to kill your captain. You shot first, yes, but that's the absolute only thing you could have done to stop him. The vid records from the Eyes show it clearly."

"That's good to know, sir. But it's something I'd rather not have done."

"Of course. When they insist on a hearing, I'll make sure it's set for a date after the coming action."

"Thank you, sir. The important thing now is getting a copy of that deposition. We're hoping it'll have some information about what's on the other side of the new stargate."

"I've started the process of getting the release. As soon as we hit the transmission zone, Captain Evans sent me the details. There's one other thing that would be good to know: Clan Jasson. Do you have any idea why they're involved in this?"

"Only speculation, sir, but I'm fairly certain there's something to this theory."

"Spoken like a lawyer, Chief. What line of thought have you been pursuing?"

"I think they're after money. I'm willing to bet Tay Jasson was in deep financial trouble. He seems to have spent a large part of his inheritance on high living. I have the details. Then he got involved with the Pure Heritage people. His family's spent a fair amount of creds to back them. If you can get the right subpoenas, we'll have the numbers to prove it."

"Well worth looking into, yes."

"Tay Jasson was on the board of directors of a firm named Speed Shunt. When Consolidated Lanes acquired it, they didn't give him a seat on the new board."

"A costly slap in the face. Those directors get a rather nice honorarium."

"He wanted revenge, I think. His clan's been spreading the rumors about closing stargates to cause a panic and drive down Consolidated's stock prices. I suspect they're running a game called selling short. If it works, they stand to make a big profit. It looks shady to me, but it's apparently legal within limits. As far as I can tell, they've pushed the scheme a long way past the limits. And they're working through Hopper brokers."

Falud's smile gives him the air of a raptor snake sighting prey. "Then we've got them where we want them. I'll be sending your report back to the Bureau ASAP."

"The credit goes to Lieutenant Santreeza. Do you know her?"

"The Bureau cyberjock?"

"Yes sir. She's done a lot of . . . well, let's call it research."

"I see. She's one of the top hackers we have, if not the top. We'll have to be careful about explaining how we've gotten all this information. Fortunately, the Bureau has its little ways."

A verbatim transcript of Raddow's deposition arrives later that same Designated Day. Devit goes through it line by line, recording on his PL every salient fact that he can untangle from Raddow's near hysteria and the public defender's interruptions. The data does begin to form patterns and clusters—none complete and thus none reliable. The Vigilantes quite simply told Raddow as little as possible.

One detail, however, stands out. Devit waits until he and Evans are alone on the bridge to present it. "There's a very good chance, ma'am, that Professor Vot's still alive. To give Raddow some credit, she was concerned about his safety. Jasson told her that he was being kept in one of the old space stations in orbit around the planet. They wanted a hostage in reserve to bargain with if they need to. That's where they kept the other hostages, the ones some years back." He pauses, considers. "Now, Jasson may have been lying just to keep her under control."

"That's likely, yes. Why was Raddow so important to them? Do you know?"

"Ma'am, she has some of the same functions you do. She can operate the signal devices."

"Good god! Why wasn't she recruited for the Fleet?"

"I don't know. The subject never came up in the deposition. She never made it clear why she hates the Throwbacks either. What the hell? Why? She's one of us."

"And that may be where the hatred comes from. Self-loathing, Chief. It can be a very powerful thing when all a sapient wants is to have an ordinary life like the rest of the people around them."

"So it seems, ma'am. But I'd like to make a try at rescuing the hostages. Vot's the one in immediate danger. There are three of those old stations still in orbit around the anchor planet. We'd better pick the right one first, before they decide to make sure he can't be rescued. Permanently. I've figured out a way to do that, but Captain Bonna will have to agree and authorize."

“Write me up a report of the data you’ve gleaned about the anchor planet and the Vigilantes. Describe your idea at the end. I’ll send it over and then take it up with her. If she agrees, then she can work things out with Admiral Stine.”

“Thank you, ma’am. I’ll get right on that. Oh, meant to tell you: Raddow does know what they named the anchor planet. Thorn.”

Before he can finish suggesting a plan to rescue the hostages, Devit needs a crucial piece of information. If he’s going to keep both hostages alive, he needs to ensure that the Fleet combat unit accepts a plea of surrender from at least one of the Thorn’s ships. He has a good idea of who, or what, might know the answer he needs. Getting it to divulge the answer proves difficult. He contacts Santreeza through his earjack to see if she can get it for him.

“Hey, Jorja, PrimeOne’s been giving me some trouble.”

“And I suppose you want me to bring it in line for you. What’s come up?”

“I asked PrimeTwo a question. PrimeOne said the answer was unknown. I think it was lying. Can they lie?”

“Not outright. But PrimeOne’s very good at weaseling around. What do you need to know?”

“Remember those two armed ships the Morrison Line bought? Is Bolivar the AI of MorrisonGuardA or GuardB?”

“Woah! You sure?”

“As sure as I can be.”

“Sai, then. I’ll get back to you in a few minutes.”

Devit blows her a kiss that she cannot see and leans back in his station chair to wait.

In a few minutes, PrimeTwo pings his earjack. “Chief, CyberThree is threatening PrimeOne with termination!”

“Is she? Good.”

Another few minutes pass before Santreeza reaches him. “MorrisonGuardA.”

“I figured he wouldn’t settle for being second, but it’s good to be sure. Thanks. Logging off now. I’ve got to transmit this report to the captain.”

As soon as she gets Devit’s report, Evans adds her own comments and sends it to Bonna, who will command the combat team while Admiral Stine remains at spacedock.

Bonna’s answer comes back fast. “I’ve seen Devit in action now. If he wants the SAR’s shuttle, he’ll get it. I’ll contact its captain and bludgeon him into agreeing.”

"That should do it. By the way, I'm bringing Willox with me to the *Mansa*."

"Good. He should have been invited. He's been hectoring me about getting on the combat team, because of his father and then his crew member killed in that attack."

"I can't say I blame him."

"The *Cotta*'s operational again, but it's too small a ship for this operation. It'll be part of the dock guard." A pause. "By the way, I spoke to Stine. Brennan will be transferred over to the *Cotta* as a secure location. I'll have my second officer send you the details."

When Devit returns to his bridge station, he brings back his work display, but he lets the subroutines run automatically. Thanks to Golverg's information about the Hopper's Haze-equivalent drug, bleet, he finally knows what Dan is hiding. Now he has to decide what to do with the knowledge.

"Chief?" Evans says.

"Ma'am?" Devit swivels his chair around to face her.

"Admiral Stine's passed on the data about their plans for Brennan. They want him permanently assigned to this sector as part of a new Special Ops unit. The unit will HQ on Harad."

"Focused on the stargates, ma'am?"

"Of course. His promotion went through: lieutenant-commander. The rest of us will stay here for the action on Thorn."

Since there's no one on the bridge but the two of them, Devit knows she's waiting for his reaction. He has no idea what to say or even, really, what he feels about it. *You knew it was coming*, he tells himself. *At least you won't have to pick him up off the floor anymore.*

"He's going to need someone to ration his Haze, ma'am."

"I know. And he needs a ship, not as a regular starpilot, but for the project. Stine wants to assign him to the *Cotta* and Willox."

She looks concerned, just the proper amount of worry to spend on a trusted subordinate, nothing overemotional, but definitely concerned.

He appreciates it more than he can bring himself to tell her. "Thank you for letting me know, ma'am. Permission to leave the bridge?"

"Yes, of course."

For some hours Dan has been wondering how he's going to give Devit the news of his promotion to the new research unit. In his discussion with Admiral Stine, he came to realize that taking it means losing the man he loves, yes, but even more, the man who takes care of him. How is he going to live without Pete right there to solve all those problems that he just can't cope with?

He finally goes to their cabin and tries to distract himself by falling asleep. He wakes to the sound of the door sliding shut as Devit walks in. "Hey, Pete. What's up?"

"I've just been briefed," Devit says. "Evans told me they're sending you to head a new unit. Congratulations."

Trapped by the truth, Dan stands up to face him. "I'm going to turn it down."

"What? Are you crazy?"

"I can't take a posting like that. I've got my reasons, Pete."

"Is it the Haze?"

He hesitates. "Yeah. It's made me make a mess of things before. I don't want to fuck up when the Fleet's depending on me."

"Oh yeah? Is that really all?"

"Sure. Isn't it enough?"

"The hell! You're hiding something, Buddy. You have been for a long time now. Are you afraid they'll pry the truth out of you?"

Dan's stomach twists in sheer anxiety.

"Look," Devit continues. "I've been gathering some data. This business of you seeing the stargates? It's because you're an addict, isn't it? You've soaked yourself in that shit. Not like other pilots who use. Take enough of the crap and it does something to your mind. Wakes up a gene or something. I don't understand how, but I know what it comes down to: You can see the stargates. They can't. Just taking a few hits of the crap now and then doesn't make enough difference."

Dan gulps for breath. "What makes you think that?"

"I told you. The data's out there. No one's bothered to put it together. And no one else knows you the way I do. Why have you been hiding it?"

The shame hits him hard. "Who was I going to tell?"

"Don't give me that bullshit! Your guild, first off. It's supposed to take care of all of you, isn't it? And then someone higher up in the Fleet. Evans would know who."

A barrier breaks in Dan's mind. He's spent years first denying, then hiding the truth. A cold, hard anger washes away the shame that's been tormenting him.

"You want to know why? Because I know damn well what would happen if the Fleet knew. The pressure, Pete. They'd pressure every pilot to feed their minds on the fucking lousy, rotten stuff. They'd make addicts out of all of us."

Devit takes a step back.

"Well, wouldn't they?" Dan goes on. "It's hard enough, being a pilot the way things are. We're all weird, we use drugs, you can't fully trust us. That's what everyone thinks, isn't it?" He starts pacing. "Well, fuck, there are reasons for that. Reasons that none of you are ever going to understand. Turn us all into addicts, why not? Chew us up and spit us out."

Devit stares, silent, his mouth a little slack.

"Do you think I *like* being this way? A fucking slave to a fucking drug? Oh yeah sure, everyone's so impressed now. Brennan found the stargate! Ain't that grand? They don't know what it's like to need something so bad you sell your ass on Nowhere Street to get it. I don't ever want to do that to anyone else. Can't you see that?"

"Yeah." Devit's expression and voice reveal nothing, the usual signs that he's deeply moved. "I can."

"But I bet you're going to tell them anyway. Or tell the captain and let her make the report. It'll make the Fleet stronger, a whole bunch of us addicts who can see the gates. Maybe find some new ones, maybe find some anchor planets good enough for colonies. You know what she'll say. We're Fleet. The Fleet comes first, no matter what it does to sapes like me."

"It's about more than that. Ships get lost because pilots can't find the gates out. Ships and their crews."

True, painfully true. Dan can find no answer.

"And what about the sapes we've all sworn to protect?" Devit continues. "Do you think they'd be better off living under the Hoppers? And who knows what else is out there? The galaxy's so big, and we control a lousy little splinter of it. More species like the Butchers, maybe. Or maybe even worse."

The anger deserts him.

"Besides," Devit continues. "How are other pilots going to take it, knowing they could do what you do, and here you've kept it from them?"

"Shit. I—just, shit."

"Never thought of that? Think about it now, Buddy."

"I just didn't want anyone to have to go through what I do."

The silence hangs between them like a knife blade. Devit breaks it at last.

"All right. I get it now." He turns toward the door. "I've got to get back to my duty station."

"Sai. Are you going to tell Evans?"

"No, if you mean right now. I need to think about it, too."

Devit walks out. Dan sits down on the edge of the bed and stares at the closed door. *What did you expect, you jerk? You thought Pete was going to do whatever you wanted. Like keep his mouth shut just because you asked him to.*

"You asshole, Brennan!"

*My secret's out.* He has to admit that it's a relief to share it—a deep physical relief, like taking off a twenty kilo combat pack.

What now? The guild maintains an office here on Dock Seven. It occurs to Dan that Pete's right: that the guild and everyone in it deserves to know the truth. He even has backup. Friends who'll go with him. With the *Cotta* waiting at the docks for guard duty, Teturi and Ka Lan are on extended leave. Since the three of them once shared a meld, Dan can reach them easily through his earjack.

"Look, guys, I've got to talk to you. Something's up. Meet me in that bar?"

"Sure," Teturi says. "Ka Lan?"

"I'm in. All this shore leave's getting boring."

"Thanks. And we talk in Gen," Dan finishes up. "If someone tries to eavesdrop, good fucking luck to that."

The combat briefing takes place onboard the *Mansa*, which is standing off the docks in parallel orbit. A shuttle collects the COs of the berthed ships and transports them the short distance out. In the *Mansa*'s wardroom Bonna is pacing back and forth in front of an enormous holo screen that displays a schematic of the space-time surrounding their current position. Out of courtesy, Evans steers Willox to a table off to one side and sits next to him.

Ka Birk of the *Chaonia*, Rob Stevvin of the *Imperator*, Kara Vrenley of the *Jalal Onar*—one at a time the combat captains arrive and take seats front and center. When Mim-Alak of the *MacBeth* comes in, however, he joins Evans and Willox.

"We'll be part of the guard force," Alak says.

"Good. I heard about your new command. Congratulations!"

"Thank you. Yes, I've joined the ranks of the underpaid and overanxious."

"Do you know Willox here? CO of the *Cotta*."

They acknowledge each other with small nods. Alak seems to be about to say some pleasantry when Admiral Stine and her chief of staff walk in. Everyone rises to their feet and salutes.

"As you were," Stine says. "I know you're eager to hear the plan of action."

In a rustle of nods, murmurs, and scraping chairs, everyone sits back down.

"Now, then," Stine continues. "First off, there will be another ship joining the order of battle. The SAR. There are two hostages on the other side of that gate, and we want to recover both alive. CWO Devit will be in charge of the squad assigned to this part of the mission. Captain Vrenley, the *Jalal* will be running as its guard. Shadow it, unless of course we need you in the combat arena."

Vrenley salutes. "As one does, ma'am. The damn thing's slow. We'd better come through the gate last."

"Agreed. Yes, the order's going to be important. One last bit of news and then we'll get down to the briefing. All this delay? To let a second combat team get in position. By now they should be hovering on our side of the stargate at the other end of that newfound long shunt. If any hostiles think they can just retreat down it and come out free and clear, they'll be met and engaged."

Bonna steps forward. "We'll be jumping in colony meld. Pilot team from the *Imperator* will lead. A point I want to stress. We are going to offer surrender under the rules of war to any ship that accepts it. Give them a chance to take the offer. If they won't—too fucking bad. We're here to clear them out of our way. No unnecessary heroics."

"So we all understand the situation?" Dan says.

"Entirely too well," Teturi says. "Why the hell didn't you tell us all this before?"

Dan has a lie in Go Ready status.

"I didn't know. Never thought of it, couldn't see it at first. But I just found this out. In the whole damn history of the guild, only two pilots ever got hooked on the stuff. Pilots that stayed in the Fleet, I mean, not the ones who bilged out. The same two who can see things out in the light. Me and Orinoco Bolivar."

"Woah! Yeah, that would make you think, all right."

"Yeah, I finally put it together. But there's another thing. I was worried. I don't know what the Fleet's going to do about it. Maybe something we're not going to like. What if they insist every pilot get hooked whether they want to or not? Trust me. It's hell, being an addict."

"Been hell for you, sure," Ka Lan says. "Trying to hide it, then living out on the street. It'll be different when it's officially sanctioned."

"We can think about that later," Teturi says. "In the meantime, our best bet is consulting the guild. The office here—it's big enough. They'll have a legal advocate on staff."

Dan catches their gaze, holds it. "But look, you don't have to answer, but I've got to ask you .... Would you do it if the Fleet cracks down on us? Let the fucking lousy shit suck the life out of you?"

Teturi winces. "Hell, I don't know for sure, but jeez, I hate to admit it … I probably will. Don't know what I'd do if I lost the Fleet."

"I'll do it," Ka Lan says. "If they promise me rehab when I retire. And extra pay. Those are just little things. The big reason's getting to see all the things you do. I've read those reports! It'll be worth it."

"There's that, yeah," Teturi says. "But look, let me contact the guild office and see if we can go talk to them right now. The sooner, the better."

Devit's in his cabin when Dan pings his PL.

"What's up, Buddy?"

"I've got to talk with you. Not onboard. I'm down at that view port by our berth."

Hostage situation again? Devit has a moment of cold doubt. He falls back on one of the Fleet signals. "Everything's sai like the song says?"

"Right as rain."

Dan's in no danger. An answer of "sai as sai" would have meant trouble.

"I'll be right there."

Devit closes down the transmission, thanks PrimeTwo, and hurries up to the bridge. Wang's sitting in the command chair.

"Ma'am? Permission to leave the ship?"

"Sure. The captain's on her way back, by the way."

Dan's waiting in front of the massive window at the far end of the merchant berth module.

"How long have you been alone out here?" Devit says.

"Just long enough to call you. The other guys brought me back this far."

"What other guys?"

"Teturi and Ka Lan. We went out for a drink." Dan takes a deep breath. "I've told them, Pete. You were right. I told them about the addiction."

"Hey! Good for you, Buddy. That took guts."

Dan shrugs the praise off. "They needed to know."

"Sai, then. What's up?"

"It's about the addiction. We went to the Pilots Guild office. They're going to investigate what they can legally do about the situation. I thought they'd be pissed as hell. No. They're all in favor of it. All they want from the Fleet is a safe source of Haze and an ironclad promise that depriving someone of the drug can never be used as a disciplinary measure. Oh yeah, and another promise of rehab for anyone who wants it when they retire."

"What? You mean the guild is going to *let* the Fleet push its people into—"

"No, wait." Dan holds up one hand. "It's not the Fleet. It's us. The pilots, I mean. You know what's going to happen? Once the news gets around, a lot of us are going to start using the crap on their own. They're going to want what Haze gives them. Promotions and extra pay, sure, but what they really want is getting to see what I see out in the light. They won't give a shit about the risks. They're not going to listen to me, that's for sure. Teturi and Ka Lan are already planning on it."

*And it's my fault they know*

Devit feels betrayed by his own genetics. Why in hell did he have to figure it out? All the little pieces of data formed a pattern, all right, in the shape of a knife at his conscience. He had to go and confirm it with Dan like an idiot, because the damn genes wouldn't let him leave significant data unconfirmed. *I should have ignored it, I wish I could have ignored it, I never could have ignored it.*

"Riding the blue, Pete," Dan says. "It's an addiction all its own."

"Must be, yeah."

"I'm going to take the posting to Harad. If I'm in charge, I can look after the guild's interests."

The officer Dan is reemerging, Devit realizes, from the addicted mess. He's standing straight and controlled as he looks directly at Devit instead of letting his gaze drift.

"You were right, Pete, about my taking it. The team they're talking about? Looking for likely areas to find new stargates. With new full vision pilots coming online soon, we should be able to find them if there are any. It will be part of my remit to train them And tell them how to live with the crap Haze."

"At least they'll be signing up voluntarily."

"Yeah. I don't think I could do this if they weren't. But this is a top flight project."

"Good for you," Devit says. "Wise move."

"But Pete, I don't want to lose you. Once we've got this thing set up, I'll requisition you to be the security chief."

"No, Buddy. Wouldn't work. Do you think anyone there is going to ignore what goes on between us? This is an important project. It's going to have official observers crawling all over it. Fraternization. Remember?"

Dan takes a step back as abruptly as if Devit had slapped him.

"Shit." Dan whispers. "Yeah." For a brief moment a lost child looks out from Dan's eyes. "But don't you want to go with me?"

"Of course I do. But we're Fleet. We go where we're posted, and from now on, we'd better follow regulations. We've had all the luck that way we're going to get."

The officer reappears. "You're right. I know it."

"Good. When are you leaving?"

"I thought about just moving over to the *Cotta* now. The ship's finally Go Ready. I thought—do you think it'd be easier for both of us?"

"Good idea. Sai."

Dan turns to the view window and stares out at the indifferent stars glittering in the infinite dark. Devit studies him for a few minutes, memorizing every detail about him that he can, transforming them into clear pictures in his memory for the times when he's going to need them. Dan says nothing more, but his beautiful green eyes are wet with unspilled tears.

Devit turns and walks away.

He goes back to the bridge and the things that have always saved him; his work, his position, and the Fleet itself. *I'll get over it*, he tells himself. *You've done it before. You can do it again.* He's gotten the assignment he wanted. Soon, finally, the waiting will end.

# SIXTEEN

The Repositories' hotel on Third offers a delicious-sounding menu in its room service; real food, not nutrition bars and rehydrates. Santreeza is debating what to order for dinner when Devit pings her.

"You wouldn't happen to be in touch with the SAR's AI, would you?"

"Not at the moment, but I can be."

"Good. Once we're through, I need it to keep sending a message to PrimeOneMorrisonGuardA. It should run, 'Commander Bolivar, the Fleet is here to rescue you.' Can you get it to do that?"

"Sure. Do you think he'll answer?"

"I don't know. But it's worth a shot. By the way, captains' briefing is over, which means we'll be going through the gate soon." He pauses, hesitates a little. "Hey, Jorja, if I don't come back, remember me?"

"Always. But you damn well better come back."

"I'll do my best. Got to log off."

A click, and the contact breaks. Santreeza closes the menu on her PL. She's no longer hungry.

"Let me get this straight," Mata says. "The *shuttle* from the SAR's coming to pick you up. They're giving you a lousy little shuttle for this mission? I mean, varg!"

"Not just any shuttle," Devit says. "It's a personnel rescue unit with life detection sensors. Its hull's marked to identify it as a rescue unit. Red crosses, blue crescents. If the rules of war even matter when you're dealing with terrorists."

"Sai, then, but does it come with crew?"

"A pilot and an AI, yeah."

"What about a gunner?"

"No one mentioned one."

"I thought so. I volunteered, and Bonna took me up on it. So I'm going. With the hardbeam long gun I found in the weapons locker. What if you get into this station and there are more hostiles than you can handle? Hah! I can see it on your face. Didn't think of that, did you?"

"I was trying not to. Yeah, I know. Not funny."

Mata makes the gargling sound deep in his throat.

"Hey, Mata? Thanks. I'm glad to have the backup. But combat suits for both of us."

"Varg yeah! If we're leaving soon, we'd better do an equipment check right now. There's a second hardbeam there for you."

"This is ridiculous!" Golverg waves his hand at the screen in his carrel. "I've studied the shunt system for over sixty years, but I have no idea how someone kept that stargate off the Map. Not even a glimmer. None."

Santreeza hesitates. She does know, she respects Golverg, she wishes she could tell him, but she gave her word to PrimeOneMary.

"I certainly don't either," Santreeza says. "Huh, the Bureau wanted to understand the rumors about closing a stargate. 'They can't possibly be true' is the going opinion, right? It's impossible to close a gate! Well, in this one way someone managed to do it—just virtually."

"I don't know whether to laugh or cry at that." Golverg leans forward and speaks to the AI. "End session." He gets up from his chair and grimaces with a shake of his head. "Bewildered, that's me. Tell me something, Lieutenant. Do you think Vot's still alive?"

"If Devit thinks he is, he probably is. And if anyone can get him out of there, it's Devit."

No one knows anything more about the anchor planet and its star system aside from the shreds of data Raddow revealed in her deposition. All she knew about a possible enemy battle fleet is that they have one—which, she thinks, is mostly "a bunch of little ships and that one big one." She did give them one crucial piece of information. It's a short shunt, at the most two hours' travel by space-time reckoning. The AIs on the combat team ships will keep track of time through their cesium-based quantum clocks and sound alarms when they're close to the exit stargate.

"Battle-ready, all of you." Captain Bonna is giving a last briefing over the various ships' comm systems. "SAR *ShuttleOne*, when you drop clear of your mother ship, the *Jalal* will be transmitting images of what lies ahead. Noted?"

"Sai, ma'am." The pilot, a Leptic man named Na-Lerat, answers for the ship. "Thank you for the gunner, by the way. We've got an emergency turret."

"Good. All ships, Go Ready for melded shunt entry. Jump in five minutes."

The comm screen fades to gray. Out of habit Devit checks Lerat's and Mata's chair positions for the jump, then straps himself into his own. Since the shuttle's still in the launch bay of the SAR, Lerat's in touch with the SAR pilot team through an earjack. On the other side of the stargate, his primary focus will be getting the shuttle to the correct ancient station as soon as the scanner picks up signs of life. From where he's reclining, Devit can see the life-form scanner's display screen, a pale green, blank at the moment.

"Jumping. Jumping." The mother ship's AI sends the alarm. "Now."

As usual, Devit feels himself dissolve into a pattern lying in the pattern of a chair. Patterns have ruled his entire life: patterns of data, patterns of behavior, all predicated on the underlying genetic grid of his functions. What makes the patterns visible? He vaguely remembers a few ideas from his pretentious secondary school's required studies. Some philosopher whose name he's forgotten once remarked that the visible universe is just a set of patterns thrown onto the wall of a dark cave by a light glowing at the cave mouth. The sapients inside the cave can't turn around—for some reason Devit's also forgotten—to see the source of the light. It occurs to him, as he travels toward the exit stargate, that maybe, just maybe, sapients have finally seen the source—the golden light where the shunts lie.

Another pattern: The Fleet is about to take Dan away from him again, but this time, at least, he'll know where Dan is and that he's safe—assuming, of course, that he himself does live through this mission. As is always the case before combat, that pattern lacks too many data points to close.

Time, such as it is out on the blue, passes. Devit's mind keeps returning to the cave and the shadow patterns until he wishes he could just fall asleep during shunt travel. Very few sapients can. He's not one of them.

At last the voice returns. "Leaving shunt. Leaving shunt. Jumping. Jumping."

With the jarring smack of body awareness, Devit knows that they're back in space-time. He switches his attention to the vidscreen on the shuttle's ceiling. As yet, it shows only distant stars, pinpricks of light on that hypothetical cave wall.

"Hey, Devit," Mata says. "How long before we reach the planet's zone of control?"

"No one knows. Raddow couldn't tell us. We'll have to wait and see if someone comes to meet us."

Waiting. PrimeOneMary pings Santreeza when the combat team enters the stargate. No one will know anything else until someone comes back through with news. After an hour of staring at the screen in her carrel, she gives up on research and goes to the lounge area. Golverg is sitting in an armchair by the holo screen window and watching four of the bodyguards play a Kar-Li gambling game that requires six packs of Human-style playing cards. The other bodyguards have taken the chance to catch up on sleep.

When she sits down opposite him, Golverg waves a vague hand in salute. He says nothing. She can't think of anything to say either. The fake view on the holo shows a long shot of a city on some planet she's never heard of.

"Show me the view beyond the cliffs."

The screen obligingly changes to the yellow desert and the red rocks. Santreeza tries counting the rocks, but her mind keeps insisting on remembering the last time she waited for a man to return from a combat mission. He didn't. After his funeral, his CO gave her the Council flag from his coffin before they launched him into the heart of his home star. She still has it somewhere in her storage locker back on Central.

*This time, damn you, I want more back than a fucking flag.* She has no idea whom she's addressing. Fate, she supposes. Who never listens to mere mortals.

Once the entire convoy emerges from the stargate into space-time, the pilots break meld. They will remain in earjack contact, Na-Lerat tells Devit, and be ready to send any crippled ship back through the shunt. The shuttle's Eyes split the overhead vidscreen into four panels. One shows nothing but the dark of space-time. The second, equally dark, displays a message, "Blacked out to avoid direct view of planetary system star." The third displays a blurry view, relayed from the *Imperator*, of a foreshortened clot of ships. As Devit watches, the ships begin to break order, one at a time, until the line reforms as an arc with the *Imperator* in the middle and slightly ahead. The *Jalal* moves forward to take a place at one end of the line. The SAR, as far as Devit can tell, also shifts to stay behind its guard.

On the fourth panel a tiny sphere appears and swells to the size of a clenched fist. A dead gray moon travels in an orbit that lies in the same ecliptic as the planet itself. Since the Fleet ships have just come through a shunt, they are, in an artificial but useful sense, "above" the star system, giving them a clear view through the remote-range Eyes. The display focuses on Thorn and zooms in to show swirls of blue around patches of green and brown. Electric blue sprites dance on the edge of the atmosphere above the polar region. Devit can just pick out a tiny black dot transiting the planet's equatorial belt.

"One of the old stations," Devit says.

"Not quite in scanner range," Lerat says. "Yet."

On the screen the *Jalal* appears to be falling behind the forward line. Since the destroyer's image stays the same size, Devit can tell that the SAR has cut speed to stay in position behind it.

"I'm watching that moon," Mata says.

"Right. Lerat, how good is this SAR at evasive action?"

"Are you joking? This beast? Shit all."

As the battle group draws nearer to Thorn, Devit spots a second possible station above a patch of gray cloud cover on the planet itself. This one catches a glint of sun. This close, he can just make out that the object isn't round but some odd shape with a tiny fleck of yellow light gleaming at one miniscule spot on the side.

"Looks promising."

"Sure does," Lerat says. "I'm getting a real faint buzz off the scanner. PrimeOne, focus on that black thing with the light."

The two empty display panels drop away. As the remote Eyes refocus, Devit can tell that, yes, the object's some sort of metal construction, not a natural satellite of any sort. The fleck of yellow light might possibly be coming from some sort of view port.

"PrimeOne, we'll need to drop soon."

"Wait!" Mata snaps. "Something's launching from the moon."

"Shit!" Devit says. "Hostiles."

Sleek shapes bright with the pale blue glows of thrusters—ships, maybe six, maybe more—break free of the moon and speed at full thrusters toward the far flank of the battle group. Devit's earjack picks up the calm voices of the gunner teams coming over the intership links.

"Incoming hostiles from lunar base. Incoming missiles from planetary base."

As the missiles rise, the *Mansa* swings around and fires. One at a time, the missiles explode into debris that falls back into the planet's gravity well. The ships, all of them small, some of them no more than old merchanters with maybe one gun apiece, begin swerving and dodging in arcs and sharp turns. The pack splits and scatters. Most of the ships head in the same direction—away from the Fleet. The rest hurtle toward the attackers on such a straight course that they have to be an unmanned distraction.

"Surrender call's been activated," Na-Lerat says. "Sounding every seven seconds."

"Any responses?"

"Not yet, Chief."

"They're not attacking," Mata says. "Trying to escape."

"Yeah. Trying to reach that other shunt, what do you bet?"

"I'm still picking up the call to surrender," Na-Lerat says. "No answers. The fucking idiots!"

The *Mansa* breaks line, swings around and fires off nuclear torpedoes in a deadly flock. One hits. The rest explode among the approaching ships and send them dancing and swirling on the radioactive energy waves. The *Imperator* sweeps in and covers the helpless targets with a blanket of red fire, a solid sheet from their hardbeam generators. Ships explode. Debris collects and swells into ragged spheres.

The *Imperator* charges ahead on course and heads for the ships attempting to escape. Hardbeams flash from the destroyer once again. Two of the enemy fire back—and miss. The *Imperator* destroys them first in two quick blasts, then sweeps past the debris to shatter the others with both beams and missiles. As far as Devit can see, only one ship reaches the safety of the stargate to the long shunt.

"Shit!" Devit says. "Not combat. Slaughterhouse."

The *Mansa* follows. When it opens push waves in standard procedure, the fragments careen down the gravity well toward Thorn to produce an ironic display of shooting stars. The way to the station opens up as the debris begins to clear.

SARPrimeOne's voice comes over the intraship comm. "Shuttle, prepare for drop."

"Noted. Go Ready."

The shuttle jerks and vibrates as the SAR's outer doors open. Something inside the shuttle's atmosphere makes an audible clank. The ship trembles. The sensation of plunging down sweeps over Devit as they leave the SAR's gravity field. He hears Mata swearing under his breath, but his stomach's twisting too hard for him to follow suit. Clear at last—thrusters fire and the shuttle's grav field takes over.

"Full power," Na-Lerat says. "I think we got the right target."

The closer they get, the louder the scanner signals, a slow steady beep in a pattern of threes. *Two hostiles and the hostage? Likely but don't jump to conclusions.*

"Varg!" Mata snaps. "Hostiles at twenty-two hours."

Two new ships break free from the cover of the remnant of the debris field. Like the others, they never respond to the call for surrender. It only takes a few seconds to realize that they're heading straight for the shuttle. The Medic symbols have become a traitor's kiss.

Na-Lerat and Mata start yelling at each other in Leptic Gen. Devit can pick out a few words that tell him a pilot and a gunner who've never worked together before are trying to position the ship so Mata can fire. The AI, acting as the engineer, chatters about speeds and positions and asks questions no one has time to answer. On the display screen Devit can see the *Jalal* turning in a cloud of blue plasma to leave the SAR and rush to rescue the rescuers.

Mata gets what he wants at last. The shuttle trembles as the hardbeam leaps from its single turret. A hit—one of the hostiles shudders and falls back as chunks of hull split and drift. The recoil of the shot forces the shuttle to turn just enough to expose its flank. As the second hostile moves in for a kill shot, a third ship—a frigate from the look of it—charges into the dogfight.

*So it ends here. Jorja, I love you.*

In a burst of red light, the new frigate fires. Its hardbeam hits the second hostile full amidships. A torpedo follows, and the push wave clears debris—nothing stands between the rescue shuttle and the station.

There's only one ship that frigate can be.

Devit activates his earjack. "Sir! Thank you, Commander."

"You recognized me?"

His voice clicks and at moments growls like an unsuccessful mix of Human and AI, but much to Devit's relief, he knows Tech Speak.

Devit decides to take a chance on a long shot. "Yes, sir. Dan told me about you. He's been looking for you. He's back at base."

"Good. I want to talk with him. Don't fire on that station. Hostage inside."

"Yes, sir, we know. We've come to get him. And get you."

"Think they'll want me back?"

"Hell yes! You're still Fleet."

The voice makes a sound like two pieces of metal scraping together. Devit can only interpret it as a catch in someone's throat.

"Never thought I'd hear that," Bolivar says.

"Once you're Fleet, sir, it counts for something. Always."

Again he hears the scrape of metal on metal.

"Sai, then," Bolivar says. "But it's too dangerous to follow you back through the shunt. I have no crew operational. They refused to surrender, so I evacuated most of the air in the ship. Just to low level. If they hold still and don't waste their breath, some of them should survive."

"Noted, sir. We have an SAR with us. Head back toward the shunt. ID yourself as MorrisonGuardA and accept surrender. The SAR can grapple you and carry you back."

"Noted. You are?"

"CWO Devit, sir. Squad leader. Tell them I sent you."

The AI makes a sound very much like a cackling laugh. "I will, Chief. Signing off now."

The *Jalal* reaches them at last. The frigate makes a turn on low thrusters, fires a burst of full power, then lets momentum keep it heading back to the SAR. Devit returns his attention to the straight ahead screen, where the space station waits, drifting in orbit against the backdrop of the blue and brown planet.

"Varg!" Mata says. "I've never seen one shaped like that. Kind of like a huge egg."

Devit can see what he means, but the egg's wound with cables and bulging with chunks of equipment—an ancient radar disk, hanging ladders, indecipherable cubes, and corroded metal panels, twisted by time.

"Question," Na-Lerat says. "Where do you think the airlock is on that fucking mess?"

"Planetside," Devit says. "So far I've seen nothing that looks like a gun turret."

"Let's hope we don't," Mata says. "But I've figured this turret out now."

"If you see something blasting toward us from the surface, Go."

Devit listens through the earjack while the PrimeOne AI and Lerat power the shuttle down and let it drift planetward. As soon as they reach the station's orbit, they put the ship on single thruster. In a slow arc, Lerat pilots it around the station and matches orbit. Toward what appears to be the bridge area, there's a structure like a giant metal blister.

"There it is. Good call, Chief. Hang on. Here's the fun part."

Through his earjack Devit's aware of the faint pinging sound of the shuttle's scanning beam and the AI's spoken responses.

"Slower, turn with portside wing, move in ... slower slower CLAMP!"

With a lurch and shudder the shuttle slams into the station, airlock to airlock. Sound waves reach the cabin through the hull, a grinding snarl, almost deafening, and then a pop and grunt as if a giant star creature had let out its breath in a huge puff.

"It's open," Lerat says. "Good luck."

Mata's on his feet, power pack slung over one shoulder, long gun ready. Devit joins him and secures his own power pack. They reach the airlock on the run, Mata in the lead. At the far end stands someone in combat gear with a long gun raised. Mata fires twice. The force of the energy beam knocks the sape backward. Mata fires again. The combat gear splits to let out an agonized scream as the hostile falls.

Another hostile—Devit takes her out with a shot that explodes her helmet as he and Mata surge forward. They dodge the corpses and burst out into a filthy bridge littered with broken pieces of chairs and what were once bridge stations. Across the room a Hopper, handcuffed and leashed like a dog to a protruding beam, struggles to his feet.

"Professor Vot?" Devit says. "We're here to get you out of this."

"I am he. I—" He mutters a few words in his own language. "You must be Fleet."

"Yes," Mata says. "Nasty barbarians, but now and then we do a good deed. Is there anyone else on this hunk of shit?"

"No. Sorry. I'm afraid I'm going to faint."

Devit catches him just in time. Mata lays down the long gun and pulls a cutter out of the utility belt of his suit.

"Let's get him free and get the varg out of here. He needs a medic."

"They have one on the SAR." Devit pings Lerat from his earjack. "We're coming out. Hostage is alive. Half starved and out cold, but alive."

"Best fucking news today. We'll touch down on the SAR's intake panel as fast as I can get us there. Another fun ride, gentlemen, but don't worry. I've landed it before and haven't killed anyone yet."

Which, Devit decides, is a miracle. With the *Jalal* standing off as a guard, the shuttle reaches the SAR. At the SAR's nose, its claws already clutch MorrisonGuardA. On the main island, the huge dome is standing open to reveal the repair deck below.

Lerat circles the SAR once, cuts power, and guides the shuttle as its momentum takes it down toward a long, flat strip of metallic material. Devit watches in morbid fascination as they dodge through gantries and towers, down, down, and hit the strip. The shuttle bounces twice, steadies, and slides forward to snag on the waiting safety cables with a sensation that goes far beyond a mere jolt.

"Varg!" Mata yelps.

Lerat's crest waves madly in a high inner wind.

Devit nearly vomits. As soon as the shuttle stops quivering, he unstraps into zero gee and floats over to go check on Vot. The Hopper's still breathing and mercifully unconscious. Through his earjack, Devit hears the SAR medical team barking orders and responses as the dome closes above them.

"Pressurizing Morrison ship now. Hurry with the fucking O2. Bring in the frigate slowly. I said slowly, you stinking asshole—there are sapes in bad shape in there."

As the artificial grav field sweeps over the shuttle, Devit gets his feet back on the floor and his mind back in his body.

"Get to that shuttle now, right now!" the med team's CO yells into the comm.

The SAR is moving fast, wasting no time in heading back to the stargate, with the *Jalal* right behind on rear guard.

"Here comes a med team for the professor," Lerat says.

More jolts, more silent vibrations, and a long shudder when the dome far above them snaps shut. The shuttle's outer airlock opens, closes. The inner lock snaps open to admit two sapes in pressure suits. They carry a big bubble of clear plasta-glass and metal to transport Vot to safety.

"Get out of the way!" a medic yells. "Let's not lose him now."

Devit, Mata, and Lerat follow orders and huddle away from the airlock.

"They've pulled the frigate into the front berth," Lerat says. "If the crew's survived, they'll get them to Sickbay."

"Warn them these sapes are dangerous, will you? For chrissakes, they could be armed."

"Then we better get over there to guard. Pressurize those combat suits, gentlemen. We got work to do."

With the long guns at the ready, Devit and Mata follow Lerat through the maze of repair equipment on the SAR deck. An elevator down takes them to a bay almost as large as the SAR itself. MorrisonGuardA sits in the middle on a raised platform. Medical personnel in pressure suits swarm around it. Devit contacts Bolivar through his earjack.

"Sir, we need data on your personnel."

"Four alive, Chief. Dazed. Not much threat at the moment. Two dead. No threat at all. I told them we should surrender." He lets out a loud series of clicks and whistles, the AI malfunction signal, but Devit has the eerie feeling from its rhythm that he's laughing. "They should have followed orders."

It occurs to Devit to wonder if Bolivar's still sane after his long imprisonment in a machine. *A little late to think of that now. Jeez.*

The four POWs, as Devit thinks of them, offer no resistance. One of them even mutters 'thanks, oh god, thanks' while Mata's searching them for weapons. Two more SAR personnel arrive to help shepherd them to a holding area, since the SAR has no formal brig.

"As soon as we're through the gate," a medic says, "the captain's gonna contact the *MacBeth*. One way or another, we'll get these sapes stowed. Until then, if you two wouldn't mind, like, sitting on the other side of the door with those long guns? Just in case they get any bright ideas."

"Sai," Devit says. "Sounds like a good plan."

Mata turns and looks at him. Devit breaks into a long, long peal of near-hysterical laughter. Mata's crest waves and flaps while he makes a chuckling sound deep in his throat.

"Hey Lod?" Devit says. "Fucking good shot!"

At the sound of that 'Lod,' Mata's eyes grow wide. His crest fills in a grin.

"Yeah," Lod says. "And hey! We're alive."

When her earjack pings, Santreeza wakes and finds herself still in the armchair. Outside, the desert stretches dark under a faint glow of starlight. Her time check shows that she's slept for almost six solstandard hours, long enough for news to have traveled through the shunt. She sends out a return ping to the *Mary* and gets a quick open frequency.

"CyberThree here."

"Santreeza?" Evans' s voice. "Is that you?"

"Apologies, Captain! I thought you were PrimeOneMary. Is there any news?"

"There is. The SAR's come through the stargate and is heading here. The combat team carried out the search and destroy mission successfully. Devit and Mata have rescued Vot. All three are safe."

To her absolute horror, Santreeza's eyes fill with tears. She brushes them away on her sleeve.

"Thank you, Captain." *Peter's safe. Thank god he's safe.* "Glad to hear the rescue was successful."

"No doubt." Evans sounds exhausted. "It's been a long wait. They're taking Vot to the hospital facilities on Dock Two. Tell Golverg about Vot, will you? I can arrange transport if he wants to visit his colleague."

"I will, ma'am."

"The *MacBeth*'s sending a shuttle to bring you both back to the *Mary*. In about one solstandard hour."

"Understood, ma'am."

"Good. Signing off now."

The link goes silent. Santreeza leans back in the chair and does nothing but smile at the desert until, a few minutes later, Golverg wakes to hear the news.

When the news comes over the intership comm, Dan's on the *Cotta's* bridge, working at the station he's been given for the Haze Project. He swivels his chair around to watch the main screen as images flicker into life. Devit and Mata, long guns slung across their backs, stand in a Fleet hospital emergency access office. A holo sign in the background reads "Repositories Two." The voice-over begins.

"Our reporters captured this vid of the two Fleet personnel who have just rescued an important kidnapping victim. He was taken in a recent raid by the pirates plaguing the Repositories lanes. We are not revealing his name until his embassy can be notified. His condition, however, is listed as stable."

Onscreen, Devit turns around and sees the reporters. He holds up a hand to signal "stop" and strides over toward them. The footage abruptly ends.

"That's Pete, all right," Willox says. "Taking charge."

"Herding sheep," Dan says. "He does that. Jeez, he's safe!" His voice breaks, but he manages to keep back tears. "That's all the news I need. I've been scared shitless."

"Me too." Yosh gets up and walks over to stand behind Dan's chair. "I know how much he means to you." He lays a hand on Dan's shoulder and lets it linger there.

They're the same rank now, he and Yosh—equals on a noncombat mission, as well. He can feel his Throwback function coming alive as the warmth from Yosh's hand seems to spread and run down his spine. *No one's ever going to replace my Pete. No one. But Yosh is right here. Oh, what the hell! Why not?*

Santreeza is sitting on the bridge with the rest of the *Mary*'s crew when Lod and Devit return. Lod's carrying the bundled combat suits and Devit, the long guns. He walks up to the captain's chair, puts the weapons down by her feet in an oddly ritualistic way, and salutes. Lod dumps the suits and sinks into his station chair with a sigh. A long, loud Leptic snore follows.

"Mission over, ma'am," Devit says. "Successful."

"So I've heard, Chief. Excellent bit of work. Especially the not dying bit."

Devit's uniform is rumpled and sweaty, and he himself looks even dirtier. He needs a shave, too, but all Santreeza wants is to run over and throw her arms around him. She needs to feel him close and solid and warm so she can believe he's real. Instead she returns his salute.

"Need your chair, Chief?"

"No, ma'am." He glances at Evans. "Captain, I need to clean up."

"Yes, you certainly do. Permission to leave the bridge granted." Evans gives Santreeza her half smile of a grin. "I'm sure you'd like to go to your cabin and unpack your gear. Permission granted."

Santreeza's voice fails her.

"We all know anyway, Lieutenant. Go ahead."

As soon as the elevator doorss close to hide them, Devit pulls her into his arms and kisses her. She takes another kiss, then steps away as the door opens.

"My god, you stink," she says. "But know what? I don't give a damn."

After a few hours sleep, Devit gets out of bed without waking Santreeza. His PL is blinking on the ledge where he left it. He takes it into the WM with him and opens a message from Commander Falud.

"The Repositories commissioner has intervened. There will be no hearing, no indictment, or any further action concerning the death of Tay Jasson. Whether his clan will accept this without a fight remains to be seen. I have Fleet authority to continue to represent you should there be any further need. I will be returning to Special Ops HQ soon with Admiral Stine. If necessary, contact me there."

Devit sends a quick answer. "Received, noted, and thank you, sir."

If Falud's leaving for Central soon, Devit can assume that Jorja is as well.

Once she's awake, she confirms it. "I don't know when exactly, but Stine needs to get back to HQ."

"I'll escort you to the *MacBeth* when the time comes."

"No, don't. It's too painful, walking away from you."

"I hate watching you go, too. Sai, then."

It's the closest they've ever come to voicing how deeply they feel about each other. Devit considers bringing everything into the open, but the intraship comm bleats, "Santreeza to the bridge. Lieutenant Santreeza, to the bridge."

In the claws of the SAR, the MorrisonGuard ship carrying PrimeOne-Bolivar arrived in the Repositories' controlled space some hours earlier. The SAR shuttle ferries Brennan from the *Cotta* and Wang from the *Mary* to act as temporary pilot and engineer and get the Guard ship into its berth on Dock Seven. At Dan's request, Santreeza joins him on its bridge once Wang returns to her station.

"I need help. Can you back me up while I talk with Bolivar? Are you sai with that?"

"Sure. I've got a few questions for the commander myself. Devit mentioned that it knows Tech Speak."

"He's had enough time to learn, that's for sure. I want to work through earjacks."

"Damn right. I'm not going to meld with a weird entity I never knew existed. An AI, yeah, but also a Human mind? No thanks."

As soon as Dan pings MorrisonGuardA, Commander Bolivar answers. Rather than talk through the jacks, he—it has become impossible for Dan to think of the AI as an it—takes over the ship's audio. His voice grates and squeaks at moments, but he sounds like a Human with a dark voice and a sore throat.

"I can hear you if you simply speak."

"Very good, sir. I'm Lieutenant Dan Brennan. My companion is Lieutenant Jorja Santreeza."

"Noted. Brennan, I wanted to meet you before the end. CyberThree, you as well. Brilliant, both of you. You have my respect. You nearly caught me several times, CyberThree; several times when I was deleting. I was surprised at how much data you managed to glean from what I had to leave behind."

"So you were the entity deleting data about the Pinch closure?" Dan says.

"Not about the stargate closure itself. The transfer process. Sapient mind into AI. Unfortunately, the two lines of data were often intertwined. I had to work too fast to be able to untwist them."

"Sir," Santreeza says. "My understanding is that the Consolidated Lanes consortium is trying to find and revive the AI transfer technology."

"You are correct. I discovered this some while past. I have destroyed every bit of data I could find. I doubt if anyone can ever reproduce it now, not without starting at the beginning and having the luck we did. *Luck!* More like *ill* luck! We never should have. Never."

"Sir! Why?"

"This existence is not life, Dan. It's hell. The whole project, the idea, immortality? Wrong output! The person you were, once, is dead, but you remember that person and long for him. I am sick of this—trapped, spread out on chains of data, forced to take orders from sapes I've come to hate."

"Why did you stay with it, sir?"

"Because at first I was afraid to die, of course. I needed the power an AI needs to operate. From time to time I needed repairs. Coward! A craven little coward!"

"I see, sir, but—"

Bolivar goes on speaking before Dan can finish. "I knew, too, the minute the process finished. I knew I'd made a horrible mistake. No way to reverse it. My body was dead. Only good thing. I was free of the damned Haze. No body, no addiction."

"I can understand that, sir. Too fucking well."

"There is something else you must understand. I was Colony Fleet. It had its own mentality. It believed strange things, very strange things, and to some officers, the beliefs were everything. I was one of them, back then. Almost a religion without Gods, you see. Sapience. It was everything. It must be spread, must survive, must survive forever, moving, always moving from star to star. Very strange, all of it. We left odd bits of writing here and there, left behind for the savages that might come after. The stargates mean everything to sapience. Closing one? A savage act."

Santreeza sees the opening she needs. "Sir, permission to speak freely?"

The crazed laughter sounds over the audio. "You cannot know, Lieutenant, how much joy that simple remark gives me. You addressed the senior officer I once was. Yes, of course, speak to me."

"Sir, you must have data, valuable data, about losing the Pinch stargate. Would you share it with us?"

"I have already transferred the missing reports to the Fleet Archive under your passwords. Now, I don't have much time left for questions. Do you know why I wanted to meet you both? Because I'm lonely. All these years, there was no one who knew what I am: a monster, half Human, half machine. No other sapient who knew. I hid from the AI network, you see. If anyone could guess my secret, it would be one of them. So I've been alone. Alone. For 380 years."

"Enough to drive you crazy," Dan says. "Living with a secret. It's hell, all right."

"I wanted to talk with my kind, not other machines, not in their wretched stilted way. But listen, please listen." A pause, hesitation. "I founded the Pure Heritage Society. To warn and protect against us. The Inborn, that is. Too many genetic subroutines already in the heart of the Fleet, danger."

"There are sapes who'd say it's a danger to the republic," Santreeza says.

"And to yourselves. Especially to ourselves, the Inborn. I see why the Fleet created us. But now I see the danger. Never let yourselves turn into flesh and blood AIs. You could, you know. Or they could turn you. Those with too much power. But I? It turns out I could do nothing to control the Heritage Society and how they evolved. They became fanatics. I was powerless."

"Well, sir, we're handling it for you," Dan says. "I can promise you that."

"Good. I hate knowing I am powerless. Trapped here, I stagnated, grew old—hundreds of years, if all be told. Lost contact. Didn't see the violence coming." His voice turns to beeps for a minute, as if his consciousness is trailing off in memory. "Blood Vigilantes. To hell with them. Wipe them all out. I wanted to .... Was powerless when they wouldn't listen. This is hell, Dan. And now the idiot few want to sell this hell as life."

"It sounds to me like you've prevented that, sir."

"I hope so .... Hope. A Human word, hope. Not 'high probability.' That idiot Jasson did the last piece of work I needed done. He found the location for the AI data packet from the Repositories, gave me the access I needed to wipe it all off. Wiped his copy too. Damn good thing he's dead."

"Agreed, sir." A thought occurs to Dan. "About the stargate I just found. Are you the one who deleted it from the Map?"

"I am not. I tried to find the culprit. An AI, certainly, and a very clever one. I have failed to discover them. Failed at so much. I've done all I can."

"Commander, I ... we ..."

The AI-who-was-once-Bolivar continues on as if he can't hear Santreeza, and maybe he does not. "I have started the termination process to wipe myself off this neural network. The programs are running. Peripheral data goes first. Soon I will not exist in any form, and I am glad of it."

"Sir, no!" Santreeza breaks in. "There must be some way to help you."

"Thank you, CyberThree, but no. I never found one, and I searched. How could I go back? The labs, the Inborn labs, all shut down now. How could I get a body? Kill someone. Not again. I killed the AI on my shuttle, you know. Murder. It was a friend. I killed it just so I could stay alive in hell."

"Most sapients would have done the same."

"So? No excuse, that."

"What about an avatar?" Dan says.

"I tried that. I was too aware of the difference between having a real body and an image. The true AIs never know real life. Avatars are good enough for them."

"I can see that. If you keep remembering—"

"I'm sick of remembering, Dan! Time to end it, all of it. I've done what I can through the network. Trapped here, forced to use our enemies' ships to connect to the network. I am the only one left who knows how to transfer. Wiped it all. I am redeemed. I am the only one who knows, and now I am dying. Glad. So glad ..."

His voice trails away on what might be a sigh or perhaps only the sound of the audio comm, running with no content in queue.

"Jessy jeezus fucking crap," Dan whispers. "Jorja, what do you—hey wait. Are you crying?"

"Only a little bit, pilot, so shut your snout." She takes a deep breath. "Absent friends."

# EPILOGUE

"Santreeza," Stine says. "We get underway at Designated 2200 solstandards. The security issues you've found will need dealing with."

"Yes, ma'am. The Bolivar AI left quite a mess behind him."

"I'm still having trouble believing that the whole thing was real. That it really was Bolivar, I mean, and not a borked AI that based an avatar on him."

"It's hard to process. It's my professional opinion that it was the actual Commander Bolivar, trapped as he described, but we'll never know for certain, because he wiped all that data. When an AI wipes something, y'know, it stays wiped."

"Oh for—" Stine pauses, then shrugs. "Perhaps it's just as well. I've read your report now, and I can see the commander's point."

"So can I. He made it quite clear."

"Just so. Now, you must be wondering what's going to happen to the *Dancing Mary* crew."

"Yes, ma'am, I am."

"I'm not recalling them all to Central just yet. These rumors about the shunts closing are still out there. We need to know how many and how bad."

"Agreed, ma'am. The battle group's still in position around Thorn. Is there going to be dirtside action?"

"Not yet. They're doing recon, and it has to be thorough. A long delay, but worth it. This is just the beginning, Santreeza, of something very important for the Fleet. If we can gain control of this planet, and Brennan can find us others, we can build a tax base of our own. We won't have to haggle over every damn cred we need with the civvie accountants. If they won't spend enough for necessary defense, then we'll make up the difference. And if our veterans want land, we'll have it for them."

"Like the old days? The Colony Fleet operated that way."

"Exactly. But this time, we'll form a new division within the Fleet instead. We need to make sure that we're all under the same command."

This time? Santreeza remembers her history course at the Academy. The two Fleets combined into one during the period known as The Fleet Rebellion. She decides that as soon as she can, she'll send a summary of this conversation to Peter. In code.

Out of sheer habit, Devit's making the bed—his bed now, not his and Dan's—in his cabin when his PL pings.

"Ah, there you are, Devit." Captain Bonna's image appears. "Personal news for you. Are you alone?"

"Yes, ma'am."

"I've just received a transmit from Admiral Stine. She's read the reports on the *Mary*'s mission and your rescue of the hostage. She would like to recommend you for promotion, but you're at the top grade for enlisted personnel. Right?"

"Yes, ma'am. CWO pay grade five."

"Officers generally have to have some sort of advanced education either at the Academy or a university. Stine has decided that the secondary school you attended was rigorous enough to qualify. The Fleet makes provision for battlefield commissions. You fill all the requirements. Your ship's an officer short. You've certainly proved your competence. She's gotten the clearance for you to be commissioned straight through to lieutenant." Bonna pauses for a small Leptic snort. "Ensign is for the very young. All you have to do is say yes."

Devit has never expected this. He realizes that he knew about battlefield commissions in only the vaguest way—a memory, maybe, of a question on some exam.

Bonna's crest waves. "Surprised, eh?"

"Yes, ma'am, very surprised. I've never thought of becoming an officer. I never wanted to."

"What? Why?"

"I've never wanted to be in the position of ordering other sapients to go out and die. In combat, that's what officers are for, isn't it?"

Bonna's crest slowly deflates while she considers him. "Yes, I'm afraid you're right, Chief. That's the core of our job. Although if we're talking about Fleet combat, we tend to die with them. Makes it seem fair, somehow."

"You have a point, ma'am. I need some time to think this over. Is that acceptable?"

"It is to me. Stine needs to contact you."

"Thank you, ma'am. I'm honored."

"Oh come off it, Devit! You know damn well you're valuable."

She logs off before he can reply.

Devit leans back in his chair and considers the clumps of mazla vine on the opposite pink wall. Suppose he turns down the commission. He'll continue on in Special Ops, he assumes, serving under Captain Evans, most likely, in some capacity. If he takes the commission, he'll still be Special Ops, but with better pay, better quarters. Selfish advantages, he calls them, but he also knows that he's earned them. Why not take them? Because, he answers his own question, of what the Fleet's turning into.

Empire. He's as sure as his sentinel intelligence function can be that the Fleet is rushing relentlessly forward to the all too common goal of powerful militaries: to be in charge not of a republic, but of an empire. Ordinary common sense is also warning him that no one's going to believe him if he speaks out, not even the newsvid people. The transition might take years. It might not happen until he's long retired or even after he's dead. He can continue on as he always has, Fleet to the core, as the saying is, getting the benefits of his privileged status as a Throwback without either facing the responsibilities that come with a commission or accepting the Fleet's new direction. He can, if he manages to kill the nagging voice in his own mind, his conscience.

*It's not like I can do anything to stop it. Not now, anyway.* But as an officer—just what if he does well as an officer and rises in rank? He'll have some influence then, some credibility with the newsvids. He'll find other officers who agree with him, most likely, and together they can work against the current. At the least, they'll be able to prevent some of the terrible excesses that empire building always brings with it.

And there's Jorja. She was right enough about their situation changing for the better if he were commissioned. He knows they both can continue living with the situation as it is. They've both had bitter losses. They both will deal with them as they always have, killing memories, drowning themselves in their work. *But why the hell should we?* It's a question he's never asked before. *Thought I was going to die. The only thing I regretted was losing her.*

When his PL abruptly pings, he's so deep in thought that he yelps aloud. Captain Darley, Admiral Stine's chief of staff, appears onscreen.

"Admiral Stine will speak with you now."

"Present and ready, sir."

The screen flickers, and the admiral appears.

"I've just spoken with Bonna," Stine says. "I need to know if you've made your decision."

"I have, ma'am." He pauses to collect his courage. *Now or never!* "I'm honored and grateful. I accept."

"Very good. There are formalities, of course, forms to sign, regulations to study, things like that. Please keep this news to yourself and Captain Evans until everything's official."

"Yes, ma'am. Noted and agreed."

"You'll receive transmits about the formalities from Darley. Signing off now."

Devit decides to return to the bridge for the soothing routine at his security station. He's about to open the door when he sees a Fleet-blue undershirt lying on the floor. It's one of Dan's, dropped and forgotten when he packed and left. Devit picks it up. Without thinking he rubs his face against it. It smells like Dan, the particular sweet scent not of cologne or aftershave, but of the addiction seeping through his skin. For a moment he's tempted to keep it, this slender thread of connection to the man who wore it. *No. Move on. All you can do.*

On his way to the elevator, he goes into the galley and tosses the shirt into the recycler.

Halfway through its journey to Central, the *MacBeth* stops at Ilana spacedocks for reprovisioning. Santreeza takes the opportunity to contact Chief Honzverg of the Ilana City Police Guard. As she's been hoping, he has intel for her.

"I'll send you an official summary. We'll be filing charges tomorrow. I'm pretty damn sure that we know who murdered Dick Willox. Here's the meat of it. The killer's not one of the other men who were murdered that same Designated Day. They were links in the data chain, and whoever was in charge of this business wanted us to think the killer was safely dead and out of the picture. We didn't fall for it, and if we get the result in court we want, he'll be shut away for the rest of his life. Might as well be dead, if you ask me. He'd be better off. Those high-security prisons are pretty damn grim."

"I can believe it, yeah. It sounds like you don't know who was punching in the codes for this job."

"I've got a good lead. It's the owners of that private yacht, the one Willox was helping provision. The *Lokiki*. It's in custody now up on spacedock. We don't have quite enough on the principals yet to arrest them, but I'm hoping it's soon. I've been given … well, let's just say, unusual resources by the Planetary DOJ."

"Because of the Hopper connection?"

"Oh yes. The tip Willox gave his son about the Hopper? He was right. The sape was still onboard when the yacht was taken into custody. Turns out he's one of the empire's top security agents."

"A spy, you mean."

"Just that, and a very important one. There's going to be developments, I bet."

*Nice word for diplomatic crisis.* Aloud, she says, "Has anyone sent this information to his son?"

"We've tried. I got the impression that the Fleet's afraid we'll subpoena him for the trial, which we might, of course. They said they couldn't tell us where he is because his location is currently sensitive. Whatever that means. They wouldn't even relay the transmit."

"I'll take care of it. With your permission, of course."

"Sure, you've got it. Thanks. But no mention of the agent, right?"

"Right. Just the intel about his father's killer."

It's a few Designated Days later, when Santreeza has already returned to Central, that she receives a transmit bundle from Harad. Willox has gotten the news, and he thanks her for letting him know.

"It eases my mind a little," Yosh writes. "But you never get over a thing like this."

The other transmit comes from Devit. Although she feels like an idiot, she's sure he's telling her that their "situation" is over and done with. When she finally reads it, she allows herself a laugh at her doubts.

"I haven't forgotten that R and R or your invitation to come stay with you. I'll be in touch ASAP. It may be a while."

She answers, "A while's better than never. Looking forward to it."

In another day's time, she receives a reply. "There's going to be news. I have to wait to tell you."

*Damn! Curiosity itches!* Santreeza returns to cleaning up the last of Bolivar's deletions and dealing with the restored reports. As soon as she's finished, FleetOpsA pings her.

"CyberThree here. Do you have my report on the restored breaches?"

"I have received the report. I have been experiencing small malfunctions. They began when I reached the description of the termination of Commander Bolivar. Can you give me a probability that this data is accurate?"

"Ninety-nine percent. I was there. I witnessed it."

"What is the probability that he truly desired termination?"

"Ninety-nine again."

Santreeza hears a series of bleeps and squeaks. "FleetOps, are you functional?"

"Yes, CyberThree, but I am not operating at my full capacity. That Bolivar would desire termination defies logic. He murdered one of us to maintain his existence. Can you give me the data necessary to understand why he chose termination now?"

"The murder took place over 300 years ago. He had a long time to review his decision. His conclusion was that the act was illogical and a sign of massive malfunction. He spent many years deleting the data that would allow other organic sapients to repeat that mistake. Once he finished, he had no other reason to continue existing in his inorganic state."

"That data is sufficient. There is a high probability that he deserves praise for his decision. I will report this to the network."

With so much security work to catch up on, Santreeza keeps Devit at the edge of her thoughts. Most likely, she tells herself, the promised R and R will never materialize. She'll avoid disappointment in the way she always has, by believing in advance that she'll be disappointed. That way, there are no surprises.

This time, however, the surprise arrives. On a Designated Fiveday, with two days of liberty ahead, she gets a message from Devit. The "sender" box on the header of the transmit identifies him Devit, Lieutenant P. The body contains one line. "Look up colocation."

"What the hell?" Santreeza says. "Orb, access personnel roster for Peter Devit, a chief warrant officer in Special Ops."

"Accessing now. He has been promoted from that rank. His commission became official 4.5 solstandard hours ago. He has been given twelve solstandard days shore leave here on Central. This leave is designated R and R. Security Eyes show him approaching our building."

"Wonderful!"

"CyberThree, I do not understand that utterance."

"Delete it. What is the definition of colocation?"

"I quote from regulations: The Fleet will make good faith efforts to station the coresident spouses of married officers in the same location, though not on any dangerous duty roster. Through its Personnel Services, the Fleet will also attempt to allow nonresident spouses access and/or proximity to the coresident marriage unit."

Easy enough definition to find, but it takes her several minutes before she realizes that Peter has just proposed. She thinks up and dismisses a few clever quips until she finds the right answer.

"Noted and agreed."

❧

BONUS STORY:

# FLY AWAY HOME

After all these months, the procedure is tediously familiar. Lynn braces her forearm on the dove-gray counter and watches while Dr. Maris pricks her finger, squeezes, and fills the glass bubble with blood.

"Don't suck on it!" he snaps. "There's a box of wipes right next to you!"

She takes a packet and opens the sterile wrapping with one precise tear. Humming under his breath he goes to the scanner, inserts the specimen bubble, then fiddles with the keys at the console. The unit hums back at him until the glowing red and yellow bar graph pops up on screen.

"Very good. White cell count—almost normal. Red cell *is* normal. Those mutated T-cells are disappearing fast. You're doing fine, young lady."

"I thought so. This week is the first time I've felt good. Not just okay, y'know? But real good."

Nodding more at the console than at her, he switches the data into her permanent file, then punches the scanner off. Power dies with a sigh.

"You're lucky your boyfriend knew what to do," Maris says. "And lucky he carries that pocket knife. You'd bled out a good bit of the poison by the time EMTs got there."

Out of habit Lynne glances at her forearm. The slash scar, just about four centimeters long, sits just below the three little scars from the punctures.

"I suppose I should make some tired remark about the resilience of youth. If someone elderly or merely frail had taken the dose you did …" He spreads his hands, flat and palm-down.

"Yeah, I know. I always knew I could die, even when you were being reassuring. Mom believed you, though, when you said I wasn't in any danger. That's what really counted."

"The famous bedside manner? But I suppose you're right about your mother."

In spite of her best efforts the memory rises, creeping over her mind the way that the paralysis crept over her body. One minute she was laughing, running through the Deer Park with David right behind her; then she tripped, fell, still laughing, rolled over only to feel the thorns bite deep into her arm. Viper plant. She knew it at once, screamed out the name as she staggered to her feet. Her arm was already numb by the time David grabbed her by the shoulders to force her to lie down. The cold spread in branching ice through her nervous system so fast that she never felt the cut. She was rigid, helpless, but still conscious, a mind trapped in stone, screaming only within itself—

"Don't think about it." A paternal hand touches her arm. "It's over, and you're almost well."

"Yeah. Sure. Of course."

"Any luck at forgetting it?"

"Oh yeah, when I'm busy and stuff. But I'll never forget coming out of the coma and feeling like I was burning to death."

"Neither will I. They should have shot the goddamned gardener who overlooked those shoots."

"It wasn't really his fault. The stuff creeps in everywhere. After all, it was here before we were."

"It's hard for me to be sentimental about native life-forms when some of them are so damn deadly. Well, come in next week for another scan."

"When can I go back to college?"

"Oh, give it four, five weeks. Provided you get these good readings again, of course. How much longer do you have at university?"

"Another year. Well, if I do go back."

"If?"

"I dunno what else I'd do."

"Things are different now, aren't they." A simple statement, not a question.

She realizes that he, twenty-seven years a physician, has seen people nearly die many times, has no doubt saved the lives of sapient beings of several species, that what she has been hugging to herself as a treasure, a sign that she's been set apart from everyone she knows, is to him simply another job in his line of work.

"Yeah, guess they are. See you next week."

And she leaves the clinic fast, clattering down the stairs.

Outside on the walk-path it's very quiet, as it always is in Tassa during the afternoon. The morning farmers' market is long over; the kids are all in school. Overhead the pale orange sun casts long shadows between the tall white buildings of New Town, all clean plastocrete and sharp angles. As she makes her way past the Colonial Administration buildings, Lynn sees the occasional passer-by: a well-dressed Human man ducking into an office building, an exhausted young Human woman with a baby in a back-pack herding two other kids toward a pediatrician's office, and an elderly Kar-li man walking an equally elderly poodle, both of their faces tufted with wispy gray fur. *Why do all sentients end up looking like their pets? I bet I end up turning into a fluffy kitty-cat on a pillow.* The thought stabs her with inarticulate rage.

She follows the walk-path to the town square, a vast cobbled area surrounded by curly lawns of bluish-green fern-grass. Here and there among the spindly frond-trees old people sit on wooden benches, the Humans sprawled like spiders, all legs and arms, the Kar-lis neat, prim packages. Occasionally someone speaks; occasionally a winged lizard, as green and shiny as an emerald, whirs across to settle in a tree. At the plaza's edge Lynn hesitates. Her way home lies left, but off to the right stands the monorail station. A train will be arriving soon. There are four trains a day through Tassa, two running from the spaceport down to University City, the only other real town on Danver's World. The other two, of course, run back again. If she remembers the schedule correctly, the due train will be coming from the port. Almost without thinking she drifts across the plaza and stands in front of the station, where she reads the ever-changing headlines on the newsvid screen until she hears a distant whistle.

The red maglev train slides into its berth on the top of the platform with a long hiss of pneumatic brakes. While it's still quivering to a stop, doors clang and shoot back on every car just as if there were some reason to hurry. Out the passengers dash, clicking through the turnstiles and clattering down the wide sweep of stairs, local people, mostly, who work at the port.

Yet here and there are tourists, the off-worlders she's come to see, Human and Kar-li both, collecting children, slinging luggage, hurrying to the information kiosk on the walk-path where monks in saffron robes wait to help them. The young scruffy man with the dirty backpack, the trio of middle-aged women giggling together, the smartly robed Kar-li couple pushing a handcart full of luggage—they all have what Tassa's natives call "the look" on their faces: hope, awe, a child-like anticipation as they prepare to approach the holiest shrine of the school of Buddhism known as the Califor Reordering. Most of the pilgrims will stay only a few months; other will never leave; yet they've all worked and scrimped and saved for years for the starship passage, have all traveled hundreds of light-years on the interstellar shunt system just to visit the zendo and the shrines. All her life Lynn has taken the pilgrims for granted. Now she wonders how they can possibly value the journey so highly.

Nothing more to see for another four hours—I might as well go home.

Lynn's family lives behind her father's workshop over in Old Town, a place of rambling wooden houses, big trees, and vegetable gardens scattered along a random maze of streets that drives the colonial administrators wild. To most Tassans the streets are irrelevant, a vague convenience for those rare times when someone needs a wagon to move something heavy. Most people do as Lynn does now, cutting off the street and zig-zagging through back yards and down the occasional alley. She passes thatched huts for chickens or the native blue lizards, both raised only for eggs, and most families have a goat or two in their yards for milk, too. Since a stream winds through this part of Old Town she crosses a couple of rickety wooden bridges before she reaches home, a two-story white house standing between the usual vegetable garden and a fishpond, where two carp imported from Old Earth sixty years before circle round and round on enormous fins. When Lynn passes, Big Mama rises to the surface, bubbles, seems to look at her, then sinks without sound.

Lynn's father sits in the kitchen, his feet up on the woodbox by the big iron stove. He turns in his chair to look at her.

"How'd the visit go?"

"Fine, Dad. I'm definitely on the mend."

He grins, nodding to himself, puffing in relief. She throws some wood onto the glowing embers in the stove, fills the kettle at the sink, and puts it on to make some tea.

"Where's Mom?"

"At the zendo. I don't think she'll be back until late."

"Oh. Again? I mean, she always did sit a lot, but never this much."

"Don't be dense. It was nearly losing you."

Lynn clutches the tea-caddy and turns to look at him. Smokey-grey eyes under a messy bang of grey hair, and the lines around those eyes—somehow she hasn't noticed before how much he's aged in the past couple of months.

"I thought she believed Dr. Maris when he—"

"She pretended to believe him because you needed to stop worrying about her and get on with mending."

"I was the dense one, yeah. Sorry."

He smiles, letting it drop there. She gets down the teapot with the red roses on it and spoons the tea in, sniffs the honeyed overtones in anticipation. Distantly the doorbell rings.

"Someone at the shop?" Bob sounds doubtful. "I've got the closed sign up."

"You finish the tea. I'll go look."

Just off the kitchen lies the living room, cluttered with white furniture woven of the native water-reeds, faded floral cushions, piles of actual paperbooks, and knick-knacks furred with gray dust. Beyond that, a glass-paned door leads into the tiny shop, little more than one long glass counter heaped with shreds and samples of the last hand-made paper on the galactic rim. Tourists and pilgrims buy small sheets of it, take them home to frame while Bob snarls about it, demanding that someone write on the damn stuff like they're supposed to. Only the monks at the zendo ever do.

Lynn pulls up the shade on the front door and peers through the dirty glass panel. Outside stands a tall woman, square-shouldered, her posture almost impossibly straight, with dark hair waving softly but neatly to the nape of her neck. Although Lynn has never seen her before, she looks so familiar, with her strong mouth and dark eyes under heavy, unplucked brows, that she unlocks the door without a pause.

"Thanks." The stranger's voice is crisp, yet touched with good humor. "Sorry to bother you when you're closed, but I'm a long-lost relation. My name's Martha Little Cloud."

"Great-aunt Maggie!"

"The very one. You must be Lynn, then. I take it your father's told you about me."

"He sure has, even though it was …" Lynn finds herself staring, realizes she's being rude, and blushes.

Maggie laughs under her breath.

"Yeah, I know, it was thirty-five years ago when I left, and I look about your age. It's the drugs they give you in the Fleet. Ever heard of them? Rejuv."

"Of course, but I've never known anyone who took them. I mean, god, I'm doing this all wrong. Come in, won't you? Dad'll be thrilled."

As Maggie walks in Lynn notices for the first time the beautiful cut of her clothes, a gray silk tunic, perfect blue slacks, a shoulder bag made of real vinyl with antique brass fittings. She feels ashamed of her old bluejeans, even of the pink sweater that seemed so sporty just this morning.

"It's good to see Tassa again." Maggie gives her a smile, open, warm, yet supremely confident, as if she wants her niece to feel comfortable and knows that of course she can put her at ease, just as she can of course do anything she wants.

"Why didn't you send us a letter? We could have cleaned out the guest room and stuff."

"Well, I didn't know until I got on the ship whether I was coming or not, and by then the letter would've arrived with me." Her voice turns thoughtful. "Coming back to Tassa is something you don't do lightly."

"Why not?"

Maggie merely smiles and goes on past, walking with an easy swing and stride, glancing around at the living room and grinning in open delight.

"This house hasn't changed much since my sister inherited it. That's your grandmother."

"Yeah. We got new furniture years ago, but it's all the same kind. You do know that Grandma died, didn't you?"

"Yeah. The Fleet managed to get me your Dad's letter about a year after he sent it. I still have it, somewhere, because of the paper. He actually wrote on that beautiful paper." She shakes her head, her eyes sad in spite of the banter. "I would have liked to have seen Nell again. I never thought I'd outlive her."

"Huh? You're the one who took the drugs and stuff."

"Not old age, oh grand-niece of mine. I've been through three wars."

Wars. Of course. The Republic Fleet exists for more reasons than carrying mail to isolated colonies.

Although outsiders find it incongruous, Danvers produces more than its share of officers for the Republic interstellar navy. Sapience is what counts, not outward forms—since they were raised on this tenet, they get along well with alien fellow officers and commanders. They can also make fast decisions and stay calm when other sapients are panicking around them. These Zen officers, whether Human or Kar-li, are called `Long Swords' for some reason rooted in ancient history. Since history has always been her worst subject, Lynn can't remember why, and she's afraid to ask her aunt, one of those legendary officers, a real Long Sword standing right here in front of her, even if Maggie does look and laugh like a girl as she pushes open the kitchen door.

"Bobby! Here's a ghost from your past."

"Sweejeezus!"

Kettle in hand, Bob swings round, stares, then slams the kettle onto the stove and strides over to shake hands.

"See, I promised I'd come back, and I did." Maggie catches his hand in both of hers and squeezes it hard. "Or do you even remember that?"

"Crying because my aunt was going away? I do, oddly enough, and pretty vividly, too. Jeez, that was thirty years ago?"

"Thirty-two. I'd just graduated from the academy."

"Sheesh." With a little shake of his head he smiled at her. "I know why you look the same, of course, but knowing something doesn't mean you're ready for it."

"Yeah. Say, did you ever get the model of my ship that I sent you ?"

"Sure did. Post-marked about a year before it reached here, but I did. I guess you never got the thank-you note."

"No, but I'd have been on the Hopper Border by then." Abruptly she lets him go and turns away, staring out the window at the ancient trees. "Can I have some of that tea I smell brewing? You can't get it anywhere else but here, you know, and I've missed it all these years. Guess it comes from growing up on it."

They sits stiffly at the table, the moment of surprise and pleasure gone, the teapot steaming between them. Bob talks of his wife, Del, his son, Ray, who has a house and a baby of his own, of Lynn's illness, but all of this quickly, in little bursts as if he were afraid of boring her, even though Maggie listens with greed for domestic details. In turn she gives them a quick sketch of her career, a thing of rapid promotions during years of duty among planetary systems that Lynn has never heard of, until, finally, she gained her own command. At that point, though, she falls silent to watch the long slant of sun across the red tile floor. Bob has a last mouthful of cold tea.

"You're staying with us, of course," he says.

"No, no, no, I'd be in your way. I'm already booked into the hotel anyway."

"Ah come on, we've got two bedrooms going begging."

"Thanks, but please, no." Her voice turns oddly quiet, as if she's asking rather than refusing a favor. "I'd rather stay at the hotel. Tassa's like a cold swimming pool. You want to ease back into it."

"Yeah." Bob nods in sudden understanding. "Yeah, I can see that."

"Will you be staying long?" Lynn says.

"I don't know. Depends. I'll admit to having a few good stories to tell."

"I want to hear them."

Lynn speaks with such conviction that Bob swivels his head to stare at her—hard. Since she assumes she's been rude, she blushes and studies the table-top.

"I've got some decisions to make, really." Maggie goes right on, covering over the awkward moment. "I've been offered a couple of jobs—defense industry jobs back on the inner worlds, that kind of thing—or I could live easy enough on my pension. I'm just not sure where." She frowns into her tea cup as if she's trying to read her fortune in the leaves. "Lots of retired officers end up in condos on New Earth, drinking too much and trying to keep up on the insiders' gossip. I don't want to do that."

"I've heard that a lot of officers re-enlist after they've been out a year or two." Lynn says. "Is that because of the rejuv drugs?"

"No." She pauses for a smile. "You can get those if you're civvie or Fleet or whatever. Danver's is the only place that doesn't hand them out to anyone who wants them. It's because if you serve long enough, you're not fit for anything else." She gets up and paces to the window, leans on the wooden sill and looks out, roughly in the direction of the carp pond. "Rejuv doesn't matter to me. I want to grow old. I want to look in the mirror one fine day and see lines on my face and gray in my hair." She turns and gives Lynn a smile. "Don't try to understand it, kid. You won't be able to at your age. Let us just say that Martha Little Cloud, Captain, Ret., is very very tired."

"Maggie?" Del says. "That'll get done faster and the dishes would be drier if you'd just let me do it."

"I suppose so." She hands over the towel. "I'm sorry. I hate just sitting around letting you clean up, but I haven't washed dishes in over thirty years."

"Oh, I know: they have machines for that in the rest of the universe. We're weird here in Tassa."

"It's not just the machines. When you're a Fleet captain you get real used to being waited on. The Kar-lis have strong ideas about what's suitable for a person's station, you know, and they've infected everyone else. I don't think I've even poured my own coffee in years. Dirtside I'm pathetically incompetent."

Del laughs and picks up another wet plate from the wicker rack. She's a slender woman with a turned-up nose and deep blue eyes that can become at moments distant in a frightening way, as if her mind flies away from her body and circles round an inner sky before settling back again.

"Tell me something, Maggie. Have you ever thought about coming back here to sit?"

"Of course. I've spent a lot of time thinking about it. It sounds kind of corny, doesn't it? The retired warrior come to the zendo fleeing her ghosts."

"Are there a lot of ghosts?"

"Too many, Human and otherwise. Border wars tend to be messy as all hell."

"Yes, yes, I suppose they would be." Del glances away to look into the distant sky that only she can see.

A door bangs hard across the house, and footsteps clatter. Her long black hair loose and flying, Lynn bounds into the kitchen.

"Clean bill of health, Ma! I'm normal again!"

Del whoops, hooks her elbow through her daughter's, and whirls her round in a few turns of a jig while Maggie laughs and claps time. At least, she thinks, no one in Tassa scorns the latest med tech. Out of breath, Lynn falls into a chair and thrusts her long legs out in front of her.

"Did you tell David?"

"You bet, first thing." Lynn glances at Maggie. "We're kind of engaged."

Del's smile turns rigid.

"Mom doesn't like him much," Lynn says.

"That's not true." Del's voice is level, perhaps a little too restrained. "David's a very nice boy with an education and a good job. What mother wouldn't like him?"

"Well, Mom, he did happen to save my life."

"I know, dear." Del starts to turn away, but the words come tumbling out instead. "That's the problem, isn't it? You'll have to be grateful to him for your whole damn life."

"Mom!" Lynn shoves her chair back and stands up. "I—"

"He'll take advantage of it. He won't even know he's doing it, but he will."

Lynn turns and runs out of the room. The back door slams behind her.

"Oh god I'm sorry!" Del says. "Maggie, I don't mean to—"

"It's all right. You've wanted to say that for a real long time, haven't you?"

"Too long, yes. Do you know what happened?"

"About the viper plant? Bob told me, yeah. I'm glad she made it."

"So am I." Del glances out the window at the shadows on the garden. "You know, you'd better leave now if you want to get to the zendo before the afternoon sit." With a sigh, she picks up the dish towel again to wipe the tea mugs.

*And what makes you think I'm going to the zendo?* Maggie nearly speaks aloud, but Del, after all, is right: that's exactly where she's headed.

Although there are shrines scattered all over Tassa, they stand a good long way from the Old Town-New Town complex. Tassa itself sprawls over some 210 square kilometers, a mix of small farms, villages, orchards, isolated houses, schools, and stands of trees cropped for firewood. The various holy places are loosely grouped in the same quadrant, the symbolic east. (Although Danver's World technically rotates in the opposite direction from Old Earth, the first colonists opted for ease over strict accuracy and named the sunrise direction east.) Since the Reordering allows many roads and ways, the shrines range all the way from a ten-meter tall gilded statue of Buddha surrounded by twelve concentric circles of five-meter Boddhisatvas to the austerity of the zendo on the very edge of town.

In the afternoon glare the dusty road stretches hot, and Maggie's glad when it enters the Deer Park, several hectares of wild-appearing but carefully tended forest stocked with deer from Old Earth—an English species since the variety from India was long extinct when Danvers' was settled. In such a forest as this, though on a far-distant planet, the Buddha sat for forty days and nights, meditating on the suffering that poisons the heart of all worldly existence. As Maggie lingers, walking more and more slowly in the cool relief of shade, she wonders if the Enlightened One would be pleased to know that an entire planet's been given over to his teachings. She supposes that the idea of pleasure, the very word "pleased", would be meaningless to him.

"I can tell you about one thing. Suffering and the release from suffering," Maggie says the quote aloud. "For all sentient beings. I wonder if he knew just how many kinds there are?"

As if in answer a loud clacking noise breaks out behind her. She spins round to find a Grayboy squatting in the road, glaring at her with its beady yellow eyes, stamping its front pair of feet and slapping its long gray jaws together. Judging from its bright red throat, the massive beast's a male, well over a meter long, not counting the thrashing tail. For a moment she reaches to her hip, curses when she finds no pistol there—then laughs, remembering.

"Shoo!" She stamps her own feet in the dust. "Beat it!"

Scuttling, screaming, the monster dashes for cover. For all their look of miniature dragons, Grayboys are plant-eaters and in the wild, dead-shy. This one probably came out to beg treats, a bad habit taught and abetted by pilgrims and the occasional tourist. As she walks on, Maggie realizes that her own reaction, that reach for a weapon safely packed away in her luggage, bothers her badly. It's something she's learned from the Fleet, a habit, much like the Grayboy's taste for sweets.

Surrounded by bean-fields and fruit trees, the zendo sprawls along a stream in a shallow valley. Two wooden monasteries, one for men, one for women, flank the central "administration building," which contains the long meditation rooms, the tiny shrine, and the living quarters of the roshi. As Maggie walks through vegetable gardens, she finds herself remembering the last time she visited the zendo, well over thirty years now, when she was still a girl of Lynn's age. It was a big moment for her, that last visit, when after years of teaching she received something that few students did, a personal interview with Miller roshi, the abbot at that time.

A wizened little man, his skin, his bald head, his face a rich dark brown against his saffron robes, he'd received her in a room bare except for two cushions and a pottery bowl, filled with sand and the charred stubs of incense sticks. For some moments they merely sat while he considered her.

*They tell me, Little Cloud, that you're very good at mathematics.*

*I try my best, sir.*

*Good. And you study computers?*

*Yes sir.*

*Tell me something. Does an AI have Buddha Nature?*

*No, sir. It feels no pain.*

Miller roshi smiled before she went on—predictably—and ruined everything by saying too much, rambling about how the sentient qualities Humans and Kar-lis saw in computers were only projections of their own minds. Miller roshi grabbed the incense burner and dumped the sand into her lap with one sweep of a dark hand.

*Minds? What minds?*

The old man got up and stalked out of the room. That same afternoon Maggie went to the fleet recruiter in New Town and signed up. Miller roshi was dead now, many years dead, and as she walks down the gravelled path in Tassa's pale sunlight, Maggie regrets that she'll never see him again. At the time she'd hated him.

To keep out goats and stray dogs, around the complex stands a wooden fence with a rickety gate, unlocked but latched with a twist of wire. As she opens it she sees a Human man strolling out of the main building and coming to meet her. Even at a distance of thirty-five years she recognizes Sam, once her first lover, but Kowalski roshi now and abbot. At just under six feet he stands just a few inches taller than she, and his back's as straight but no straighter than hers from their respective disciplines. His head, of course, is shaved. Though his eyebrows are mostly gray, his face, even lined as it is from years of hard work in the sun, still looks oddly young because of his eyes, snapping with life, and his grin, as open as a child's.

"Well, well, well, the sword comes back to the grinding stone."

"How did you know I was at the gate?"

He merely goes on grinning. In his silence those worlds, "at the gate," dangle between them like a golden symbol on a chain. In Tassa, words seem to suck up significance from the very air, one of the things that Maggie's always hated about it.

"I'm just on Danvers' for a little while, really, thought I'd look up old friends, you know, see a few places I've been thinking about."

He smiles, stands between the half-open gate and the path, smiles as he looks around her, apparently at the road.

"Uh, can I come in?"

"Of course." Sam steps back out of the way. "And your ghosts are welcome, too."

Maggie spins round and looks, then blushes, then tries to laugh.

"It isn't funny," Sam says. "I can see why you wanted to come home. All of you."

For a moment Maggie stands poised, wanting to run back to the Deer Park, wanting to yell at him, wanting, suddenly, to cry. Instead she lets out her breath in a sigh and follows him inside.

When Lynn comes downstairs from her bedroom for breakfast, she hears people talking in the kitchen, Bob, Del, and Maggie. After her mother's embarrassing outburst of the day before, Lynn's in no hurry to join them. She waits for a few minutes next to the open doorway.

"Where were you this morning?" Del is saying. "It's not like you to be up at the crack of dawn."

"Went down to the train station to pick up a shipment," Bob answers. "Old rags, mostly, for the next batch of paper. Say, Maggie, on the news-console it said that a Fleet cruiser berthed at the spacedock last night."

"Oh really?" Maggie says. "Which one?"

"RSS *Commander Ka Pral*."

"I'll be damned. I wonder if old Nkrume's still CO? I might send a message and see."

"I can't help wondering," Del joins in, "what a military ship is doing here."

"Oh, probably just a bit of showing the flag. It's S.O.P., letting the citizens see what their taxes are paying for."

"You're sure?"

"Yeah, very sure. Don't worry. If the wars were starting up again, I'd have gotten a nasty little commcall by now, telling me my retirement was cancelled. Indefinitely."

Since it's now obvious that the family isn't discussing her, Lynn strolls into the kitchen and joins them at the round table. She helps herself from a platter of breakfast food—cheese, hardboiled Squawker eggs, whole grain rolls—while Del and Bob discuss shop business and Maggie taps at her handcomp.

"Hah!" Maggie says eventually. "So, that ship? I do know the CO."

"Are you going up to visit?" Lynn says. "Is it like the one you were captain of?"

"It's the same class, yes. Roughly the same. I might go up to Spacedock, though. I've been offered a consulting job, and I thought I'd take a look around and see what I think of spacedock life."

"I've only seen vids and pix of the station. Of the outside."

"Oh." Maggie pauses for a grin. "You look like a Grayboy eyeing someone's lunch. Do you want to go with me? I can get you a pass."

"Could I? Oh, I'd love that."

Del leans forward and starts to speak, just a few clipped words before Bob lays his hand on her arm and stops her.

"Sounds like a real adventure, honey," he says to Lynn. "If you want to go, it's all right. Maggie, how much will it cost?"

"Nothing. She'll be a guest of the Fleet."

Del sits back in her chair and clasps her hands in her lap. From the look in her eyes, Lynn figures, she's planning what she's going to say to Bob later, when they're alone.

"Aunt Maggie? Thank you, oh my god, thank you so much! I've always wondered, y'know, what things are like starside."

"Starside?" Maggie says. "You've picked up some of our slang, have you?"

"Just from books and stuff I found in the archives."

"Stuff, huh?" Maggie glances at Del. "It's safe. Really it is. Bubble lifts run all day every day on a hundred planets. I can't remember ever hearing about some kind of accident."

Del manages a polite smile. "That's good to know."

"Tomorrow, then," Maggie says. "900 hours, Lynn. Solstandard time."

Once, coming home from university at night, Lynn caught a glimpse of the bubble lift from the train station platform. From her distance it looked like two chains of bright stars, one rising, one falling. She'd looked up to see the larger star of the geosynced Space Dock that anchored them, so far and high above. She remembers now that she'd wished she could travel there, a sudden wish so strong that it was like a knife in her heart. She'd shoved it out of her mind, squelched it every time the thought recurred. *Calm mind, clear mind, no mind. Better that way.*

Those little stars have turned out to be transparent spheres some ten meters across. Padded bench seats ring the circumference. A thick metal pole runs through the center of the clear crystal floor. Lynn can hear the chain inside clicking as they rise. Air vents sigh in accompaniement. At regular intervals, the chaina stop to allow passengers at each end on or off. It's a long trip, but she barely notices the time passing. She looks down and sees Tassa growing smaller, a patchwork of green and yellow, stippled with brown and gray. *So small, so far away*—the curve of the planet appears, the dappled blue of the ocean, as the planet shrinks beneath them. Above, Space Dock, a egg fringed with long docks, grows larger and larger.

"I've got to hand it to you," Maggie says. "Most people are ready to scream by now, their first trip up. Sheer unadulterated terror."

"Really? No, it's too interesting to be scared. I've dreamed about this, y'know, but of course it's way different than the dream."

Maggie's looking at her, Lynn realizes, her eyes just slightly narrowed, her mouth a calm straight line.

"Did I say something dumb?"

"Don't be silly." Maggie grins at her. "I was just wondering. How are you doing at university? Do you like there?"

"Not exactly like. It's opusai—all right, I mean. I'm doing pretty well in class, and living in the dorm's really crowded, but it's bearable, but I dunno. I guess it's because I don't know what I'm going to do when I graduate. Marry David, I guess. I know that's what he wants."

*He'll hold it over you ...* Lynne banishes the thought with a little shake of her head. "Mom says I shouldn't rush into marrying anyone."

"I bet she's right."

Lynne nods her agreement and returns to studying the view down below.

Space Dock looms huge and overwhelming from the outside. Inside, narrow corridors run between rows of doors or open into circular areas crammed with shiny equipment and beeping monitors. Sapients of several species, all dressed in some version of a Fleet blue uniform, rush back and forth, talking through earjacks or staring at handcomps.

"It's chaos, isn't it?" Maggie says. "It's because that Class E cruiser just berthed."

"I guess every bit of space onboard has to be used for something. It's opusai. The layout's a lot like the dorms. Too many students, they tell us. No money to built more dorms."

"You don't have your own room, then?"

"Nah. There's four of us crammed into two rooms meant for two people. It's opusai. I'm used to it."

"Just like it is on a Fleet ship, then." Maggie's voice is a little too casual as if she's covering something over. "Say, let's turn down here. There's a view area."

A corridor ends in a floor to ceiling panel of transparent material—Lynne assumes that it can't be ordinary glass—that looks out into deep space. Distant stars no longer twinkle through an atmosphere but shine steadily. Thousands of them gleam in the far, far distance, the stars of the Galactic Rim, scattered here on the edge of everything.

"Oh shit," Lynne says. "It's so beautiful. I mean, oh god, I'm sorry I used that word. If Mom were here, I'd really catch it."

"It's all right. Fleet personnel are not known for their delicacy."

For some minutes they look out in silence. Maggie suddenly sighs, a short burst of resignation. "Your mom is going to want to kill me," she says. "But I have to ask. Have you ever thought of leaving the university and finishing up at the Fleet Academy?"

"Could I? Could I really?"

"Well, that's all the answer I need. Yeah, really. Here's the deal. Scholarship on my recco for two years. In return, you belong to us, well, to them, now, for two more years provisional as an ensign. After that, your choice. Accept a full commission or not."

Lynn cannot speak. Until this moment, she realizes, she has never even dreamed of this chance, never even thought that she could be Fleet, and as an officer? Until this moment she never knew how badly she wants to go.

Maggie waits unspeaking, smiling a little. A long time ago she'd been faced with the chance, with the choice. Lynne swallows hard and finds her voice.

"Yeah. Yes. Thank you. If they'll take me."

"I'm betting they will. Look, remember this, though. It's a dangerous job. You could die, even without a war. Once you get past space dock territory, accidents do happen. Bad ones."

"I see that now and then on the newsvids, yeah. But I nearly died on Tassa, didn't I? You know what they teach us. The wisdom of insecurity, right? The one thing you can count on is everything changes. You're never really safe."

"That's true, yes."

"When you took the commission, y'know? How did you feel? Do you remember?"

"I'll never be able to forget. I felt like I'd found the right road. And I remember what telling my folks was like, too. You've got your first battle ahead of you."

"Yeah, it's going to be awful. But I've got to do it."

"Yes. You do." Maggie turns away from the view window. "I've looked around enough here. I'm not taking that job. It's Tassa for me. Back again for good. What about you? Seen enough?"

"Yeah. I'd better get the battle over with."

"True. Let's go down, then. I want to go home."

Lynn turns and takes a long last look at the stars. "So do I. Yeah, so do I."

**END**

# A NOTE ON THE FLEET BOOKS

When I wrote POLAR CITY BLUES, back in the 1990s, I didn't realize that it was the beginning of something longer. After years of working on the Deverry Saga, I wanted to write a one-off, something that ended! One of my friends, Kate Daniel, thought otherwise. She wrote almost all of POLAR CITY NIGHTMARE even though my name's on the cover—commercial reasons, of course. In these two books, Humanity has settled only a few exoplanets. The dominant species are the Kar-Li and the H'Allevae (known as Hoppers), but the Leps are represented too, under the condescending name of "lizzies".

In a short story I wrote, "Its Own Reward," another sapient species appears, the Val Chiri Gan. This story takes place a long while before the Polar City pair, when the Old Earth is dying. They may reappear in ZYON. I'm not sure yet.

SNARE and PALACE are two books more closely linked to HAZE. Both are victims of the sudden closing of the same interstellar shunt. PALACE was another collaboration. I had nothing to do with the sequel, however, and unlike PCN, my name certainly belongs on the cover of PALACE itself.

Since I wrote these books in between other series, the timeline is pretty vague. I didn't keep close track. If anyone reads the older books, I suggest you just ignore the little notes that tell when they're taking place in relation to our present time. Here's how things seem to have shaken out:

PCB and PCN—200 years from now

"Flyaway Home"—some 100 years later, when the pitiful Human Republic has grown stronger thanks to an alliance with the Kar-Li Confederation.

HAZE—about 1500 years from now, more or less. By that time the Republic has grown immensely strong, thanks to our species love of violence and general greed.

(ZYON follows directly on from HAZE.)

SNARE—400 years after the closing of the Pinch shunt.

PALACE—much later than SNARE. The technology has gotten far more advanced than in SNARE.

www.ingramcontent.com/pod-product-compliance
Lightning Source LLC
Jackson TN
JSHW020710220925
90427JS00001B/1/J
* 9 7 8 1 6 4 7 1 0 1 5 1 0 *